FITTING THANKS

"I might expect a little gratitude for saving your hide," Judge ground out.

"Then I fear you are going to be sorely disappointed," Victoria returned haughtily.

If she were a man, Judge would have punched the truth out of her. Instead, he found himself being drawn into the depths of those incredible blue eyes and said softly, "No, I don't reckon I am."

He ran his hands up her arms before gathering Victoria into his embrace. When she didn't resist, he murmured, "I've been wanting to taste those luscious lips of yours since the moment I saw you. I reckon a kiss would be gratitude enough—for now."

"For now?" Victoria wondered. Then his hands were roving up her back, his lips were crushing hers, and the inexperienced young lady couldn't think another thought as her body gave itself up to the most delicious sensations she had ever felt . . .

HEARTFIRE ROMANCES

SWEET TEXAS NIGHTS   (2610, $3.75)
by Vivian Vaughan

Meg Britton grew up on the railroads, working proudly at her father's side. Nothing was going to stop them from setting the rails clear to Silver Creek, Texas—certainly not some crazy prospector. As Meg set out to confront the old coot, she planned her strategy with cool precision. But soon she was speechless with shock. For instead of a harmless geezer, she found a boldly handsome stranger whose determination matched her own.

CAPTIVE DESIRE   (2612, $3.75)
by Jane Archer

Victoria Malone fancied herself a great adventuress, but being kidnapped was too much excitement for even Victoria! Especially when her arrogant kidnapper thought she was part of Red Duke's outlaw gang. Trying to convince the overbearing, handsome stranger that she had been an innocent bystander when the stagecoach was robbed, proved futile. But when he thought he could maker her confess by crushing her to his warm, broad chest, by caressing her with his strong, capable hands, Victoria was willing to admit to anything. . . .

LAWLESS ECSTASY   (2613, $3.75)
by Susan Sackett

Abra Beaumont could spot a thief a mile away. After all, her father was once one of the best. But he'd been on the right side of the law for years now, and she wasn't about to let a man like Dash Thorne lead him astray with some wild plan for stealing the Tear of Allah, the world's most fabulous ruby. Dash was just the sort of man she most distrusted—sophisticated, handsome, and altogether too sure of his considerable charm. Abra shivered at the devilish gleam in his blue eyes and swore he would need more than smooth kisses and skilled caresses to rob her of her virtue . . . and much more than sweet promises to steal her heart!

Available wherever paperbacks are sold, or order direct from the Publisher. Send cover price plus 50¢ per copy for mailing and handling to Zebra Books, Dept. 2906, 475 Park Avenue South, New York, N.Y. 10016. Residents of New York, New Jersey and Pennsylvania must include sales tax. DO NOT SEND CASH.

VICTORIA'S ECSTASY

GWEN CLEARY

ZEBRA BOOKS
KENSINGTON PUBLISHING CORP.

For Amanda,
who has brought me
only joy and love.

ZEBRA BOOKS

are published by

Kensington Publishing Corp.
475 Park Avenue South
New York, NY 10016

First printing: February, 1990

Printed in the United States of America

Chapter One

Wyoming
1883

The crusty old cowpoke watched the letter being furiously crushed between Judge Colston's fingers. Ozzie rubbed his protruding Adam's apple. It was as if he could feel his own neck being squeezed in that huge, vise-like grip. He swallowed hard, trying to think up a reasonable explanation. The big rancher might very well strangle the life out of him when he discovered that Ozzie was the one who'd gone and done it. It wasn't as if he'd *purposely* set out to do it; it'd just sort of happened.

"What does this . . . this old prune think she's going to gain?" roared Judge, stomping back and forth in the plush parlor of his ranch house, waving the crumpled missive in the air.

Ozzie watched as the six-shooter strapped to Judge's hip jarred with each pounding step. The entire house seemed to rock under his fuming strides. Ozzie'd only seen Judge this all-fired worked up a time or two, but the man could be deadly with a gun when provoked. The blaze in those azure eyes reminded the old timer of flames from a prairie fire gone wild.

Although usually a reasonable and compassionate man, despite a sorry upbringing and all, when Judge's temper erupted and he got his dander up, the rest of the household would suddenly remember chores which took them scrambling to the far corners of the ranch. Damn all tarnation! Judge could be so stubborn and hardheaded when he got a burr in his craw. The trail-worn lines on Ozzie's leathered face deepened. How was he ever going to make that son-of-a-bear listen to reason?

Visions of having his hide strung to the nearest fence post caused Ozzie to gulp down his thoughts of blurting out the truth. "Judge, maybe ya might oughta sit down and write out a answer. It could just be a mistake 'n all."

"I'll *write out* an answer!" Judge spat, his temper near exploding.

"Now don't go forgettin' how t' be reasonable," Ozzie counseled, rubbing his sweaty palms along his worn buckskin trousers.

"Reasonable. Reasonable! I haven't built this ranch from nothing but a lot of sagebrush and rattlesnakes in order to be *reasonable* when, out of the clear blue sky, some scrawny, withered English bitch writes me a letter and says she has some legal paper which gives her the right to part of my land."

"She might be a downright nice lady, ya know," Ozzie offered meekly.

"Ha! Don't try to tell me that any female who

states she has handled her father's investments for over ten years and signs her name 'Miss' could be anything but a dried-up, bitter old maid."

Ozzie sagely kept his tongue from further comment. From the tone of Judge's voice, he knew it was no use trying to talk some sense into the man — whose dark mood so perfectly matched his physical features — until he cooled down.

Judge glared at the gnarled old cowpoke who had been his father's friend and had known his mother before that. Ever since Judge had returned from the East, near twenty years ago, to work as a young ranch hand on Luther Jessup's spread, Ozzie had been with him.

For an instant Judge wondered if Jessup had something to do with the old spinster's attempt to claim part of his ranch. It would be just like Jessup to try and pull something underhanded. Judge took another look at the letter, postmarked England. A feeling in his gut told him this wasn't the work of Jessup, although Jessup had made several business trips to that country over the years. No. Somehow the old maid must have heard about the Brits investing heavily in ranches in Wyoming, then thought up the scheme to try to claim a part of his. Well, she'd picked the wrong ranch to sink her greedy claws into!

Judge stuffed the letter in his vest pocket and headed for the door.

"Where ya goin'?" Ozzie called out to Judge's back.

"For a ride."

"Wait. I'll saddle up and come with ya."

"No," Judge shot back, whipping his hat off the six-point deer horns near the doorway and crushing

7

the flat brim down on his thick black waves.

Seconds later, Ozzie heard the pounding of hooves. He looked out the window to catch a glimpse of dust swirling a path from the house, as Judge drove the stallion at full tilt toward the river.

Ozzie sighed and shook his head. "Just like when ya was a young 'un."

He plunked down on the horsehair couch and rested his head on his palms. His thoughts drifted back to how, as a boy, when things got under Judge's skin, he had raced his horse to the riverbank to sit there for hours, staring at the Sweetwater River. He wasn't one to come right out and spill his gut or complain when things didn't go his way.

In some ways Judge was so like his ma. His ma. Ozzie grimaced. Sometimes he wished he didn't know the truth about Judge. To the dying woman, Ozzie had sworn that he would keep his lips sealed unless, of course, it was a matter of life or death. He'd kept the secret all these years. Yet that letter from England had unsettled the old timer and set his mind to spinning all over again.

The spring air was sweet and cool against Judge's face as he rode over the rolling hills gilded with wildflowers and gently waving grasses. Vast herds of cattle peacefully grazed the land, dotting the country-side brown. For as far as he could see, the land belonged to him. All the thousands and thousands of fertile acres, every rock, every boulder, every fistful of dirt he'd sweated for, was his and his alone. The ranch was his dream; he'd put his life's blood into building it. No one had ever handed him anything. He had pulled himself up by his own boot heels by starting as a cowhand earning twenty-five dollars a month, and no one . . . *no one* was going to take even the smallest part away from him.

Judge drew to a halt next to a bend in the river where the water ran deep and swift. This was his special place, its scrub cottonwoods and hefty granite boulders secluding it from prying eyes. Often when he had a decision to make, he came here to think.

With a fluid motion, Judge dismounted. He patted Firebrand on the rump, sending the spirited palomino on its way to graze nearby. A grouping of three huge rocks formed the perfect place to rest, and Judge settled down to reread the letter and contemplate his next move.

All afternoon Judge remained at the water's edge. At times, he thought of strangling the scheming bitch; at others, he gave her the benefit of the doubt. If she had made an innocent mistake, he ought to answer her letter with a civil but firm reply. By the time the sun was about to dip behind the mountain peaks to the west, Judge had made a decision.

Firebrand whinnied and stamped the ground after answering Judge's call. "Good boy." He stroked the golden mane and the horse snorted and nuzzled Judge's neck. "It's time we head back."

Judge gave the animal its head and returned to the ranch house in record time. Ozzie, his pet goose honking noisily at his booted heels, and Chang, Judge's houseboy, were standing on the porch nose to nose, arguing as usual.

"Look, ya little pigtailed devil, I'll snatch me some

vittles from the kitchen any danged time the spirit moves me, whether ya like it or not, Chinaman."

The wiry, small-boned man, dressed in loose-fitting black cotton shirt, pants, and shoes, and menacingly waving a kitchen knife the size of an axe, shot daggers at the towering, snow-haired cowpoke. "This my kitchen. You ask befole you take or I chop you thieving hand off."

"*Rrrr,* not *Llll,* Chinaman." Ozzie rolled the correct English pronunciation off his tongue for the man who had difficulty with *r's* and *l's.*

Ozzie then narrowed deep amber eyes. "Ya come at me again with that dadblamed meat cleaver and I'll shoot that friggin' pigtail of yours clean off your heathen head 'fore ya come within another inch of me, ya hear?"

With a protective gesture, Chang grabbed his queue, the symbol of subjugation forced upon the Chinese by the ruling Manchus. Although Chang detested the queue, he continued to wear his hair long and plaited since he, as well as the majority of his countrymen, hoped to return to his homeland someday.

Judge sat astride his horse listening to the two men sling insults, until he'd had enough. Those two cussed, old geezers were never going to learn to live peaceably under one roof, he concluded. "Will you two stop that infernal bickering! I have enough on my mind right now without having to put up with you two carrying on tonight."

Ozzie immediately forgot about Chang. The little man snapped up his chin with a defiant grin across his lips, gave the menacing goose, which hissed at him, one last narrow-eyed glare, and went proudly back inside the house.

Ozzie knelt down and stroked the ill-tempered bird. Once it calmed, he asked Judge anxiously, "Ya decide what ya're goin' t' do 'bout that there letter?"

"Yeah," Judge answered darkly.

"Well? Ya goin' t' let me in on it or keep it t' yourself?"

Judge frowned, thinking of the nerve that prune of an Englishwoman possessed, then broke into a grin in spite of himself. The old timer acted like a doting father. Ozzie'd never let him have a second's peace until Ozzie found out what he had in mind. He pushed his wide-brimmed hat back on his head.

"Why don't you go tend your business, old timer. I've got a letter to write."

Chapter Two

England
1883

Victoria Elizabeth Torrington looked out the window of the palatial manor, watching the stodgy solicitor alight from his conveyance and lumber up the massive steps in the front of the house. Rain splattered against his pinched face and drawn, pouchy cheeks. The aging man's appearance on such a gray, stormy morning, coupled with his tight expression, warned Victoria that their meeting could mean only one thing: the reply to the letter she'd had sent the American juror was not what she had been anticipating.

"Bloody determined vultures," she mumbled. With an impatient sigh, she adjusted her rigid, high-necked collar, checked the pins holding her blonde locks back in the severe hairstyle she wore. Then she went to face the man who for so long had faithfully represented the family's business interests. He now headed the pack of creditors demanding settlement from her father's estate.

"Victoria, I say, if you are not up to this, I will see that you are not disturbed until you feel up to facing Hampton," Gerald Pelthurst hesitantly offered, as Victoria neared him in the hallway.

The slender Milquetoast had looked for an instant as if he wanted to console her, but now his shoulders drooped and he stepped back to allow her to pass.

To his surprise, she stopped. With that take-charge style which made him emasculated she said, "It is quite all right, thank you, Gerald. I shall see Mr. Hampton now. Do show him into the library, though, won't you?"

"Miss Chastity Iron Drawers," he muttered under his breath, as he dropped his head and went to carry out her instructions.

With hurried steps Victoria entered the richly decorated room. She positioned herself behind the enormous desk and primly smoothed her starched black skirt, taking a deep, calming breath. She was a Torrington, after all, and would face the man proudly.

She ran her fingers over the smooth polished surface of the mahogany desk. Memories of going to her father's office flooded her mind. She had so loved watching him handle all the intricacies of business. He had been such a strong man before her mother's accident five years ago. She considered herself fortunate that he had endowed her early on with the importance of self-reliance.

"Never come to rely too much on another, my child," her father had lectured. "I depended entirely too much on your mother." Sadly, she thought of how he had withered from an aggressive, self-assured man

13

to a mere twig of his former self before dying. Setting aside any personal feelings of loss, Victoria squared her shoulders as Gerald ushered the man into the room and faded into the background.

"Miss Torrington." Weatherby Hampton shrugged out of his soggy overcoat and nodded as he came into the room, "I want you to know once again that you have my deepest sympathies. Such a terrible misfortune, Charles's heart giving out so suddenly the way it did." Nervously, he stopped to wipe his forehead. "Pity your father had invested so heavily in . . . ahem . . . such an, shall we say, untried venture before he died."

Under the tightening of Victoria's lips, Hampton shifted from foot to foot before blurting out, "I am sure you are aware your father's creditors have been most patient." He glanced in Gerald's direction. "Of course," he paused to clear his throat, "if you and Mr. Pelthurst," he dipped his head at Gerald, "were to set a wedding date, placing a male at the helm of Torrington Limited, I might be able to persuade the creditors to be patient a little longer."

Victoria thought she saw her slightly-built fiancé flinch. She ignored her inclination to place the blame for this pickle at Gerald's feet; it was he who had convinced her father to back that scheme to secretly buy enough stocks to gain the controlling shares of their nearest competitor, only to lose everything when the company went bankrupt. But what had been done was done. There was nothing she could do to change the past.

"Please, do sit down, Mr. Hampton. Tea?"

"Yes . . . yes, of course." The cool-headed woman

had no intention of making it any easier for him, Hampton surmised.

Victoria pulled a cord, summoning a skittish young maid. "Yes, miss?"

Victoria ordered a tray of refreshments, then turned her attention to the perspiring man. "If it is too warm in here for you, Mr. Hampton, I shall be happy to have Gerald open a window."

"No. No, thank you."

"Mr. Hampton, I realize how very difficult this must be for you. But I can only assure you I would prefer that you come promptly to the point of this visit, which I suspect has something to do with the letter we have been expecting from America." She had returned to the desk and sat primly proper, her back erect, her delicate hands clasped in front of her.

"Right you are, Miss Torrington." He again was forced to clear his throat. "I fear the letter I sent in your name informing one Judge Colston of your partnership in his property, did not produce the reply we had desired." He unfolded the letter and fumbled with his spectacles.

"*We*, Mr. Hampton?" Despite the crumbling of her father's empire, she still continued to control what was left of it, even if it were nothing more than a portion of land in the former colonies. She had no intention of letting anyone else assert his interest.

Hampton's index finger anxiously ringed the inside of his collar. "I . . . I merely meant it figuratively, of course."

"Of course. If you will allow me." Victoria held out her hand. "I shall read the response myself."

"Yes . . . yes, naturally." He quickly handed the

15

letter over to her, heaving a sigh laced with relief. He glanced from Pelthurst to the Torrington woman. The young man's narrow face displayed his quivering nerves, while she did not give away the slightest hint of what she was thinking. Theirs was a match which threw more than a few people into a quandary. She was hard and cold, that one, with an incredible business acumen that many privately envied. Pelthurst was soft and pliable as an infant.

"I fear the American juror is being most uncooperative," Hampton ventured to add.

"Quite the contrary, Mr. Hampton." Victoria looked up; her face remained a placid picture of unfathomable beauty. "From this letter Judge Colston would seem an honest man not given to relying on hearsay. Undoubtedly loss of memory—most likely brought on by advancing age—has occasioned this disavowal. I am certain that, as a man sworn to uphold the judicial system of his country, he will strictly adhere to the legal agreement once he has had the opportunity to study the document." Although she did not appreciate the American's reply, from the letter's tone it appeared more than likely that its author was the perfect gentleman, a kindly, aging, thoroughly tractable juror.

Hampton's eyes bulged. "No offense, Miss Torrington, but I fear I received quite a different impression." He squirmed under Victoria's steady gaze. "Of course, no one knows better than I your persuasive powers once you have made up your mind," he amended. "Please do be reminded though, the man states quite firmly that there is no such partnership and never has been. At such distance, it could take

16

years of litigation to prove otherwise."

"But we know he is mistaken," she said with conviction, firming her resolve. "Since this property, located in some God-forgotten place called Wyoming, appears to be all that is left of my father's estate, I fully intend to claim it." She raised her chin. "And I have no intentions of waiting years. Have you ever been to America, Mr. Hampton?"

"I should say not! Quite an uncivilized land, I am told. It is difficult to believe the British would want to invest in such properties."

Gerald hesitantly stepped forward, his voice filled with dread. "Victoria, do be reasonable. The American must have been quite shaken to learn that he has a partner he knew nothing about. Another letter imploring him to listen to reason might well suffice, what?"

"That sounds most sensible," put in Hampton, wringing his hands nervously. "Or perhaps you might be able to trade the documents to another party with the finances and time to pursue the matter."

"Am I to presume that would be your advice, Mr. Hampton?"

"Of course, having only your best interests in mind, Miss Torrington."

"No doubt."

Gerald caught the implacable gleam in Victoria's blue eyes; his own eyes registered his sense of foreboding. With halting steps, he made his way over to the reference books and got down an atlas from one of the many leather-bound volumes adorning the shelves. Flipping through the pages, he quickly found what he was looking for.

17

"I jolly well hope you are not entertaining the idea of going to America. Why, Wyoming seems to be located in what has been termed the Wild West. Cowboys and wild Indians — unmitigated lawlessness, you know."

"Do be realistic, Gerald. After all, the man is a juror. Furthermore, *I* have no intention of going to America."

"*I?*" He gulped, loosening his tie, which suddenly seemed to have grown too tight.

"*We* shall leave as soon as enough family treasures can be liquidated to finance the trip. I shall not have our creditors kept waiting any longer than necessary." A wide smile of triumph spreading her lips, she turned to Weatherby Hampton. "Mr Hampton, you will kindly inform the creditors that as soon as my fiancé and I return from America with the proceeds from the sale of our portion of the land, all accounts will be settled in full. Torrington Limited will be on its way to being quite solvent once again."

"I do not mean to pry, but the sooner you two are wed, the better for business," awkwardly offered Hampton.

That was the second time the man had suggested she marry Gerald without delay. His insistence troubled her for an instant, but she was quite aware of the prevailing opinion on the subject of women heading business enterprises.

For a moment, Victoria wished that she were not the level-headed one in the family. Gerald was pleasant enough looking, of medium height, with muddy brown hair and eyes. A rather nondescript sort, actually. But wasn't that what she had wanted? She had

18

picked him, from the clerks in her father's shipping office, as someone who would not attempt to assert himself over her decisions. She was getting exactly what she had asked for, wasn't she? She studied him. It certainly was no love match. But she had learned that love could destroy a person. In that way, she had no intention of following in her father's footsteps.

Sporting a sharp-edged smile, she said, "I am pleased that you do not intend to pry, sir." Her response sounded more biting than she had intended, and tact demanded that she quickly amend, "You needn't overly concern yourself, Mr. Hampton. This trip to America could very well serve as our honeymoon." She linked her arm with Gerald's. "Wouldn't that be nice, dear?"

"Q-quite so," he stuttered, appearing more a condemned man than an expectant bridegroom.

"Very well. I am pleased that is settled. We leave for America as soon as our affairs are in order. Would you be kind enough, Mr. Hampton, to handle the details? Oh, and do write to Judge Colston advising him of our arrival date, so he can meet our ship when it docks in New York. I expect that, as we are partners, the gentleman will wish to personally escort us to the ranch."

The matter closed as far as she was concerned, Victoria swept from the room, leaving the two men staring after her, mouths agape.

Chapter Three

Victoria neatly folded and packed the last of her things in her trunk. Never in her worst dreams had she envisioned having to dismiss the household staff and sell everything they owned. But she had had to finance the trip to America so she could save the family's name, and salvage the business she had worked so hard to build from behind the scenes.

Her thoughts drifted to her younger sister, Alayne. What a soft life the girl had led. At seventeen, she seemed more a child than a young woman. Victoria looked in the mirror. Her fingers smoothed at the faint under-eye circles which in too few years would probably deepen to match the blue hue of her irises. The first hint of feathering lines whispered out from the corners of her heavy lashes. At Alayne's age, Victoria had already been working with their father for two years. Maybe taking Alayne along as Gerald had suggested would help her mature. Heaven knew, Victoria could use some help to get the business back on its feet; Gerald was not much good.

Gerald. She bit her upper lip. Why had her father

been convinced by that man and that group of American investors to commit his funds to such a scheme? Her anger welled for an instant. She had no one to blame but herself. She had selected and quietly pursued Gerald against her father's advice that the man was no match for her in inner strength or character. She sat down on the bed and put her face in her hands. With her father's death, her secure world of finance and shipping had crumbled like a tower built of cards.

"Excuse us, lady, we've come for the bloomin' bed," the burly man, who reeked of sweat, barked. "You'll have to sit yourself somewheres else." He turned to his equally filthy partner. "Come on, 'Arry. We ain't got all day."

Victoria cast them an indignant look and moved over near the window. "I hope you do not mind—"

"Oh, but I do mind!" Alayne swept into the room, bedecked in yards of ruffles and peach satin which complimented her green eyes and soft beige ringlets.

"Lani, what are you doing here? You should be at school."

"Should I, sister dear? Did you really plan to leave me there while you and Gerald merrily sailed off to America?" The young girl pouted and dealt Victoria an assessing eye. "I do hope you plan to discard that dowdy black frock. It is not at all becoming with blue eyes. Gives you a rather washed-out appearance, actually. Of course," she cutely pondered, the devil dancing in her eyes, "that severe hairdo you wear would better fit some gray-haired widow than an attractive blonde."

Scandalized, Victoria pressed her hand to her

chest. "Our father has not been dead long. It would not hurt you to honor his memory, too."

"I do honor his memory. I simply choose not to dress in black. But do not try to change the subject. Why wasn't I invited to go with you? Or am I no longer a member of the family?"

"Do not be absurd. I do not know how you found out about the trip. But since you have, you must know Father left us virtually penniless except for a partnership in a ranch in some far-off place called Wyoming. This trip to America is not a pleasure trip. I intend to claim what rightfully belongs to us. You needn't worry, though. I have left enough money with Miss Ernestine at school to cover your expenses until we return." Taking Lani to America would be a mistake; Victoria could see that by the girl's behavior. "Now, I suggest you return to school where you belong so I can get on with what needs to be done."

"Lady, you got enough to pay us?" intruded the mover, setting the heavy four-poster bed back down.

Impatiently Victoria turned to the men. "You will be paid."

"That's what all them blokes say that lives beyond their means. Try to pretend they're better than their kind, they do," he grunted. "We want our money now, or not another stick of furniture leaves this 'ere 'ouse."

"Oh, very well." Her head beginning to split, Victoria picked up her bag to get the money she had carefully set aside, only to discover it was gone. "Gerald." She let out a frustrated sigh, remembering how he freely helped himself when he needed money. Quickly recovering, she said to the smirking men, "I seem to

22

have left the funds with my banker."

Not fooled for a second, both men crossed their arms over barrel chests. " 'Ow many times 'ave you 'eard that one, 'Arry?"

Lani quickly dug into her purse and handed the men several bills. "Will this be enough?"

"Yeah. Come on, 'Arry, let's get movin'. Doesn't look like they got a extra shillin' to their bloomin' names. By the way ducks, this 'ere ain't enough to move that trunk of yours. You'll 'ave to shove it out to the top of the stairs yourself." The man gave a belly laugh and picked up his end of the bed.

Victoria ignored the rude remarks and returned her attention to Lani. "Where did you get that money?"

"You gave it to Miss Ernestine. She returned it to me when I told her how destitute we are."

Mortified, Victoria arched her brows. "Alayne, how could you?"

Lani made a jaunty pose. "It was really ever so simple. I am not going back to that stuffy girls' school. And now it looks as if you will not be able to make me." She smiled through her teeth in victory. "Furthermore, I intend to go to America with you."

"You are only seventeen. America's Wild West is no place for a properly reared young lady. No. I shall work something out with Mr. Hampton so you can return to school."

"*You* are only twenty-seven," Lani snipped, jutting out her chin. "If you try to send me back there, I will . . . I will run away and join a troupe of performers, that is what I shall do."

"There is not enough money," Victoria persisted, feeling frazzled and worn down.

"I have just enough left over." Lani grinned and handed Victoria the rest of the bills.

Victoria sighed and took the money. Lani was young and so given to whims. If she did not get her own way, she probably would run off to join some lowly group of performers.

"Oh, very well. Hurry and gather your things and have them sent down to the *Seahorse*. We sail tomorrow morning with the tide."

An impish twinkle lit up Lani's green eyes. "My things are already on board."

"Of course," Victoria sighed. "In that case, you can help me with my trunk."

"You know I would love to. Really I would. But I simply must go tell everyone that I am leaving for America. Won't they simply be oozing with envy?" Lani danced from the room. "Let me see, there is Margaret, and Jessica, and Diane, and . . ."

Left alone, Victoria bent over and dragged the heavy footlocker toward the door. Her back ached, and a sudden stab of resentment bolted through her. Neither Gerald nor Alayne seemed to worry whether they would be able to salvage the family name or not, although Victoria knew they depended on her. She had always been the one to take over, the caretaker of the family. She thought about it as she inched the heavy trunk along. It was not as if she had been forced to help out her father. She enjoyed the complexities of business, the challenge. And she had promised her mother, long before the dear woman died, that she would always look out after the family.

She unexpectedly felt very weary. Perhaps becoming engaged to Gerald had been a dreadful mistake.

He was almost like having another brother to take care of. Well, there was no time to dwell on that now. At least Edward would be spared knowledge of the family hardships; he was safely attending school on the continent, and there he would remain. Letting herself feel overburdened was merely giving into a self-defeatist attitude.

She had made her decision ten years ago, when Sir Geoffrey Helmsley had wanted to marry her and she turned him down. There had been several suitors after Geoffrey, but they too had given up eventually, turning to more certain prospects. No. Gerald was from a good family and would prove a respectable husband. And once this partnership in America was settled, she could return to the life and business she so loved. Tomorrow they would leave for America, and soon she would have enough money to pay off the creditors, salvage the family name, and take care of her sister and brother.

She straightened and rubbed the small of her back, before heaving the trunk toward the top of the stairs again. She was a strong woman. She had not relied on anyone thus far, and by God, whatever it took, she would put the family empire back together!

Ozzie sat on the edge of the bed in Judge's bedroom watching the big man storm about, throwing his things into a suitcase and cussing like a tornado on a rampage. It was a man's room, no mistaking it, from the solid, clean-cut lines of the heavy walnut wardrobe and dresser, to the massive elk horns which hung regally over the head of the bed. Even the rugs signified a man who lived without the female influence, their bold design in reds and blues matching the quilted bedspread and draperies.

"When I get my hands around that Englishwoman's throat I am going to *squeeze* the truth out of her!" Judge raged.

"Don't go forgettin' her age," Ozzie hedged, wishing like hell he wasn't the one responsible. He rubbed his throat, wondering about his own neck when Judge found out he really did have a partner.

"She won't have to worry about growing any older when I get through with her." Judge glared at Ozzie. "What are you sitting here for? You're going to New York with me."

"Shouldn't I oughta stay here?"

"No. I want you along. After I take care of Miss Victoria Elizabeth Torrington, we'll make a swing down to Texas and check out that prize bull Bridgewater has for sale. I'll need your help in case I decide to ship more cattle up this way."

"But—"

"No buts. Besides, you might come in mighty handy to prevent a murder." Judge gave a harsh laugh at the irony of it. "Somehow I doubt that those fancy Easterners mete out justice quite as swiftly as we do out here. And I'm afraid they wouldn't much like the idea of seeing a woman's neck stretched even if she deserved it. Now, get going and get packed. We leave for Cheyenne in an hour, right after I give a few of the hands special instructions in case that old prune somehow manages to reach the ranch."

"I won't have to get all duded out none, will I?"

"If you mean you'll have to look respectable, yes.

26

Pack that suit I bought you."

"Ah, shucks." Ozzie forced himself off the bed, shot Judge a look of disdain, rolled his eyes, and left, muttering to himself about the evils of not being his own boss.

Hidden, Helene Jessup watched from around the corner until Ozzie closed the door behind him and disappeared into his own living quarters. She then slipped into Judge's room and threw her arms around his neck.

"I waited down by the river, but when you didn't come I was worried that something had happened . . . to you." Her lusty smile faded when he peeled her arms off him and turned to latch his bag.

"Are you going somewhere?" She frowned and sensuously tossed her dark hair over her bare, white shoulders, which reeked with the heady scent of her perfume.

"Yeah." He ignored her attempts at seduction.

"Why don't I tell Luther I need to go to Casper and buy some of those frilly little underthings he likes to see me wear, then I can come with you," she purred. Feeling secure she was the only one Judge Colston bedded, and intending to keep it that way, she stepped back up to him and nuzzled his neck. Oh, how she loved this man! Almost as much as she loved money. Pity he hadn't had any before she had married that crude old Luther Jessup.

"Don't you think you should be home tending Jeremiah? A little boy needs his mother."

"Luther'll see to him," she defended with a shrug. Motherhood had never been one of her main interests in life; it was an annoyance, actually. But the boy

27

would someday serve her purpose.

Judge shot Helene a look of disgust. "I don't have time for you right now, Helene. I've got business in New York."

Her dark eyes leaped open. "New York?" A calculating glint slipped over her expression. "My cousin, Clarissa, lives in New York. What business could you have there?"

"Some old crow thinks she can send me a letter and claim part of my land. I intend to meet her there and send her packing back to England before she ever gets anywhere near my ranch."

"How old?" Although Helene tried to hide it, her jealousy and possessiveness were all too clearly visible in her sharp tone.

"You don't have to worry. I have little interest in women."

"Except in me, of course." She giggled and pulled down the top of her gown, exposing two luscious, rounded breasts. Not satisfied to let Judge go off to New York and be surrounded with all those beautiful women without first giving him something to remember her by, she grasped his hands and drew them to her hot flesh. "Say you don't want me," she throatily challenged, squeezing his fingers tighter around her hardened nipples while she gyrated her hips against him.

Judge stared down at the beautiful, wild, dark-haired woman. She had been the only woman he had ever loved. There was a time when he would have killed for her. That was before he'd learned that a woman's heart was little more than a money belt to be bought by the highest bidder. Now he accepted what she had to offer, sating little more than his male hungers. She was exciting and totally uninhibited, never seeming to get enough of him. Yet sometimes he wondered why he continued to see Helene. She was beginning to bore him with her constant demands for attention.

"I don't have time."

Ignoring him, she settled onto the bed like a lazy cat and drew her skirts up to reveal a mound of thick brown hair curling at the apex of shapely milk-white thighs. "By the look of your body, you'll make the time." She leaned over and took his hand, pulling him to her. He was hers; she could tell by his body's reaction. And someday, some way, she would be free of Luther so she wouldn't have to sneak around any longer. "Judge, honey, I want to give you something to think about while you're gone."

A triumphant smile lit upon her full, red lips as she felt Judge's hard body succumbing to her seductive powers. With precision, her greedy fingers began working the buttons on Judge's trousers.

Ozzie burst into the room.

"I'm as ready as I'll . . . ever . . . be. S-sorry," he stammered when his eyes fell on the tangle of legs and arms on the bed. His lips broke into a broad grin. "How do ma'am. Good to see ya again. Been seein' quite a bit of ya around here lately," he said straight-faced, his amber eyes sparkling with insinuation.

Helene scrambled to cover her nakedness. "You old fart! Get the hell out of here!"

"Helene," chuckled Judge, unaffected, "remember, you married Luther to become a lady." He casually got up and refastened his pants. Shrugging into his shirt, he turned to Ozzie. "Take the bags down to the buckboard. I'll be there shortly."

Helene held her tongue until that irritating old coot had left the room. She got up from the bed, letting the blanket slide to the floor, and walked boldly over to Judge. She pivoted before him, and then lubriciously drawled over her shoulder, "I'll show you just how much a lady I can be, if you'll come back to bed."

"I know exactly how much a lady you are, Helene," Judge drawled. For a moment, his hatred of Luther Jessup—a man driven to destroy Judge—almost turned to pity for the man who was bound to Helene. Had she been wed to anyone else, Judge would never have touched her. The thought fading, Judge's fingers gave a familiar squeeze to Helene's rounded backside, and he followed her back to bed.

Chapter Four

New York City
1883

Ozzie took off his crumpled, well-worn felt hat and scratched his head. "Kinda fancy, ain't it? Look at all that marble, will ya?" He squinted into the sun as he counted the horizontal divisions of the immense hotel. "And eight stories high. Well, I for one ain't plannin' on lettin' any city slicker put me up no eight flights in some man-made mountain."

"Don't worry, old timer." Judge laughed. "I already made arrangements. You and I are on the second floor. I asked for a room on the eighth floor for this supposed partner of mine. I want her as far away from me as possible."

"Can't we just mosey on over to some boarding house that serves up plain old rib-sticking grub, where a man can get himself comfortable?" Ozzie complained.

"You'll live. Besides, you might grow attached to the Grand Central Hotel by the time this is over. You might not want to leave."

"Don't go countin' beans on it! A man ain't got room t' breathe in the city. Why, there's more people rushin' about here than cows on the ranch."

Ozzie followed Judge inside and set his bags down while Judge registered. When a boy came and tried to carry Ozzie's luggage to the room, the old timer pulled his gun. "Put them there bags right back down where you found 'em, sonny. Ain't no young whipper-snapper in brass buttons goin' t' make off with my duds."

The young boy's eyes bulged and he dropped his load as if he'd been shot.

Nattily dressed women screamed and men looked on horrified. The concierge stared down his long nose, cleared his throat, and was about to venture that perhaps Mr. Colston and his man should find other accommodations. But he hesitated. Judge Colston was known to be an exceedingly wealthy rancher who tipped well. All the same, the concierge much preferred to cater to the wealthy patrons from more civilized regions.

"Put that peashooter away before you get us both thrown out of here," Judge directed in an even voice. He then handed the trembling boy a coin. "You can take care of my bags. My friend here will handle his own."

The boy's eyes brightened at such an enormous tip. "Yes, sir!"

Judge turned back to the ruffled concierge, ignoring the whispers of outrage buzzing about the lobby. "Has a Miss Torrington checked in yet?"

"Just a moment and I'll check." The stuffy man

with the big carnation in his lapel quickly scanned the register. "No, Mr. Colston. But you have several other messages, one from the Vanderbilts." Obviously impressed, he handed Judge the neat stack.

Judge smiled to himself. The old hag was about to be in for her first surprise. He offered the man a generous tip. "When Miss Torrington arrives, let me know." The man beamed his agreement. "Oh, and if anyone asks about me, you don't know a thing."

"You can count on me, Mr. Colston, sir." With the sly grin of a satisfied conspiritor, the man pocketed the money.

Once Judge and Ozzie were settled into their rooms, Judge scribbled a curt note to Miss Torrington informing her that he had been detained and would meet with her at the hotel later in the afternoon. He called for a messenger and sent the man to meet the *Seahorse* at the docks.

He watched the slender man scurry down the elegant hallway. That note should give the scrawny old maid something to think about. He'd show her he was not going to trot to her tune! Her letter instructing him to meet her ship had sounded like a summons. Well, let her find her own way to the hotel. He'd meet her when he was damn good and ready — on his terms!

Off in the distance, a clear blue sky glistened over a city which Victoria had learned was in excess of one million people. The snug New York harbor loomed ever nearer, as the tug maneuvered the steamer toward the enormous wooden shed which would be its mooring place at the pier. Anticipation sprouting within her, Victoria silently watched as the ship was secured at the dock by a blur of workers. She then turned to disembark.

"I say, quite a bustling place, what?" Gerald observed, as he followed Lani and Victoria down the gangplank. Fascinated, he gaped at the flags waving from nearby ships of foreign nations; the huge ferry boats busily carrying hordes of passengers; the vast numbers of palatial river craft docked further along the Hudson and Long Island Sound.

"I have little interest in this country. I intend to claim what is rightfully ours as soon as possible and then return home," Victoria said shortly, although she could not deny the twinge of excitement she felt. They were surrounded by the vessels of the steamship empires: Cunard, Guion, White Star, National, and Torrington Limited. Somehow, she had to salvage the family business and save the proud name of Torrington.

"Well, I, for one, am glad we are here!" squealed Lani, taking in her surroundings. "I cannot wait to check in at the hotel so I can begin exploring the city. Isn't this ever so exciting?" She grabbed Gerald's arm and gave it a familiar squeeze before she realized Victoria might have seen her. She quickly shot a glance at her older sister. Luckily, she seemed preoccupied and had not noticed.

Gerald quietly listened to the exchange between the two siblings. It was hard to believe they had been spawned from the same parents, though that both were beauties, no one could dispute. Lani's rounded rosy cheeks appealed to him much more than the hollows under Victoria's high cheek bones. Victoria was so capable and strong. She didn't need anyone—no doubt, never would.

That dreadful nickname, *Miss Chastity Iron Drawers,* seemed to fit Victoria, who stood, stiffly erect, in a tailored gray striped traveling suit. Thank goodness, Lani had insisted she don that, instead of those ghastly black frocks she had been wearing. Lani herself looked delicately feminine in billowing layers of pink satin and lace. She looked up to him with adoring eyes radiating an innocent dependence. Victoria, he was sure, had never depended on another human being in her entire life.

A big bruiser of a dock worker lumbered over to Victoria and picked up the traveling case she had carried with her. His eyes roved over her gently curving body. "How 'bout letting me escort you into the city, lady? I could take real good care of a woman like you."

Lani shrank behind Gerald, who stood still, trying to decide which tactic to take with the muscled man.

Victoria cast Gerald a disgruntled frown. It was clear he was not going to intercede. She turned her attention to the leering man.

"From the filthy look and odor of you, sir, I seriously doubt your ability to take care of yourself, much less be of assistance to anyone else," Victoria said. She snatched the valise from the shocked man's hand. "Now, if you will kindly step aside." She raised her chin and walked past the now bewildered worker.

Gerald swallowed a lump of fear, expecting to be forced to defend Victoria's sharp tongue. But the man just laughed and moved off, muttering some-

35

thing about Victoria being more than he'd want to take on.

They stood on the wharf, waiting, until the sun was directly overhead, heating the already sweltering docks. Lani wiped her forehead with a lace handkerchief. "Could he have forgotten us? Why, we do not even have hotel reservations. What are we going to do?" she whimpered.

Victoria sent Lani an impatient glower. "Mr. Hampton's letter specifically instructed Judge Colston to meet us here and make arrangements for our lodging. I am certain—"

"Did you say Judge Colston?" interrupted a grimy little man dressed in a red coat with shiny brass buttons.

"Surely you are not Judge Colston?" Victoria put her hand to her throat, fighting a sudden desire to hold her nose. It was evident the man hadn't bathed for more than a week. Didn't anyone bathe in America?

"No, ma'am. He couldn't come to meet you. Said to give you this." He held out a note covered with smudged fingerprints. "Says to meet him at the hotel—that's the Grand Central Hotel, the best one in New York City."

"Since you took the liberty of reading my message, are you willing to escort us to this Grand Central Hotel as well?" Although Victoria sounded perturbed, she was more annoyed at the judge than with the messenger.

"No, ma'am. I'm on my way home. You'll have to get there yourselves. Won't be any trouble though. Just ask. Folks'll be happy to direct you." Before

Victoria could protest, he tipped his hat and disappeared among the freight containers.

"Are you still so sure the man is going to be receptive to your demands?" Lani squeaked.

"They are not demands!" snapped Victoria over her shoulder as she walked. "I am merely claiming what is rightfully ours."

"What about the bags?" Gerald asked, thoroughly bewildered by the enormity of the new country.

"We'll send someone back from the hotel."

Hot, tired, and thoroughly angered by the judge's lack of etiquette, Victoria and her entourage finally reached the hotel and checked in. After making arrangements for their luggage, she and Lani left Gerald at his door and entered their room.

The room was small, yet tasteful and comfortable. The lush, lime carpeting and draperies matched the flowered wallpaper, and a maple vanity stood regally in the corner, its ruffles coordinated with the bedspreads. Lani hurried to wash her face while Victoria sat down on the bed and took off her shoes. Victoria was overheated and exhausted, but had no intention of letting Lani see how unsettled she felt.

"Gerald has offered to escort me—that is, us about town this afternoon. Isn't that ever so kind of him?" Lani sheepishly said, after sitting down at the vanity to brush her hair and adjust her ribbons.

"You two go along. I am going to take a hot bath and then go downstairs for a spot of tea." Victoria yawned and stretched out on the luxurious satin coverlet.

"I wonder if Judge Colston is staying in a room this small?" ventured Lani, still stinging that they had not been given a suite. She had hoped to be treated like royalty, after having had to watch every cent since their father died. Victoria could be such a damper, worrying about money and propriety all the time. What if the judge did not escort them to all the fine restaurants and theatres? Victoria would never allow Lani to spend their own money on anything enjoyable. Lani pinched her lips. "Victoria?"

"Yes?"

"Do you think the judge is going to be very frugal toward us?"

"He may be as frugal as he desires with his money, as long as I get what is rightfully due us."

Judge glared at Ozzie from across the hotel room suite. "It doesn't matter what you say, old timer, I aim to make sure that Miss Victoria Torrington gets exactly what's coming to her. And letting her find her own way from the ship is only the beginning."

Ozzie tossed his hat on the bed in disgust. "If I'd a knowed ya was goin' t' do that, I'd a met the lady myself. Ya ain't goin' t' get her t' go quietly back across that there dadblamed ocean by treatin' her like that."

"This is my room, old man," Judge grunted. "Don't come in here and try to tell me what to do. I'll treat her the way she deserves."

Judge was going to lose his patience if this conversation went any further. He had been meeting with an attorney most of the day, which left his nerves frayed. From what he had been told, if the woman did indeed have some type of legal paper it would have to be proved a forgery before he could send her packing. He had been advised to proceed cautiously with the woman. Well, caution hadn't built the J Bar C ranch, and the need for it now grated on Judge. He was a man of action, used to taking risks. A man didn't keep his empire by sitting idly by. No. He wasn't going to hang around New York City and play games. Dammit, he had business to tend to.

"All I'm tryin' t' say is, don't go off half-cocked." From the look in Judge's eyes Ozzie knew the hard-headed rancher was going to do exactly as he pleased, no matter what anyone else said.

"If you've had your say, how about heading down and getting something to eat?" Judge set forth, effectively changing the topic of conversation.

"Down in that fancy eatin' place?" Ozzie croaked.

Judge looked Ozzie over with a chuckle. "You are the one who looks dressed to go to the finest dining room in the city."

The old timer's face reddened. "Well, what ya waitin' for then? Let's go get us some grub." He picked up his hat and motioned for Judge to lead the way. "Puttin' on the feed bag and a couple of double shots of gut-warmin' whiskey is just what I need. And it cain't hurt your temper none neither."

Judge sent Ozzie a daunting frown, then left the room shaking his head. There was no curbing the old timer's prickly tongue.

Having had his say, Ozzie quietly followed Judge down the thickly carpeted hallway and through the public rooms filled with elegantly clad men and women. As they were passing the desk, the concierge waved Judge over.

The man slyly scanned the area and then whispered, "Mr. Colston, sir, the lady you have been expecting is in the dining room."

Judge's eyes narrowed. "How do I recognize the old crow?"

The man's mouth dropped in surprise. "She is not exactly an *old crow,* sir. She is—"

"Save it. I know what she is," Judge said shortly. "Just tell me what she's wearing. And remember, you don't know me." Judge handed the man another coin.

A conspiratorial grin slanted the man's lips. After describing Victoria's high-necked, blue suit and braided jacket, he said, "Sir, I've never laid eyes on you before in all my life."

The concierge watched the wealthy rancher, dressed in a fringed leather jacket, western-cut shirt and trousers, and pointed boots, head for the dining room. For an instant, he pitied the lady. There was no mistaking the stern, set line to the rancher's jaw. The concierge breathed a sigh of relief; he certainly was glad that he wasn't the one Mr. Colston was looking for.

At the entrance to the spacious dining room, Judge stopped to scan the patrons positioned at the numerous linen-covered tables set with fresh flowers. His eyes came to rest on a lone woman, who fit the concierge's description, sitting near a window.

"Well, I'll be damned." He rubbed his chin and muttered, "Old maids sure aren't what they used to be."

Chapter Five

Victoria sat primly in the hotel's dining room, quietly sipping her cup of tea. Without appearing to eavesdrop, she strained to listen to a couple of middle-aged matrons discussing how some crude cowboy had pointed a gun at a helpless bellboy, in the lobby this very morning.

The tale left Victoria feeling shocked and unsettled. If such a lawless thing had happened once, it could happen again. Or worse yet, that type of thing might take place on a regular basis in this country. What if the gun discharged? Lani could be hurt, or worse. Victoria troubled about what she should do. Perhaps the judge did not realize what unsavory clientele this hotel attracted. She would have to inform Judge Colston as soon as he returned. Undoubtedly, he would want to change hotels.

As Victoria proceeded to stare into her teacup, continuing to trouble over events, she did not notice the big man standing at the entrance contemplating her.

"Which one of those old vultures is she?" Ozzie

asked, nodding toward the overfed, aging matrons sitting near the window.

When Judge failed to answer, Ozzie followed Judge's line of vision. Judge was staring at one of the most stunning women the old timer had ever seen. Her beauty was not derived from the first blush of youth, but from the full bloom of womanhood.

Ozzie's lips broke into crooked grin. "Don't tell me that that right purty little gal over there is the scrawny, old maid you've been flittin' 'round about. Boy, was you dead wrong!"

Ozzie was inwardly pleased. She just might be able to give Judge something else to think about other than that scheming she-devil, Helene Jessup.

"So it seems." Judge rubbed his chin again, ignoring Ozzie's barb. After a long moment, he added. "Let's go see what she's up to."

Ozzie followed close behind Judge's long strides until the two men were standing in front of the blonde woman. She might be downright gorgeous if she were dressed in something bright and frilly, Ozzie thought.

Victoria looked up at the strangers before her. She was about to demand an explanation for their uninvited presence at her table, when her eyes caught with the tall man's. He was dressed like the cowboys she had read about. For the longest time, they gazed at each other. Victoria seldom, if ever, was at a loss for words. But all rational thought had seemed to leave her, replaced by a quickening heartbeat and a spreading warmth.

Ozzie looked from Judge to the lovely young woman and back again. There was a gleam of attraction sparking between the pair of obviously untamed hearts. He couldn't remember Judge ever looking at a woman like that before. Judge was too used to women throwing themselves at his heels, and had developed a rather jaded attitude about him where women were concerned. Yessiree, any woman spunky enough to write the kind of letter this one had to Judge Colston might very well give him a run for his money—*or land*. Maybe the tough rancher was about to meet his match, Ozzie chuckled to himself.

The old cowpoke's stomach roared. If they wanted to stand there and gawk at each other, let them. He had a gut which was crying to be filled, and he was going to fill it! He reached out to grab a tea cake from off the table.

Victoria blinked to clear the unbidden thoughts about the cowboy which had so suddenly dominated her mind. She wasn't a silly schoolgirl inclined toward instant crushes and romantic nonsense. She was a mature woman engaged to be married. She took a cleansing breath and turned her attention away from the magnetic stranger. Something in her mind clicked when she noticed the neatly dressed older man standing next to the big, handsome cowboy.

She gave the man her brightest smile. "Judge Colston?" She offered her hand to him, thinking that he had intended to introduce himself when he had reached out. "Your honor, I am so very pleased to make the acquaintance of such a highly esteemed juror," she said, before the elderly man could say a word.

Judge's first thought had been to correct her amusing mistake. But when she turned on the charm toward Ozzie, Judge narrowed his eyes and knew he had been right all along. She was nothing but a fortune huntress in an exceedingly pretty package.

"My honor?" Ozzie nearly choked.

"Yes . . . *your honor.*" Judge gave Ozzie a hard slap on the back. My God, the woman thought Ozzie was a judge. That could very well work to his advantage, Judge decided.

Ozzie threw Judge a look of bewilderment, but the expression on Judge's face warned him to keep his tongue. "Miss Victoria Torrington?" Ozzie managed.

"Yes. Please, won't you join me?" She motioned to one of the three unoccupied chairs at the table, all the while feeling foolish at having to act enchanted with the elderly juror. She had learned long ago that men could often be charmed to her cause. And what cause could be more important than concluding this business transaction as quickly as possible?

Ozzie was still somewhat confused, but he pulled out a chair and sat down. This little gal sure was being awful social toward him.

With an indifference she did not feel, she glanced up at the cowboy, who had been left standing. "Is this your man?"

Ozzie's bushy eyebrows darted up in astonishment. *"My man?"*

Maybe she hadn't made herself clearly understood. There was, after all, a difference in their cultures. "Yes . . . your servant."

Jumping polecats, she's really gone and said the wrong thing now. "My servant?" Ozzie swallowed hard, his Adam's apple working up and down. He could see Judge's forehead crinkle, and knew Judge was having a time of it restraining himself. Judge had never let anyone accuse him of being a hired hand without a fight. Judge was too proud; always had been, even as a young 'un. Once he'd blacked both eyes of another boy who had teased him for helping his ma mop floors in the big house Luther Jessup's family owned.

"No," Ozzie blurted out, gaining his voice again. "He's—"

Judge interceded, a lopsided smirk settling on his full lips. "In a way I suppose you could say I am. I'm Judge Colston's foreman back at the ranch." This was going to work out even better than he had originally planned. If he pretended to be the foreman, he might just be able to get her to confess what she was up to.

"If I have offended you, I apologize. It is simply that one would not expect to see a man in such attire in New York City." Her comment about his clothing reminded her of the conversation she had just overheard between the two matrons. When the cowboy shifted positions she saw his holstered gun. Her eyes rounded. "You are not that crude cowboy who drew his pistol on some poor helpless bellboy earlier today, are you?" She asked before realizing that, if he were, the man could be dangerous.

Judge's eyes shot to Ozzie, who was now desperately trying not to laugh. "No, ma'am. I can quite honestly say that I was not that crude cowboy."

From appearances, she knew it was no use suggesting they change hotels. She exhaled a breath. At least they should be able to handle any such situation should one arise. "I am relieved. But I suppose that sort of thing is quite common in the Wild West."

"There are those one is better off not tangling with, no matter where one meets up with them," Judge answered cryptically.

"No doubt." Victoria put her hand on her chest. "I hope you will forgive my manners, Mister—?"

"JC," Judge mumbled very quickly, for want of a better response.

"Mister Jesse. Won't you please join us?"

Jesse? She had misunderstood. Jesse. Not bad though. Actually, Judge admitted to himself, she had come up with a better name than he. "Just Jesse," he added.

"Well, won't you join us . . . Jesse?"

"Don't mind if I do." Deliberately, Judge pulled out a chair, turned it around, and straddled it. She looked shocked, which, although it galled him, only served to make him more determined than ever to enjoy the little ruse he had begun. He would unmask her for what she really was and send her back to Britain with her tail between her legs.

The thought of her legs turned his attention to her body. Although she was seated, what he could see was put together without a flaw. Too bad she was wearing such a high-necked jacket. It looked as if she were trying to hide a figure which would turn any man's head.

It might be rather pleasant to get a better look at her. From the proper way she was sitting, he wondered if she owned anything but prudish clothes. Maybe if he took her somewhere which required that she wear a ball gown, he could find out if the rest of her was as striking. The idea recalled to mind the invitation he had received this morning, requesting his attendance at a fancy charity ball being given tonight by William Vanderbilt. The idea of seeing this woman in something more alluring intrigued him.

After a few moments of polite conversation Victoria said, "I do hope you will excuse us, Jesse. Judge Colston and I have a mutual business venture to discuss."

She had been scandalized when the blue-eyed cowboy had turned his chair around and sat down, but she must learn to make allowances. After all, the man was employed by the judge, and she must remember that if she kept their relationship amicable, they could conclude their business dealings much faster.

She squirmed in her seat as a second flush of warmth invaded her body when she glanced at the bronzed cowboy. She quickly looked away. She must just be overtired from the trip, she attempted to convince herself. But she knew the truth. Quite simply, she found that she was attracted to the American cowboy. At least she was not addlepated. It was only a fleeting attraction and would soon pass.

"You go right on ahead, ma'am. I don't mind none at all," Judge said, with such a twang to his voice that it flipped Ozzie's gaze to him. "I'll just mosey on over there," he pointed to where a lovely brunette sat sweetly smiling in their direction, "and set a spell." Judge rose and tipped his hat. "Ma'am."

Momentarily forgetting her intent to settle the matter of the ranch as soon as possible, Victoria watched Jesse saunter over to the brunette's table and be most cordially received. A stab of jealousy picked at her, and she had to force herself to remember that it was the aging judge she was here to see.

Out of the corner of her eye Victoria saw Gerald and Lani approaching the table. They were walking arm and arm, laughing and smiling at each other. Why had she been jealous of a perfect stranger, while seeing her fiancé appear a little too friendly with her sister did not faze her in the slightest? Gerald was merely being kind to Lani, that was the answer. But that did not explain her reaction to the cowboy, which continued to disturb her. Attraction was one thing; jealousy, quite another.

When Lani and Gerald reached the table, Victoria promptly introduced them. They were chatting when Jesse returned minutes later, stuffing a slip of paper which reeked with perfume, into his pocket. Victoria thinned her lips at the overpowering fragrance, then reached out and took Gerald's hand in a sudden display of affection.

"Gerald dear, I want you to meet Mister Jesse. He is Judge Colston's foreman at the ranch. Gerald is my fiancé."

Gerald rose and held out his hand. "It is quite nice to meet you." His smile faded and he retrieved a hand which throbbed. "That jolly well is quite a grip you have. Do sit down, won't you, old man?"

"Good to make your acquaintance, Harold, old man," Judge mimicked the man, whom he had sized up as a sissified pipsqueak of an English dandy.

"*Gerald,* Mister Jesse," Victoria corrected.

"*Jesse,* Miss Torrington," he returned, arching a dark brow in a challenge of sorts.

Lani was closely watching the exchange. Their reaction to one another stirred her thinking. Could that unmannered cowboy possibly be a solution to the

48

dilemma facing her and Gerald? Oh no, she could not be so cruel as to encourage such a match, could she? After all, the American was nowhere near the man Gerald was. It would not be fair, would it? Well, she would just have to get to know the man.

"Do forgive my sister, Jesse. I am Alayne Torrington." She dimpled. "But you may call me Lani."

"Pleasure, Miss Lani." Judge nodded, with an easy, sparkling grin.

"Oh no, I think the pleasure is mine." She tittered and sneaked a wink at Gerald.

Victoria mistook Lani's intentions and began to worry. What if her younger sister were enamored of the cowboy? It would be just like Lani. What was she going to do? She could not let such a man take advantage of Lani. Quickly, Victoria resolved to turn the conversation back to business. "Now that we all seem to be here, perhaps we should discuss the matter of the ranch."

"The ranch?" Ozzie choked.

Judge wasn't ready to hear anything about her claim to his land. First he had to find out more about this woman. "It's getting late, judge. There's no time for talk of business now."

"Late?" Confusion was overtaking the old timer again. He had come to the dining room to eat. The only thing he'd had his fill of so far was words.

Judge gritted his teeth as all eyes turned to him. "Yes. Don't you recollect the party you're going to tonight?"

"I reckon I don't."

"The one at the Vanderbilts. You planned to escort Miss Torrington, remember?"

49

"Oh . . . that party." Finally the boy was starting to make some sense. Judge must want to get the pretty little gal alone. "Miss Torrington, I'd be mighty honored if you'd consent t' go with us." Judge kicked Ozzie under the table. "Ah . . . I . . . I mean me."

"Thank you, but actually I am quite exhausted from the trip."

"It's a charity ball to raise money for orphans. You do believe in charity, don't you ma'am?" Judge challenged.

Victoria opened her mouth to respond just as Lani interrupted. "Victoria! Before we left England, Margaret told me that William Vanderbilt is the richest man in New York! She would be ever so envious if I . . . I mean, if we attended one of his balls! For a charitable cause, of course," Lani squeaked, her eyes as big as saucers at the thought of attending a magnificent ball given by the Vanderbilts. Silently, she shot Victoria an imploring plea before turning her gaze on the judge. "We would ever so much love to go with you. Wouldn't we, Victoria?"

Before Victoria was given a chance to decline, Judge said, "Good. It's all settled. Be ready by nine."

the term in the phrase. "Only you ya was butted in the—" "Aw, hell. And ya sounds off'n some fancy French school as if yer in his boots. Who gave him a wild ass idea t' sue their ass. After they did say—anyway, I should let me way they done. Why d'ya and ya comin'?"

"Oh, ya because ya haven't given me a chance. Before—"

Chapter Six

Judge and Ozzie, finally left alone, grabbed a bite to eat, then left the dining room to start back to their rooms and get ready for the Vanderbilts' ball.

"If ya think I'm sashayin' that little gal 'round one of them fancy shindigs, ya better think again. 'Cause I'll hightail it outta here so fast—"

"You needn't worry, old timer." Judge assured him, as they headed up the stairs toward their rooms. "I never had any intention of you taking our Miss Victoria Torrington to Vanderbilt's ball."

"God almighty! Ya ain't goin' t' stand her up, are ya?"

"Would I do something like that?" Judge had a devilish grin which did little for Ozzie's peace of mind. But at least he didn't have to escort her himself.

Ozzie looked suspicious. "All I got t' say is, it's a good thing ya ain't goin' t' let her down again." Then his brows spiked together as a thought hit him. "Another thing, what's with ya masqueradin' 'round as a ranch hand, *Jesse? My* ranch hand at that! The way you're talkin' she's sure t' think you're as unlearned as me. Tsk, tsk. And ya goin' t' one of them fancy Eastern schools as a young 'un 'n all. Why, your folks would turn plumb over in their graves after slavin' t' send ya away t' school the way they done. Well? Why ain't ya answerin'?"

"Probably because you haven't given me a chance."

"Humph!" Ozzie scowled and crossed his arms over his chest. "Never shoulda worn these duds. Now you're goin' 'n makin' me part of your guldurned games. Why don't ya just come right out with it and sit down and do some palaverin' with her?"

"You listened to the woman. You think she has the slightest intention of being reasonable? Hell no! She's prepared to fight this all the way." They stopped outside Ozzie's door. "I hadn't planned to become 'Jesse.' But when she mistook you for me, I thought it'd give me a chance to learn more about her and maybe trick her up."

Ozzie scratched his head. "Trick her up?"

"Yeah. She might confide in someone she considers a lowly ranch hand. If she does, I've got her. As far as you pretending to be me—who better? You know everything there is to know about the ranch." Judge dug into his shirt pocket and pulled out a cheroot. "Here," he handed it to Ozzie, "puff on this. It'll calm those jitters you're having about being a wealthy ranch owner."

Ozzie shot Judge a disgruntled look, then sniffed the length of the cheroot. A smile broadened across his lips. "Ahh, it's goin' t' be a mighty fine smoke. That's downright righteous of ya."

The old timer opened his door and stepped inside.

An instant later, he turned and stuck his head out. "Don't go enjoyin' that purty little gal's company too much, ya hear?" He chuckled at Judge's deep frown, which only served to goad him into making another comment. "I ain't set eyes on such a looker for nigh on forty years now. Why, she's the most purtiest woman I ever did see, what with that thick yella hair and those big blue eyes, the color of a Wyoming sky in summer. She's so beautiful that if I wasn't so danged old I'd—"

"I didn't notice," Judge said lamely, knowing damn well Ozzie knew better.

"I'll just bet ya one of them good bottles of whiskey ya didn't." Ozzie laughed and shut the door, leaving Judge in the hall glaring at him. "I'll just bet ya didn't."

Judge crammed his hands into his pockets and went to his room to get cleaned up. What *would* Miss Victoria Torrington do if she were stood up . . . ?

"Will you please hurry?" Victoria chided Lani. "Judge Colston will be here any moment, and you are nowhere near ready."

"Then you will just have to go on ahead without me. Gerald can bring me later," Lani blurted out, then pressed three fingers to her lips.

Victoria stared into the mirror, smoothing the lace frills and ruching of her midnight blue gown from Worth. She fussed with the extreme décolletage which accentuated the lush curves of her breasts. She adjusted the heartshaped neckline which exposed incandescent shoulders. She turned, wondering if she would be able to breathe, the bodice was so tight.

"You look marvelous! Stop making such a fuss with your gown," said an exasperated Lani, standing proudly in a fluffy mint crinolette by Doucet, with its profusion of laces, froufrou, and ruffles.

"I am only going to this ball because it seems to be important to you," snapped Victoria. "You know I prefer a tailored look."

"Why? So you can hide the fact you are an exceedingly attractive woman underneath those dowdy suits of yours? At least you are not wearing black any longer."

"I think that is enough from you, young lady!"

"I do not know what you are so afraid of?"

"I said that is enough!" Victoria was beginning to get angry. But when she stopped to think about what her sister had said, Victoria wasn't sure whether she was perturbed over Lani's comment or because she was closer to the truth than Victoria cared to admit.

Lani ignored Victoria, took a seat at the vanity, and began toying with the small curls framing her face. She looked in the mirror to see Victoria attempting to smooth her thick golden tresses. "At least I managed to coif your hair into a bouffant of curls. If you do not attract that gorgeous Jesse the way you look tonight, then the man is simply not human."

"Alayne Torrington, I am surprised at you! I am quite happily engaged." As soon as the words darted from her lips, Victoria turned from Lani so the girl would not see the troubled expression which shadowed her face. A rap at the door saved her from being further probed by her all-too-blunt sister.

Lani watched Victoria stiffly walk to answer the

door. Never one to let anything slip by without a comment, Lani remarked, "If you were just more feminine in your attitude toward life, you would have married years ago." Victoria shot Lani a piercing look. Lani shrugged. "My goodness, you even walk like you are an old lady."

An impish curve turned the corners of Lani's lips upward at a calculating angle which warned Victoria that the girl was up to something. She swallowed a retort, and turned her attention back to the door.

When Victoria opened the door she stood mute, her lips parted in wonder, her pulse pounding.

"Is standin' there with your mouth open like that considered a proper greeting in your country, ma'am? Or did a wolf bite off your tongue?" Judge drawled, leaning against the door frame.

Victoria blinked. She had been expecting Judge Colston, not the paradigm of male sensuality standing arrogantly before her. "No. And I do not intend to let one dressed in gentleman's clothing close enough to attempt it, either."

"Yes, I reckon any wolf who would get involved with a lady like yourself would have his work cut out for him, ma'am."

"I have no intention of involving myself with anyone, wolf or man." Lamely, she stood still, mesmerized by the handsome cowboy.

"No offense ma'am, but that is obvious from your selection of Harold."

She took an indignant breath. "Gerald."

Judge stared into the fire in those snapping blue eyes. This was a multifaceted woman worthy of exploration. The attraction he felt irritated and excited

55

him at the same time. "May I come in while you get your wrap, or are you going to leave me standing out here in the hall?"

"Please, do not put forth such a sage suggestion or I might be tempted to adhere to it."

"I'll keep that in mind, ma'am," Judge lazily drawled, undaunted by her attempts to put him in his place.

Victoria felt her neck grow warm. Before their exchange got completely out of hand, she quickly gathered her pelisse with the wide sleeves designed to create a cape in back, while Lani grinned at the intriguing change of events.

Her eyes gleaming, Lani stepped up to Victoria and whispered cutely, "Why, sister dear, I have never seen you lose your cool demeanor so easily before."

Before Victoria could object, Lani moved toward Jesse and gave him a seductive smile, letting her eyes openly take in the big man from head to toe. "Umm, why, hello there, Jesse. You look utterly irresistible. Isn't what you are wearing called a tuxedo?"

"It sure is, miss. It's the latest in formal duds," Judge offered, with a crooked grin. Maybe he was planning to pursue the wrong sister. Without a doubt, he could get more out of the one who was throwing herself at him. But she was little more than a child, and he had to admit that the older sibling was the one who sparked his senses. He reminded himself he wasn't here looking for female companionship; he was fighting a fortune huntress. It would be a pity to use the girl, Lani, as a weapon against her own sister. Yet a child with a loose tongue could prove helpful with his cause . . . The thought gave Judge something to ponder.

"It surely does wonders for you, Jesse. And I simply love that black silk tie and tailless evening coat. I must say, men's wear has improved. Or could it be due to the man who is wearing it?" Lani coyly tittered.

"Alayne!" Victoria was shocked by her sister's bold display.

Lani knew Victoria was ruffled and decided to egg her on. "Didn't Mother used to say to Father that the man inside the clothing was more important than the clothes? Wouldn't you agree, Jesse?" Lani was shamelessly flirting, thoroughly enjoying the pink blotches beginning to adorn Victoria's cheeks.

"I guess I'd say that you can't always tell how a badger will fight until you invade its territory." He looked straight at Victoria then, an accusing gleam in his blue eyes. She sure was packaged nicely! He'd thought so earlier. Why did he find her so fascinating when the only feeling he should have for her was an enemy's animosity?

Victoria was horrified by her sister's outrageous behavior, as well as the receptiveness of the cowboy to such blatant overtures. Then again, weren't all men the same? Hadn't she learned that from her father's business associates, constantly making advances toward her when their wives were not around? She couldn't control Jesse's reactions to Lani. But she could not let it continue, either. Victoria knew not to confront the whimsical girl directly, so she said, "Alayne, shouldn't you hurry so we do not keep Jesse waiting?"

"Oh, dear." Lani pouted. "You only call me Alayne

when you are angry. Did I do something wrong?" she asked innocently, baiting Victoria without mercy.

Victoria looked from Lani to Jesse. Embarrassed, but intending to give the girl a good dressing down when they got back to the hotel, she answered non-committally, "I think you had best hurry."

"I am nowhere near ready. You two go on ahead." She smiled coyly at Jesse. "You will save a dance for me, won't you, Jesse?"

"Why, Miss Lani, it'd be my pleasure." An ulterior motive flickered in the blue depths of his eyes, which gave Victoria further cause for concern.

Despite her trepidation, Victoria took Jesse's proffered arm. A bolt of heat flashed through her. It made the spasms in her stomach, which had begun when she opened the door, quicken. It must be something she had eaten, she fretted, trying to convince herself that what she was experiencing had nothing to do with Jesse. As they walked out the door, she sent Lani a piercing look over her shoulder. Surely the girl could not be interested in some American cowboy, could she? Lani was so impressionable. Victoria must not let such a flirtation progress any further.

"Mr. Vanderbilt certainly has a palatial home," observed Victoria as the coach drew to a halt in front of the impressive residence on Fifth Avenue.

"I reckon, if a person wants to live in something like that. He's busy building two more further on, between Fifty-first and Fifty-second. One's for himself and the other's for his married daughters. Two of his sons are building places higher up the avenue."

Victoria silently studied the elegant mansion. Although her family home was not as enormous, this house brought back memories of a way of life so suddenly lost to her. Not that money was the most important thing. No, it was the security and freedom wealth provided which she longed to regain. Somehow she had to get enough money from the ranch property to rebuild Torrington Limited so she could buy back her family home. The thought strengthened her resolve to convince Judge Colston to be reasonable.

Once inside, Judge whisked Victoria out onto the dance floor before she could go through the receiving line. They glided amidst women elegantly clad in fashions from Paris and sparkling with jewels, and men attired in the latest formal wear. The crystal chandeliers above glistened, casting a shower of lights around the room. Tableaux of rare flowers displayed an unbelievable wealth of color.

The orchestra was playing a waltz, and Victoria felt herself being drawn close against Jesse's hard chest. His scent of fresh lime encircled her senses. In no time, all thoughts she had had of protesting such intimacy faded off into the distance.

She had seldom enjoyed dancing before, the men always grabbing or holding her so stiffly. But with Jesse, it was different. There was no awkwardness, no tenseness. They melted together naturally, swaying about the floor with the ease of long-time familiarity.

Judge looked down at his dancing partner. Why did she have to feel so good in his arms? "Victoria Torrington," he murmured absently, before he realized what he'd said.

The sound of her name brought her back to reality. "Yes?" When Victoria noticed the music had ended, she felt a strange rush of disappointment.

"The music has stopped." He looked amused when she discovered that they were the only ones left on the floor.

Victoria looked about her. Clusters of guests were staring at them, whispering. Her fantasies immediately crashed. How could she, even for a moment, have imagined that she had feelings for this man? He was nothing but a crude cowboy dressed as a gentleman, and she was an engaged lady.

"How could you! You . . . you cowhand!" Embarrassment heightening her color, she hurried from the dance floor, Judge chuckling as he followed her.

"What's the matter, Miss Torrington? Did you go and forget yourself? A lady like you shouldn't be seen with the hired help. Particularly since you were starting to enjoy yourself," he added, annoyed by her attitude and by the enjoyment he had derived from holding her in his arms.

Victoria gasped, then whirled around and rushed toward the huge, bubbling fountain of champagne. She had hoped to get lost among the throngs, but felt stifled, surrounded by the horde of people. Passing the enormous double doors which led out onto a magnificent veranda, she slipped outside to compose herself.

Judge followed close behind, berating himself for antagonizing her. He had to gain her confidence so she would let down her guard and confide her little scheme. He filled two glasses with champagne, intending to make amends.

With ease, he wove his way through the clusters of guests toward Victoria, who was standing with her back to him at the edge of the veranda. A breeze was gently teasing her golden curls as she leaned against the wall, seemingly lost in thought. Judge found her a most fetching sight. He had almost reached her when a voice behind him caused him to change course.

"Is it really you? Ju—," a pleased feminine voice began.

"Clarissa." Judge cut her off. "What are you doing here?" There was a note of annoyance to his voice. He inwardly heaved a bored sigh. Now he would be forced to court Clarissa's attention away from Victoria all evening. He couldn't let Clarissa spoil his masquerade. Damn Helene for siccing her cousin on him back at the hotel!

"For me?" She took a glass from Judge's hand. "Cousin Helene telegraphed me that you were the very sweetest, otherwise I should never have sent you that note to meet me at your hotel." She ignored his irritation and continued. "When I saw you in the hotel dining room this afternoon, you didn't say one word about coming to the party tonight. I really should scold you, you naughty boy. If I'd known, I never would have come with that dreary Teddy Benderson." She took Judge's arm and, sipping champagne, led him back inside so she could be seen with the most handsome man in attendance.

Victoria turned in time to see the pair stroll inside, arm in arm. It was just as well. She had come to America to see Judge Colston, not spend time with his foreman. Yet annoyance and another unrecognizable emotion held her as she watched the cowboy waltz the stunning brunette around the floor, the woman laughing at whatever he said. She was the same women he had met in the dining room at the hotel. Had he planned to meet her all along? He must have been furious when Judge Colston had forced him to be her escort.

It seemed like hours before Lani and Gerald appeared. Victoria had forced herself to dance nearly every dance with the array of men who had asked her, just to prove she was having a good time. She had been introduced to the Vanderbilts and a variety of unassailable society barons and their pompous wives, as well as bevies of sparkling debutantes and their escorts. Boring conversations had assaulted her while she watched that irritating Jesse ignore her and delight in the brunette's company.

"What a grand ball!" Lani exclaimed, dazzled by the pure, unadulterated opulence. Victoria seemed annoyed, so Lani added, "I am ever so sorry we were late, Victoria. The judge was feeling a bit under the weather. And we had such a dreadful time getting lost on our way here." Lani looked contrite, but she secretly sent a smile to Gerald when Victoria glanced at the dance floor. Lani followed Victoria's gaze. A calculating gleam entered Lani's eyes when she saw that Victoria was staring at Jesse.

Chapter Seven

The rising outlines of the city were etched against the lightening skyline when she tried to rouse Lani from her bed.

"Ge—" mumbled Lani, pulling the satin coverlet over her head.

"What did you say?" Victoria asked, suspicious that her sister had been about to say Jesse's name in her sleep.

Lani sat bolt upright when she realized she had been dreaming about Gerald. "Oh." She rubbed her eyes. "Victoria. What are you doing up so early?"

"You know very well we were told last night that we would be leaving early this morning. Do not try to change the subject. What were you saying when I woke you?"

"Is it all right for you to change the subject?" Lani attempted to put Victoria off.

"You are not going to divert my attention, if that is what you are trying to do. Now, what were you saying?" demanded Victoria.

"I . . . I was merely dreaming about Jesse, if you

must know. I guess I must have said his name," Lani said coyly, watching for Victoria's reaction.

The man was insufferable. And now there was no doubt he had captured her sister's admiration. "I certainly cannot imagine why," Victoria said shortly. "He did not pay any attention to you until he was taking us back to the hotel. And then he had the nerve to inform us that we would have to accompany him and Judge Colston to Texas, to look at some cow, before the judge will agree to look at the legal documents I have."

"It is a bull," Lani said dreamily, and rose to begin dressing.

"Who cares what it is. I do not want you mooning over a man at least twice your age."

Lani stuck her head out of the dressing room door, a wicked smile on her lips. "I do not intend merely to moon over him, sister dear." Lani watched Victoria furiously throw things in her bag. It was a good sign. A good sign indeed.

"Why did ya go and put them duds on for?" Ozzie shook his head. "Them's your work clothes." He looked puzzled.

"Exactly. And you can get that good jacket I got you back out and put it on. Appearances, remember," Judge shot back, stuffing the last of his clothing into a suitcase.

Ozzie grumbled but did as bid. "Did you learn anything last night?"

"Looks like you will just have to be Judge Colston a little while longer. That damned cousin of Helene's showed up and ruined everything. I spent most of the evening keeping the prying witch away from the Torringtons. When I get back to the ranch I'm going to wring Helene's neck for siccing Clarissa on me."

"Sounds like the smartest thing ya could do t' Helene," Ozzie put in.

Judge knew Ozzie didn't approve of him dallying with Helene Jessup. But it was none of the old timer's business.

"Save your tongue, old man. We've got a train to catch."

"We finally goin' home?"

"No. I told you I want to keep that schemer as far from the ranch as possible."

"So where we goin'?"

"To Texas. We'll check out Bridgewater's prize bull, and lose one Miss Victoria Elizabeth Torrington along the way."

"I wouldn't go countin' on it if I was ya."

Judge and Ozzie did not reach the station until the train was nearly ready to pull out. Victoria had been impatiently pacing back and forth, her jabot cascading over the pouter pigeon bosom of her suit blouse, her skirt bouncing in beat with each step. "Judge Colston!" She rushed past Judge, ignoring him, and took Ozzie's arm. "Lani told me you were ill last night. I do hope you are feeling better this morning."

Ozzie patted her arm. "Much better, darlin'."

"I say, I do believe we should hurry," announced Gerald, checking his pocket watch.

Ozzie turned to Judge. "Jesse, get them there bags so we don't miss this here train."

Judge scowled, mumbling, "Scheming bitch."

"I beg your pardon?" Victoria looked back over her shoulder.

"I said I got me a itch," Judge answered in a grating voice.

"I will be ever most happy to scratch it for you, Jesse," cutely piped in Lani.

Gerald looked shocked and Victoria shot the girl a look of disapproval. Ozzie chuckled at Judge's deepening scowl and let Victoria help him onto the train.

The conductor directed them toward two drawing rooms near the dining car. "Here youse is, two of the line's best." The man's black eyes expectant, he clasped his arms behind his back, rocked back and forth on his heels, and waited.

When none of the men bothered to tip the man, Victoria shot them a disgusted pose, dug into her reticule, and offered the man a coin. "Thank you."

"Yes ma'am," he nodded. After sending the men a haughty look, he disappeared down the long narrow corridor

Gerald gazed at the two doors for a moment, then said, "I had not planned to spend my time with you, sir. But I fancy it will be fine, what?"

"I fancy it won't," Judge snapped. "You'll be spending the seven hour ride to Washington, D.C. in the parlor car, with the rest of the people who haven't paid for a sleeping bunk."

Gerald's eyes slitted. "You, my good fellow, are rather a crude bloke. You could use a right good thumping."

"You want to try?" Judge took a menacing step forward. For some reason, the idea of beating the pulp out of Victoria's fiancé greatly appealed to him.

66

"Gerald, ignore the man." Victoria linked her arm with Gerald's. "He is only the hired help."

"Right you are, dear." Gerald breathed a sigh of relief. He knew he wouldn't stand a chance up against a man of Jesse's size, not to mention the man's muscular physique. But Gerald didn't like the way Lani was behaving toward the American at all.

"Tell ya what, Gerry. Just to show there's no hard feelin's, the little miss here," Ozzie looked at Lani, "and me will go with ya and get ya all settled in."

Gerald looked to Victoria for approval. "It is all right, dear," Victoria said. "Lani will help you 'settle in.' It is only for seven hours." Gerald gave Victoria a chaste peck on the cheek, then meekly followed the judge and Lani toward the back of the train.

Judge picked up Victoria's bag. "Well, which one of these do you want?"

"Thank you. But I do believe I can manage," she said curtly. "You may set my luggage down."

"I wouldn't think of it."

"Oh, very well. This one." She stepped inside the door on the left. The interior finish was a rich walnut with carved inlay and lacquer work. An oil lamp was fastened to the outer wall, providing a soft yellow glow about the carpeted room.

Judge set her bag inside the room and then stood there. She was standing so close that he inhaled her fragrance of crushed roses, which sent his senses roiling. He had to fight an inner battle to keep up the pose he had adopted. Warring nerves in his fingers twitched to feel the satiny smoothness of her skin on his. He forced himself to swallow the inclination to take her into his arms.

Victoria was trying to ignore the warmth his presence exuded and so busied herself by reaching up to pull down the bed. No matter how hard she tugged, the stubborn berth would not budge.

"Do you plan to help me, or are you merely going to stand there," she finally said tartly.

"Oh, I don't know. I think I might just stand here and enjoy the view." He smiled, his eyes fastened on the slender bit of ankle protruding from the bottom of her skirt.

Victoria quickly smoothed down her skirt, shooting daggers at him. "My ankles are none of your business."

"I'm afraid they are."

"They most certainly are not!"

"As long as you plan to use them to set foot on Colston property, they are."

"That is none of your business either," she sputtered.

" 'Fraid it is."

"Perhaps we should have a little chat with Judge Colston about that."

"If you want. But since I plan to stake a claim on that ranch myself, you might as well tell me exactly what you are up to. Or did you think you could steal it out from under some poor, dumb rancher's nose? If that's the case, you better think again. 'Course, if you want to throw in with me, and tell me what you have planned, we might be able to come to terms." Judge had not meant to blurt out such a story. But after he thought about it, it didn't sound too bad. Might be better than playing up to her harebrained sister. If Victoria Torrington thought he was after the ranch maybe she would lay her cards on the table.

So he was trying to cheat the judge out of his land, Victoria surmised. Maybe if she went along with him she could find out what he was up to and alert the judge. "I do not know what you mean, but if you are to tell me what you have in mind—"

Her attempts at playing innocent had so incensed Judge that he lost the cool, detached control he was known for possessing and snatched her into his arms.

"I'll tell you what I have in mind." In a swift motion his lips swooped down over Victoria's, effectively cutting off the rest of her sentence.

At first she struggled against him. But he held fast, his lips tasting, teasing, softly pressing, inviting and tantalizing her to respond. Daring her to deny the sudden sensuous rush wildly tracing a path throughout her body, Judge coaxed her lips open and slipped his tongue inside her mouth. As he tasted the sweet cavern, he felt her resistance slacken and an undeniable response, at first hesitant and then more bold, took over.

"Ah-hem." Ozzie cleared his throat. Standing in the doorway, both the old timer and Lani wore pleased smiles.

Victoria was mortified by her response to the big American and immediately broke away.

Judge stood still, nonplussed, yet he continued to feel the soft texture of Victoria's lips against his.

"I . . . we were just discussing business," Victoria stammered, an embarrassed pink blotching her throat and cheeks.

"Victoria dear, Judge Colston and I can see for ourselves what kind of business you two were *discus-*

sing." Lani tittered and stepped up to Judge. "I hope you do not mind if I *discuss business* with you, too." She smiled wickedly and threw her arms around Judge, giving him a smacking kiss.

The older sister wasn't about to tell him what she was up to, so Judge took full advantage of the younger girl's boldness and thoroughly kissed her back. It was a pleasant kiss, no more, no less. Judge was not affected by it the way he had been with Victoria, damn her!

Victoria could see that Lani was getting out of hand. Jesse, too, seemed to be enjoying himself. She had to save Lani from making a terrible mistake, and find out what Jesse was up to. If she had stopped to analyze her distress, she might have realized it was the fact that Jesse had just kissed her and now was kissing her sister which disturbed her so much.

Ozzie watched the whole scene with quiet interest. Judge was getting himself in a lot deeper than he knew. The old timer just hoped that the big rancher was smart enough to pick the right sister.

"Would you like to see the rest of the train, Miss Torrington?" Judge asked Lani when they broke apart.

To Victoria's chagrin, Lani took his arm. They strolled toward the parlor car. Victoria sucked in her cheeks and sat down, Ozzie plopping down across from her. "I wouldn't go worryin' none 'bout that little sister of yours. She looked like she can handle herself right fine."

"Not from where I was standing," Victoria said, a bit too sharply.

Ozzie's lips curled into a satisfied grin. There was

definitely more to this filly than met the eye. A calculating twinkle sparked into his amber eyes. "Don't ya go givin' them another thought. If Jesse gets her in a family way, I'm sure he'll do right by the little gal."

"What?"

"I said, he'll do right by your sister if he—"

Scandalized, she stopped him. "I heard what you said."

"Then what'd ya want me t' repeat it for?"

Ignoring him, Victoria jumped to her feet and started for the door.

"Where ya goin'?" Ozzie asked innocently, delighted by her reaction.

"Where do you think? If that man has any designs on my sister, he is in for a big surprise!"

After Victoria hurried away, Ozzie took a cheroot out of his pocket, bit off the end and chuckled out loud. "I think this trip is goin' t' give us a few more surprises than we expected." He struck a match and puffed contentedly.

Chapter Eight

The warm scent of spring blossoms hung invitingly in the late afternoon air as the train pulled into Washington, D.C. Gerald and Lani pressed near the open windows, absorbing the ambience of the United States capital city, while Victoria worried over the documents she had tucked inside her luggage.

An expressman had given them medal tags with a number for their luggage and a promise to deliver their bags to the hotel before they arrived. Victoria sat troubled, unable to fathom how Gerald and her sister could so easily hand over claim to their possessions.

Still concerned about their bags, Victoria looked back over her shoulder three times as they left the train station for the hired carriage which Jesse had insisted on driving. They passed through heavy traffic as they headed toward Wormsley's Hotel.

Victoria found the nation's capital a charming city. The streets were paved with asphalt, and well planned, Victoria observed, viewing the assorted buildings and spreading trees which shaded the capital's many inhabitants. There was an electrifying excitement about the city which captured her attention and held her mesmerized for some time.

"How long will we be here?" Victoria finally asked the judge, growing impatient to conclude this ridiculous side excursion to Texas and be on their way to the ranch.

"Not very," Judge drawled from the front of the carriage, where Lani sat beside him in orchid frills, resting a possessive arm on his shoulder.

"I would like to conduct the preliminaries of our business, at least." Victoria's words were directed toward the judge, but her eyes remained on Lani and Jesse.

"I say, that does sound like a jolly good plan," put in Gerald, who shrunk in his seat when the rest of the party shot him quelching looks in unison.

"You were already told you would have to be patient," Judge said, snapping the reins over the rumps of the matched sorrels. "So I suggest you enjoy the city in silence."

Victoria burned inside. Since it was obvious that Judge Colston had no intention of rescuing her from Jesse's cutting remarks, she would keep any further remarks concerning the claim to herself, for the time being. "What is that white marble building up there on the hill? It is most inspiring."

"The Capitol Building," Judge offered dryly. "Much of the country's business is handled there."

As Victoria stared at the impressive structure, an idea flashed into her mind. Why should she remain patient? If the judge was not willing to discuss her claim, maybe she could force the issue.

They drove on in silence until Judge said, "Over there on the left is the Executive Mansion."

Not to be outdone, Victoria responded, "I understand the Executive Mansion was nicknamed the White House after it was painted white in order to conceal the aftermath of a fire set by British troops in 1814."

"The British repeatedly failed in their attempts to conquer the Americans and bring them to heel. You might keep that in mind before you try to insist that you own part of the J Bar C," Judge glibly shot back.

Victoria bit her lip to keep from retorting. After all, why should she debate the issue with a disgruntled ranch hand? Judge Colston was the one she had to deal with. And he was sitting beside her without comment.

They stopped in front of a plain but pleasant hotel. Three attendants lumbered out to take care of the carriage and escort the party inside and to their rooms.

Concerned that the luggage had not yet been delivered, Victoria sank down on the bed with a sigh of exasperation. "I should have kept the documents with me. The English method of handling one's own luggage is much more efficient. I am going right back to that train station to personally see that our baggage is delivered promptly, before it is lost. Then I have business to tend to at the Capitol Building."

"What if I go? You can rest, and then take care of your business. Gerald can accompany me," Lani offered eagerly.

"That is the most responsible thing I have heard you say since we arrived in America. Do stop and check at the desk before you leave, just in case that fool expressman has delivered our things."

"Do not worry, sister dear. I shall be ever so happy to take care of everything," Lani chirped, flitting from the room.

She practically skipped down the hall toward Gerald's accommodations, a pleased smile on her lips. Out of the corner of her eye she glimpsed Victoria watching her, so she stopped at Jesse's door and knocked.

Naked from the waist up, displaying a chest of rippling muscles, the width of it peppered with thick, curling, black hair, Judge answered the door with a towel in his hands. Was he going to be hounded to the ends of the world by these English bloodsuckers? "What can I do for you, Miss Lani?" he asked less than enthusiastically.

Victoria was shocked and dismayed that Lani would lie to her and then immediately try to sneak into Jesse's room. Victoria rushed to join her sister in a panic that Lani would do something rash, and mindful of what the judge had said about Jesse doing right by the girl if he got her in a motherly way.

Lani fought a bubble of laughter as she said, "Victoria needs an escort to accompany her on a visit of the Capitol Building. Since Gerald is going to help me try to locate the luggage, I thought you would not mind protecting my sister."

"I do not need protection," Victoria insisted, glaring at her well-meaning sibling. When she looked at Jesse's nakedness, a deep red crept up her cheeks. Warmth spread once again throughout her body, and an urge to stroke her fingertips through the dark curling hair on his chest threatened to overtake her.

Judge looked from sister to sister. There was something about Victoria's stance, stiff and uneasy, which made him suspicious. The last thing he needed was to cart an Englishwoman in a red suitcoat around Washington. But a voice inside his head warned him that she was up to no good. Her name and outfit caused the perfect nickname to drop into his head. "You needn't worry about your sister none, Miss Lani. I'll be glad to stick to Tori's backside like a tick on a pesky dog."

Victoria's eyes rounded at his blatant disfigurement of her name. "What did you call me?"

"Tori. You have hearing problems?" Judge grinned, pleased that the nickname seemed to have struck a nerve.

"I hear quite well, thank you. But it seems I must remind you that you are the hired help. Therefore, when you find it necessary to address me, sir, you may refer to me as Miss Torrington." She lifted her chin into a haughty pose.

"Since I'm not *your* hired help, I'll call you anything I damn well please, Tori. Can you think of a better name to call an Englishwoman wearing a red coat?" Judge chuckled mischievously.

"If you are referring to British soldiers, I had not realized you would be so well versed in lessons of history."

"There's a lot of things I'm well versed in," he wolfishly crowed. "Take, for example, the lesson I gave you this morning."

Victoria didn't have to search her memory. "This morning?" she whispered, feigning innocence before realizing the error she had just made.

Judge took a step toward her. "Don't try to tell me you have forgotten? Maybe I should refresh your memory."

Victoria absently touched her lips. The recollection of the soft texture of Jesse's lips pressing, pressing, against hers lingered still. She gasped, then quickly sought composure, stiffening her spine.

"That will be quite unnecessary. My faculties of retention are quite intact, thank you."

He shrugged. "Your loss."

"You overestimate your powers of appeal, *Mister* Jesse."

"I certainly do not think so," interjected Lani.

Victoria gritted her teeth to quiet her nerves. She stepped back, further experiencing the remembrance of his fiery kiss and the effect it had had on her. Not about to allow herself to be kissed again, and still reeling from the feelings he had elicited from her so easily, she swung around and stomped back toward her room. Garnering her strength, Victoria stopped. Stiffly, she turned and said, "If you must use my given name, do try to remember I was named after two queens, Victoria and Elizabeth."

"Maybe that explains your priggish behavior."

"You are undoubtedly without redemption, sir!" Victoria huffed, and started back down the hallway.

"Tori," Judge called out, "don't think you're going to sneak out of that room without me. And the name's Jesse."

"You may be at each other's throats now, but I have not seen Victoria display that much fire toward any man before. If you are interested, I would say it is a

77

good sign. Thank you, Jesse. I am sure you will take good care of Victoria for me," Lani said.

Noting Victoria had looked back over her shoulder, Lani stood on her tiptoes and placed a kiss on his lips. An instant later, she flinched, as Victoria's door slammed shut.

"By the way, Jesse, you had better watch your diction. That lowly cowhand talk seems to come and go." Lani gave him a calculating smile and winked. "But you need not be concerned that I would expose you. I would not think of telling another living soul that you may be trying to hide something."

"I suppose I should thank you." Judge's tone sounded bored and not the least bit ruffled. "Instead, I'll do you a favor."

"Oh?"

"I won't say anything about you and your friend, Gerald."

"He is Victoria's fiancé," protested Lani, no longer quite so confident.

"So I've been told."

Judge followed Victoria up the steps of the Capitol Building, watching the inviting sway of her hips as she walked. He wondered what it would be like to have the nicely rounded hips he imagined encased in that skirt, writhing nude in rhythm beneath him on a soft mattress. She was so proper, yet the fire he saw in those blue eyes led him to believe that if unleashed, Victoria Elizabeth Torrington could fulfill a man's wildest desires.

Why that fool Gerald Pelthurst would want to look

at that empty-headed sister when Victoria had spunk, intelligence, and beauty, made Judge wonder. Then he thought of Victoria's other side: the stubborn, take-charge, overbearing portion of her which could threaten to strip a man of his masculinity. If she were his woman, he'd know how to handle her. *His woman?* What an unsettling idea. What could he be thinking? Just must be a notion left over from that annoying conversation he'd had with the lawyer, who had noted that one option would be to marry the woman. She was his adversary, and he had better not let his guard down for a minute.

Judge looked up from his reverie to see a good-sized man with mutton chop whiskers coming down the steps toward him. It was President Chester Arthur. Judge had known the man for years, and feared he would be recognized. As the president drew near, the recognition in his face warned Judge that his masquerade was in jeopardy.

"Ah, one of my favorite supporters," President Arthur smiled and held out his hand.

Judge pumped the proffered arm. "And how are you, Mr. President?"

"Well as can be expected."

"Pity the senate overrode your veto of the Chinese Exclusion Bill. It was a crashing blow to Chang Sung back at the ranch. He had hoped to bring the rest of his family to this country."

"Yes, it is a pity that any Chinese who works with his hands is denied immigration." He let out a heartfelt sigh. "But do tell Chang I look forward to sampling his cooking again next time I visit Wyoming. I have fond memories of his suckling goose with fried

79

rice."

Victoria's ears perked up. Jesse had just spoken to the President of the United States? She had heard that the handsome, genial man nicknamed "The Gentleman Boss" ran an honest administration. Perhaps she could enlist his aid, since Judge Colston did not appear to be in the slightest hurry.

"Mr. President?" Victoria stepped forward.

"Yes?" President Arthur looked askance at Judge.

"Mr. President, may I introduce Miss Victoria Elizabeth Torrington from England. Named after two queens, but better known as Tori."

"Tori," chuckled the president. "An Englishwoman wearing a red coat. How utterly charming, my dear Tori."

At first Victoria was furious with Jesse. Since the president appeared to find Jesse's remark amusing she would not dispute the nickname. But as soon as she got back to the hotel, she was going to put the red suitcoat inside her luggage for the remainder of the trip—that is, if Lani and Gerald had been able to locate the bags. Tori, indeed!

Trying to put the irritating misnomer out of her mind, she asked, "Mr. President, I know how busy you must be, but I wonder if I might make a request?" When the president did not say anything, she pressed forward. "Since you seem to be familiar with Judge Colston's ranch and have past experience as a member of the bar, and since I recently inherited a portion of the property, I wonder if you might be so kind as to look over the documents I have and reassure the elderly juror of my claim's validity."

"The *elderly juror?*" President Arthur's brow shot

up and he sent Judge a bemused look.

"Why, yes. Judge Colston. I assumed you knew him," Victoria added, "since you were referring to his ranch a moment ago."

"The *elderly* Judge Colston's ranch." President Arthur caught the tightening of Judge's lips and held further comment behind his amusement. "Why, do forgive me, Tori. Of course I am acquainted with the man. And while I wish I could be of service, to you, I am certain you understand that the pressing affairs of state must take precedence. I might suggest you speak directly," he looked squarely at Judge, "with the man. Or perhaps you might try our American court system if you do not find satisfaction. I must say, it was a pleasure meeting you, Tori." He then turned to Judge. "You, my son, seem to have your work cut out for you. You will write and let me know how *the elderly Judge Colston* fares up against this formidable young lady, won't you, sir?"

"It will be my pleasure, Mr. President." Judge frowned at the enjoyment the president seemed to be deriving from his discomfiture. He watched the president continue down the steps before he realized that Victoria was disappearing inside the building. "What the hell are you up to now?" he grumbled, rushing after her.

Chapter Nine

With a determined click to her heels Victoria headed toward the Senate Chamber of the Capitol Building, where the Supreme Court convened. A man dressed in a black robe was walking toward her. Judge caught up with Victoria before she could approach him.

He grabbed her arm. "What do you think you're doing?"

"Not that it is any of your concern," she sent him her most wintery look, "but since Judge Colston does not seem to be able to find the time to discuss my claim, I intend to take my plea to someone who will listen."

"Oh? And since you began at the very top with the President of the United States, does that mean you plan to work your way down? Chief Justice of the Supreme Court perhaps?" he threw back sarcastically.

"How observant of you, Jesse," she answered in kind. "That is exactly what I intend to do!"

As she stood there bandying words with him, Victoria realized that her pulse was fluttering. Yet her expression remained piqued, and she turned to put an end to their exchange.

"You can't be serious," he yelled after her. "And I thought your sister was the harebrained one," he grumbled, following her once again.

A bespectacled law clerk stopped the distinguished gentleman in the black robe in front of Victoria. "Excuse me Mr. Chief Justice, here is the brief you asked for." The clerk scurried away after handing over the bundle of papers.

"Mr. Chief Justice?" Victoria inquired before Judge could stop her.

"Chief Justice Waite," the lackluster man answered.

"Chief Justice Waite?" Judge choked, kicking himself for putting the idea into her stubborn head.

"Yes. May I be of assistance?"

"No —" Judge stepped forward to intercede. Yet he had a sinking feeling she was not going to be convinced to leave meekly. No, she would be more like a wildcat, fighting all the way.

Victoria was not to be put off. "Yes, sir, I do believe you can."

"Well, young woman, how may I help you?"

Judge rolled his eyes. Victoria Elizabeth Torrington, named after two queens, was more determined and high-spirited than he had originally thought. How aptly she'd been titled. He had to give her credit for her perseverance, even if it were at his cost.

"Mr. Chief Justice Waite, I understand that your Supreme Court handles cases involving foreign matters."

"Yes, but only those affecting foreign ambassadors and ministers."

"I think that leaves you out," Judge said, a relieved grin crossing his lips. "Now come on, Miss Tori, we should get you back to the hotel."

The drab figure of a man nodded. "Good day." He walked three steps down the hall toward the chamber door before Victoria caught up with him.

"Sir, I think if you will only listen to me, you will agree that I do indeed have a claim worthy of a hearing."

"I am afraid I am due in court. Have your lawyer draw up a writ of certiorari. I will try to see that it comes up for review."

"But I do not have time. I have a valid claim to property in Wyoming Territory and this man's employer, Judge Colston, refuses to discuss it with me," she blurted out, despite the amazed frown crossing Jesse's dark countenance.

A glimmer of recognition sparked into the man's eyes. "Judge Colston? Why I have an appointment with him at his hotel this evening. But I am afraid that if your case involves a dispute with another party, you will have to take that up in the territorial courts."

The chief justice stepped into the court chamber and Victoria followed him, determined not to let him get away so easily. "Sir, you are being most unreasonable."

"Young woman! You can't come barging in here like this." Justice Bradley raised his brows and pounded his gavel from the bench. "You will have to leave. This tribunal is not in public session right now."

As the justice was chastising Victoria, a reporter heard his angry, booming words and sneaked inside the chamber in search of a story.

"Mr. Justices, if you gentlemen will only be reasonable and listen to what I have to say . . ."

Murmurs buzzed around the room and the angry justices rose to join in the budding fray. A gavel beat against a table, as Judge restrained Victoria from going up to look the men in the eyes, as she had threatened.

"If you do not leave quietly, miss, you will be arrested," warned one of the justices.

"I am not leaving until someone agrees to listen to me," Victoria shot back. But her intentions were thwarted when Judge grabbed her around the waist and practically swung her outside the doors, effectively putting a halt to the escalating commotion.

While Victoria and Judge stood arguing, they paid no more than passing notice to the shadowy reporter carefully listening to their words. His eyes glittered with delight as he thought of the ammunition the scene was going to provide for his exposé on the corruption of the legal system.

Victoria experienced the bitter taste of defeat as she conceded that to return inside the chamber would probably prove futile. Those men had no intention of listening to her plight. Judge Colston seemed to have far-reaching influence. He knew the president and was meeting with the chief justice of the Supreme Court. But why would he be conferring with such a high-ranking officer of the court? Could it have something to do with his holdings back in Wyoming? She had noticed the look in the chief justice's eyes when she mentioned Wyoming. Could they be conspiring to cheat her out of her rightful inheritance? Even if they were not, if their meeting had anything to do with the ranch, she was a partner and she had a right to be involved.

As their carriage rolled back toward the hotel, Victoria finally broke her enforced silence. "I cannot understand why you decline to tell me what this conference between Judge Colston and Chief Justice Waite is about."

"Don't you ever think about anything but your damned partnership with Judge Colston?" he snapped, not even sure why he should care if she had any other thoughts.

"That is all that is important."

Judge noticed Lani and Gerald strolling arm in arm, engaged in what looked like a very cozy conversation on the opposite side of the street. "Aren't you the least bit jealous at your fiancé gallivanting all around town with your sister while you play at business?"

Victoria sucked in her cheeks. How dare he ask her personal questions! Besides, she had no intention of telling him that, while Gerald might be her fiancé, he meant little to her. "Why should I be jealous of my sister?" she demanded. "And, for your information, I am not *playing* at business."

"Maybe . . . maybe not." He shrugged. "But if you were my wife, you'd be home where you belong."

Judge knew before Victoria stiffened that he had made a mistake. "Mister Jesse. First of all, this is where I belong. And secondly, being your wife is something I would never want to happen to me."

Judge narrowed his eyes. What had made him say such a stupid thing in the first place? Having a wife, even a compliant one, was the last thing he needed or intended. No matter. He had just been making a point. What an insufferable woman.

"You needn't worry none, ma'am. Any man with balls would have to be crazy to get tangled up with the likes of you."

Judge's crudely caustic comment played on her nerves. Victoria drew in an indignant breath and swung around to look out the window without retort. She had, at one time, been considered quite desirable, back home in England.

The coach stopped, and Victoria jumped out before Judge could offer his assistance. She lifted her skirts and nose, and marched past him toward the hotel entrance.

Judge laughed. "Turned-up noses are kind of cute." When Victoria didn't respond, he added fuel to the angry fires simmering between them. "Always have enjoyed a nicely turned ankle, too. Good of you to give me another glimpse."

Seething, Victoria stopped in her tracks. She heaved down her skirts without looking back, before furiously throwing open the door, and practically sending it crashing shut in Jesse's face.

"My word, it appears as if Victoria and that cowboy are having a bit of a tiff once again," observed Gerald, who stood across the street, his arm linked with Lani's.

Lani turned to face the slight man, her eyes filled with adoration. "I do hope we have done the right thing," she worried. "When Victoria finds out, she is going to be ever so upset, and with so much on her mind right now, too. Oh, Gerald, should we go to her and tell her the truth, pleading for her understanding and forgiveness?"

Gerald peered down at the young girl who was now his wife. His wife. She was so sweet, so truly special, and he loved her above all. He hadn't been able to resist her pleas that they be wed, as their carriage had passed a justice of the peace's quaint cottage just two hours earlier.

He had so wanted his precious Alayne to have a grand wedding, but after watching the way that disgusting American lusted after her, he couldn't take the chance of losing her. He sighed. There was still the matter of breaking Victoria's heart when she learned he had preferred Alayne from the moment Victoria had introduced them. Well, Victoria would be forced to understand.

"Gerald, what should we do?" Lani beseeched, looking to him for guidance.

"I trust you realize Victoria will be heartbroken, I must say. And we should have a care for the pickle she is in right now. Although I certainly do not condone the likes of it, perhaps we should wait to break the news to her until we see to it that her claim is settled. Then the poor old girl will have something to take up the lonely hours in her life, since she won't have me," he announced.

"Gerald, that is awfully decent of you. Of course

we shall wait. We must make the sacrifice for Victoria's sake."

"The devil take me, it will be ever so difficult to keep from announcing to the world that you are mine. But we must be strong. Come along, Alayne, I am certain that Victoria must be expecting us by now."

"Alayne?"

"You are no longer a child; you are a married lady now. My wife." He patted her hand and stepped into the street, feeling the sweet taste of protectiveness and responsibility for the first time in his life.

Victoria paced the floor waiting for Lani and Gerald to return from their excursion to locate the missing luggage. She stared at the red jacket laying over the edge of the chair, where she had tossed it as soon as she had entered the room. With her luck, she would be stuck wearing the jacket, which had given that insufferable Jesse the idea to start calling her Tori, for the rest of the trip. A smile came to her lips. Tori. No one, not even her father, had ever called her by a nickname before.

She had always been the prim and proper Victoria Elizabeth, named after two queens. While such an over-familiar form of her proper name had been appalling at first, she now found it rather amusing, if not endearing. She shook her head in an attempt to shake the thought of Jesse's inviting blue eyes from her mind. But the harder she tried, the clearer his image entered her consciousness to taunt her.

Lani's laughing voice drifting down the hall finally

provided an end to the swirling visions of the big cowhand.

"Why, Gerald, you are so wicked," Lani was giggling when Victoria opened the door. Lani's mouth dropped into a startled line, and she swooped her hand behind her back in an attempt to hide a bouquet of baby's breath and white roses. "Victoria, we . . . ah . . . I thought you would be out all afternoon with Jesse." Lani sent a disappointed look to Gerald.

"As you two can clearly see, I am here — alone." Then, as if realizing she had forgotten her manners, she said to Gerald, "Thank you for watching out for my sister. Did you locate the luggage?" she added.

Gerald smiled fondly down at Lani. "It was my pleasure, what, to keep a watchful eye on Alayne. As for the baggage, we located all but yours. I rather think it is on its way to California by now. Seems the ignorant blokes have misplaced it."

Victoria was so absorbed with the idea Gerald's words had put into her head that she missed their secret exchange of roses and their longing glances at one another.

"I say, you seem to be in a bit of a fog. Did you hear what I said about the baggage?" Gerald questioned, relieved he did not have to explain why he and Alayne had been gone for so long.

"What? Oh. Yes, yes, I heard," she offered absently. "I suppose I shall continue to wear my red suitcoat until the luggage is located." A hidden smile edged toward her lips, although she could not quite force herself to admit why the thought of wearing the red jacket pleased her. Then the realization hit her: the legal documents validating her claim were lost.

Well, she would get her inheritance, with or without them.

Ignoring proper etiquette further, Victoria dismissed Gerald and pulled Lani into the room, effectively shutting the bewildered bridegroom out. Victoria closed the door and sat down on the bed.

"I need your help, Lani."

"My help?" an astounded Lani returned, slapping her palms to her cheeks. "You have never needed anyone's help in your entire life." Then a knowing sparkle lit her eyes. "It could not have something to do with that mysterious dark, handsome Jesse, now could it?" Lani let out a yearning sigh for Victoria's benefit, all the while watching her sister very closely for her reaction.

"As a matter of fact, it does."

Chapter Ten

A balmy evening breeze fluttered the lace curtains when Victoria opened the window and leaned out. While she checked the ledge, she inhaled the sweet scent of spring flowers beneath the third-story window. Purposely, she kept her mind clear of all thoughts which threatened to remind her of the wild thing she was about to do.

"Victoria, this is absolutely insane." Lani bent out the window beside her sister and looked down. "You cannot be serious about going out there on that ledge. You will be killed."

"Do not be so melodramatic," Victoria countered as they drew away from the window. "I shall be fine. I simply intend to find out what our Judge Colston is planning."

"You have never even climbed a tree in your life, not even when you were young."

"Well, maybe now that I am *old,*" Victoria snapped, "it is time to start."

"You know what I meant." Lani tried to redeem herself. "You are not old. It is just that you are a mature woman." Lani cringed and looked outside the window again. "Why not let me go out on that ledge?"

"Stop arguing and help me tie my skirts back."

The job done, Victoria sat on the window sill and swung her legs out. "Do not forget to open the window once you get inside Judge Colston's room," she instructed her nervous sister.

"I shan't. But I do not like this."

"Now that you have registered your complaints, please do not dawdle. I do not plan to spend any more time outside Judge Colston's window than is absolutely necessary in order to find out what he is planning."

Lani rolled her eyes and walked to the door. "And to think I was always considered the flighty sister," she mumbled.

Lani was almost to the judge's door when the door across the hall opened to admit a rather distinguished, yet lackluster man. She watched in dismay as the man said Judge Colston's name and entered Jesse's room. Stumbling, Lani rushed back to the room she shared with Victoria and cried out the window, "Victoria, they are all in Jesse's room. What do we do now?"

"Use your head. Just make sure you leave a window open in Jesse's room," Victoria said sharply. "What are you standing there for? Go see to that window."

Victoria leaned her head back against the bricks and inhaled deeply, in an effort to calm her nerves. Now she would have to make her way all the way around the building. She looked down. A scream threatened to roar from her throat but she swallowed it. It had to be done.

With hesitating steps, she made her way around the ledge, grasping the bricks which protruded at every third block to help steady herself. Her foot slipped.

"Oh!" she cried and clung to the edge, panting. She regained her sense of equilibrium before continuing to inch her way along.

By the time Victoria had worked her way around to Jesse's room, the window was open as if it had been waiting for her. Lani could charm the wings from a bat, Victoria thought. She drew closer to the window until she was right next to it.

The sounds of male voices discussing problems with land sales in Wyoming floated out the window. Jesse had such a warm, pleasant voice; it was almost a caress. Yet there was a commanding strength to it.

She heard her name before their voices grew inaudible. Blast! They must have moved away from the window. Carefully, Victoria crouched down and peeked inside. The three men were seated in a corner of the spacious room sipping amber-colored liquid. The two elder men were puffing on cheroots. Why had she been a topic of conversation?

The man Victoria recognized as Chief Justice Waite was speaking to the other men. "I've no doubt that what you say, Judge, about Jessup using his cowhands to make fraudulent claims on meadow lands instead of desert lands, as required by law, and then transferring the titles to himself, is indeed true. Since this problem involves a public issue it may be possible, eventually, to bring it to the court's attention, but I am afraid this may be an issue for Congress. As I told the young woman this afternoon, you will first have to take cases such as this up in the territorial courts."

She was right. Judge Colston was not above trying to use all his influence when it suited him. She would have to remember that. But why had Chief Justice Waite been addressing Jesse? Could Jesse have some hold over Judge Colston? Now more than ever, it seemed vitally important to Victoria that she get to the ranch in Wyoming, the sooner the better. Somehow she had to figure out a way to shorten this side trip of theirs. Her mind spun with ideas until she settled on the perfect plan.

Victoria waited until she heard the two men leave, then began inching her way back toward her room. But when she slid her foot along the ledge, she scraped some loose gravel over the edge. The noise made her heart pound and she plastered herself against the side of the building before looking down to check if anyone had seen her. The only person she noticed below was a man with what looked to be a sheet of paper in his hand, scurrying into a coach. The man seemed somehow familiar, but she dismissed the thought. She had more pressing matters to worry about.

Judge heard the noise. Living out West had taught him that his life depended on the keenness of his senses. In three strides he was across the room and leaning over the casement.

"Now let me see, what do we have here? A little too large for a pigeon, I'd reckon." What the devil was Victoria Torrington doing outside his window? How much had she heard? Could she be in cahoots with Luther Jessup after all? Maybe she'd been sent to spy

95

on him and report back to Jessup about Judge's efforts to stop him from illegally claiming more and more land. Judge clenched his teeth. He knew trying to stop Jessup by legal means was a waste of time.

"You are not at all amusing, Jesse." She paused, expecting him to offer his hand. When he did not, she said hotly, "What are you waiting for? Help me inside."

"You got out there by yourself. I'm sure you're capable of getting back inside the same way."

"You cannot be serious. I almost lost my step once. If I try to go back to my room, I shall surely fall."

"Have to admit that would be a waste of a beautiful woman. Would solve a problem though," He hesitated. " 'Course, if you'd like to tell me exactly what you are doing out there, you might be able to convince me to reconsider."

"Will you stop this nonsense and help me in?" Victoria sputtered.

"Look lady, I didn't put you out there in the first place. If you wanted to spend time with me so badly all you had to do was say so. I'd have let you in through the door," Judge said wolfishly.

"You are insufferable!"

"Most don't think so. But have it your way." He swung from her before turning around and shutting the window. He had intended to help her inside at once. This way, though, he might be able to get her to confess. Despite a stab of guilt, he crossed his arms and waited.

Victoria gulped in big breaths of air to help steady her raw nerves. Afraid to move, and not daring to look down again, she remained plastered against the side of the building. How was she ever going to explain what she had been doing outside his window?

It seemed that an hour had passed as she waited. When that impossible cowboy made no effort to help her inside, she swallowed her pride, and forced herself to slowly reach out and tap on the pane of glass.

Judge slid the window open. "I was beginning to wonder if you planned to stay out there all night. Have a change of heart, Tori?"

Victoria glared at him, swallowing a retort. "Please, help me inside," she said coolly.

"Always was a sap for a sweet talkin' woman." He grinned, relieved to get her off that ledge before her stubborn pride caused her to get hurt.

Judge reached out and snatched Victoria inside before she could protest. He held her, staring down into frightened blue eyes. Her eyes seemed innocent, which momentarily confused him. He had always been a pretty good judge of character, and she was a schemer. Yet he saw no sly, calculating look in those blue depths. She was shaking. In that moment something about her seemed so vulnerable; it touched him. Was she afraid of him, or that she'd been caught?

Victoria, too, was aware she was trembling. But she was not sure whether it was that she could have fallen or whether it was the warmth from Jesse's strong arms which held her so tightly. She looked up into his face. Strangely, his countenance held a concerned warmth before turning cold.

"You're inside." He reluctantly released her, towering over her. "Now, tell me what you were doing outside my window."

"Listening," she offered curtly, brushing her skirts

97

into place in an effort to regain her control.

"Just exactly what did you hope to learn?" Judge demanded, his fists clenching.

From his tense stance Victoria could tell that he wasn't going to let her out of there without an explanation. "While we were at the Capitol Building this afternoon, I heard Chief Justice Waite say he had an appointment with Judge Colston this evening."

"So?" He dropped his hands on his hips, unmoved, unconvinced.

"So I thought it might have something to do with my claim."

"Is that all?" he asked, incredulous at the simple honesty of her explanation. She was so forthright that he almost believed her.

"Of course it is," she said shortly. "What else would you expect?"

"I might expect a little gratitude for saving your hide."

"Then I fear you are going to be sorely disappointed," she returned haughtily, hoping to bluff her way out of his room by maintaining an indignant pose.

She was straining his patience beyond endurance. If she were a man, he'd punch the truth out of her. Instead, he felt himself being drawn into the depths of those incredible eyes. He said softly, "No. I don't reckon I think I am."

Judge ran his hands up her arms before gathering Victoria back into his embrace. When she did not resist, he murmured, "I have been wanting to taste those luscious lips again since the moment I first kissed you on the train. I reckon a kiss would be

98

gratitude enough — for now."

"For now?" She mouthed the words, quietly staring up at his handsome face, her heart pounding madly.

He stood gazing down at her; the look in his half-lidded eyes was scorching, hypnotizing. He held her firmly, but gently as he slowly lowered his head. She should fight him, yet something inside her issued a wordless yearning to taste, to sample, to revel in those full lips again. Victoria lifted her face and closed her eyes as their lips met, and she relished his soft moist texture and inhaled his manly scent.

If Judge had expected to teach Victoria a lesson, the minute their lips met, he discovered that he was the one being taught. It was the sweetest kiss Judge had ever experienced, and he sought to savor and extend the moment, his hands roving up her back.

A knock at the door harshly broke the fragile web of enchantment which had so completely ensnared them. Judge cursed under his breath and went to answer the door.

Lani was standing in the hallway looking guilty. "Yeah?" Judge said gruffly. Why the devil did Victoria's damned sister have to pick the most inopportune time to show up?

Lani caught a glimpse of Victoria red cheeked and awkward as a schoolgirl found cheating on an exam. An impish idea welled up from inside her.

"I saw Judge Colston and the other man leave and thought maybe you would like some company, Jesse," she purred, trying to look around him to see if what she had said had the desired effect.

"I seem to be getting plenty of that tonight," Judge said blandly, stepping aside for her to enter. He had planned to use Lani to find out exactly what Victoria was up to, but now, when he saw the strangely disappointed expression on Victoria's face, was no longer sure he could.

Instead of entering the room to join Victoria, an idea flashed into Lani's head, and she snaked her arms around his neck and kissed him properly. "I hope you did not have to wait too long." That should give Victoria something to think about. Then she moved in plain sight of her sister. "Oh? Victoria? I thought you would be back in our room by now."

The crimson blotches on Victoria's cheeks darkened. "Yes, of course you did." Her heart sank. They had planned to meet.

Victoria could still feel the soft tingle of his kiss on her lips. But why had he bothered to kiss her when he was planning to meet Lani all along? Jealousy reared up. It was a new sensation for Victoria. She was an engaged woman. Even if she had not been engaged, why should she feel envious over a man her sister found attractive, an American cowboy, no less? She breathed a silent sigh of relief that she had not told Lani about the documents. Infatuated Lani might very well have told the American.

"Come along, Lani, I think it is time we return to our room," Victoria finally said, when she had regained her senses. Now was not the time to attempt to question him further about his conversation with the chief justice.

When Lani balked, Victoria added, "I do believe we've both had enough excitement for one evening."

"Maybe you have. As for me, I had barely begun," whined the younger girl as she trailed behind Victoria's stiff strides.

Judge begrudgingly opened the door, wishing Miss Alayne Torrington had not intruded upon him and Victoria. Then he recalled why he was here: to keep Miss Victoria Torrington away from his land.

"At least you didn't do any harm by that dumb stunt you pulled earlier," he said to Victoria. "Chief Justice Waite is a good, honest man who was merely offering some personal advice as a favor to an acquaintance. It would be a pity if his conversation with Judge Colston were misconstrued by the wrong people."

Victoria stared at him for a minute. The vehemence of his statement told her it would be useless to pursue the truth of their meeting, even at a later date. Advice for a friend, indeed. "You needn't worry yourself unduly. I would not think of mentioning his visit to anyone."

Judge stood watching the two women retreat. Lani's walk was sensuous and slinky as a cat, a young woman most men would be panting after. Yet it was Victoria's squarely erect gait which drew him. Victoria, with her yellow hair the color of wild sunflowers, her gentle curves, and her strength and determination, who continued to creep into his mind. The sooner he sent her packing back to England, the better!

Victoria stopped mid-stride when she heard Jesse's door close and turned to Lani. "You go on to bed. I have something I must take care of."

"What are you up to now?" cried Lani, secretly delighted. Victoria's absence would allow her to finally spend time with her bridegroom of less than eight hours.

Victoria smiled wickedly over her shoulder. Quickening her steps toward the stairs, she called out, "You will find out soon enough."

"Judge!" Ozzie burst into Judge's room, interrupting his bath. "Ya seen the mornin' newspaper yet?" He thrust it into Judge's hands, causing wet blotches to spread over the newsprint.

"What's so important it can't wait?"

Ozzie gulped down a hard lump. "Ya better read it."

Judge skimmed the headlines splashed across the *Washington Post*. "Damn rag!" Judge raged, totally livid, then hurriedly read the first couple of paragraphs of the article. "I should have known better than to let that Torrington woman go last night. After leaving my room she must have gone directly to the newspapers with the story."

"She was in your room last night?"

Judge ignored Ozzie's question and read further, cursing his stupidity for believing her when she had promised not to mention yesterday's events to anyone. On the front page, bold print screamed of yesterday's encounter at the Capitol Building. The confrontation with the Supreme Court was detailed, and Victoria's excursion out onto the ledge was said to be in an effort to find out why a certain unnamed chief justice was meeting with the very wealthy Judge Colston of Wyoming Territory. The article concluded by raising the question of corruption in the courts. "This goddamned article must have the town buzzing."

"Gosh, I kinda liked that purty little filly." Ozzie scratched his head. "Sorta thought ya was gettin' a hankerin' for her too, the way ya been lookin' at her lately."

"Don't be a fool, old timer." Why had he thought last night that Victoria Torrington could be different than what he had originally suspected?

"I ain't the fool. Ya been spendin' so much time with that Jessup woman all these years, I figgered maybe ya finally got some smarts and decided t' look elsewhere."

Judge flew into his clothes, spurred on by his anger. "Maybe you're right. I have been stupid, only not the way you think. But no more. If your precious Miss Victoria Elizabeth Torrington wants war, then war is what she is going to get!"

Chapter Eleven

"After spending hours undoing what you attempted to do, I don't give a goddamn whether you're ready to leave Washington or not!" Judge took a menacing step toward Victoria, his fingers itching to wring that beautiful neck of hers. "If you aren't out of that bed, dressed, and ready in ten minutes you will be boarding the train just as you are." His eyes rolled menacingly down Victoria, who still lounged in bed wearing a pale pink satin robe fringed with lace.

The vivid dreams of Jesse which had crept so stealthily into Victoria's mind last night, crashed to the floor. Was this the real Jesse? This . . . this beast, dressed in somber dark trousers, who had just burst into her room like the wrath of the devil? Well, he was not going to try to intimidate her and get away with it!

"And exactly what did I try to do?" she demanded, becoming wide awake and jutting out her chin.

"You have all of Washington in an uproar. From the president on down," he ground out.

Victoria thought he was referring to their episode

in the court chamber the day before. "If Chief Justice Waite would have agreed to listen to me, I would not have had to resort to such tactless methods."

Judge was further infuriated by her open admission of guilt. So. She had deliberately seen to it that that damaging story got into the newspaper. "Lucky for you, your methods did not work," he snapped, remembering his early morning excursion to the newspaper office. He'd had a time of it convincing the editor to retract the story and print an apology. "I was able to see to that. Before you can cause any one any more trouble, you'll be leaving this town."

Lani rolled over and sat up in bed. "What is going on?" she asked, wiping the sleep from her eyes.

"Your sister is leaving Washington . . . now! If you and Pelthurst want to go with her, I suggest you gather your things and be on the train to Cincinnati when it pulls out in half an hour."

"I do not understand." Lani looked genuinely confused.

"You don't have to." Judge spied the floor-length, pelisse which Lani had tossed over a nearby chair. "Hand me that coat," he said in a low voice which brooked no question. When Lani stretched over and offered him the hooded garment, Judge held it out to Victoria.

"If you think I am going to put that on and leave with you now, you are—"

"I don't give a cowpoke's damn what you think I am, Miss Torrington. You'll put it on or go without it."

He had pricked her pride and she stood her ground, her eyes silently challenging.

Not one to engage in empty threats, he roughly wrapped the fur-trimmed coat around her and practically dragged her out of the room and down the hall.

"You are not going to get away with this!" she screamed at him, struggling, as two richly dressed hotel guests passed, their necks craned.

"Help me. This man is forcing me to go with him," she entreated the bewildered couple.

Judge tightened his hold on Victoria and grinned through his teeth. "Now, now, my dearest, you know the sanitarium will help cure your drinking problem." He gave the couple a look of hopelessness. "I apologize for my wife. But I'm sure you understand how difficult it must be for me to commit the mother of my six children. I am doing this for her own good."

"Six children! Why you! I do not have any children," she sputtered.

"See?" Judge gave the couple a most forlorn look. "She does not even remember her children."

The shocked couple shook their heads and whispered amongst themselves before hurrying away in the opposite direction.

As Judge and Victoria were about to reach the exit, Gerald came out of his room. "I say, where do you think you are taking my fiancée?" he blustered.

"Go ask Miss Lani if you want to know," Judge barked. When Gerald just stood there, stiff as a wad of dried-out clay, Judge impatiently added, "You better be quick about it unless you want to be left behind."

"Are you just going to stand there?" Victoria demanded, expecting the man to make at least some attempt to defend her honor.

Gerald looked down the hall toward Lani's room, then back at Victoria and Jesse. "Ah . . . no. No! I suppose I had best hurry on down to Alayne's room. I jolly well would not want to be left behind." With that, Gerald scurried off from a thoroughly demoralized Victoria.

Seething, Victoria sat in the train's drawing room car. She tried to focus on the American capital rapidly disappearing in the distance, but the windows were so small and low that she had difficulty enjoying the passing scenery. She felt like a prisoner. Jesse had unceremoniously dumped her on the train shortly before it pulled out, and now stood over her like a gigantic guardsman from Buckingham Palace.

"Oh, Victoria dear, here you are," squealed Lani as she neared the pair. "Isn't it ever so romantic, having some devastatingly handsome man carry you off, and you wearing nothing at all but your flimsy night clothes under that coat?"

All eyes in the crowded train car swung around to stare at Victoria. She shifted uneasily in her seat, her cheeks crimson. Why hadn't Lani ever learned to hold her tongue? "Did you bring my clothing?" Victoria whispered.

"Your clothes? Oh. Of course I brought you some clothes to wear," she announced loudly. "I gathered everything from the hotel room, just as instructed," Lani continued with ample volume, flashing Jesse a bright smile. Muffled chuckles sounded throughout the drawing car.

"Just give them to me," Victoria snipped, embarrassment threatening to cause her to do something quite rash. She snatched the clothing from Lani. With as much dignity as she could muster, she raised her chin and walked past the amused passengers and a broadly grinning Jesse to the wash room at the far end of the car.

"Got t' hand it t' the little filly," Ozzie observed. "That one's a thoroughbred for sure. She's got guts t' strut past everybody gawkin' at her like they's doin'."

"Why do you think the men at the club call her *Miss Chastity Iron Drawers*," remarked Gerald, discounting the judge's admiration for Victoria.

"Miss Chastity Iron Drawers?" Judge remained unmoved, annoyed at the Englishman's levity at Victoria's expense. "I'll just bet it fits her, too," he muttered to himself. He filed the amusing nickname in his memory for future reference. He just might use it to take some of the flutter out of her wings. Then his eyes narrowed. "Just don't ever let me hear you call her that again."

Lani shot Gerald a disgusted look. "Victoria does not know about the name," Lani put in, trying to protect her sister. "You won't tell her, will you?"

"Miz Lani, Jesse'd never stoop that low," Ozzie said, shifting worried amber eyes toward Judge, who maintained an impassive stance.

When Victoria returned, she was once again wearing the red suit jacket. Without a word to anyone, she took her seat next to the window, concentrating her attention on the passing pines and giant clumps of rhododendrons which clothed the steep sides of the hills. She was too angry to even attempt an intelligent conversation. If Jesse and Judge Colston thought

108

they were going to force her to accompany them to Texas, they were going to be in for quite a surprise. She had taken care of that last night when she'd left Lani. Jesse may be wearing a self-satisfied smirk of triumph now, but not for long.

All afternoon Victoria tried unsuccessfully to talk to Judge Colston without Jesse present. The irritating cowhand was constantly by the judge's side. To make matters worse, Lani seemed to be mooning over Jesse more than ever. The thought had entered Victoria's mind before; now she realized she *had* to reveal Jesse for what he was. Who was Jesse? She didn't even know his last name. There might not be anything she could do about getting her inheritance money just yet, but nothing was going to stop her from finding out more about the man who had introduced himself as Judge Colston's foreman. Heat slid up her neck when she caught Jesse intently gazing at her.

The sun had begun to sink into a fire-streaked sky when Lani, following Victoria's counsel, (and with Gerald's hesitant blessing once he learned why Lani had been paying attention to the American) finally succeeded in coaxing Jesse to walk out onto the car's platform on the pretext that she was afraid to go alone. Victoria watched, as Jesse had suggested that Judge Colston accompany them, but the elder man held fast to his seat.

After Jesse ushered Lani outside, Gerald moved to a seat closer to the door and sat staring purposely, as if he expected something dreadful to happen and wanted to be prepared. This was the chance Victoria had been waiting for. Knowing Lani — she could chatter on endlessly — Victoria was sure she would have enough time to pry some information about Jesse out of the judge.

Unable to enjoy a swig while Judge was around, due to Judge's feelings about liquor since his pa had drank himself to death, Ozzie now took a hefty flask from his bag and gulped down a good slug. "Ahh." He smacked his lips and swiped his sleeve across his mouth. He looked up to see Victoria studying him. "Forgive me, Miz Victoria, I almost done went and forgot my manners." He wiped off the neck of the bottle with his hand. "Ya want a swig?"

Victoria was about to decline when an idea came to her. "Why, thank you, sir." Forcing herself to appear amiable, Victoria lifted the flask to her lips. Then, in a gesture to throw the man off his guard, she mimicked him, wiping her sleeve across her mouth.

"I knowed ya was all right since the first time I laid eyes on ya." Ozzie laughed. Awkwardly he bent down and retrieved a slender book from his bag. A sly grin curved his lips. "I'm gonna do ya a little favor. Before we get t' Texas, ya might want t' read this. It'll tell ya what ya need t' know 'bout cattle. Don't tell *Jesse* I let ya see this here little book."

Victoria accepted the offering. "Thank you. I shall read it thoroughly and return it to you without anyone the wiser. Here," she handed the flask back, "have another." When the judge took the bottle, Victoria tucked the volume into her reticule.

Ozzie's mouth watering, he asked, "Ya don't mind none?"

"Not at all," she reassured him. "While my father

was alive he enjoyed a little nip every evening."

Ozzie brightened. "In that case, don't mind if I do." He guzzled a good portion, then grew somber. "Sorry 'bout your pa. Is that why you're after the land?"

"It is all Father left me," she admitted in a weak moment.

"Guess I can't blame ya none then." He squirmed in his seat and looked over his shoulder toward the rear of the car before saying uneasily, "We'll talk 'bout it soon."

She wanted to ask why he had been refusing to discuss the land if he truly felt that way. But he hadn't yet drunk enough to thoroughly loosen his tongue. She held hers.

Again and again they passed the flask back and forth, Victoria taking small sips to the judge's long pulls. Yet she could feel the effects of the strong brew.

The judge's eyes were beginning to look glassy, and his speech grew slurred. If only Lani could keep Jesse outside just a little longer. The judge appeared as if he was about ready to tell her anything she wanted to know. Victoria sneaked a glance at the door. She could see them standing with their backs to her. She took a deep breath. Now was the time.

"For the life of me I cannot understand why your foreman, Jesse, seems to take my claim to the ranch so much to heart."

Ozzie hiccupped and attempted to focus on the beautiful blur before him. "I'll be a dadblamed son of a gun, you're so purty." Then as if he had suddenly recalled what Victoria had said, he looked sheepishly from behind the empty flask. "I don't know why ever not. If I was Ju . . . ah . . . Jesse, I'd be frettin' your claim, too. 'Course, I'd know how t' settle the problem right quick."

"You would?"

"Dadgummit, sure would."

Tense excitement surrounded Victoria now and she urged, "How would you do that, Judge Colston?"

"Why, I'd marry ya."

She let out a breath of disappointment and ignored the comment about marrying her. But why had he said if he were Jesse he would be worried? Victoria leaned forward in her seat, certain she had stumbled onto some important bit of information. If only her mind didn't feel so fuzzy, she was certain she could connect the pieces. She should never have indulged in those spirits. She tried to clear her brain to think. The man had also tripped over Jesse's name. Why? Slowly, so the judge could clearly understand her, she asked, "What do you mean, if you were Jesse? Who is Jesse?"

Ozzie grinned slyly, shifting his eyes from side to side as if he were about to divulge a secret and didn't want anyone else to hear what he was about to say. "Ya won't go lettin' the coon out of the sack if I tell ya, will ya?"

Victoria leaned forward. "No. No. I would not think of it." Please hurry, she wanted to shout, her heart pounding with a flurry of expectation that she was so easily about to learn what she had set out to discover.

Ozzie scooted forward and whispered, in a voice heavy with alcohol, "Jesse is—" He stopped in mid-sentence and keeled over.

Victoria let out a frustrated groan and tried to help the judge back into his seat, but he lay in a heap, out cold — dead drunk.

"I say, the bloke does not look too well, does he?" Gerald observed, having left his seat when he saw the old man slump from his position.

"Will you hurry up and help me?" Victoria shot Gerald an annoyed grimace, and then went back to her efforts to right the judge. "We have to get him back into his seat before Lani and Jesse come back. He was about to tell me something about Jesse when he passed out. I do not want Jesse to find out what I was doing."

Strong arms helped Victoria put Ozzie back into his chair.

"And just exactly what were you doing?" Judge asked, his dark brow rising.

Chapter Twelve

Ignoring Jesse's demands for answers concerning what she had been trying to find out from the judge, Victoria tried to stand, but teetered against Jesse's strong, muscled chest. His warmth caused a heady sensation before a pressing awakening hit her cold in the stomach. She must have consumed more than she realized, and suddenly she felt sick — very, very sick.

"If you will excuse me, Jesse, I do believe I am about to be ill."

She put a hand against her throbbing temple and unsteadily weaved toward the washroom. It was occupied, and a woman and small child stood outside the door impatiently waiting their turn.

Despite Victoria's resistance, Judge grabbed her about the waist and quickly ushered her outside onto the platform. Once outdoors, the cooling evening air only served to make Victoria feel worse. She clasped her hand to her mouth, desperately trying not to vomit. But the effects of the liquor were now hitting her full force.

"Come over here to the rail and lean over," Judge

ordered, remembering the time he had similarly helped his father.

"You are not going to throw me off the train, are you?" she asked, the whites of her bloodshot eyes rounding. Judge Colston had begun to tell her something about this man who called himself Jesse. Jesse had demanded to know what the judge had told her. Oh dear God, what could it have been?

"If I wanted to toss you off the train, I wouldn't have brought you back here quite so publicly. Now quit fighting me and lean over."

Judge did not get her into position any too soon. She completely lost the contents of her stomach.

Expecting to be hounded by Jesse as to what the judge had started to tell her, Victoria steeled herself. She was surprised when instead he held her to him, took out his handkerchief, and gently dabbed at the corners of her mouth.

"You feel better now?" Judge asked quietly.

There was a note of concern in his voice. Victoria was grateful for his gentleness, which only served to confuse her. "Yes, thank you." She looked up into his face. His expression was void of the hardness which only a short while before had characterized his features.

He took her elbow. "Let me help you back inside. I'll have the conductor make up your berth so you can lay down and sleep it off."

Victoria did not protest. She felt too weak from vomiting, and her head continued to spin.

Settled in her small berth in the pullman, Victoria closed her eyes. She had not been asleep long when, out of the mists of her dreams, Jesse came to her. Dressed in a blue cambray shirt open at the neck, a leather vest, denims, and pointed boots, he held out his hand. Without hesitation, she placed her small hand in his large one and their fingers entwined. A warm breeze swirled about them, ruffling the frothy azure gown she wore. In each other's arms, they waltzed across gently rolling golden hills, the only two people in the world. The music stopped, but she remained wrapped in his embrace; his hands stroked her back, her shoulders, igniting her flesh. Her skin was afire with his touch, and when he slowly lifted her chin to join their lips, the scene was so real, so vivid, that she awoke with a start.

With a jolt, Victoria sat up and promptly hit her head on the ceiling of the small cubicle. She was panting, and felt disoriented for a moment, until she realized it had been a dream, all a dream. She absently rubbed the knot on her head, which had already begun to rise. Feeling strangely hollow for the first time in her life, Victoria silently settled back and tried not to think of the implications the dream held for her.

Long after the other passengers had retired for the evening, Judge remained in the drawing car listening to Ozzie's drunken snorts, lost in troubled thoughts. At one time, Judge would have stood by and laughed at Miss Victoria Torrington's distress, or condemned her for her drinking. But earlier, seeing her in such a sorry state had given him no pleasure. No. Instead, he'd felt only the need to help her, to reach out, to protect her despite what she had tried to do back in Washington. She had been so vulnerable. She had needed his help and he had offered it.

Ozzie woke with a jerk, sure the clatter of the train was about to send the mighty engine roaring through his head. He yawned and looked out at the darkness.

Judge sat with his boots up, leaning on his elbow. He seemed to be deep in thought. "What ya doin' still up? It wouldn't have nothin' t' do with that there little filly, Miz Victoria, would it?"

Judge scowled. "What if it does?"

"I'd say it's a mite better than thinkin' 'bout that she-devil what belongs t' someone else."

"Yeah? Not that it's any of your business. At least Helene isn't a schemer trying to get her fingers around my land."

"I wouldn't be so sure 'bout that, if I was ya." Ozzie snickered.

"Enough of your observations. What did you tell Victoria about me?"

" 'Bout ya?" Ozzie groped through the thick haze of his memory. "Sure's purty smart, that one," he mumbled.

"So you've said. But what did she get out of you?" Judge pressed.

"She almost got me to spill my gut. But I guess I got too likkered up and passed out 'fore I let on who ya is." Ozzie paused before continuing. "Consarn it, why don't ya tell her the dadblamed truth? Ya might even find her reasonable if ya'd give her half a chance." He hung his head and added, "Sorry I drank too much, knowin' how ya feel about it an' all."

Judge splayed his fingers through his black waves. "Forget it, old man."

"What 'bout Miz Victoria?"

Judge did not respond to the old timer. He didn't like the effect she had had on him earlier. In his mind he had been wavering. Somehow, it was becoming more and more difficult to imagine that such a high-spirited

117

woman as Victoria Torrington could be trying to swindle him. He shook his head to clear his brain. He didn't really even know her. What was wrong with him? She hadn't changed overnight. It wasn't his way to discuss his inner feelings with others, not even Ozzie. Then again, it wasn't his way to let a woman get to him, and Victoria Elizabeth Torrington seemed to be doing just that.

They reached Cincinnati shortly after six in the morning, and were bustled off the train onto a long, dirty platform. Lani complained constantly about the early hour and how she was not in the habit of rising before the sun made its appearance. Gerald maintained a stiff upper lip and, for once, held his tongue. Both Victoria, wearing the only jacket she had now, and Ozzie, looked as if they would have been happier dead, but neither one complained while they waited for over an hour in the bone-chilling cold. All but Judge were jostled toward a huge four-horse omnibus, to be transferred to another station. Judge's size alone warned others from messing with him.

When one of the men grabbed Victoria's arm a little too roughly, she let out a startled scream.

"Hurry it up lady, we ain't got all day," the behemoth sneered at Victoria instead of offering an apology, and promptly gave her a shove.

Judge was a short way behind and witnessed the scene. He was through the crowd in a flash and clamped an iron hard hand on the man's shoulder. "I suggest you try remembering she is a lady, mister," Judge said in a deadly voice.

"Yeah? And who's gonna make me?" the man scoffed and put hurting fingers around Victoria's arm.

Not one to waste time with needless words Judge spun the man around and landed a fist square to his jaw. The man never saw what hit him. The crowding passengers scattered as the man crumpled to his knees, his big fist relaxed, and sprawled, face down, on the ground.

Victoria watched in horror at the confrontation. She had always been shielded from such unpleasantries in life. She had not thought Jesse capable of such unmitigated violence. It suddenly struck her how dangerous he could be. Instead of thanking him for protecting her, Victoria bristled. "How dare you strike that man. You might have hurt him." She bent down to offer her assistance.

Judge angrily yanked her back. "Maybe you would have preferred it if I'd let him rough you up," he snapped, not understanding why she wasn't thankful he had just interceded on her behalf.

"I could have handled myself," she countered, pride demanding her response, yet knowing what she said was untrue. She noticed Gerald standing behind the judge and Lani. Although the violence bothered her, something inside her registered that it was Jesse, not Gerald, who had been quick to defend her.

"No doubt. I suppose you would have asked him nicely to *unhand me, please,*" he mimicked in a feminine voice. "And, of course, he would then have been the perfect gentleman and offered to carry your hand luggage." Scathing sarcasm filled every rich syllable.

"Perhaps." She pulled a face, unwilling to admit any differently.

"For someone your age, you don't know a thing about human nature, do you?" He shook his head tiredly.

"My age?" she snorted, all too aware of another reference to her age.

"Well, you aren't exactly a child."

"Maybe not." The cadence of her tone honed into a biting point. "But I know quite a bit about human nature! And you should not have used undue force."

"Undue force?"

Gerald finally stepped forward. "I say, if you two are bloody well done arguing, we should hurry along or we shall miss the omnibus."

"Thank you for your timely concern." Victoria sent Gerald a frown of disapproval, then stuck her nose in the air and moved on.

Pleased as the dickens over the chain of events, Ozzie moved over to Judge. "Ya best watch yourself with that one." He nodded toward Victoria. "Ya may not be able t' handle her as easy as ya think ya can."

Judge narrowed his eyes and snorted, "I'll handle her."

"Somehow I get the feeling there might be a bit a handlin' on both sides 'fore it's all said and done." Yup, two untamed hearts, Ozzie grinned to himself, and followed Judge, the last one to climb on board and take his seat. The more Ozzie saw of the little lady, the more pleased he was with himself that he had forgotten about getting that money from Miz Victoria's pa years ago.

At a grimy restaurant next to the platform they had transferred to, they stopped for a hot cup of coffee and stale roll while they waited to change trains. It was still blustery and cold on the platform when they left the restaurant. Victoria shivered, her breath plainly visible. She had insisted Lani take the pelisse, leaving herself only the red jacket as protection from the elements. Gerald stood wrapped up to his ears, his hands in his pockets, seemingly oblivious that Victoria's lips were turning blue.

Judge had left the others to check on their train connections. When he returned, he noticed Victoria's sorry attempts to warm herself. In his bag he had an ankle-length, buffalo skin overcoat. Used to the extremely bitter cold winters of Wyoming, Judge was quite comfortable in his worn buckskin jacket. He dug into the bag and pulled out the heavy garment.

"Here, Tori." He wrapped the overcoat around Victoria's shoulders before she could protest. For an instant Victoria had felt herself warm toward Jesse, until he said dryly, "With your icy disposition you need it more than I do."

"I am just as capable of withstanding the elements as are you, regardless of your opinion of my disposition — which, incidentally, is quite unfounded." Why couldn't she just accept Jesse's offerings gracefully and ignore his jabs? Why did she take offense at everything he tried to do, every kindness he showed despite his barbs? After all, wouldn't she fight just as hard if some outsider were trying to claim part of her family's land? Although Jesse wasn't family and the land did not belong to him, she had seen how much the old judge and the ranch meant to the man.

"A woman as soft as you? Ha!" Why couldn't he ignore her retorts? No other woman had been able to get such a rise out of him since Helene, years ago. Of course, he could have merely offered her the coat without remark. Why did he delight in goading her?

"There is not a soft spot on my body."

Judge could not help himself. He did a slow assessment of Victoria from head to toe. "Oh? I don't know about that." His face registered aroused amusement. "If I had to venture a guess, I'd say you probably have several very appealing soft spots. 'Course, it's hard to say for sure with those dowdy clothes you wear."

"No one asked you to 'venture a guess'," she snipped, embarrassment turning her cheeks crimson. "And there is nothing wrong with my choice of attire."

"No. Not if you were a seventy-five-year-old spinster."

Lani giggled. "I told you your wardrobe needed attention."

Victoria sent the girl a quelling look. "I do not believe your opinion was invited. May I suggest you join Gerald and the judge over there on the bench?"

"I beg your pardon. How utterly rude of me. I should have known you two would want to be alone," Lani bristled impishly, swishing away.

"Wait. I did not mean I wanted to be alone with Jesse," Victoria called out before she realized the insult and turned to look directly into his face.

They stood in the early morning light, their eyes locked, blue on blue. Her heart suddenly began to miss its beats. This man so utterly irritated her, and yet he caused her to feel like no other man ever had.

Judge, too, was pondering over what was happening to him as he gazed into the depths of Victoria's incredibly beautiful, innocent eyes.

Chapter Thirteen

All day the train rumbled down the track toward Saint Louis, their next stop before heading on to Texas. Victoria was thankful they were traveling in a Pullman. Now she could direct her attention out the windows, and the arm chairs were more comfortable, too. But the porters and conductors made constant trips down the aisle, banging doors and interrupting her efforts to get Jesse out of her mind. Worse yet, every time she looked up, she noticed Jesse studying her, staring quite openly.

"You know, you wouldn't be a half bad-looking woman if you stopped dressing like an old maid and let your hair down, instead of acting so prissy all the time," he said bluntly. He gazed at her delicate hands with their long nails, her turned-up nose, long slender neck, hair the yellow color of a meadowlark's breast, and her full, sensuous mouth. It was her mouth which held his attention; those were lips he wouldn't mind exploring further.

"You have a kissable mouth, too. Pity though," he rubbed his chin.

"What is a pity?" she asked, realizing too late that she had fallen into a trap.

"Your sharp tongue keeps getting in the way."

"Your opinion of how I dress and act does not interest me in the slightest," she sputtered. But a short while later she stood gazing in the washroom mirror, studying her reflection and fussing with her hair.

Lani, who had followed Victoria toward the washroom, creaked open the door when her sister had not emerged after a reasonable length of time. Victoria was so intently posturing that she did not notice Lani. Lani stifled a satisfied giggle at her sister's sudden self-awareness and shut the door quietly.

With lively steps Lani pranced past Gerald, giving him a saucy wink, and entered the next car. Gerald looked about him. The judge and Jesse were engaged in conversation and seemed oblivious to Gerald's presence. Ever so nonchalantly, Gerald slid from his seat and followed Lani, at a respectable distance, of course.

Judge watched the young pair disappear. It didn't take much to see that they were quite taken with each other. He could not fathom why the puny pipsqueak was engaged to Victoria; he was so obviously in love with her sister. Either Victoria was blind when it came to her sister, which he doubted, or she didn't give a hoot about the Englishman, which Judge found suited him just fine.

"Cain't quite figger 'em out none neither," put in Ozzie, scratching his head. He cut off a good-sized chaw of tobacco and popped it into his mouth. "But it sure does make one's 'pinions 'bout that purty filly sit up and take notice, now don't it?"

124

Judge scowled. How was it Ozzie seemed to know what he was thinking lately? Judge was starting to get the distinct impression that the old timer had taken more than a liking to Victoria, and was looking to match Judge up with the Englishwoman. Well, he'd soon straighten that notion out! He ignored the fact that she had a way of getting to him. They wouldn't be in Saint Louis until tomorrow. That would give him time to come up with a way to demonstrate exactly what he thought of Victoria Torrington. He would stop that conniving old matchmaker plumb short in his tracks.

Lani looked about her. Thank goodness. The car held only three men; one was slumped in his seat snoring and the other two were hidden behind the morning newspapers. She and Gerald would be able to share a few minutes before they would be missed. She eased herself into a chair in the farthest corner from the men, waiting for Gerald to arrive, totally unaware that the men sitting behind the newspapers earnestly waited to hear what she and Gerald would say.

Gerald slipped through the door and slid in next to his darling wife. He clasped her hands and pressed urgent kisses along her fingertips. "My Alayne, how I wish we did not have to deny our love to the world."

"And I as well. But you know we cannot hurt Victoria." Not one to remain daunted for long, her bleak mood lifted and she brightened with enthusiasm. "We may not have to wait much longer though."

Gerald looked directly into the vibrant green eyes he loved so dearly. "How is that?"

In her usual animated fashion, she explained, "I think my plan to make Victoria jealous of me and Jesse is working. She makes an effort to monopolize his attention when I am around. And have you seen the way Victoria and Jesse look at each other? I caught Victoria preening before the mirror in the lavatory a few moments ago. I cannot ever recall her worrying about her appearance the way she has since Jesse came into her life, let alone how easily rattled he can make her." Then she frowned. "Do you not think you should have stepped forward and defended Victoria against that rude man on the platform this morning? Unless we can get her and Jesse together, you are all she has left. Oh . . . and Gerald, would it not be wise if you continued to call me Lani until everything is settled?"

Momentarily, Lani's observations pricked Gerald's ego. "You are the only one I would risk life and limb for." He abhorred violence of any kind, and had no intention of defending anyone's honor if he could help it. "Besides, everyone knows *Miss Chastity Iron Drawers* can take care of herself."

"Oh, Gerald, please," Lani pleaded. "Victoria is not that way at all. You know she had little choice but to help Father after Mother died. We would have lost all our money then if it had not been for Victoria."

Gerald hung his head, stung by her remark.

Her soft heart went out to him. She placed a comforting hand on his shoulder. "Gerald, I am sorry. I did not mean to imply that losing our money was all your fault. I know your intentions were honorable, just . . . misplaced."

He heaved a frustrated groan. "You bloody well know it was my fault. But, I say, those investments

126

seemed to be such a marvelous opportunity." He hugged Lani to him.

He seemed so guilt-ridden that Lani tried to make him feel better by chattering against his shoulder. "It is just that it is ever so difficult having to do without the latest fashions and having to wait on myself. But I am learning to curl my own hair, and I even sewed on a button all by myself last night. Why, I feel as if I have accomplished so much just since arriving in America. I may even learn to cook." She crinkled her brows and looked wistfully down at her soft hands. "That is, if I must."

She was such a helpless child, so full of life, so deserving of the best. Somehow he would see that she had everything she desired. "Do not worry . . . Lani." She sent him a smile when he returned to calling her the endearing childhood name. "You will again have all your dear heart wishes in life." A thought came to him. "Once Victoria receives her share of Judge Colston's property, she can sell it, use the money to rebuild her precious empire, and you and I can be together openly, at last."

"Oh yes! Oh, yes, yes, yes!" squealed Lani. She exuberantly threw her arms around Gerald's neck, trusting that everything would work out all right.

"You hear that?" one of the unshaven men behind the newspapers whispered to the other.

"Shur 'nuff did. The boss should find that bit a palaverin' 'bout that bastard, Colston, most interestin'. Soon as we gets to Saint Louie, we'll send word like we was told. Should earn us a mighty hunkerin' big bonus."

"Yup, it should oughta. I'm a'gonna use my share

and get me two willin' sportin' gals all at once; one to dip my stick int' while sucklin' at the other one's big titties."

"Sheeit. All you ever think about's big tits and that dick a'tween yore legs. Come on, we's got us work to do." The two men folded their papers and slithered past the pair into another car.

Feeling awkward for the first time in her life, Victoria left the washroom and returned to her seat across from the big cowhand. Jesse was talking with a big man whom he introduced as a member of the fire brigade in Saint Louis. Buck, so named for his efficiency with a bucket, and Jesse had known each other as young ranch hands years ago, Jesse explained. Buck remained only a few minutes, inviting them to inspect the firehouse in Saint Louis if they had time, then rose to leave. There was amusement in Buck's gray eyes when he nodded cordially to Victoria and ambled toward the next car.

She had a thousand questions to ask about Jesse's friendship with Buck, but swallowed the urge. She certainly did not want Jesse to think she was interested enough in him to want to know about his early life! Pity she had not had the opportunity to talk to Buck alone. Victoria felt her cheeks redden under Jesse's silent stare, until she could no longer abide his scrutiny. "Well," she raised her eyebrows impatiently, "what are you staring at?"

Judge grinned. "Like I said before, you're not a half bad-looking woman when you fix yourself up."

"I did not *fix myself up*," she protested, shifting in

the chair. Underneath, she secretly delighted he had noticed.

"If you insist, Tori." Judge pulled his hat over his eyes and crossed his arms along his chest.

"What do you think you are doing?" she demanded, indignant that he was dismissing her so easily.

"Getting some shut-eye," he answered, without removing his hat.

Victoria tried to make herself comfortable, but found that ease eluded her. Irritation racking at her, she snipped, "It must be nice to be able to sleep sitting in a chair. Strange how some people can sleep no matter how many others are deprived from their rest. And then there are those who can sleep despite what they have done to others," she added for good measure knowing she was being a bit of a shrew but unable to help herself.

Too tired to listen to her sharp tongue any longer, Judge reached out and scooped Victoria into the seat next to him. "Put your head in my lap."

"What?" she asked, startled by the strong arm which held her so close to him.

"I said, put your head in my lap," he repeated blandly.

"I will not."

"You will put your head down, and at least rest your tongue, or I'll—"

"Or you will what?" she snorted.

"Or I'll tie you up and gag you," he warned. "Thanks to you, I haven't slept for two nights, and I don't intend on making it three."

Victoria could see by the tension lines in his face that he would very well do just that. Not wishing to further bear the brunt of his crude actions, Victoria reluctantly curled her feet beneath her skirt and settled her head against his hard thigh.

She closed her eyes, but the warmth of his leg and the hardness of his muscles sent her mind racing. When he rested his calloused hand against her shoulder, she thought her heart was going to leap out of her chest. Even in her prone position, tension rippled through her body, and sleep remained out of reach while the man who called himself Jesse bombarded her senses.

Despite the exhaustion pervading his bones, Judge could not ignore the closeness of such a beautiful, spirited woman. For the third straight night he could not sleep.

By morning, Judge was feeling like a rankled grizzly bear. The only plan he had formed to demonstrate what he thought of Miss Victoria Elizabeth Torrington involved tasting those luscious lips and possessing her, body and soul. It had to be the loss of sleep, he grumbled to himself at the thought of wanting more than just her body.

Careful not to disturb her, he silently watched the other passengers move about the train. She remained resting in his lap. Why was he being so considerate? He should simply dump her on the floor and be about his business. But instead, he absently stroked her hair, enjoying the smooth, soft texture of the long silky strands escaping in golden threads against his fingers.

Victoria's breathing was slow and even. After long disturbing hours, she had finally been able to turn off the questions about Jesse. But she had not been able to control the warmth spreading from her cheeks and down her spine to wash over her. She felt his thigh tense. He was awake. She knew she should sit up and move away from him. But she made no effort to stir.

He represented everything she had always shied away from: a man with a mind of his own and the capability of getting whatever he desired, a man who saw what he wanted and took it, a dangerous man who could ignite a woman's passions. She had prided herself on keeping to the secure life. Why, look at Gerald, she thought, glancing at his stiff, scrawny figure from beneath long, dark lashes. Wasn't he the type of man she had chosen for herself?

Victoria Elizabeth Torrington, named after two queens, would never allow herself to be attracted to anyone as dangerous or enigmatic as Jesse. Security. The known. The tried and true. A safe, comfortable, companionable existence. Those were the values which had ruled her life. Yet a voice inside her asked if she wanted to spend the rest of her days never knowing what life could hold for those who took the chance.

If Judge and Victoria were not willing to admit to themselves the growing feelings they held for each other, there were others more candid. Lani and Gerald exchanged pleased glances at the sight of the pair. Ozzie wore a complacent grin across his gnarled face. And two shadowy figures, lurking in the back corner of the car, found the scene even more interesting than the conversation they had overheard the day before.

Chapter Fourteen

Shortly after passing a sign heralding the city of Saint Louis, Victoria looked out the window as the train ground to a halt. A number of passengers were getting off. She glanced over at Jesse and the judge. They had not even bothered to look up. The sooner they got to the hotel, the sooner the judge would discover that he could not dictate to her. Without consulting her better judgment as to why the others were remaining in their seats, she impatiently jumped up.

"What are you waiting for?" she demanded when she caught Jesse's eye. When he didn't bother to answer her, she said to the judge, "We are in Saint Louis. Did you not say we would be stopping here?"

"That I did, but—," Ozzie began to explain until Judge's warning look stopped him.

The perfect way to show the old timer what Judge thought of Victoria popped into his mind. "If you are in such an all-fired rush to get off the train, go right ahead," he said levelly to Victoria.

She glared at him for a minute, then directed Lani

and Gerald, "Hurry and collect what luggage we have left. We are leaving the train." With a swish of her skirts, she regally swept past Jesse and the judge and down the aisle.

Lani and Gerald looked bewildered, but compliantly did as bid, handing the luggage down to Victoria, who was now standing on the platform.

"What ya doin'? Ain't ya goin' t' stop her?" Ozzie choked, astonished by Judge's cool demeanor.

"If Miss Victoria Torrington is so determined to take charge, let her." Judge shrugged and forced himself to remain impassive in spite of the comically frantic scene on the platform outside his window.

"Well, I, for one, ain't goin' t' let her —," Ozzie started to rise, but Judge clamped steely fingers around the old man's arm before he could finish his sentence.

"Yes. You are," Judge said in such a low tone that Ozzie uneasily settled back in his seat.

"What's we a'gonna do now? They're a'splittin' up," whined the smaller of the two rough-featured men who had been keeping an eye on Judge and the lady.

"You get off and try t' find out what you can from the gal. I'll stick t' Colston."

Judge noticed the tall, lanky man in the ill-fitting suit get off the train and walk toward Victoria. There was something vaguely familiar about the man's stride. Judge never forgot a face, but the man kept his head down and turned away from him.

Even before the train pulled out, Judge had felt a twinge of regret and now, as he watched the distance separate them, he got an uneasy feeling all the way down to the heels of his boots. If he could just recall where he'd seen that man before.

In disbelief, Victoria watched the train chug away with Jesse and the judge on board.

"I say, where do you suppose they are heading off to?" asked Gerald, in a voice brimming with confusion.

The lanky man stepped forward holding a well-worn hat. "Gosh, ma'am," he said to Victoria. "I don't mean to be a'listenin' to youse. But that train's a'headed into Saint Louie."

"What?" Victoria's eyes rounded and she felt the veins in her neck stand out, she was so angry.

His eyes shifted over the foreigners. A sly edge hovered about his thin lips. "Shur 'nuff, it is."

"That is impossible," cried Lani, clutching Gerald's arm.

Victoria noticed the possessive hold her sister had on Gerald. But Lani had always been excitable and given to histrionics. Victoria ignored the pair.

" 'Fraid it ain't. You's a mile from the main depot."

"A mile? How ever are we going to get into town?" Lani wailed and looked to Gerald, who appeared at a loss for words.

Victoria stared down the tracks, eyes murderous and glittering with rage. How ever could she have thought Jesse had one decent bone in his body? The beast. He had deliberately let them get off the train, knowing full well they would be stranded. Yet even as she burned over their situation, the mere thought of the handsome cowhand started her body throbbing in that secret place. She had to remind herself what a rotter the man was to stop the sensations.

"Ma'am?" When Victoria did not answer he cleared his throat and said louder, "A'beggin' your pardon, ma'am."

A scratchy voice intruded into Victoria's thoughts. Trying not to appear rude, she quickly dragged her attention from the tracks to the lanky man. "Yes?"

She looked perturbed. He'd have to handle her right careful. The other two would be easy to pump for information, but not the lady Colston seemed to have his eye on. No. That one was no pea-brain like the one hanging onto that fancy-dressed dude. His eyes raked Victoria. She was a mighty handsome piece of woman-flesh under those ugly duds. A bulge grew in his crotch, and he was forced to slide his hat in front of it in order to cover the desire he had to dip beneath her skirts.

"The name's . . . Clancy."

"Yes, Mr. Clancy?" Victoria prompted, feeling impatient at the man's intrusion.

"I couldn't help but see how that man back on the train hoodwinked youse. If youse let me help, I can see that youse get into town in one piece and show him up at the same time."

Victoria looked about her. They were the only ones left on the platform now. The streets were muddy from a recent rain. Walking a mile with the luggage was out of the question. Lani looked about ready to cry, and Gerald, as usual, was not going to be any help. She glanced back at Clancy. She did not like what she saw. His expression could best be described as a leer, which made Victoria unwilling to be at his mercy. She gazed at the train tracks again, reminding herself of what Jesse had done. She would best him. They would find their way to the station without his assistance.

Victoria flashed Clancy a charming smile, which she did not at all feel. "Why, thank you, Mr. Clancy. We would appreciate a lift to the station."

Any thoughts of arriving at the depot in style were dashed when Clancy returned with what he said was the only available mode of transportation. Before Victoria stood an open wagon which both resembled and smelled like a pig cart.

Victoria's pride demanded that she refuse to ride in anything so filthy. But now was not the time to let her pride get in the way. After a lengthy argument, she overruled Lani's protests and Gerald's hesitance, and they climbed on board.

The wagon bumped and jolted the mile to the depot, splashing mud into the cart. "It's right up ahead there." Clancy pointed. He cursed beneath his breath. Here he had paid good money to get the driver to take the long way to the station, and he hadn't learned a damned thing from the closed-mouth bitch. Pity she wasn't alone. He'd know just how to handle her if she were.

Before Clancy could offer further assistance, Victoria leaped out of the cart and headed at a brisk pace toward Jesse and the judge; Lani and Gerald scrambled from the cart and struggled with the luggage, trying to catch up with her.

"If there's anything else I can do fer youse, youse just holler fer ol' Clancy," he yelled to the retreating figures.

"What you learn?" The other man slipped out of the shadows, his scraggly dirt brown hair hanging over one eye.

"Sheeit! I learned nothin', Mort. You?" Clancy paid off the driver and followed his cohort back into a dark corner.

"Not much, 'cept Colston was mighty edgy. Got me t' thinkin' he's got hisself a itch fer that one gal—the bossy one with the brains."

"You saw too? That one was 'alookin' mighty hard after the train back there, too. You think they could be sweet on each other to boot?"

"Don't know, but let's us mosey on over to the telegraph office and let the boss know we's a'keepin' our eyes peeled open."

Clancy shot one last look at the pretty women before he caught up with the other man. He spit a brown stream of chewing tobacco on the ground. "Sure wouldn't want to be in Colston's boots right 'bout now. That yella-haired gal looks like she's a'gonna kill. Let alone what the boss's a'gonna want t' do t' him when Colston gets back home." He shook his head. "What a woman that foreigner is. She'd be right fun to tame." He gave a longing sigh and slurped his tongue across his lips.

Her face heated with anger, Victoria marched up to the judge and demanded, "Would you be good enough to explain what prompted you to allow us to disembark a mile from the depot?"

The color drained from Ozzie's face and he looked helplessly to Judge for support. Judge leaned lazily up against the wall, his legs crossed at the ankle, his blue eyes taking in Victoria thoroughly.

"If I remember rightly," Judge said amicably, "it was you who insisted on getting off the train. We merely let you have your own way." When Victoria made no attempt to retort, he changed the subject. "No use standing around here any longer, let's head for the hotel."

"What about my luggage? At least we should inquire whether it has been located yet." Victoria started for the office.

"Already checked. Afraid you're stuck in your red coat a little longer . . . Tori," he taunted. Although Judge had coined the nickname to deride her, he found he was beginning to like the sound of it.

Victoria inwardly smarted at Jesse's smug tone, but rather than shred words with him, she quietly trailed behind the others to the awaiting coach.

Her mind swirled with thoughts as the coach clattered through town toward the Southern Hotel. She was so absorbed in trying to sort out the recent events that the passing scenery escaped her notice.

If Victoria had before suspected that something was awry between Judge Colston and Jesse, now she was certain of it. There was more than an employer/employee relationship between them; Jesse was definitely in control. Henceforth, she was going to remain close to Jesse in order to find out why. Yet, even as she formulated her plans, she couldn't ignore the sensations that just thinking about Jesse elicited. Against her will, she was being drawn closer and closer to the man.

She looked over at Gerald. He sat staidly, his hands clasped in his lap. A surge of guilt washed over her. She had been so wrapped up with her own problems that she had been ignoring her fiancé. Her glance caught with Jesse's as she shifted closer to Gerald. She locked her arm with Gerald's, and he patted her hand absently, not even bothering to look up.

When Victoria looked back at Jesse, her momentary feeling of triumph vanished. The frustrating man merely gave a silent nod, then shook his head; an arresting grin settled across his disgustingly captivating lips. She determined to ignore him, and turned to blankly stare out of the window.

Go ahead and laugh now, Jesse, she thought. But we will see who's laughing when we get to the hotel.

Chapter Fifteen

Judge glowered at the telegraphs Ozzie had collected at the reception desk and handed to him. "It's got to be a mistake," he muttered. "Bridgewater knows I . . . ah, you," he amended quickly when he noticed Victoria, "inspect all purchases before taking delivery." The other wire he stuffed into his pocket.

From the dark look on Jesse's face, Victoria decided that there was prudence in making a timely exit. "Come, Gerald," Victoria took his arm, "you may escort me to my room. I want to check on Lani."

Judge noticed the all-too-knowing expression on Victoria's countenance. She had to have something to do with the telegram from Bridgewater.

"Judge Colston?"

"Yes, Miz Victoria," Ozzie responded after a moment's hesitation.

"Will we see you for tea this afternoon?" Victoria smiled much too sweetly for Judge's liking.

"You can count on it," Judge answered for Ozzie. They watched the grand exit. "You know, Judge," Judge began for Victoria's benefit, "I thought we'd only be returning to the ranch with one bull. But it looks like there may be two."

"Two?"

"Yeah." Judge looked directly at Gerald. "The one out in the stockyard, and the other gelded one with the ring through its nose being led away before our eyes."

Gerald cringed at hearing the remark. "Ignore the bloody comment, Victoria," he urged, although he knew he had not been much of a man.

She stopped. "I will not." Her face reddening, she pivoted around to face Jesse. He was standing with a red handkerchief dangling from his fingers. With deliberate steps, she moved to come face to face with Jesse and snatched the crimson cloth out of his hand.

"I have found you to be intolerably rude from the first moment we met."

"Oh? Have you now," Judge returned easily.

"I most certainly have."

"You didn't seem to find kissing me intolerably rude."

Gerald's eyes bugged. "You let him bloody well kiss you?"

"And I'd say she *bloody well* enjoyed it, too," Judge chimed.

Victoria looked truly flustered. "I did not!"

"Come, come now, Tori," Judge chided. "You know you enjoyed it as much as I did."

She opened her mouth to retort, but not a sound left her lips. What Jesse had said was true; she had enjoyed it, even reveled in it. Instead of allowing further entrance to her feelings, she practically whispered, "You did?"

Judge moved over to her and silently delved into her searching blue eyes before she dropped the stiff veil into

141

place. "Yes, I did," he murmured. Then, suddenly aware that he had let down his own guard, he grabbed her hand roughly and began to drag her through the lobby.

"Have you taken leave of your senses?" Gerald shouted at the retreating couple, but wisely remained stationary, in a position of safety away from the angry cowboy.

"What do you think you are doing?" she demanded.

"Since I have no doubt you somehow managed to send a telegram," with his other hand he waved the crinkled sheet of paper at her, "instructing Bridgewater to ship the bull from Texas so you would not have to waste time traveling there, the least you can do is come with me and take a look at your first purchase for the ranch. And for our sake, I hope you chose well." There was a furious hiss to his voice.

"But I . . ." Being marched through the lobby against her will, Victoria held her hat to her head with one hand.

"Don't try to deny you're responsible."

She tugged out of his grasp. "Of course I shall not attempt to deny it."

"How did you know where to send the telegram?"

She thought of the book the judge had loaned her and the man's address scribbled inside. "I have my sources," she said evasively.

Not allowing him the opportunity to question her further, she said, "You yourself said the man was honest, and the creature has won prizes." She bluffed indignation. "And since I do own a portion of the ranch, I am well within my rights to take an active part in the decision-making process."

"Maybe where you come from. But where I'm from,

we have other ideas about our women."

"I am not your woman!" she sputtered.

"Maybe not yet," Judge said before thinking.

Startled faces settled on Judge after his unintended disclosure.

"Sounds like a right good idea t' me." Ozzie chuckled, although his Adam's apple was bobbing up and down from the tension of the moment.

Judge narrowed his eyes at Ozzie.

"I say, old man, do be good enough to remember that Victoria is engaged to marry me," Gerald blurted out, playing the bruised suitor for all he was worth, but taking care not to get too near the furious cowboy, and thinking how he'd have the opportunity to visit his bride once they were out of the way.

"So I've been told," Judge said, in a low voice which would not brook further interference. "But for now the future *Mrs. Pelthurst* is coming with me."

"I am not," Victoria protested.

"Oh, yes you are." Unceremoniously, Judge tossed Victoria over his shoulder and stomped outside, past astounded hotel guests. With a whistle, he hailed a coach.

"Sir?" The whiskered driver hesitantly brought the coach to within two feet of Judge and a struggling Victoria.

"How much to rent just the carriage and horses for the day?" came the gruff question from Judge.

"What do you think you are doing?" screeched Victoria, abashed by the crowd of onlookers beginning to cluster, yet not about to remain meekly still.

"Ignore her," Judge said casually to the bewildered driver, pulling a wad of bills from his pocket. "It's a game we play." When the driver looked skeptical, Judge added, "Can I help it if she likes the strong-man type?"

"I do not," Victoria retorted, scandalized. "I command you to release me this instant."

Judge calmly ignored her.

The driver scratched his head, greedily eyeing the money. "My old lady gets off on a spanking, she does," he snickered. "But I don't know about letting you take the carriage." He watched while Judge placed bill after bill on the seat. It was more money than he made in a week. "I just don't know."

"Make up your mind," Judge said impatiently, setting another bill on the stack. When the man still hesitated, Judge looked him straight in the eye. "That's all I'm offering."

The man snatched up the money and jumped from the coach. "You got yourselves a carriage. Just return it here to the hotel when you're done with it."

Judge gave a curt nod to the man. "Show's over folks," he announced to the milling assembly of people. He dumped Victoria on the seat and climbed up next to her. "Don't even think about it, Tori," he warned when Victoria edged away from him as if prepared to take flight.

She turned her back to him and crossed her arms, silently fuming at such an undignified exit from the hotel. But his words *maybe not yet* charged before her eyes. Her mind swirled with thoughts of how different Jesse was from Gerald. She had always been in control with Gerald; there had never been any question of their relationship being otherwise. But Jesse was not a man to be dictated to — by anyone. What would it be like to be married to someone like Jesse? she suddenly wondered.

Victoria steamed beneath her collar as she flatly

144

refused to look at the man, instead steadfastly keeping her eyes averted. In her blinding anger, coupled with her unbidden thoughts about the cowhand, she entirely missed all the beauty the scenery had to offer.

Snapping her attention back to him, Judge said, "And just when did you have the time to send that damned telegram?"

"I went straightaway to the telegraph office after I left you in the hotel that night in Washington, D.C. But I do not see what difference it makes now," she snapped.

"No. Unfortunately, you wouldn't," he grumbled, thinking that her actions had put him in a difficult position with Bridgewater. Doing a slow burn over her selfish deed, he added, "And I suppose you don't see what difference your giving that libelous story to the newspaper makes either."

Victoria's haughty expression went blank, which took Judge by complete surprise. "What story?"

"The story about your little side trip to the Capitol Building and the meeting with the chief justice, that's what story."

"I have no idea what you are talking about."

He studied her. There was a simple honesty to the way she had answered him, and her features were relaxed — not at all tense like they would be if she were lying. "There was a derogatory article in the paper yesterday morning about corruption in the courts, which included your little jaunt out onto the ledge. Lucky for you, I managed to extract a retraction from the editor."

Victoria stared at him, expressionless for a moment. Then it came to her. "That reporter at the Capitol Building, of course. He must have been the one I saw

145

scurrying into a carriage when I was on the ledge," she half mumbled to herself, only now realizing who that shadowy man at both sites must have been.

She proceeded to explain the incidents to Jesse, absolving herself from responsibility for the damaging article. To her chagrin, the cowboy remained rigid, refusing to understand why she had felt it necessary to take such drastic measures. In other words, she determined, the coldhearted lout had not one ounce of sympathy.

Although Judge continued to hold her partially accountable — she had provided the reporter with more ammunition by her dumb stunts — he was relieved that she had kept her word and had not gone to the newspaper office behind his back. This revelation gave him further pause for thought, causing him to sink into mute contemplation for the remainder of the trip.

After a lengthy silence, they arrived at the stockyard to find a short, squat man in dusty denims standing beside a pen which enclosed a black bull. Judge left Victoria sitting in the carriage and greeted the middle-aged man.

Bridgewater gave a jovial laugh. "Judge, you son of a sidewinder."

"Can't explain now, but the name is Jesse," Judge said in a choked voice, looking back over his shoulder to see if Victoria had heard the rancher call him by name.

Bridgewater looked past Judge to Victoria, who was sitting primly, having opened a white, frilly, lace-trimmed parasol to shade her creamy complexion from the warm rays of the sun. "It wouldn't have nothing to do with that right nice heifer you've got with you, now would it?"

146

"Heifer? Ha! A Texas tornado would be more like it."

"Met yer match, huh?"

Judge glared as Bridgewater rushed past him to help Victoria down. "Mighty nice to meet you, ma'am. Bridgewater's the name. I was wondering why *Jesse* here didn't want to take the time to make the trip to Texas to take a look-see at my MacTosh." He pointed to the bull. " 'Course, seeing you explains why the lad's so galldarned anxious to get back to Wyoming. You know, there's them of us who would of took odds that *Jesse* would never tie the knot. But if you aren't the prettiest — "

"Mr. Bridgewater," Victoria raised her chin, her tone imperious. "I am *Miss* Victoria Torrington. I most certainly am *not* Jesse's intended. I am here quite simply because I happen to own a portion of Judge Colston's property."

"Why, if that don't beat all." Bridgewater's utter shock was plainly visible. "That true, *Jesse?*"

"This supposed partnership remains to be seen," Judge said dryly. "Since the judge's new partner took it upon herself to send you a telegram instructing you to meet us here, let's see what you've got."

"You mean to tell me that it weren't you what sent the message?" He turned to Victoria, who remained silent. "Knowing Judge Colston and all, I think the two of you is going to have a right interesting partnership, if you know what I mean."

"Mr. Bridgewater, I do believe we are here to conduct a business transaction. Shall we inspect the MacTosh, Jesse?"

Annoyed by the man's flippant manner, Victoria stepped past him to view the bull.

Bridgewater sniggered and slapped his thigh. "Mac-

Tosh is his name, miss. He's a cross between an Aberdeen-Angus and a Texas Longhorn. The Aberdeen-Anguses was first brought from Scotland in '73. I've been crossing them with Longhorns to increase beef production."

"Of course. It is obvious the animal is an Aberdeen-Angus by its smooth, black coat and hornless head." She stepped around the animal. "A first-rate specimen, I would venture to say." Frantically, she searched her mind to remember what she had read in that book the judge had slipped her. She pretended to study the animal further. "Good, sturdy legs, and a well-developed back and loins. Its rear quarters are nicely wide and deep, too."

Judge cocked his head sideways at Victoria, ignoring the bull. "Never a doubt in my mind," he quipped, sending Bridgewater into spasms of rollicking laughter.

Victoria was not going to let Jesse's ribald remarks concerning her person deflate her. She hesitated only long enough to issue a searing squint in his direction. "The *animal's* black skin should lessen the eye troubles which plague so many beef cattle. And since the breed matures early, it will mean an increase in profit. It will prove an excellent choice, I should think. We shall take him," she said, before Judge had had the opportunity to speak for himself. "Only if the price is not overly exorbitant, of course."

Bridgewater stood, his mouth slack, too impressed by her knowledge of the breed to respond.

When she'd stepped in and taken over, Judge's first inclination had been to wrap his hands around her neck and squeeze. But he had to give her credit. She had done her homework — with Ozzie's help no doubt. And now she was prepared to haggle with Bridgewater.

Although he had good quality cattle, Bridgewater was a real hustler. It was a rare occasion when anyone came out ahead of the man. Judge stepped back. He'd just see if she was as accomplished a businesswoman as she had led him to believe.

Judge swung out his arm. "This party is all yours, Tori."

"What're you doing?" Bridgewater asked Judge, thunder-stunned. "You going to accept a female making a deal for the J Bar C?"

Judge shrugged. "She insists she's a partner. If she makes a bad deal, then the loss will come out of her share."

Victoria pursed her lips at his condescending comment. She'd show him!

For an hour she persisted, finally leaving Bridgewater feeling as if he had been turned inside out, hog-tied, and hung out to dry.

Bridgewater took out his handkerchief and wiped the perspiration from his forehead, his amusement vanquished. "Well, if you didn't bring in a real ringer and hornswaggle me. I oughta take MacTosh and hightail it back to Texas before I end up paying you."

Judge stepped in. Despite his anger at her presence, he wasn't going to let Bridgewater slither out of a deal with one of his nasty displays of temper. "What's the matter, Bridgewater? You having a hard time taking it kindly when you're on the other end of a deal? Or can't you admit that the little lady bested you fair and square?"

Bridgewater sucked in a hard defeat. "Fair and square? Ha! Swindle's more like it. Next time I aim to deal directly with *Judge Colston*."

"Think you'd of done any better?"

"No. Don't think that I would've. Never thought I'd lose out to a woman, though." Forcing the appearance of being good-natured, Bridgewater said to Judge, "Between the two of you, the J Bar C's bound to become the largest spread in the Territory of Wyoming. If I was Judge Colston," he looked directly at Judge, "I'd marry her."

At Bridgewater's comment, Victoria's head snapped up in surprised shock, only to look straight into blue eyes dancing with an inexplicable gleam.

Chapter Sixteen

"If you two are done gawkin' at each other, I could use something to drown my tonsils with. You don't even have to buy. *Judge Colston* can foot the bill. After he finds out the bargain he got with my MacTosh, I know he won't kick. That right, *Jesse?*" Bridgewater gave a hearty laugh.

Within ten minutes they were again settled, or rather, squeezed, into the rented carriage and on their way to a local tavern.

Victoria experienced a great sense of exhilaration. It was as if the deal she'd made with Bridgewater signified a greater triumph — one which had nothing to do with bulls. Jesse had suddenly become more relaxed around her; perhaps she had won a small measure of acceptance. Whether he accepted her or not should not make the slightest difference, but deep in a chamber of her heart she admitted to herself that it did.

They arrived at a pleasant tavern and in short order were seated at a table set with two bottles of wine. Victoria quietly waited as Bridgewater sloshed three mugs full of the fiery liquid that she had insisted Jesse

151

order. Bridgewater pulled a face at the wine bottles, plainly conveying that he'd rather have a drinking man's liquor.

"Here's to the little lady even if she don't know how to celebrate right proper with a good slug of hard liquor." He lifted his mug and guzzled down its contents. "Sure have to hand it to Colston. It was quick thinking on his part." He looked pointedly at Judge. If the man hadn't sent me that telegram instructing me to pack up my MacTosh and rush right on up here, I might still own the animal or at least have ended up gettin' a better price."

Judge shot Victoria a knowing glance. "Surprised me too, Bridgewater. Colston doesn't usually do business that way," Judge added dryly.

Victoria could have sworn that Jesse had winked at her, and his lips curled up ever so slightly. She absently ran her index finger around the rim of her glass as the men continued to converse. She was pleased with herself, and the thought that Jesse, too, seemed gratified secretly warmed her heart. She studied his profile. His features were expertly crafted. His hair was so black it had a blue cast to it, and his skin was tanned, his eyes deep blue. His muscular body demonstrated the benefits of years of hard work. He was all male; there was no mistaking that. Not wanting either man to notice she had been scrutinizing Jesse, Victoria brought her attention back to what they were saying.

"When I got Colston's telegram I thought to myself, Bridgewater, what if you hurry on up to Saint Louis with MacTosh and Colston changes his mind? So I says to myself, if Colston don't take MacTosh after that long trip, you'll have wasted a lot of time, not to mention money. You know I'm a man with a healthy respect for the dollar and I don't waste time by taking needless chances. So before I trailed on up here, I sent Luther Jessup a telegram telling him I was meeting up with Colston, and if Jessup was interested in MacTosh, he'd better hightail it out here to get his bid in. Lucky for you two, he and that pretty, untamed wife of his ain't arrived at the hotel yet."

"Yes, lucky," mumbled Judge. In his pocket, he fingered the telegram he had received from Helene, informing him that she would be seeing him soon. He looked over at Victoria. Helene would have a fit when she met her. Judge knew Helene's quick temper could ruin everything. All that possessive she-devil would have to do is take one look at Victoria and she'd spoil his masquerade. Hell, Helene would never keep her lips shut and go along with his plan. Not when another woman, more beautiful and younger than she, was involved. She'd believe the worst, Judge knew that.

Judge looked at Victoria again. Strangely, the thought of the Englishwoman warmed his blood. He found himself thinking it was a pity Helene's suspicions would be unwarranted. Of course, who knows, he let his eyes slide over Victoria's curves, by the time Helene met Victoria, things could be different. He shook his head. What was wrong with him? He'd made a decision a long time ago; he'd be well advised to stick to it.

For the time being, he had to keep Helene away from Victoria if he was going to succeed. A comparison between Helene and Victoria flashed before Judge's eyes. They both were motivated by a need for money. Helene had married for it, sold her body and soul, whereas Victoria's scheme was to insist that it rightfully belonged to her. But he grudgingly had to admit he had a growing respect for Victoria. She had driven a hard bargain with Bridgewater, which would add to the worth of the ranch.

"Ain't you going to celebrate with us, Miss Tori? Or you think you're above tippin' a mug or two with a couple of trail hands like us?" Bridgewater egged her on. Bridgewater hailed the tavern keeper. "Keep the bottles coming, man. We still got us a bit of real celebrating to do, if you get my drift." He nodded toward the hard liquor.

The last time she had overindulged with the judge had had disastrous results. Victoria looked from man to man. Bridgewater had a firm set to his features, as did Jesse. She lifted her mug. This time she would gauge her sips with care.

Two hours later, Victoria's lifelong belief in proper deportment was rapidly diminishing. Although she had dutifully nursed her mug, Bridgewater had stealthily seen to it that the wine was liberally spiked with doses of whiskey, which had left her feeling utterly giddy. When a group of hefty firemen entered from the nearby firehouse and sat down at an adjacent table, Victoria recognized the man from the train. She stood up feeling free from all constraint.

"Hello, Buck," she said cutely, waving at the big fireman she'd been introduced to on the train.

Buck nodded in their direction, hefted his glass, and sauntered over to their table. Acquaintances were renewed and Buck sat down.

"I'm glad to see you decided to take me up on my invitation to view an American firehouse," Buck said, proceeding to describe in detail the last call he'd answered. Once he'd finished with his tale, he asked, "You all celebrating something special?"

"Well actually, we just, or rather I just, bought a

MacTosh for the ranch. Now we are here commemorating the event — and since we seem to be so close to your establishment, we can stop for that visit," Victoria explained happily, the strong spirits loosening her tongue and keeping her from fabrication.

Buck's face fell into a quizzical angle, forcing Judge to elaborate, all the while simmering inside. Bridgewater and Buck smirked into their cups as Judge's impersonation led him in deeper and deeper. Judge ended up cornered into promising Buck, before he stood to rejoin his companions, that Victoria and he would stop by the firehouse on their way back to the hotel.

"Buck, I do ever so want to meet your associates." Victoria popped out of her seat, tipping the chair over in her exuberance and sending it crashing to the floor. "Oh, my." She hiccupped and slapped gloved fingers to her lips. "I seem to be causing quite a stir."

All eyes turned in Victoria's direction, and Judge had to grab her around the waist to steady her as she bent to right the upset chair. Victoria took a moment to focus on the handsome blur before her. She giggled and wagged a finger in his face. "You really should not do that."

"Do what?"

She sent him a conspiratorial smile. "Touch me."

He cocked a brow and shot Bridgewater a look. "Touch you?"

She glanced around, then leaned close to his ear and whispered, "It does strange things to me — much like when you kissed me. But not quite as tingly." She furrowed her brows, swaying precariously. She tittered. "But do not tell anyone."

"I wouldn't think of it. Now, sit down before you fall down."

155

A satisfied grin to his lips, Bridgewater abruptly stood up. "I think this is my cue to mosey on over to the bar so I can do some serious drinking. Catch you two later. Or maybe I should say, hope I don't catch you two later. It's been quite an experience doing business with you, little lady. *Jesse,*" he nodded, grinning slyly and moved off.

Victoria sat primly proper, blushing, until Bridgewater left, then edged closer to Jesse. "Did you hear what I said before Mr. Bridgewater left?"

Judge sat still, astounded by the sudden change of events, but aroused nonetheless by her confession and altered demeanor. "If I didn't know it was the liquor talking, I might be tempted to do something about it."

Victoria shifted her eyes to make certain no one would overhear her, then rasped, "What would you do?"

Judge stared at the beautiful woman; she was shamelessly flirting with him. In order to put a halt to the unbidden thoughts invading him and heating his senses, he reminded himself how he felt about liquor, and how it had destroyed his father. "Come on. We're getting you out of here." He grabbed her wrist and began dragging her from the tavern.

Bridgewater lifted his mug in salute. "Ain't love grand, *Jesse?*"

Judge sent the man a scowl and pushed Victoria out into the fading sun. Get up on the seat," he commanded.

"Aren't you going to offer your assistance?" she cooed, feeling strangely free-spirited for the first time in her life.

"Chrissake!" Judge circled Victoria's waist to help her up. She immediately slid her arms around his neck, her big, innocent eyes looking up into his. Judge groaned and raked his fingers through his hair. She leaned against him. Her face was so close to his he could smell the scent of rosewater dabbed along her invitingly long, beautiful neck. Her full, sensuous mouth was set in a pout of expectation. Despite an inner warning, Judge circled his arms around her. He had meant to immediately send her packing, back to England. Now, he literally found his hands full.

Gerald straightened his collar, glanced over his shoulder to make sure no one else was in the hallway, and scratched on Lani's door. He fidgeted with his fingers. He could hear her moving about inside the room. Just when he was about ready to give up in defeat, the portal opened and Lani peeked out.

"Gerald? What are you doing here?" she squeaked.

He straightened his stance. "I daresay, you are my wife, after all."

"But what about Victoria? She might come along at any moment." Her green eyes were wide with fear of discovery.

"No need to worry about her for hours. That Jesse fellow just led her from the hotel — quite unwillingly, I might add. Seems he accused her of sending a telegram to that chappie with the bull, and the fellow is here. So he forced her to accompany him to view the bloody animal."

"What about the judge?"

"I watched him go across the street to a tavern. I well believe we shall not see him all afternoon."

Satisfied that they would not be found out, Lani pulled Gerald into the room and began planting kisses over his face. Gerald awkwardly stepped back to catch his breath. "I say, you will doubtless make a rousing wife."

"I apologize if I seem too forward." She dropped her head.

"No. Not at all. Shall we get on with it?" He unbuttoned his jacket and carefully laid it on the chair, smoothing out the wrinkles.

Lani's lips slid downward. "It?"

"My love, I did not mean it that way at all." Gerald ushered her to the bed, swiftly removed her skirts and began kissing and nibbling her neck.

"Oh, Gerald, you are not sorry you married me, are you?" she said, while undressing him in a heated panic.

"Never." The rest of his words were muffled as she tossed his starched shirt in a heap. They fell onto the bed, and as he began showing her just how much becoming man and wife meant to him, he couldn't help but remember their wedding . . .

"Are you quite certain we are doing the right thing?" Gerald looked rightly shocked at Lani's suggestion. They stood fidgeting in front of the white picket fence surrounding the justice of the peace's house.

Lani pouted, remembering how Gerald's gaze toward Victoria had seemed much too fond. "It must be fate that we happened by this house on our way back from the train station. Besides, I thought you wanted only me," she implored.

"My dear girl, you are the only one I shall ever desire," Gerald offered, with all the sincerity in his heart.

"Then let's hurry so Victoria and Jesse do not return to the hotel before we do. Once we are married, I shall never again have to worry about losing you," cried Lani.

"What about Victoria?" interjected Gerald, fearing the elder sister's reaction when she learned she had lost him.

"You have seen the way Victoria looks at Jesse," she said, deflating his ego. "Everything will work out, I know it. We shan't tell a soul. You can remain engaged to Victoria until she gets the money from the ranch. Then we can tell her. If she's still madly in love with you, you can let her down easy."

His pride reinstated, Gerald hugged Lani to him. "I could never refuse you anything. Shall we pay a visit to the minister, what?"

Lani smiled triumphantly as Gerald swung open the gate to their future.

Abruptly, Gerald's attention returned to the present as Lani's breast thrust against his hand. Unable to hold himself back and go slowly, he quickly raised up over her and plunged into her woman's depths, sealing the futurity of their life together.

Chapter Seventeen

Sitting in front of the tavern in the carriage, Judge lowered his lips and gently pressed them to Victoria's. In her hazy state of mind that didn't satisfy Victoria. Her arms slid up his back and she grabbed the back of his head. His soft mouth tasted so good that she sought to deepen the kiss.

Judge could hardly believe it. The beautiful schemer was practically forcing herself on him. Her enthusiasm left no doubt in his mind that he could whisk her back to the hotel and bed her before she had sobered up enough to change her mind. He had to put all his energy into denying his arousal, or his body would override his head. His control was rapidly dissipating as she ran fiery fingers down his chest and slipped them inside his shirt.

Buck walked outside the tavern with his companions and immediately howled out a whistle. "I like the way you two picked to wait for us to return to the firehouse."

Victoria and Judge immediately broke apart. Gaining his head once again, Judge gazed into her glazed eyes, a wolfish grin settling over his countenance despite his resolve. "If you're not through kissing me yet, we can forgo the side trip to the fire station and head back to the hotel."

"*I* was kissing *you?* I must say I am quite certain it had to have been the other way around."

" 'Fraid it wasn't."

"I never!" She clutched at her throat trying to clear the fog from her mind.

"Well, fact is, you just did. But we'll have time to pursue this topic in more depth at a later hour—after you've visited a genuine American firehouse."

"We most certainly will not."

Not five minutes from the tavern, Judge halted the horses in front of a good-sized building. The engines stood in rows on each side of the shed, the stables, at the back. As Victoria stepped from the carriage, Buck set a helmet on her head over the delicate hat she wore.

"We've all decided to adopt you, if that's all right, Miss Victoria," Buck offered timidly.

"Why ever would you think it would not meet with my approval?" She straightened the oversized headgear, feeling quite like a schoolgirl on her first outing.

"Why don't you show us around so I can get Miss Tori back to the hotel by supper time," Judge recommended, expecting her to have a dreadful headache as the influence of the liquor wore off. That is, if she didn't up and unload her gut like the last time she had overindulged.

Buck showed them how the horses were already harnessed, waiting to be pressed into service by a chain which passed in front of a row of boxes. He explained that when the alarm bell sounded, the chain dropped down and the horses were raced to be hitched to their own engine. He ushered them through the station, making introductions and describing how the men of the brigade slept above the fire engine shed.

"How do they get down that ladder so rapidly when there is a conflagration?"

"A what?"

"A fire. She means a fire, Buck." Judge rolled his eyes at Victoria but secretly admired her knowledge. She was not only bright, but well-educated as well.

Buck grinned. "You want I should show you, ma'am?"

"I don't think that would be such a great idea in Miss Tori's condition," Judge cautioned.

"Whatever do you mean? I am in perfect shape. What is it you have to show me, sir?"

Buck shot a questioning look at Judge. Swallowing back his trepidation, Judge nodded his approval. Scratching his head, Buck led them to the loft. Victoria marveled at the way all the clothing and gear stood in readiness. The dormitory room reminded her of Miss Ernestine's school. She stepped over to a smooth wooden pillar and fingered the satiny finish. She was about to ask its use when the fire bell clanged. An orderly chaos erupted and Judge was forced to snatch Victoria aside as the men slid down the pole in answer to the call.

"Sorry I can't finish the tour, but duty can't wait or someone's family's likely to be burned out of their home," Buck hollered, wrapping his legs around the pole and disappearing through the hole in the floor.

"My word, that looks as if it would be ever so much fun." Victoria was fascinated with the column, and moved nearer to peer down to the scurrying teams below. An impish glow colored her cheeks and she said, "Why don't we try it, Jesse?"

"I don't think that's such a wise idea." Judge moved nearer Victoria to stop her should she attempt something rash.

"Well, I do."

Judge put his hand on her arm to halt her. "Okay, okay. If you insist on this foolishness at least let me go first, so I can be there to catch you if I have to."

"You will not have to." She raised her chin and tried to focus on the pole, which suddenly seemed to have duplicated itself. "Which one are we going to use?"

He rolled his eyes. "There's only one, Tori. Why don't you forget it and I'll let you climb a tree or something when we get to the ranch."

"Not very amusing, Jesse. Now hurry along, or I shall not wait for you to go first."

Judge glared at her, grasped the pillar, and slid easily to the floor. "Carefully grab the pole, then wrap your feet around it and hang on," he shouted up at her, enjoying the glimpse of stockinged ankle and lace petticoats.

Before he could step aside, Victoria gave a squeal and glided down the length, only to plop right on top of Judge, knocking him to the floor with a hard thud.

Sitting astride the fuming cowboy, she swivelled her head until they were nose to nose, and announced, "That was such fun. Shall we do it again?"

Victoria could not understand Jesse's sudden brooding animosity toward her. She certainly couldn't fathom why he had limped up behind her, grabbed her by the foot, and yanked her off the ladder without the least bit of delicacy as she was attempting to climb back up to the loft. *She* should be the one who was ruffled, when she thought of the way he had rudely clamped hurting fingers around her arm and forced her to leave the fire station. Then a smile tugged at her lips. Since she'd arrived in America, she had inched her way around a third-story ledge, slid down a fire pole, talked to the president, and created a stir in the Supreme Court—not to mention being kissed by a real, live American cowboy!

Once Judge turned the carriage back over to the driver Victoria pursed her lips toward him. "Does that mean we are not going to have any more fun today?"

"I don't think my body can take you having any more fun today." He rubbed his aching backside as they entered the hotel.

Victoria was feeling woozy and quite upset to her stomach as they climbed the stairs, but what made her feel particularly awful wasn't her physical ailments—it was her shocking behavior earlier. How could she have ever acted so . . . so common?

"What time would you like to meet for supper?" Judge asked, causing Victoria to turn away from her door.

"I wouldn't," she replied, holding her temple and feeling a trifle green. "I fear you will have to dine without me this evening."

Her head was thumping loudly between her ears, and she had to strain so to focus her attention on Jesse that she entirely missed seeing Gerald cautiously creak the door open.

He froze when he caught sight of Victoria and that crude cowboy. Fortunately, Victoria's back was to him, and the American did no more than cock a brow in his direction. His heart pounding, Gerald darted back into the room and returned in a flash, with his shirt and coat

164

slung over his arm, frantically fastening his trousers.

Judge knew there was something between Victoria's sister and that dandy, and had half a mind to show him up for what he was. But Judge liked the harebrained sister and wasn't sure what feelings Victoria had for the man. Despite a flaming desire to see Gerald Pelthurst out of Tori's life, he held Victoria's attention while Gerald tiptoed down the hall and into his own room.

"Victoria?" squeaked Lani. Her color was high and her beige tresses were in a state of disorder. She wiped a stray lock back behind her ear, secretly breathing a sigh of relief that she and Gerald had heard Victoria's voice before she had walked in on them and caused a dickens of a scene. Then she pinched her lips. If Victoria weren't so tight with their money, they wouldn't have to share a room and she and Gerald wouldn't have to risk being caught. Next time she would have to go to Gerald's room, rather than chance discovery.

"Where have you been all afternoon?" Lani tried to sound worried and perturbed.

"Oh, please, not now," begged Victoria. She swept past Lani and collapsed on the bed.

"What did you do to my sister?"

"I think a better question might be: what did you and that Englishman do to your sister?" he shot back.

Lani blushed purple before she said, "It is not what you think."

"And just what exactly is it that you think I am thinking?" he demanded.

"Alayne, would you be so kind as to fetch me a cool compress for my head?" Victoria requested from across the room, sure her head was going to split in half.

For the second time today, Lani was rescued. "I shall be right there, Victoria." She turned pleading eyes on

Jesse. "I must go to her now. Please, Jesse, do not tell Victoria you saw Gerald leave our room."

A whole new set of questions occurred to Judge as he returned to his room to bathe and change for supper.

In spite of himself, Judge was thinking more and more about Miss Victoria Elizabeth Torrington with each passing day. When he'd originally received that infuriating letter, he could have squeezed the breath out of the woman he was sure was a scheming old maid. Then, when he'd walked into that dining room in New York and spotted that lovely vision sitting so stiffly alone, his breath had been nearly kicked out of him. But that was only the beginning of the surprises she had meted out.

Although he still firmly believed her claim was bogus and doubted her motives, he was coming to admire her tenacity and determination. But that was only one facet of the lady which intrigued him. Earlier in the day he had witnessed another. There was a very human side to her when she let her guard down. Thoughts of her efforts on the ledge, as well as at the firehouse, caused him to chuckle.

His grin faded when he thought of another aspect of her personality. There was a hidden passion within the woman waiting to be unlocked. Without even trying, Victoria Elizabeth Torrington, named after two queens, managed to arouse him like no other woman had. Not even Helene had ever touched the part of his heart that Victoria — Tori — had. For an instant, he found himself wanting to make love to her, to protect her so she'd never have to concern herself about anything but him again.

His musings abruptly ended at the thought of being her protector. She was a shrewd businesswoman capable of dealing with the most difficult adversaries. Hadn't she herself stated that her only interests were business and the precious corporate empire her father had created? Judge's lips tightened. He went to the window and looked out in the direction of Wyoming and the land he treasured. Showing that side of her had been a fatal mistake on her part. She had demonstrated to him that he would have to pull out all the stops in order to beat her at her own game. To save his ranch, he would do just that.

"Judge! Judge! You in there?" Ozzie pounded against the door.

Judge let him in and immediately swung on him when he smelled the whiskey on the old man's breath. He grabbed the bottle from his hand and smashed it against the wall. "If you can't hold your liquor, you had better not let me catch you taking another sip until I'm through with the Englishwoman. And you'd best remember your tongue before you slip up and call me Judge again where someone might overhear you."

"Ah geez, I didn't mean no harm." Ozzie shuffled a booted foot and settled a hip on the edge of the desk.

"Yeah, I know." Judge's expression was hard, unforgiving. "But if I lose even a handful of my ranch due to your damned drinking, I'll have your hide. Now go take a cold shower. Sober up and get ready to go to supper."

Ozzie hung his head. "I won't let ya down again, ya'll see. I know how ya feel 'bout drinkin' 'cause of your pa an' all."

Lani pushed herself away from the cowboy's door and darted back to her room. She had been leaving her room as the judge began pounding on Jesse's door, and had paused to listen. Hearing the judge call out the name "Judge" had caught her attention, and when the

167

elder man went inside, she crept to the door and pinned her ear against the frame. She had heard enough of the conversation to set her mind spinning.

Once Judge had cooled down, he got cleaned up and checked on the ladies. Victoria was sleeping soundly and Lani, suspicion glinting from her eyes, pleaded a headache. After leaving the two Englishwomen, Judge went to Gerald's room. The dandy stood awkwardly, embarrassed, and insisted on keeping his own company, apparently so he wouldn't have to answer any incriminating questions.

"I guess it's just you and me tonight, old timer," Judge mumbled to himself, thankful for the reprieve. He went to collect Ozzie. Tonight he could be himself and enjoy a quiet meal; he could relax and forget about his problems.

As Judge and Ozzie made their way to the entrance of the dining room, Judge stopped flat in his tracks. There, not more than twenty feet in front of him, sat Helene Jessup, as regal and proud in her black, low-cut gown as the most formidable predator.

Chapter Eighteen

Judge's mood turned black as he watched Helene ply her wiles on the dozen formally dressed men present at her table. Luther, his gut stuck out over his belt, a cigar hanging from his thick lips, looked as if he would enjoy stripping her naked right there so he could show off his beautiful possession.

Helene was like a cat; she always managed to land on her feet regardless of what life tossed at her. She was a gorgeous, greedy schemer. Thoughts of the poor childhood she'd had caused Judge's stance to soften. In many ways he could not blame Helene for what she was. She had clawed her way into the wealthiest family in the territory, and was determined to have it all: Luther, his ranch, his money, her son, and Judge.

"Come on, let's us go on somewheres else t' fill up," Ozzie recommended when his eyes settled on the Jessups. "Ya don't need t' get yourself in a deeper tangle with both them gals while we're here."

Ozzie stepped back at Judge's venomous look of warning, which astounded Judge almost as much as it had the old timer. It was one thing to have Ozzie voicing his opposition to Helene, but Judge was not about to accept him saying anything about Victoria in the same breath with Helene—that was between him and the Englishwoman. His protective instinct, too much like that of a wild animal's for its mate, disturbed him to the core, and he absently stepped into the dining room without thinking about Helene.

Ozzie called out, "Where ya going?" but it was too late. Helene eyed Judge and was barreling down on him just as he glanced up.

"Judge, darling." She grasped his arm with such a grip that Ozzie could have sworn her fingers were lethal talons. "I sent you a telegram and left half a dozen notes. Where have you been all afternoon?"

Judge stared down at Helene. She was exquisite in the form-fitting, black, velvet and lace gown glistening with golden sparkles. Her ample bosom threatened to pour from the décolletage of her bodice. Her wealth of dark hair was piled into the latest fashion and twined with fancy gold ropes. Diamonds dripped heavily from Helene's neck, ears, wrists and fingers—an ostentatious display of her wealth, and a rebuke to anyone who would dare remember her dirt poor upbringing.

"I told you I'd be away on business. I don't have time for you now, Helene."

"Make time," she said, smiling sweetly up at Judge, but her face was a murderous red. Judge started to pull away, causing her to hiss, "I'll make a scene."

"Go ahead, Helene. I told you I don't threaten."

She glared at him. She never could control the man like she could Luther. She forced herself to relax her posture. "Very well. But Luther will be out all day tomorrow. I'll look for you. I want to hear all about how you fared with that *old maid* you met in New

York."

There was a strange inflection to Helene's voice which gave Judge pause. She evinced a new hardness, calculating coldness, deadly seriousness. It made him wonder if she knew more than she was letting on. "Don't change your plans for me, Helene. I told you I don't have the time."

"You have to eat. We'll have breakfast in the morning. I'll wait for you."

"Luther is looking this way. You'd better go to him."

Judge watched her stroll through the clusters of tables back to the crude rancher. She leaned over Luther, giving him a view of her breasts, and kissed his ear, all the while watching Judge.

Disgusted by her actions, obviously meant for his benefit, Judge made his way over to a far table. He sat down in time to see the same two men he had noticed on the train before it had stopped outside Saint Louis. The pair was standing between Jessup and Helene. Judge knew those two had looked familiar and now he knew why: they were two of the Jessup's hired gunslingers. This further development gave Judge something else to consider.

Ozzie slid into the chair across the table from his boss. "Ain't we goin t' go elsewheres? I downright don't like the way that she-devil was actin'. Somethin's been mighty peculiar 'bout that one the last few times I's seen her. In a ways, it's kinda like when her boy was born but different somehow. Cain't rightly put my finger on it exactly. But I don't like it. Don't like it none at all. She's gettin' t' think of ya as her private property."

"You don't have to worry about Helene." Judge kept his tone unconcerned, but he too had noticed the change in her; he didn't like it either.

171

Ozzie gawked at the Jessup party. "Do ya see those two men? Thems the same ones what was on the train. What do ya make of that?"

"Don't know. But no doubt they're up to no good."

"My thinkin' exactly. What ya goin' t' do?"

"Order supper." Judge wasn't about to encourage further discussion about the men, for he wasn't quite sure what Jessup was up to. At present, he didn't have the time to find out. He filed the information in the back of his mind.

They ordered steak and potatoes, and while they waited to be served, Judge told Ozzie about the trip to the stockyards and the deal Victoria had hammered out with Bridgewater. They had a good chuckle over it, the way Bridgewater was and all. But Ozzie roared when Judge described the incident at the firehouse with Buck, causing the other patrons to send daunting looks in their direction. Judge ignored all but Helene. She stiffened and sat staring at him, her intensity penetrating.

All the while the two men remained in the dining room, Judge kept the conversation light, directed away from further discussion about Helene or the gunslingers. It was after midnight when Judge left Ozzie at his door with orders not to sneak out for anything stronger than sarsaparilla.

"I was beginning to wonder if you ever were going to return. May I have a word with you, Jesse, or should I say, *Judge?*" Lani sauntered toward him, a new confidence in her stride.

Judge grabbed her arm and shoved her into his room. "What are you talking about, Miss Lani?" he drawled once he was assured they would not be overheard.

"You need not continue with that uneducated act of

yours any longer. I know better. Remember our previous conversation on the topic?"

He shrugged and leaned across the bed on his elbow. He was tense. Every muscle in his body had been ready to flex into action the instant he'd heard the girl call him by name. Yet he gave the appearance of one bored and totally relaxed. Lani bit her lip and edged to the desk near the door, not taking her wide eyes from the cowboy.

"Since you went to all the trouble to wait up for me, I suggest you say what's on your mind. We're going to have a busy day tomorrow and I need some sleep."

Lani swallowed the urge to run to Gerald and seek his protection. She had tried all evening to get away from Victoria and talk to Gerald about what she'd overheard. But each time she'd inched toward the door, Victoria had stirred and she'd been forced to tend to her older sister.

She wrung her hands. "I — I want to know who you are."

"Name's Jesse."

"That's not what the judge or whoever he is called you earlier this evening."

Judge remained impassive.

"I heard him in the hall beating on your door. He said the name Judge. I — I listened outside your room and he . . . he apologized for. . . ." Her voice faded away with her last ounce of courage.

"Please. Continue."

Lani hung her head, wishing she had consulted Gerald or told Victoria before confronting the man. The American frightened her, the way he was acting, so nonchalant. She'd read stories about the Wild West and the untamed ruffians who roamed freely there.

"I could not hear the rest," she admitted, certain she was about to faint.

"Why don't you go back to your room and get some sleep," Judge advised, choosing to ignore the girl's accusations for the moment.

"But what about what I heard?" She was proud of herself for standing her ground despite her trembling knees.

"You must have misunderstood. The judge was merely identifying himself, and then apologized for behaving so rashly."

Lani's brow creased in confusion. Perhaps she had been mistaken. "But what about your speech?" she cried.

"What's the matter? Isn't a lowly cowpoke supposed to know how to put words together? Or is that supposed to be reserved for wealthy Easterners and the English?"

Lani apologized profusely and hurried back to the room she shared with Victoria, thoroughly daunted and exhausted by the ordeal.

Judge stood in his doorway and made sure she didn't change course and go to Pelthurst with her story. He raked his fingers through his hair. Victoria. Helene. And now Lani. Just what he needed: another female to worry about. To top it off, Jessup had two gunslingers standing by — for what purpose, Judge did not want to consider.

Until the wee hours of the morning, Judge lay on his bed, his arms folded behind his head, sleep eluding him. He had told Victoria she could spend their last day in Saint Louis shopping, while he made arrangements to have the bull shipped back to the ranch. Helene and those two gunslingers had changed all that.

174

He had to keep Helene away from Victoria, while watching for those two gunmen to make their move. Victoria and that entourage she was traveling with made things all the more complicated. Lani and her accusations added another problem. The girl was a breath away from the truth, and when she related her suspicions to Victoria, which she was sure to do, Victoria wouldn't waste any time putting it together.

Judge looked at his watch; it was three-thirty. Another few hours and all his carefully laid plans would fall apart, unless . . .

He strode to the desk and scribbled out a couple of hurried notes. Without wasting another moment, he tossed a few essentials into a bag and left the room.

The sun poured into the room, causing Lani to blink open her eyes, sit up, and stretch. Her gaze caught on the porcelain clock on a nearby table. "Oh dear, I overslept," she grumbled to herself. "Victoria, I —" her voice broke off when she noticed that Victoria had gone down to breakfast without her.

Lani finished her toilette and put an extra ribbon in her hair before making her way to her husband's room to seek his advice. She prettily smoothed her skirts and adjusted the lavender ruffles along her bosom, then rapped, her face glowing in anticipation. When Gerald did not answer, her smile wilted into an annoyed frown. He hadn't waited for her either.

The thought of walking into the big dining room unescorted prickled Lani's sensibilities. She thought of seeking out Jesse, then decided against that course of action; he was much too dangerous to be around unless there were others present. The judge seemed harmless enough, she would go to him.

He was not in his room either.

Feeling utterly frustrated that no one had bothered to consider her delicate constitution and wait for her, Lani ran back to the privacy of her room. Tears flowed down her cheeks as she waited. When no one came to her rescue, she was forced to dab away the salty streaks and strengthen her mind.

She was a married lady now. She was no longer a girl. She was forced to go downstairs and join the others by herself, and Gerald was to blame for this breach in etiquette. Lani took a fortifying breath and nervously made her way down the stairs and to the entrance of the great room. She put her nose in the air and swished over to the table where she recognized familiar faces.

The men stood when she approached, and Gerald held out a chair for his perturbed bride. "You could have had the courtesy to wait for me this morning, Gerald," she whined.

"The note you slipped under my door told me not to disturb you," he protested.

"I did not write you any note." Lani ignored the implications of the missive and, without giving thought to the possible consequences, proceeded to tell them in detail what she had overheard.

As the young English twit told of her late night discussion with Jesse, Helene's attention was captured. Seated at the next table with her back to them, she leaned nearer to listen. She pulled her bonnet down and turned her face away so she wouldn't be recognized. What she heard made her blood boil.

As if something had just struck Lani, her eyes opened wide and she slapped her little hands to her cheeks.

176

"Why ya suddenly got t' lookin' like a mountain lion just cornered ya, Miz Lani?" asked Ozzie, taken back by the frightened gleam in her eyes.

"Where are Victoria and Jesse?"

Chapter Nineteen

The two men stared at Lani until Gerald gathered his wits about him. "In your note, you stated that Victoria would be out early shopping and that since you were feeling quite exhausted, I should not interrupt your beauty sleep," supplied Gerald, defending himself. He took the bit of hotel stationery from his breast pocket and offered it to Lani as evidence he would never have neglected his precious bride purposely.

"I did not write this!" she exclaimed, close to hysteria. "And this is not Victoria's handwriting either. We must call the constable. That cowboy, Jesse, or whoever he is, must have kidnapped my sister," she squealed, beside herself with fear.

She was halfway out of her chair when Ozzie clamped a reassuring hand on her arm. "Ya sit yourself back down, Miz Lani," consoled Ozzie. "I think I can shed some light on what's goin' on."

Hesitantly, Lani settled onto the edge of the chair, her eyes silently beseeching Gerald to wave some magic cane and make everything better. He placed his hand over her trembling fingers, but appeared as much at a loss.

"I got a note too," Ozzie announced, totally unaware that Helene was waiting as anxiously as Lani and Gerald to hear of its contents. He pulled the sheet of paper out of his hip pocket and slowly unfolded it.

"Give it to me," Lani blurted out. Unable to stand the suspense any longer, she snatched it from the old timer. She scanned the simple message, then her breath caught in her throat. "This instructs you to see that the bull is sent back to the ranch, and escort Gerald and I to Cheyenne without Victoria. It says they will meet us there." Her eyes came to rest on the signature. "I knew it! There is no Jesse, is there? That man is Judge Colston, and he has taken Victoria, hasn't he?" she cried.

"If Jesse is Judge Colston, then who are you, my good man?" Gerald uneasily shifted in his chair. He had been against this bloody trip to America all along. He had known something terrible would happen. The American Wild West was no place for a lady; he'd warned Victoria of the ghastly things which could befall them. He thanked God that it was Victoria who had been abducted and not his sweet treasure, Lani.

Ozzie motioned with his gnarled hands for the two to cease their accusations and wild questions. "Calm down. If ya give me half a chance I think I can put your minds t' rest."

"Who are you?" implored Lani, crazy with worry.

"Name's Ozzie, Miz Lani."

"You lied, too?"

"Let me handle this, love," Gerald advised. Then he turned on Ozzie. "I think we have had enough of given names, my good fellow." Gerald straightened his posture to put forth a more intimidating appearance. He had to be strong for his fragile, young wife. "What is your full name? And do not lie to us."

"Makes no nevermind t' me if ya know who I am. This weren't my idea in the first place," he grumbled to himself, thinking about Judge and his plan. "The name's Aloysius Osborne," Ozzie gritted out the hated given name few people knew.

"Your name is the one on my father's papers," Lani said, suddenly remembering it from the files she had helped Victoria prepare for the solicitor.

"This mess is my fault, not Judge's. Years ago Judge needed money when he was just a young'un startin' out, so I borrowed it. No bank would loan the likes of me a penny. A neighboring rancher, Luther Jessup, fixed it so Judge couldn't get no help neither."

Gerald blanched and furrowed his brows at the name, wondering where he'd heard it before, but swiftly directed his attention back to the old man.

"I heard 'bout Brits puttin' money in land in Wyoming so I got a friend who could write t' send a letter t' your pa—he was recommended by one of the bankers who turned Judge down—and he sent me the money I gave t' Judge t' start his spread. I never told Judge how I got the cash. Forgot all 'bout it, truthfully, Miz Lani.

"And then after all them years Judge got that letter sayin' he had a partner. Guess I don't got t' tell ya how mad he was t' learn some gal owned part of his spread. Well, when he saw Miz Victoria in New York and she thought Judge was me and I was some fancy dude who sits in a courtroom and decides who's right and who's wrong, well he decided t' find out what she was really up t'."

"Victoria was not up to anything. Why didn't he sit down and discuss it with her?"

"Judge's had t' work hard for everythin' he's got.

180

Havin' t' give up part of his land's the same as cuttin' off his arm. But I think there's more t' it now than just the land. If ya ask me, I think that after he saw how galldarned purty your sister is an' all, he's developed a hankerin' for her—even though he's too blasted stubborn t' admit it t' himself yet."

Lani sat and digested the incredible story. As outlandish as it sounded, it made sense. She studied Gerald a moment, then a smile of an idea crept up to Lani's eyes.

"What ya grinnin' for, gal?"

"Ozzie, if we confide in you, do you think we could reach an agreement?" she asked slyly.

"I say, what—?" stammered Gerald.

"Hush up, Gerald. Ozzie?"

"What kind of agreement?" He scratched the snowy thatch atop his head.

"Gerald and I have also noticed the way Victoria and Jess—ah . . . Judge look at each other. You may not know it, but Gerald and I are—" Gerald nudged Lani under the table and shook his head against confiding their secret to the old man. "Are quite *interested* in each other." Lani edged closer to her husband. "What if we give you our solemn promise not to tell Victoria about Judge, in exchange for your help?"

"My help?" Ozzie swallowed hard, his Adam's apple bobbing furiously up and down.

"Yes. If they end up together, the problem with the land will be settled. And then Gerald will be free. He won't have to hurt Victoria's feelings and we," she squeezed Gerald's hand, "can be *married* with Victoria's blessing." An air of conspiracy surrounded the two lovers.

"Just what exactly do ya want for me t' do?"

Helene remained in her seat, rigid with an overwhelming, all-consuming rage. There was no doubt in her mind what had transpired now, and there would be hell to pay before she was through. Judge was hers, and as soon as he got back to the ranch she would see to it that there'd never again be anyone else. Her lips curled into a smile of victory. The knowledge she harbored left no doubt of success in her mind. If she had to, she wouldn't hesitate to use what she knew — regardless of how many lives it'd destroy. She wanted Judge, and she would have him!

The sun was climbing high in the sky, heating up the rolling plains, when Judge and Victoria stopped for a break. They dismounted under a clump of spreading trees near a gurgling creek. Victoria, sweltering inside the red suitcoat, shed the jacket. She dipped a delicate lacy handkerchief into the cool water and swabbed her throat and face, before turning to her companion.

"I think it is time you tell me what this is all about," she demanded.

Judge ignored her and led the horses to the stream's edge. Then he knelt down, cupping his hands into the pool and splashing water on his face to wash off the dust. He then refilled the canteens and settled underneath one of the trees, pulling his hat down over his eyes.

"I will not be ignored, sir," Victoria spat out. Stomping over to the big cowboy, she grabbed his hat and tossed it aside. "If you do not see fit to offer a full explanation, and promptly, I shall return to Saint Louis immediately — with or without you."

Judge jumped to his feet and grasped her arms. "If

you value your life, you'll stay here with me."

"My life?" she choked out, clutching her throat.

"As I told you when I woke you early this morning, I was sitting in a saloon down by the river when I overheard those two men from the train talking about kidnapping you," Judge fabricated, hoping the outlandish story would satisfy her. "They seemed to think you were a very wealthy foreigner, and that they could collect some quick cash from your Englishman."

"You mean one of the men who gave us a ride into the city?" she asked, remembering that the man had had a shifty look about him. And he had met another equally seedy man in the shadows after leaving them at the train depot.

"The same."

"Then why didn't you wake Lani and bring her along? They might mean to harm her too," Victoria worried, her concern for her young sister deeper than it was for her own safety.

"No. It was you they were after. I told you that when I snuck you out of the hotel room."

Once Judge had woke up the man at the livery stable, hurriedly paid the man's exorbitant price for two good saddle horses, packed two saddlebags with food obtained from the hotel's kitchens, and tied his bag on his horse, he had quietly made his way into Victoria's room, using his expertise with locks to open the door. Putting his hand over her mouth, he'd briefly explained the situation to her in hushed tones and had convinced her to leave with him.

"But what will Lani and Gerald do when they discover we are missing?"

"You don't have to worry about that. I left Gerald and the judge a note. The judge will see that your sister

183

and fiancé get to Cheyenne safely, and we'll meet them there." He was careful to skirt what he had actually written in those notes—especially the one to Gerald.

"Won't those dreadful men simply follow them and pose the same threat in Cheyenne?"

"No, not their kind. They were looking for quick money. They'll probably spend a few days searching for us, then look for some other unsuspecting victim. If you stay with me, you'll be fine. Then we can go on to the ranch from Cheyenne."

Victoria stood, stunned into silence. She'd known there would be hazards traveling through the wilds of America, but she'd never dreamed the kind man who had given her family a lift would turn out to be such a terrible sort.

Judge could see the play of emotions across her face. He hated himself for having to scare her with such a lie. But he had to keep her away from her sister, as well as Helene, until he had managed to get her to sign over her rights to his ranch. That he intended to do somehow, once they reached Cheyenne.

"If I agree to this, how will we travel?" She was weakening, Judge could see it in her face.

"We'll catch a steamer to Independence, then rent a wagon. And you needn't worry, I won't touch you," he said, wondering what made him say such a thing.

She bristled at his last comment, but a gentle warmth ran down her spine remembering the tender touch of his lips on hers. Yet now was not the time to bother about the danger Jesse posed—or to think of the impropriety of traveling with a man unchaperoned. The safety of her person was at stake. "Won't they be looking for us, though?"

"We could travel by horseback. But I doubt if you'd

make it all the way to Wyoming."

Victoria stiffened at the suggestion she was too soft to withstand the rigors of such a trip. "For your information, Jesse, I am an accomplished equestrienne."

"Good. We'll take the horses on the steamer with us, just in case we're followed. Now, let's get going before they pick up our trail. No telling how many men they've got looking for us."

Victoria hesitated as Judge strode toward the horses. "What you waiting for?"

"I — I need to use the facilities," she ventured, looking around her in dismay.

"Go ahead."

"There does not seem to be any."

"Come with me." Judge held out his hand and led her over to the dense bush nearby. "Here you are." He fanned his arm.

Shock registered on her face. "But there are no facilities here."

"Sure there are. All around you."

She attempted to swallow her apprehension of the obvious. "The bushes?"

"Pick any one that suits your fancy, Miss Victoria Elizabeth Torrington, named after two queens."

"Your amusement at my expense is not particularly appreciated, Jesse." She stood there with her arms folded over her chest, embarrassment coloring her cheeks.

"Don't let me keep you from your task." He gave her a lopsided grin. "And don't waste time."

"You needn't concern yourself on that account."

"Good. We need to put as many miles between us and Saint Louis as possible."

Victoria grimaced, but chose the biggest and thickest

of the bushes, and gingerly lifting her skirts before seeing to her needs.

Judge was holding the reins to both horses when she stepped from the bush. "Ready?"

"No, not quite, actually."

He looked skyward. "Now what?"

"If you will remember yesterday afternoon and the celebrating we did with Mr. Bridgewater, you will also recall that I have not eaten anything for nearly twenty-four hours. I feel quite faint from hunger."

"My God, why didn't you just say you're hungry instead of going into such a lengthy explanation."

"I thought it necessary to explain my reasoning, since you are in such a hurry."

Judge raked his fingers through his hair. She was going to prove a right royal pain in the backside. Then the thought hit him. She was proving a right royal beautiful pain elsewhere as well, and it gnawed at his heart that she was such a schemer.

"Mount up, Tori."

"But my stomach," she pleaded, her empty digestive organ rumbling loudly.

Judge dug through his saddlebag and tossed her a chunk of jerky. "Here, chew on this. It's all you're going to get until tonight."

Victoria was so perturbed that she climbed into the saddle and ripped into the leathery meat with a vengeance.

They traveled all afternoon, stopping only to give the horses a rest. All the while they rode, Victoria shot periodic glances over her shoulder, fearing the two men had picked up their trail and were following them. Once she even thought she caught a glimpse of someone behind them.

When she brought her suspicions to Judge's attention, he laughed, since he'd made the entire story up, and ignored her protests, telling her not to worry.

But she continued her vigil nonetheless, certain someone was indeed following them, but for some strange reason had chosen not to confront them yet.

Chapter Twenty

By the time Victoria and Judge stopped for the night, Victoria was ready to drop, she was so weary. Her nerves were unraveling, and she found herself imagining shadowy images behind every shrub and rock. Eerie night sounds became clandestine forms of communication, and each snap or rustle of a branch signalled unshaven captors sneaking closer to spirit her off into the wilds of America, never to be seen or heard from again.

As she eased down on a rotted log near the fire Jesse had built, every muscle in her body screamed out. She was used to riding in the park, a thoroughly civilized sport, not this hard-driving traveling they had been doing all day with mere brief respites to rest the animals. Never once had he considered her needs, but she wasn't about to admit to Jesse that she was certain she had developed calluses on a most private portion of her anatomy.

"Where are you going?" she asked harshly, in an attempt to disguise the fear in her voice.

Judge shot her an amused look. The way she was

seated, half resting on her hands, left no question in his mind that she was not saddle hardened. Something inside him longed to stretch her out on his blanket so he could massage all those sore muscles of hers, but instead he barked back, "Down to the stream to get some water for coffee."

"Coffee?" Her voice cracked. "No tea?"

"Americans switched from tea to coffee 'round the time of the Revolutionary War, remember Tori?"

"Even if I did not, no doubt you would find a way to remind me." She brushed off the blasted red suit coat, wishing at that moment that she had held fast to wearing mourning for her father instead of allowing Lani to talk her into a more fashionable wardrobe for the trip to America.

She looked nervously about her.

"What's the matter? You afraid that imaginary person who's been following us will make his move while I'm gone, Miss Torrington?"

"I am not imagining things," she protested, leveling him a cool stare. "There was indeed someone there."

"Indians maybe."

"Indians?" She flew up off the log and picked up the battered tin pot.

"Sit back down. You needn't worry about Indians. Most are on reservations now, their spirit broken by the white man's broken promises."

"I think I shall go along with you just the same. I would not want you to think I cannot be useful."

"Oh, I know you could be useful." He grinned wolfishly, and let his eyes roll down her curvaceous form. "Not a doubt in my mind."

"Not the way you may have in mind," she spat, her spirit returning.

"How do you know what's on my mind, Tori?" he taunted, enjoying the sway of her hips as she grabbed the pot and marched off ahead of him toward the stream.

"Quit calling me that . . . that name," she snipped over her shoulder.

"Sorry. Can't."

She stopped and swung around on him, her hands balled on her hips. "Why ever not?"

"First off. You keep wearing that red jacket. Secondly, I like it. The name fits you."

"Fits me?" she said incredulously.

"Sure. You're a soldier of sorts."

"Of sorts? What sort?" she delved, not realizing she had just fallen into another trap of his humor.

"Soldier of fortune—Judge Colston's."

Victoria thought a moment about what he'd said. Then her eyes narrowed to mere slits. "I only came to this country to claim what is rightfully mine. I will not be accused by a disgruntled ranch hand. And when we get to the ranch I intend to see that Judge Colston comes to fully understand that fact."

"Never give up, do you?" he grated.

"Not when I am in the right."

"And you think you are this time."

"No. I know I am."

"Guess time will have to settle it. Now, are you going to stand there all night or get busy and make coffee? We need to get some sleep. Got a busy day ahead of us tomorrow. With any luck, we'll meet up with the steamer up river a ways."

Judge walked past Victoria and didn't stop until he got to the stream. While she fetched the water, he washed with a vengeance, trying to get the beautiful maddening Englishwoman off his mind.

As the fire died down, the single blanket Jesse had tossed to Victoria after supper seemed less than adequate. She huddled nearer the cowboy, unable to sleep, ever alert to each sound.

"Bring your blanket over here and come lie next to me. We'll keep each other warm," he recommended, when he noticed her shiver.

"No, thank you. I shall manage," she retorted, unsure whether she was more afraid of the strange sounds or of being so near the big American.

"Suit yourself." He edged his hat over his eyes and was soon snoring softly.

By morning, Victoria was stiff and not sure she could ride another foot when Jesse announced, "Get your horse saddled, we move out in ten minutes."

"But what about breakfast?"

"You chose to sleep in," he said with a shrug. "If you're hungry, you can gnaw away on some jerky while we ride."

"Not again. . . ."

The puff of smoke and clang of the ship's bell was like a soothing balm to Victoria's nerves by the time they rode their weary mounts to the dock tucked along the Missouri River. She had tried four times during the day, without success, to draw Jesse's attention to the riders she was certain were trailing them, but gave up as the steamer came into view.

She breathed a sigh of relief: civilization, and an opportunity to be away from Jesse. She would lock herself in her own stateroom and become reacquainted with the luxury she had nearly forgotten existed.

Victoria's daydreams crashed to the plank flooring as she stood next to Jesse and the captain of the *River Belle*.

"That's right, Captain Brady, one room to Independence," Jesse said, holding her so close to him she thought he would squeeze the breath out of her.

Once the captain had accepted Jesse's money for their fare, boarded their horses, and directed them to their cabin, Victoria whirled on Jesse. "What do you think you are doing, securing only one cabin? You know perfectly well we require two."

Judge was in no mood to have the other passengers listen to her tirade, and he headed up the stairs to the cabin, leaving her to stand by herself.

"Where are you going?"

"To the cabin."

"What about me?"

"You have a choice. You can stay on deck and keep the livestock company, or you can come with me. At this point, I don't give a damn what you do."

Victoria ceased further argument and followed the utterly rude man to their room. It was small. A compact dresser and washstand stood against wall underneath a draped porthole; a thick carpet covered the floor, and flocked, flowered wallpaper disappeared behind the sole bed.

The bed seemed to grow in proportion to the size of the room, until thoughts of it overshadowed all her other concerns. "There is only one bed," she choked.

"Yeah. So?"

"So there must be some mistake," she insisted.

"These rooms usually only have one bed."

"Then you had best go secure another room. This simply will not do."

"Well, I'm afraid it is going to have to *do*. We didn't exactly leave Saint Louis with lots of money stuffed into our pockets. And until we get to Cheyenne, *you* are the one who is going to have to adjust. Or you can take your chances with those imaginary men you keep insisting are following us," Judge set out, confident he had thrown enough of a scare into her to cause her to be compliant.

Victoria mulled over his scathing lecture, then conceded defeat. She hated to admit it, but whether she liked it or not, she needed the big American cowboy and had no choice but to follow his directives.

"Oh, very well," she said, exasperated at his bullying ways. "We shall share the room, since it appears we must. But due to the murderous pace you set today, I am quite exhausted. Therefore, I would like the use of the bed first."

Judge rubbed his forehead. She was giving him a two-queen headache, and he'd had about all he was going to take of the priggish Englishwoman's demands for one day.

"You're tired and want to get some sleep, right?"

She stiffened. "Yes. Your powers of observation are simply overwhelming."

"One has no need of observation with you. Your nonstop tongue gives everything away."

"Why you—"

He put up a hand to stop her indignant response. "Look, I am as tired as you are and intend to get some sleep as well. And since there is only one bed, whether you like it or not, we are going to have to share it."

Victoria perched on the bed rigidly, her arms crossed in defiance over her chest. "Absolutely not!"

Judge glared at her. He took a threatening step toward her. "Move over and make room for me or I'll dump you on the floor, and you can sleep there—alone."

Victoria seethed, her color heightening to near fuchsia. "I am entitled to this bed. And I do not intend to allow you to use your brutish ways to unseat me from it."

"I wouldn't think of it." Judge moved swiftly, shoving her into the corner and plunking down on the edge of the bed before she could offer further protest. He removed his gun, boots and shirt and lay down next to her. "There. Now isn't this cozy?" he set out, waiting for her to rebel.

He pulled his arm over his eyes and lay still. He fully expected her to come up with some dumb stunt in defiance. But as the minutes passed by, the heat of her body next to his, other ideas entered his mind. He found his respect and admiration for the feisty Englishwoman continued to grow.

"Aren't you going to remove your trousers?" she asked when she finally broke the tense silence.

Judge choked, not quite sure how to answer her question. He turned his head toward her, coming face to face with the woman. He was sorely tempted to kiss her, then undress her slowly and make love to her. He had to restrain himself.

"What did you say?" he questioned with a sheepish twist to his full lips, to make sure he had heard her correctly.

"You can get those base ideas from your mind. I suggested that you remove your trousers because they are scratchy and will surely rob me of my beauty sleep."

"I wouldn't think of doing such a thing."

Grinning, Judge stood, unfastened his pants before

her with great pomp—one button at a time—and stepped out of the denims. Victoria knew decorum demanded that she avert her eyes. But she was so fascinated by his male form, the strength of his thighs and the outline of him, that her eyes remained where they were.

Not waiting for further comment, he folded himself next to her and laughed softly, "Does this satisfy you, or would you prefer I removed my longjohns as well?"

Scandalized, Victoria gasped, "I most certainly would not!"

As Jesse drifted to sleep, his breathing shallow and regular, Victoria lay stiff, her arms straight at her sides, afraid to move for fear she would touch the slumbering cowboy. She attempted to analyze her fears and had to admit to herself that the big man made her feel things that Gerald never could. Jesse made her senses come alive and cry for his touch without even trying. She battled with these realizations as the gentle rocking of the ship finally lulled her into the thankful oblivion of sleep.

In her dreams, Victoria faced her fears head on and gave in to the yearning of her heart. Jesse came to her and she opened her arms to him, caressing and accepting his embrace without hesitation. She nuzzled his neck and let her fingers drift down, down, ever downward, until she touched the hot flesh of his thighs. She moaned at the delicious sensations her exploration of the man wrought through her.

The dream was so real. She basked in its glow until an amused male voice intruded rudely into the world of her design. Slowly she blinked open her eyes, a satisfied smile on her lips, until she realized where she was, now clad in only her thin chemise. Her eyes popped open, and she struggled in earnest to get free of the arms which held her pressed tightly against a naked, rock-hard chest.

"Release me at once, you . . . you beast, or I'll cry rape and have you arrested!"

Chapter Twenty-one

Judge lay next to Victoria, incredulous. She was threatening him with the charge of rape.

"You'll what?" Judge gave a harsh, raking laugh.

"I said I would cry rape and have you arrested," she persisted, raising her gaze until it was level with his. She was not about to let the man see he intimidated her.

"Before you begin exercising your lungs, lady, I suggest you take a good look at who is holding whom."

Victoria looked down, mortified when she discovered that her arms were wrapped around Jesse, her fingers pressed into the flesh of his back. As if she'd been scorched, she snapped her arms back and scooted to the far edge of the bed. The outline of her breasts plainly visible through the thin fabric of her chemise, she tried to cover herself.

"Then how. . . ." She swallowed her shock. "When did I come to be in this . . . this state of undress?" she demanded. Feeling demoralized at her apparently unconscionable behavior toward a member of the opposite sex, she tried to keep her nerve from deserting her.

That maddening grin she'd come to detest took over his lips again. "You mean to tell me you don't remember?"

"Of course I do not remember!"

"Well, it was your idea, Tori. I was sleeping soundly when all of a sudden you were all over me with those hot little fingers of yours. Next thing I knew, you were stripping away your clothes."

"I would never, never do you hear me, be a party to such an act!" she insisted, aghast. But in the back of her mind, the dream about Jesse she'd just had came before her.

"Honey, you not only were *a party to such an act*. You were the perpetrator. You're such a prim and proper little thing, it kind of surprised me."

Judge was enjoying her discomfort; it was time she found out she was a warm-blooded woman, capable of great passion. He decided to push her a little further. "If anything, I should have been the one hollering rape."

Victoria's eyes rounded, the blue deepening with her sinking state of mind. "I would never knowingly do such a thing," she sputtered.

Judge's mood shifted to one of seriousness and his eyes fastened to hers. "You might find that someday, when you fall in love with a man, making love will be the most natural, desirable thing in the world."

"I—I have Gerald."

He let out a frustrated sigh. "Yes. Gerald."

Judge's hand came up to stroke her cheek, and he slowly bent his head forward and joined their lips. Despite her protestations of a moment ago, there was no hesitance, no argument. Judge deepened the kiss, his tongue outlining her lips, sucking, tasting, and silently urging her to follow his lead.

"Open your mouth to me, Victoria," he murmured against her lips, using her given name rather than the teasing nickname he had pinned to her.

Almost against her will, Victoria's lips parted.

Judge plunged his tongue into her heated depths. Their tongues parried and he explored each inch of the smooth, wet, inner recesses, running his tongue over her teeth and along the inside of her cheeks.

"Use your tongue, Victoria, and kiss me too," he directed, wanting to introduce her into the exquisite pleasures of lovemaking slowly, so as not to frighten her defenses back into place.

Tentatively at first, then more boldly, Victoria slipped her tongue into his mouth and learned of the sweet male texture of him.

Breaking apart, he asked, "You like that?"

A smile spread across her lips before she drew him to her and savored his mouth again.

He pulled back. "I take it that was a yes."

She kissed him again blindly, fiercely, all restraint shattered by the surge of searing desire this man provoked deep within her, and kindled by the expert ministrations of his tongue, mouth, and hands.

The sensations racing through her had completely erased the last lingering thought of protest, when he reached up and lightly brushed her breast. The nipple puckered into an erect little peak. His questing fingers circled and toyed with the other breast, and he dipped his head to run his tongue down the length of her neck to the hollow where her pulse raced.

Victoria felt herself surrender her body into his hands, and arched her neck backward taking in gasps of air. Of their own volition, her fingers wound in his hair, delighting in the coarse strands.

"Victoria . . . ," her name was a whisper on his lips. "My Victoria, I want you."

Slowly, with deliberation, he slid one strap off her creamy shoulder, kissing her steamy flesh. Then he directed equal attention to the other shoulder, stripping the lacy ribbon and releasing her from the chemise. He hesitated and let his eyes feast on the beauty of her full, high bosom. After relishing the sight, he took the soft mounds into his hands.

He worshipped at her breasts, the moist heat of his tongue causing her whole body to feel as if she were ablaze in an all-consuming fire. His long, curling lashes wisped across her nipples and she gasped at the feathery sensations which rippled down to her most secret feminine core.

"Oh God, I want you," he rasped.

Slowly, tenderly, his hand descended in a silent litany as he pushed her back against the pillows. When she made no objection, he dropped his hand still further, onto the wiry, furred mound. Then his fingers floated over her inner thigh until he reached the apex of her legs.

"Open for me, Victoria. Open your legs for me."

He nudged at her thighs, but they remained clamped shut.

At his gentle probing, Victoria's half-lidded eyes flew open, and the moment of enchantment which had overridden her sense of the decorum proper for an engaged lady, was brutally torn from her.

She swatted his hand away and sat up, clutching a pillow in front of her as if it were a shield. "How dare you!"

Judge, too, was suddenly brought back to the real

world. For a short while, he had forgotten what she was and why she was here with him now. There had been those few moments when he was just a man and she a woman; a few moments when he'd thought their hearts had touched; a few moments when he'd thought he could fall in love again. Well, he'd been saved from making that mistake again! His face turned torrid, thunderous.

"What's the matter Miss Victoria Elizabeth Torrington, named for two queens, get more than you planned?" he spat. "Or were you just playing with me? Did you have this burning desire to know what it was like to taste a lowly American cowboy, so you can go back to your chaste little life with Gerald back in England and sit around with tea and crumpets and gossip with other dried-up prunes like you'll become? Or did you lure me on for the thrill of it, Victoria?" He grabbed her and shook her unmercifully. "What was it? Tell me. Did you get what you expected?"

Victoria was stunned into silence at his vehemence, the fury of his wrath. She stared into his face; it was hard, glacial. His lips were set into a cold, rigid line. His eyes were aquamarine stones beneath brows furrowed by his building rage.

"Well? Did I perform up to your expectations?" he sneered, sinking bruising fingers further into her arms. "Or maybe you didn't have any expectations. Maybe you *are* no more than *Miss Chastity Iron Drawers,* the coldhearted Englishwoman whom no man will ever touch."

"Miss Chastity Iron Drawers?" Victoria mouthed, stung. "Where did you. . . . How could you. . . ?"

Judge glared at her. "Where? Your precious fiancé, that's where. You earned the illustrious title from your

201

precious driving need to outperform all men in the business world, and your attempts to deny you're a woman—a very desirable one at that. Or do you know how desirable you are and use it to get what you want? Only this time maybe you got more than you wanted."

Victoria dropped her eyes but he grabbed her chin and swung her head up to glare into her face. "What is it, lady? You get more than you bargained for?"

"Perhaps I did," she said, in no more than a whisper. "Maybe I never expected to want you to—to make love to me," she admitted, unable to come up with anything more eloquent or harsh in her state of confusion.

Judge was still reeling from what he had interpreted as rejection. He picked up her rumpled chemise and threw it at her.

"Cover yourself!"

Victoria scrambled to hide her humiliation, her eyes blinking at a rapid rate, her lips trembling. "Jesse, I—"

"Don't even try to come up with some lame excuse. You wanted to use the bed." He dragged his scathing gaze from her and looked at his watch. "Well, Miss Torrington, you have three hours. Then I'm coming back and it's my turn. And if you're not up and dressed by the time I get here, maybe I'll remember you think of me as nothing but a lowly cowhand and act accordingly. You understand?"

"Perfectly."

Judge slammed into his clothes and stomped out, sending the door crashing behind him. He stood at the rail, watching the muddy waters lap against the giant paddlewheel which churned the river. He mashed his fist onto the balustrade.

What was wrong with him? He'd let his bruised pride get the better of him and had lashed out to hurt her by

202

calling her that cruel name. Dammit! Of course she had spurned his advances. She was a virgin, and had lived in an ivory tower all her life. And suddenly she had found herself in a room alone with a man intent on making her his own. His own. The truth of the thought stabbed at his heart, and Judge headed for the ship's saloon hoping to obliterate the haunting images of the beautiful Englishwoman from his mind.

Victoria remained curled around the pillow, stunned at the events which had just transpired. She should be livid at him for calling her that terrible name. Her properly rigid upbringing told her she should experience shame for her part in encouraging the man. But her heart cried out that there was no shame in love and wanting to give of herself to that love.

A voice inside her chastised her, an engaged woman, for so wantoningly disregarding her prenuptial vows to another. She had let Gerald down. A louder, stronger voice cried out that it wasn't Gerald she loved; it was Jesse.

From the first moment she had set eyes on the man back in New York, something within her had reached out to him. She had felt his attraction for her as well. She chided herself. She was an Englishwoman. She could not fall in love with an American cowboy—they were worlds apart. Even if he wanted her, which she sorely doubted at this moment, she could not expect him to live in her world. And she certainly could not live in his.

For hours Victoria warred with herself, carefully weighing the positives against the negatives. She stoutly reminded herself that she was here in this country to claim what was rightfully hers—not to fall in love, lose her heart and her good name at the same time.

Judge sat in the saloon at a polished oak table with a bottle. He stared at the firewater. His pa had died a drunk, and at the time Judge had sworn never to drink himself into a stupor like his pa had nightly. But he was angry, angrier than he'd ever thought possible—as much at himself as at Victoria Elizabeth Torrington.

Despite all the years of carefully keeping that wall around his heart, despite all the talking he'd done to himself about the Englishwoman's motives, he'd gone and lost his heart. Despite the fiasco of their first attempt at lovemaking; despite the frustration he experienced on a daily basis over her antics, he'd gone and fallen in love—he could not deny it.

He poured a hefty slug of gin. It burned as it went down his throat. He looked around him. Men and women sat together, happily enjoying each other's company in the gold and white room. And he sat alone! He ran his fingers through his hair. Why, he'd never even had a reasonable conversation with the Englishwoman without it degenerating into an argument, and he was in love. Damn!

He returned his attention to his glass, but out of the corner of his eye he caught sight of two shadowy figures slinking toward the door. They were the same two gunslingers who had been on the train to Saint Louis; the same two he had seen talking to Luther and Helene Jessup, in the dining room back at the hotel.

Judge's senses immediately became alert, and he pretended to drop his head on the table, drunk. One eye closed as if he'd passed out, he watched with the other eye. The men, whispering between themselves, took seats two tables away and finished the drinks they had been enjoying before having recognized him.

Every nerve in Judge's body tensed. Victoria had been right all along. They were being followed. He should have listened to her — been more cautious. Hell, he'd made up that story about the men back in Saint Louis to keep Victoria away from Helene and Lani.

The thought of beating the pair to learn why they were dogging them took root in his mind. Then Judge realized he didn't know how many men there were. At this moment, Victoria could be in trouble, while he had been attempting to drown in his own foolish self-pity.

As nonchalantly as possible, Judge swayed to his feet and zigzagged from the room, tripping and swaggering to put on a good show for the two, so as not to let them know he was on to them. Once outside, his heart thudding wildly with fear that Victoria may have come to harm, Judge made a dash toward his stateroom.

Chapter Twenty-two

Victoria was still huddled in the corner of the bed, hugging the chemise and pillow to her, when Judge burst into the room. She set her back stiff and raised her chin. In her present state of disarray, her hair hanging around her shoulders, she was even more beautiful. The firm line of her jaw caused him to have more regard for the woman. He respected her strength; most women would have succumbed to tears after that encounter.

"What are you doing here?" she demanded, in a cold voice. "It has not been three hours yet." Her eyes sparked with blue fire. "The bed and the room are mine for another hour and a half," she announced regally.

Judge looked down at his watch. "An hour and twenty minutes, Tori."

"I beg your pardon," she snapped. "But if you have nothing further to say, then you may kindly remove yourself until it is time for your turn."

Judge let out an exasperated sigh and rubbed the stubble on his chin. "Sorry. But we don't have time for games right now." He shut the door and moved toward the bed.

Victoria's blue eyes shimmered with anger as the unkind name he had called her came to mind. It was all a game to Jesse. She knew Gerald had a loose tongue. After Jesse had managed to learn all he could about her, including how the men at the clubs referred to her, he probably placed a wager with the judge on whether he'd be able to get *Miss Chastity Iron Drawers* into bed with him.

"You keep your distance," she instructed, drawing back her arms, clutching the down-stuffed cotton.

"Look, we've got trouble." He took another step.

Victoria took aim and struck him quite royally in the stomach with the pillow she had been holding.

The blow momentarily knocked the wind out of Judge, and made him just angry and frustrated enough to forget she was a lady.

He pounced.

Pinning her hands above her head, his muscular body lying the length of hers, he grated out, "Quit fighting me, Tori—"

Her chest heaving from their bodily contact as well as from her ire, she said, "Isn't that what you would expect from *Miss Chastity Iron Drawers?*"

At the shock registered on his face, she went on. "Do not appear so surprised, I have known about the unpleasant title for years. I may not be as well versed in man's baser needs as are the harlots on the streets, but I am not totally oblivious to their coarse ways."

Judge loosened the hold he had on her, longing to make love to her. "Victoria, I'm sorry. People often say things when they're angry and upset."

"Fine. We shan't mention it again," she said coolly, still burning.

"Agreed."

"Since that is settled, will you kindly unhand me? This bed is mine for another . . . ," she craned her neck toward the clock, "hour and five minutes."

"God almighty, you can be infuriating." He released her and moved to the edge of the bed. "I came back early because we are being followed."

"I have been telling you that fact for some time. Perhaps from now on you will try listening when I speak."

"Chrissake, stop it, Victoria! This is serious. Those same two gunslingers from Saint Louis are on board the ship, sitting in the saloon."

"Just two? You mean you could not single-handedly take care of two men?" she asked cutely, attempting to mask her dread.

Judge itched to take her over his knee. "Even if you don't give a damn about your hide, I do. Get dressed. We're getting off this tub. There may be more than two men out there, and if we stay on board, there's nowhere to run if we have to."

"Somehow I cannot imagine you running from anything, Jesse."

"If I had only my own hide to look after, I wouldn't be."

The amusement faded from Victoria's face and she began to gather up her clothes, forcing herself to ignore the impropriety of having him in the room while she dressed. "Why not inform the captain?" she suggested, frightened now.

"And tell him what? That there are two men on board who we saw in Saint Louis and who we think might be following us, but we're not sure why?".

She slipped into her blouse and worked the buttons. "I thought you said you overheard them planning to

208

kidnap me. Isn't that evidence enough?"

"That's not evidence. Not out here," Judge said. He'd made that story up, and now wondered why they were being tailed. Whatever Jessup was up to, Judge didn't like it.

Victoria stepped into her skirt and bent down to pull on her shoes. "What are we going to do until the ship docks?"

Judge stared at her; she was valiantly putting on a strong front. For a moment he hated himself for what he was about to put her through. Then his resolve tightened and he grabbed her hand. "Come on. We've wasted too much time on talk already."

"Where are we going?"

Judge ignored her question. He creaked the door open slowly and checked the corridor. It was deserted. Stealthily, they crept down the stairs and out to the rail.

The night was black. The darkness enveloped the outside world except for the faint outlines of brush on the distant shore, which seemed to reach up and touch the stars. Ebony, swirling water they knew was there merely because they stood on the deck of a paddlewheeler, splashed beneath them. A breeze ruffled Victoria's hair, and she caught up the escaping strands she had hurriedly tied back.

Rounding the corners at the far ends of the deck, Judge caught sight of the two gunslingers. From opposite directions, the pair came toward them. The hard-cut men pulled their guns, the evil grin of easy victory crossing their grim faces.

"Now where?" Victoria asked, her heart hammering inside her chest as she looked down at the fathomless depths.

Judge turned her face to his and searched her eyes,

partially shadowed by the warm yellow light glowing from the cabins. "Over the side."

"You have a boat waiting?" She barely mouthed the words. Before he could answer, she shifted her gaze to the river.

Inside she cried, *Not the river!* Tears of utter fear swelled behind her lids. Her mother had drowned when the carriage she was riding in had run off the road and overturned into the Thames. She hadn't been able to escape the carriage, which had become her watery grave. Victoria imagined how her mother must have died, scratching and gasping for her life's breath. The dear woman had been hurrying home to be with her daughter. Victoria had been very ill and had called out in her delirium for her mother until the household staff had sent word that she must return to care for her daughter. It was her fault her mother died that day, her responsibility. She was to blame. The sound of Jesse's voice brought her back to their dire circumstances.

"No, Victoria. There's no boat," Judge said, tightening his grip on her hand.

She froze, terror and blind torment in her eyes. "No!" she screamed, and began to fight him as if her very life depended on it.

"Sorry. There's no time to argue." As she struggled frantically against him, Judge picked her up. Holding fast to her, he managed to heave her over the side and jump at the same time.

The gunfighters ran to the rail and peered over into the night.

"What the hell? You see that, Mort? The dumb fools flew over the rail," Clancy rasped, shocked at Colston's quick thinking. Think they know we're after them now?"

"Yup. Looks that way. Quick. If they bob to the surface we can pick 'em off like at a duck shoot."

"Yeah. Only we cain't see the ducks."

They aimed at the river flowing swiftly behind the ship and peppered the dark current with lead.

Clancy quit firing and shoved at his partner's hand. "Wait up, Mort. We got orders. If we kill the wrong one we could be in big trouble and runnin' to save our own skins for the rest of our lives."

The captain and six passengers rushed out on deck as the two men were holstering their guns.

"What's goin' on here? What's all the shootin' about?" ordered the captain, fastening his meaty fists at his bulging belly.

Clancy leaned his lanky frame against the rail and shrugged. "Just a little sport's all."

"We's just havin' a little fun. . . ."

Experiencing complete panic for the first time in her life, Victoria found that she was going down, down, down into a watery grave. Her lungs were about to burst; she was going to die. In those moments, her life sped before her. The spectre of her mother came to her.

"Victoria, my child. . . ." The glowing, fluid apparition reached out a comforting hand.

Mother, I am so sorry Victoria screamed inside, before a quiet calmness seemed to descend over her.

"No, child. There is nothing to regret," the waving vision soothed.

"But I never had the chance to tell you how much I loved you," Victoria sobbed, her tears mingling with the black waters. "I shall never have your loving help and support to guide me. I shall never have you at my side when I marry. You will not be there to hold my first child — the grandchild you always wanted. And I shall never be able to thank you for giving me life."

Time seemed suspended as Victoria cried for all those lost years, for all those lost moments with her mother which could never be recaptured.

"No, child. Do not mourn me. You are the best part of me. You are the love your father and I shared, and I live on in you and in the children you will have some day. Always remember, my precious child, that those who have passed away from this mortal world die only when those whom they loved forget them."

The figure began to fade and Victoria struggled to reach out, to take her mother's hand. Before she could embrace the gentle form, she was wrenched backwards, as if fate had declared she must live to fulfill her destiny, whatever it might be. Victoria was still fighting, struggling in Judge's arms, when they broke the surface of the Missouri.

"Holy hell. Hold still," Judge hollered against the roar of the current, grappling with the wildcat Victoria had become.

Judge had held fast to Victoria when he'd tossed her overboard and together they'd plummeted into the drowning darkness of the river. He'd fought with all his strength to return them to the choppy surface where they could fill their lungs with life-giving air. For some reason, she had quit battling his efforts temporarily, allowing him to reverse their descent before they both drowned.

Gasping and choking, he grabbed at her flailing arms. "Victoria, we have to swim or we won't make it."

A bullet shot past their heads and she screamed louder, hysterically wailing something about blame.

212

Judge forced her along as he tried to get them toward shore, away from the pair of gunmen.

Victoria continued to wrestle against his efforts.

"Forgive me, Tori." Judge hauled back and brought a fist to her jaw.

Victoria sank back into peaceful oblivion as Judge toiled against the odds. Victoria's heavy skirt was pulling them back down despite his efforts, and Judge was winded. He could have sworn he'd swallowed half the muddy river. As he held her, laboring even closer to the bank, he did not see the felled log and other debris floating toward them.

"Aargh!" The stump smashed into the back of his head, instantly hurtling him toward the same black void Victoria occupied.

Chapter Twenty-three

Just as the water threatened to close over her head, Victoria regained consciousness and her feet hit the bottom of the river bed. Her hands seemed to be permanently clamped to Jesse's arms. They were being dragged along by the current, not more than five feet from the bank.

"Jesse! What are you doing?" she shouted at him, stumbling shoulder height above the surface.

No answer came in return. It was then Victoria realized his body was limp against hers. Fighting to keep her wits about her despite her fear of the water, she inched them into a shallow pool. Her lungs heaved as she dragged him onto dry land and collapsed at his side.

Night dissolved before the light of morning, when Victoria finally came to again. Jesse was sitting quietly at her side, rubbing the back of his head.

"Where the devil are we?" she groaned, and massaging her aching jaw. Her memory of last night was returning, and suddenly she became furious with the big ranch foreman. "You had no right to throw me into the river like a piece of discarded luggage."

Judge shot her a look of disbelief. He had saved her life and there she sat, regal in spite of her bedraggled appearance, berating him. "You're welcome, your highness."

"Look at me." She lifted her straggly locks and smoothed at her damp blouse. "I have nothing to thank you for."

"Nothing 'cept saving your life."

"I seem to recall our misadventure somewhat differently."

"Oh? And how do you 'recall our misadventure'?" he grated out, feeling the strings on his temper about to break.

"You tossed me overboard, and then fell asleep, leaving me in the position of having to literally lug you on shore."

"I fell asleep?" he shouted. "For your information, something clobbered me from behind before I could pull you out of the water." He showed her the back of his head.

"And am I suppose to feel responsible?" she retorted.

"You lost control and forced me to put you out of your misery back there," he pointed, "in the middle of the river. We both could have been killed."

Victoria burned. "You did this to my jaw?"

"You left me no choice."

"And if you had not thrown me overboard in the first place, none of this would have happened."

"No. We'd be dead instead. Those were real bullets those two gunslingers were firing at us from the steamer."

215

Her eyes saucered. "They were sh-shooting at us?"

"That's what I said," he expostulated.

"Well, then, why did you not shoot back?"

"Chrissake." He slicked his fingers through his hair. "I had my hands full with you." His hand unconsciously snaked toward his holster. It was empty. His language became even more foul when he had realized his gun was missing.

She ignored him. "Fine excuse. You should have been defending me."

His face turned murderous. "Why is it that every time you open that luscious mouth of yours something disagreeable comes out?"

Victoria was stunned by the virulence in his tone. She realized then that she had come to rely on her sharp wit whenever she was frightened or unsure of herself, so no one would see that she wasn't always capable and in control.

Jesse had been protecting her; she was the one those men were after. She owed him gratitude instead of a tongue lashing. She lowered her eyes.

"I am sorry. It is simply that I am terrified of the water, and you were the one who tossed me in." Jesse opened his mouth to protest, but she cut him off. "No. You do not have to say anything. I realize you did what you had to, in face of the danger we were in." She paused to take a breath. "You see, my mother drowned five years ago when her carriage overturned into the Thames, and I have . . . ah . . . never fully recovered from the tragedy."

Her voice broke and Judge went to her, pulling her into his embrace while she cried against his shoulder.

In agony, Victoria remembered the unearthly spectre

of her deceased mother, and, in between wracking sobs, related it to him before she could compose herself.

Judge's heart went out to her. What a burden of guilt she carried over something that wasn't her fault. He recalled how she'd stopped struggling for those few seconds in the river, and was astounded by the story she had told. He had to wonder if they'd been closer to death than either had realized.

He held her tighter and stroked her hair and back, crooning, "It's all right now, Victoria." Although he believed she'd imagined the strange occurrence, he sought to relieve her burden. "Your mother must have been a special lady. It sounds as if she wouldn't have wanted you to blame yourself. You're not responsible, honey. No one can foresee accidents. They are a part of life."

"I know," she whimpered.

"Of course you do, sweetheart. Of course you do."

Slowly, the sobs lessened and trailed off. Judge rocked her and dropped consoling kisses against her temple, until she sought the comfort of his strong arms to erase the pain of memory.

"Jesse?"

"Ymm?"

"Make love to me. Please."

Judge held her from him and delved into her tortured blue eyes. He wanted her more than he'd ever wanted a woman in his life. He wanted to give her a part of himself, to take away some of her suffering.

"God, Victoria." His lips swooped down on hers, grinding and tasting the urgency of her need.

His hands tangled in the spun gold of her hair, his

217

entire body suffused with the incredible tension between them. He wanted to throw her down on the sand, strip her of her clothes, and ravish every inch of her, every curve. Yet this would be their first time together, and it had to be special. He had to hold himself back and lead her from her pain with care, so as not to leave her with an additional burden of guilt.

He scooped her up and headed toward a patch of nearby grass which provided a thick, cool carpet beneath the heating sun rising overhead.

"Wh-where are you taking me?"

"Over there, my love," he whispered, and swung her around so she could see he was thinking of her.

"But there is no bed," she squeaked.

"Victoria, sweetheart, when people need and want to be together, it doesn't matter if there is a mattress. All that is important is the two people involved."

"And we are those two people?"

"Yes. You and I," he murmured.

Without further delay he strode to the green mat, lay Victoria down, and kissed her. "Put your arms around me, Victoria," he instructed, nibbling at her lips. After she snaked her arms about him, he said, "That's good."

After long moments of caressing kisses, Judge eased his mouth from hers. With one hand he peeled the clothing from her body, while the other hand skimmed down her neck, over her collarbone and shoulder, to her breast. His fingers twirled around one peaking bud, then shifted to the other. Victoria moaned and waited for him to continue.

The aching memories fled before the pleasure washing through her. This is what she needed, and she reached up and drew his other hand to her bosom, pressing him to her hot flesh. "Do not ever stop touching me."

"No. Never." His voice was hoarse, thick with passion.

Judge sat back and hurriedly stripped off his clothes. He then spread his length next to hers in the grass. He groaned words lost in his throat as his fingers made their bold descent to the nest shielding the hotbed of her desire.

This time when he nudged at her thighs Victoria did not hesitate. She gave a moan of pleasure and opened to his questing, probing fingers. His index finger rode back and forth along the outside of the folds serving as gates to the core of her womanhood, causing her to arch and writhe against his hand. All the while he drove her from her mind with ecstasy, his tongue and teeth pulled and nipped at her distended nipples, sucking in her sweetness.

She dug her nails into his shoulders until he took her wrist and guided her toward the male of him. "I want you to know me, too."

He closed her fingers around his flesh, causing her to jerk back. "No, my queen, do not pull away," he breathed and returned her hand to him.

"Oh, Jesse, you are so velvety hard," she throatily said. "Show me what to do."

"Squeeze me gently, love." Victoria followed his instruction, all the while certain she was about to explode from the sensation hurtling her toward some unknown end. Feeling took over her consciousness and left her with only a mindless hunger which demanded to be satiated.

"Oh God, Victoria, what you are doing to me," he

groaned, forcing himself to switch his focus back to pleasuring her before he could no longer hold back.

He dipped one finger into her. She was ready for him. Another finger joined the first, and another, sliding in and out in preparation. She was so tight, and her muscles constricted around his fingers, causing him to quicken the pace as she bucked wildly against his hand.

Judge was near the brink of losing control and spilling his seed before he was ready. He stopped his ministrations and stilled her fingers. He looked into her glazed eyes. He saw a raw passion flaming there, waiting to be fed until the blaze would erupt.

Victoria focused her heavy-lidded eyes on him as he was drawing his finger to his lips. "What are you doing? Why did you stop?"

"I am savoring your juices, love." He partook of the spice of her being. "You are sweet, all of you."

"All of me?" she muttered, awed by him.

"Yes. Every part of you," he whispered against her lips, thoroughly kissing her.

Victoria tasted herself on his mouth, and sought the center of his maleness to give back a portion of the splendor she was receiving.

"No. Let me sip the rest of you." He stayed her hand, then lifted her hips in his arms and bent his head to fasten his lips to her feminine source. Over and over he dipped into her, taunting Victoria with the precision of his expertise until she cried out for sweet surcease.

Nearly driven over the edge by her reaction, Judge poised himself over her and tenderly lowered his shaft into her searing heat. Slowly, so as not to hurt her, Judge eased inside until he felt her virgin's barrier. He gathered her tightly into his arms and pressed his lips to hers. With one swift movement, he claimed her as his own.

Victoria jerked once against the powerful onslaught. Then her body took control and ground against his. She drew him in deeper, luring him, summoning him to possess her. He filled her so fully, so completely that she felt whole for the first time in years. With Jesse within her, there were no longer any empty places waiting to be filled. She was now a woman in every way.

She hugged him to her as the intensity of their rhythm built into a driving frenzy, propelling them until extraordinary sensations burst within. She strained against him, panting her exquisite release. He stiffened, gasping her name and slumped on top of her to nuzzle her neck.

As they lay together, the peaceful silence of absolute contentedness encircled them. For some time they remained as one, needing no words to express what they had experienced.

The sun had risen high over them when Judge moved to Victoria's side and toyed with her earlobe. "You are quite a woman, Victoria Elizabeth Torrington, named for two queens."

A woman. She was now a woman. She had just lain with a man other than her husband to be. It was against all the teachings she'd always believed, and she did not care. She did not care! Since she had come to this country she had undergone so many changes. She had needed Jesse. They had made love. Did that mean he was supposed to marry her now? Her mind spun.

Dried leaves on a nearby branch rustled, distracting Judge's attention. "I think we best get going, before those men find us." He left to gather his clothes, tossing

Victoria's to her.

Perhaps it was the casual quality to Jesse's voice, or the ease with which he had left her side without a word, without any attempt to further explore what they had just shared. But Victoria's spine went rigid as she began to dress, and she snipped at his back, "Doesn't this mean you are obliged to marry me now?"

"What?" Judge swung on his heel, only one leg into his trousers. Then his eyes slivered. "Does what mean I am obliged to *marry* you?" The word marry came out rough and forced.

He could have at least offered some semblance of feeling for what they had shared. She had not expected a proposal; nor had she anticipated the glacial stare he had just affixed upon her. Highly offended, she bristled back, "You seduced me and took my virginity."

"I what?"

"I said—"

"No need to repeat it, *lady,* my hearing is perfect. So are the rest of my senses. And to set the record straight, it was you who seduced me—again, I might add."

"Why I allowed you to touch me, I shall never understand. You are the last kind of man a woman would want. You . . . you American cowpuncher!" she spat.

"If you couldn't lower yourself from your throne, your highness," he bowed, a smirk on his face, "to stand the touch of one of America's untouchables, how did you ever expect one to marry you?"

Each stood before the other now, hands on hips, partially dressed, too furious to abandon the silent contest. Their cobalt eyes fixed on one another, each wondered what would happen next.

In answer to their question, a shout rang out and a

bullet whizzed past Victoria's ear. "Get down!" Judge shouted.

An instant later, Victoria found herself pinned beneath Jesse again. Only this time, she was belly down, her face shoved into the grass.

"Jesus! How could they have found us so soon?" worried Judge.

How the hell was he going to defend Victoria? He had lost his gun to the river, and the killers were rapidly closing in on them.

Chapter Twenty-four

"Stay here and keep your head down," Judge harshly commanded, then sprinted into the brush.

Victoria thrust her hands over her head, keeping flat against the ground, too afraid to move.

A blast of slugs slammed into the sand not more than two feet away. Victoria screamed and frantically looked around for Jesse, as a ball ricocheted off a boulder to the left of her. The brush seemed to be closing in on her. Leafless branches became guns pointed at her. Each unfamiliar sound was someone sneaking nearer. Her mouth was so dry she could not swallow; her palms were drenched. Worst of all was the hammering of her head. It threatened to drown out the last of her senses.

Judge looked up to see a bullet tear into Victoria's skirt. A shriek ripped from her throat as he scrambled back to her. "Come on, you've got to take cover!"

"They are trying to kill me," she cried.

He grabbed her wrist and yanked her behind a nearby boulder.

"Oh, Jesse," she reached out, "do not leave me."

"Hold that thought, highness." He forced a grin,

tweaked her chin, and was gone again.

Despite the temptation to return to Victoria, now huddled to the rock, Judge knew he had to act or they'd both be dead. The hard life on the frontier had taught Judge that there were many ways to survive using no more than one's hands and a little ingenuity.

Fearing for Victoria's life, Judge frantically dug at some half-buried rocks. His fingers bloodied, but he ignored the pain and snapped a good-sized branch, fashioning it into the semblance of a spear.

On his stomach, Judge inched in the direction of the two men. One man was casually leaning into a cottonwood, his back to Judge. The man's scraggly, dirt brown hair gave him away. He was one of the men from the ship. Judge scanned the area for the other man; he was nowhere in sight.

Noiselessly, Judge crept to within three feet of the man before he swung on Judge. "I was wonderin' when you would get here." He cocked the gun and aimed it directly at Judge's heart. "Now drop that there little twig."

The gleam of a man about to kill was missing from the gunslinger's eyes. Judge's reaction was lightning quick. He faked to the right. The gunman's aim was off by a breath when he fired, giving Judge the moment he needed. He lunged at the man. They grappled until, with one swift blow, Judge stabbed the branch into his neck.

"Mort, you all right?" called out Clancy. When his partner did not answer, Clancy turned his attention from the Englishwoman and stalked in the direction where he had left Mort, his confidence puffing out his chest.

Colston had just finished dispatching Mort when

Clancy's hard eyes caught upon the grisly sight. Clancy crouched down and checked the ammunition in his pistol. Colston had slit Mort's throat with his own knife, and was gathering up his weapons.

"You bastard," Clancy sneered. "You killed Mort."

Judge's head snapped up and his grasp tightened around the grip of the gun he'd taken off the man named Mort.

"Don't even think 'bout it, Colston. Nothin' I'd like better right now than t' blow yer friggin' head off. Now drop it."

"Since you seem to know who I am, why don't you introduce yourself and tell me why the two of you were trailing me and the lady."

"One would think you got the drop on me from all the questions you's shootin' at me." Clancy gave a hearty laugh. Then his grin faded. "Why ain't you laughin'? Don't you get the joke . . . Jesse?"

"You apparently know more about my activities than I would've given you credit for," Judge goaded, hoping to trick the lanky killer into supplying him with the name of the person he suspected was behind this.

"Shur 'nuff. I ain't as dumb neither as you be thinkin'. You ain't gonna trip me up int' tellin' you nothin' more'n lettin' you know that it's gonna be Clancy what kills you and that high 'n mighty lady you's got with you."

"I wouldn't be so sure about that, Clancy. Your partner thought he was pretty clever, too. Look wha' happened to him."

Clancy's eyes briefly slid over the gory remains of hi' counterpart. "Where'd you learn to finish a man off s' tidy?"

"A man does what he must. Maybe you're afraid yo'

might end up the same way, the way you are beginning to twitch."

Clancy's eyes flashed at that. "Don't waste no more of my time. Turn 'round," he ordered.

"You aim to shoot me in the back?" Judge was stalling for time when he glimpsed a shaky figure sneaking up on them. It was Victoria, limping, a rock in her tiny hand.

"I said turn 'round, 'fore I up 'n shoot you right now."

Victoria gasped and swung her arm up. "You are not going to shoot anyone!" she snapped, ignoring the danger they were in.

Judge couldn't believe it. A short while ago she had been panic-stricken, quivering like a leaf. Now she was advancing on a killer with a gun in his hand.

Clancy whirled on Victoria. "You think you's gonna help Col—" Judge flew at the gunslinger before he could unmask him.

Clancy got off two wild shots before Judge's fist mashed into his face, knocking him out just as Victoria joined the fray and crowned Judge with her stone-age weapon.

"Oh, no!" she screamed as Judge dropped to the ground. He lay next to the man who had given her a ride to the train depot back in Saint Louis. Upon recognizing the man, Victoria's nose crinkled. "That will teach you to rent a pig cart for a lady."

Judge groaned.

"Thank the Lord. I thought I might have killed you," she offered meekly, when he opened his eyes.

"You may just find yourself wishing you had." Judge touched the pair of bumps adorning his head. "Ouch! What's the matter? Were you sorry you missed your chance to give me the first blow to the head, or did you

227

decide that two is always better than one?"

Victoria was stung. She had been trying to save his miserable life. Instead of a thank you, he was lounging on the ground complaining about a little mishap. "Perhaps we should try for three," she threatened.

"Don't even think about it. Now hurry down to the river and get me something wet for this cut on my head." He touched the gash, wiping at the sticky, oozing blood.

"Too bad we do not happen to have a bucket," she said tartly, ignoring the powerful urge to minister to his needs and cradle his head in her arms.

"Yes, it is, isn't it? I could use it to sit on while I tan your English hide. Now get going," he directed.

"Very well."

Despite the pain to her leg, Victoria swished back to the river, dipped the hanky from her skirtpocket into the cold water, and strolled back to Jesse, fighting off a flash of wooziness. She stood over him, and with the most innocent smile she could muster, dropped the cloth in his lap.

He grabbed the soaked handkerchief up. "What are you trying to do to me, cool my ardor for you?"

Victoria's eyes snapped fire. "You are incorrigible."

"With your support to foster me, how could I help but be?"

"I did not say 'encourageable'," she corrected, close to losing her temper. "I said *incorrigible,* which means you are incapable of being reformed."

"Now, I thought that's what you liked about me." He swabbed at the cut on his temple. "Or are you trying to create another Harold?"

"Gerald. You big oaf! Gerald!"

He had managed to make her lose her temper. He

wasn't quite sure why. Perhaps it was that he needed to push her past arms' distance after realizing his love for her. Or perhaps it was simply that she managed to make him furious every time she opened her desirable mouth. Or it could have been that she had needed him for a few moments. Before turning back into a self-sufficient English businesswoman, she had been helpless, vulnerable, and he had had an overwhelming urge to protect her. Any of the possibilities fouled his own temper further. He had not experienced such strong feelings for a woman since Helene, years ago.

As Victoria watched Jesse clean the blood from his face, a wealth of emotion threatened to erupt around her. He had such a wonderful face: eyes which could devour the soul, a nose out of a Roman history book, a mouth so full and sensuous that she unconsciously touched her lips, remembering the passion he had wrought.

Feeling desire rise in her, Victoria turned away from Jesse. Her gaze fell on the bloody body of the other gunslinger. She had to clamp a hand on her mouth to keep from retching.

"Oh, Jesse, how utterly horrible," she cried.

"Killing is never pretty, Victoria. I did what I had to do." Judge came up behind her and laid his hands on her shoulders. "I'm sorry you had to see that. Here," he directed her away from the body, "sit down while I see the man gets a proper burial."

"It is big of you to bury the man, the way he was attempting to kill us."

"I don't intend to do the digging, merely to supervise it while I grill old Clancy as soon as he wakes up. Just listen to me this time and stay here, will you?" She had turned green when she'd seen the body, and now seemed to sway as if she were going to faint—an unexpected reaction for someone with Victoria's inner strength.

He was pretty sure she wouldn't overhear his conversation with the gunman if he left her a safe distance from Clancy. Clancy knew his identity, and Judge did not want her hearing it from anyone but him. He glanced back at her. She was massaging her thigh through her blood-smudged skirt. He wondered what her reaction would be when she did discover the truth about him.

Judge prodded Clancy with his boot and the gunslinger groaned. "You've had enough rest. Get on your feet. You have a bit of digging to do."

Clancy's muscles tensed and he grudgingly crawled to his feet. "You should of killed me, Colston, when you had the chance," he sneered.

"Who knows, I may still send you to hell."

Clancy rather fearfully asked, "What you gonna do with me?"

"We're going over to that tree, and while you give your friend, Mort, a proper burial, you're going to tell me why you were trailing us and who hired you. Looks like you two were prepared. Here." Judge thrust the shovel he had procured from one of the horses tied nearby into Clancy's hands. "Get going."

Clancy banged his boot onto the shovel and scooped out a shallow grave. Judge gave him a nudge with the rifle he had taken from Mort's horse. "If you don't want to dig your own grave, you'd better start talking."

"If I spill my guts, I've already dug my own grave," Clancy jeered, starting to sweat. "My life wouldn't be worth a scrap from a female's love letter." He lifted the body and heaved it into the pit without reverence.

"So you know Jessup will hound you to the other end of the universe," Judge said, and noticed that Clancy flinched. "I thought so." For some unknown reason, Jessup had always seemed driven where Judge was concerned. But such a blatant attempt on Judge's life seemed bold even for one audacious as Luther Jessup.

Clancy finished filling in the hole, then arrogantly leaned against the shovel. "You don't know nothin', Colston."

Judge kicked the shovel out from under the gunslinger. Clancy grabbed the handle and swung at Judge's head. "I'm gonna teach you good now, then I'm gonna take real nice care of that there lady, if you know what I—"

A fist again smashed Clancy's face, and Judge proceeded to beat the bastard for what he'd said.

"What are you doing?" Victoria demanded of Jesse, who had stripped the unconscious gunman down to his red longjohns and was dragging him to a tree which banked the river.

"I'm making sure he won't be following us." Judge propped his limp form against the trunk, retrieved a rope from the saddle, and trussed the man up like a Christmas turkey. "Don't look at me like that, Tori. One of the steamers'll pick him up. That's why I chose this particular tree. With his red underwear, he'll be spotted a mile away."

"What's going to keep him from coming after us when he's freed?" Victoria worried.

"This." Before Victoria's humane side could come to the fore, Judge disabled the gunslinger with a shovel to his knee.

"Jesse!" she cried at his violence, putting fingers to her temple. A sudden dizziness threatened her for a

231

second before her head cleared. "How could you?"

Judge went to her. "Are you all right?"

"Yes. It is just the strain of the last twenty-four hours, I am certain."

Judge searched her face, then offered, "Look, Tori, the man is a killer. I should have killed him. But I spared his life." *Because you were with me.* "Come on," he offered his hand, expecting another battle, "I need to get you as far away from here as possible, before Clancy can send reinforcements after us."

On wobbly legs Victoria rose, holding out her hand to Jesse without protest. But when she put her weight on her left foot, a white-hot pain speared through her thigh. Her vision blurred, and she collapsed into his arms.

Chapter Twenty-five

Victoria awoke to strong arms banded around her. Slowly she fluttered her eyes open and tried to focus. She was seated in front of Jesse, atop a horse. Her leg felt like a bolt of lightning shot through it with each jarring step the animal took. When she tried to shift her weight she discovered her leg was strapped tight between two sticks and encased in what was left of her petticoat.

She managed to swivel her head around toward Jesse. "My leg. Where are we?"

Judge pressed a light kiss on her temple. "It's all right, Victoria. One of the gunman's bullets grazed your thigh. That's why you fainted. You should have told me you'd been hit instead of forcing yourself to be so brave back there at the river."

"In all the confusion I did not realize. I—"

"No. Don't try to talk. I'm here for you and I'm going to take care of you, so don't even attempt to think otherwise. Relax and let me worry about both of us until we get to Cheyenne."

Relax and let me worry about both of us until we get to Cheyenne. The words sounded so comforting. Victoria turned her attention back to the rolling hillside and leaned against the solidity of his muscled chest. She could sense the inner strength of him, and felt the tension drain from her body. For the first time in years, she could allow someone else to take care of her instead of being the caregiver. A quiet peace pervaded her mind and she rested her head on his shoulder.

Judge could feel the surrender of her body against his. A smile caught his lips. She wasn't fighting him. He had actually managed to call a truce.

It was a great pleasure to hold her in his arms and let his mind wander to thoughts of home. Despite himself, he could visualize her standing on the porch in a crisp white apron, waiting for him to return from a day on the range. Of course, he knew she would more likely be the kind of wife to spend the days on the range with him.

He'd known there was a passion inside her waiting to be released, and she had proved him right when he'd made love to her. If only she weren't after part of his ranch. In answer to that threat, coupled with his other thoughts, he found himself thinking about what that lawyer in New York had advised. Perhaps he *should* marry her.

Reflections about marriage and all its ramifications, as well as the problems surrounding Victoria and him, assaulted Judge as he kept the horse's pace steady. She slept so peacefully in his arms that he was watchful not to wake her. She would need rest to regain her strength from the nasty wound she'd received. Judge's eyes narrowed at the thought of what the gunman had done to her. He silently vowed that if he ever saw the man again, he'd kill him.

They didn't stop until it was nearing evening. Judge

wouldn't have stopped at all except that he'd noticed the muffled moans Victoria tried to hide. She was in pain. Knowing she did not want to burden him with the knowledge only served to increase his admiration for the spunky woman.

He found a suitable campsite beside a trickling stream with a canvas of cottonwoods. He helped Victoria down and carried her to a soft bed of grass beneath the tarp of trees shading them. Although he knew they should keep moving, she needed rest. "We'll stay here tonight."

Judge gathered dried twigs and branches and started a fire. He got supper going, and scooped up dried leaves and grasses into a bed not far from the warming flames. He pulled the bedrolls off the gunfighter's horses and spread the blankets over the soft mounds.

Standing over Victoria, he reached out his arms. "Ready for supper in bed tonight?"

"You are going to spoil me."

"That's the idea."

He was being so kind and patient that tears threatened to escape the deep blue of her eyes. She could not help herself, she loved the man. Why did it have to happen after she had selected Gerald, and in a country so far away from home?

She lifted her arms to him and clung to his neck as he carried her to the bed and set her down, plumping her skirts about her until he seemed satisfied she was comfortable.

"You relax. I'll be over at the stream. Call if you need me. I'll be within shouting distance."

Victoria desperately longed to know if he had the same feelings for her as she did for him. But she could not just blurt out all the questions in her heart. What if he were merely following the judge's instructions, taking something for himself by sampling her charms along the way? He was a very dangerous man—she had been witness to that, on more than one occasion. The ache in her heart would not subside, despite her efforts at hardheadedness.

She had to force herself to remember her family's name. The pride of all she'd built and was trying to hang on to was at risk.

Jesse returned hauling a canteen of water. "Will you tell me about the ranch?" she asked almost before realizing what she had said.

Judge's eyes sparked before he turned to the fire and poured the water into the battered coffeepot he'd gotten off the horse he'd had tethered behind them.

He still refuses to discuss it, she surmised. He was going to continue to deny she had a claim to the judge's property.

Chrissake, won't she ever give up? Why in the hell couldn't she just forget about his blasted ranch and her intent to claim part of it? "How's your wound? Is it bothering you?"

"Please, why can you not answer me instead of changing the subject?"

He straightened and stared at her for a moment, finally accepting that she would not let the subject die. "Because the ranch belongs to Judge Colston."

"That does not answer my question," she persisted.

She looked so earnest that Judge was almost tempted to describe the rich beauty of his land. If she hadn't been so insistent, he might have done just that—in time. Until he decided what he was going to do about the change in his feelings toward the Englishwoman, he cautioned himself that he must proceed with care.

"It's not much to look at, actually. Just a bunch of tumbleweeds, brush, and rattlesnakes. A few scrawny cows and a one-room shack that leaks when it rains, lets in the cold in winter and the heat in summer. There's little water, and it's far out from civilization. Not worth a whole lot, but it is all the man has."

"My father's will described it as a sizable holding."

Judge held her gaze. Persistence was one of her strengths, as well as one of her annoying qualities, at times.

"It's smaller than some, bigger than others."

"I see." She nodded. It would be difficult to learn much from Jesse.

"Maybe you do."

"What is that supposed to mean?"

He paused to formulate a response. "The land is like a woman to some men out here in the West. Men fight and die over it. They covet it. And some men manage to possess it. The ranch is like that to the judge. It's been his life, his mistress if you will. He's married to it. And to him, it's like you are trying to take a part of what he loves away from him."

Victoria watched his face as he spoke. His eyes were so expressive. If she did not know better, she might have sworn he was talking about his own ranch. "But does the man not remember that it was my father who loaned him the money to start his ranch in the first place? Without my father's investment, he never would have what he has today."

"How do you know that isn't something your father made up?"

"My father was an honest man. But I also have all the documents signed quite legally."

Judge's eyes narrowed. "Well, the judge said he never

237

signed any papers, if they do in fact exist."

"They do indeed exist, Jesse. The papers were signed and notarized by the judge's intermediary, one Aloysius Osborne. I have been trying to show them to the judge since we arrived in New York, but he has continually put me off."

Judge kept his expression bland, although now that she'd said Ozzie's name Judge understood why the old timer had been after him to "listen to reason." Then the recollection of how he'd borrowed the money from Ozzie years ago hit him. Of course he had paid it back many times over. Ozzie had forgotten to take care of the loan, Judge realized. This put everything into a different perspective, one which, at the moment, Judge was uncertain how to handle, so he said, "I'm sure everything will be ironed out at the ranch."

"It has to be. It is all that is left of my father's estate. You see, before he died, my father and Gerald invested in some scheme presented to them by a group of Americans. Needless to say, it failed. My part of the ranch is all I have. With the proceeds from its sale, I will begin rebuilding the family shipping business." Victoria spoke candidly, secure in the knowledge that Jesse was the man who had saved her life and was now taking care of her.

Judge's eyes flared, then he dropped his lids over them and studied the ground. He did not want her to see his reaction to this additional bit of dynamite.

"It'll be dark soon. I'd best finish getting supper so we can eat before it gets late. I need to tend your wound before we bed down for the night."

They ate in companionable silence, a few birds overhead punctuating the evening with their songs. She was thankful that Jesse had had the forethought to go through the gunmen's supplies. He had also checked the men's pockets, so they were no longer without cash once they reached a town. Oddly, the thought of quickly returning to the outside world no longer appealed to her as it had this morning.

After he had packed everything away so they would be prepared to move on at dawn tomorrow, he knelt beside her and lifted her skirt.

"What are you doing?" she asked, startled.

"I told you earlier. I need to tend that bullet hole you have in your leg. You needn't worry."

"I am not worried," she said softly, letting him slide the fabric up her thigh. His callused hands were scraped and cut, and were rough against her bare skin. She flinched when he stripped away the bandage.

"I'm sorry. I didn't mean to hurt you. We should have stopped sooner," he said, dabbing at the angry gouge.

Victoria hesitantly laid her hand on his, the sensation mind-searing. "You have not hurt me."

"I should have protected you better."

"I should think you have been doing a pretty good job of it." She turned his palm up. Her breath caught at the raw, red skin. "You are injured and did not say anything. Let me see your other hand."

"I'm supposed to be taking care of you, remember?" He laughed off her concern and withdrew his hand.

"But—"

"No buts. I've had a lot worse. I'll be fine."

Victoria wanted to protest. But it seemed important to him that she not, so she leaned back and watched as he tenderly cleaned her wound, applied the salve he'd found in the saddlebags, and rebound it.

"You were lucky I discovered you'd been hit before you lost any more blood than you did," he said, and rubbed some of the balm into his palms.

A blush warming her cheeks, Victoria asked, "How did you *discover* I had been wounded?"

He had a lopsided grin on his face. "I wasn't taking advantage of you while you were unconscious, if that's what you're concerned about."

"No ulterior motive, then?" She wasn't sure whether she was disappointed or not.

"No. Not that time at least. The bloodstain on your skirt was too wet to have come from anywhere except from your leg."

"Oh."

" 'Course, now that you're conscious. . . ." He let his voice trail off.

Her breathing quickened. "I am quite that now."

Judge ran the back of his hand along her silken cheek. The sensation was almost enough to induce him to take her where she sat. He was tempted to do just that.

Victoria could see he was struggling with himself. She was experiencing the same inner turmoil. They both wanted each other. It was evident. He was a man who seemed to take what he wanted. So why was he holding back now? As she speculated why he was not kissing her, it occurred to Victoria that perhaps he was taking her feelings into consideration. The possibility sent a new surge of feeling charging through her veins. The man was setting aside his own desires to consider hers.

In answer, Victoria put her hand on his and nuzzled her face against him. "I need your comforting arms around me tonight. Will you stay here with me?"

Judge's lips found hers. He nibbled at the top, then the bottom lip before opening his mouth and kissing her with a tenderness he hadn't known he possessed until now. His fingers caressed her chin and glided down her neck to her breasts. She was aroused. Her nipples stood erect and she pressed herself to him. He delved between the buttons on her blouse and brushed the satiny skin. Without breaking their kiss, he moved lower until he came into contact with her wound. Ever so slightly, she winced.

He drew back to gaze into her eyes. The glow on the campfire across her face left him close to breathless with longing.

"Victoria—"

"No. Do not pull back," she said in a small voice.

"I have to until your wound heals. I already hurt you a moment ago and I could hurt you again, even if I were very careful."

Victoria wanted to instruct him to ignore the wound. But instead she remained mute, letting him take the lead, confident in the knowledge that they would share their passion for one another again—soon.

He drew her into his embrace and lay down with her in his arms. She was soon breathing evenly, asleep. She had entrusted him with her life. Judge lay next to her warmth for hours, unable to fall asleep. Tomorrow they would move closer to unearthing a secret; would it rip his world apart?

Chapter Twenty-six

Victoria awoke feeling as if she had been reborn. Her wound no longer pained her when she moved her leg, and her inner fears and suspicion were gone. The world about her looked a lot brighter, the birds' songs seemed happier. Most important, she was still in Jesse's arms.

"Morning, Tori. I was wondering whether you were going to try to sleep the day away."

"I do not know about sleeping, but I might be convinced to remain here a while longer," she purred.

She was truly amazing. A few days ago she had been at his throat and now she was as tame as a kitten. Judge drew himself up on his elbow and looked down at her. He knew this enchantment was fragile—they could be snarling at each other again before long. "If you're not careful, we just might."

Startled by her own boldness, Victoria added, "My leg feels much better this morning." Then she dropped her eyes, realizing that what she'd said in innocence sounded like further invitation. "If you do not mind, I would like to wash before we leave."

"I'll get the horses saddled."

He headed off before she could retract her words. She seemed to be making a royal pickle of their new relationship, but she was not worried. Despite her inexperience with members of the opposite sex and her awkwardness, she refused to be daunted.

Victoria saw to her grooming the best she could. Jesse had brought her a bar of lye soap he'd taken from the saddlebags, and with this she scrubbed her body and cleaned her wound. She wanted to hold her nose as she slipped back into her clothes, they were so filthy. If her family and friends could see her now, they would be shocked at the way prim and proper Victoria Elizabeth Torrington looked. The thought made her smile.

"What's so amusing?"

She looked up to see his grinning face. "I was musing at the stir I would create if the people I knew could see me in my present condition."

"You look beautiful to me," Judge observed, wondering about the differences which existed between their worlds.

Not half an hour had passed before he was helping her onto the horse's back. "We are not going to ride together?" she asked when he climbed onto his own mount.

"Nothing I'd like more." *Unless I was inside you.* "But we'll make better time if we ride separately."

They did not travel as fast as they should have, and Judge spent time backtracking and covering their trail. He also made sure to stop and give Victoria a chance to rest, although she protested that she did not need it. A week's riding brought them just outside Topeka. Victoria had no idea where she was, and Judge hesitated to tell her for fear that, once back in civilization, she would again become the proper spinster he had first met.

Her wound was pretty much healed, and Judge was nearly mad with desire. It had been a hell of a week staying away from her, and he was determined not to spend another sleepless night lying beside her with an ache in his gut.

He reined in his horse. "How does this spot suit you? Lots of grass for the horses, a stream complete with a pond big enough to bathe, and plenty of privacy."

"I think this will do nicely," Victoria returned, feeling giddy at his last remark.

They dismounted and went about setting camp for the night. They had mastered the routine, and the sun was still shining when all was ready. "I think I shall take advantage of that pond now," she announced, moving to the water's edge.

Without looking back, Victoria stripped off her clothing and stepped into the cool water up to her waist, careful not to go in too deep. She heard splashing sounds behind her and turned around in time to see Jesse dive beneath the surface. She watched his masculine form swim in the crystal pool until he came up in front of her.

"I want to make love to you, lady," he rasped.

Victoria's heart threatened to race away with her. Long moments stretched the tension burgeoning between them, until she answered, "Well, then, what are you waiting for?"

Judge drew her to him and thoroughly kissed her before suggesting, "How does a watery bed sound?" The look on her face reminded him of her great fear of the water and he amended, "No. I want you on solid

244

ground."

Relief flooded through her. She smiled her gratitude, then took the bar of soap and began lathering the hairs on his chest. "How does this feel?"

Her fingers were instruments of exquisite torture as they glided over him, and Judge had to force himself to stand still while she reacquainted herself with each part of him. When she drew him back to knee-deep water and soaped the standing male portion of him, Judge thought he was going to lose control. Slowly, methodically, she massaged his length, then took him between her hands, rubbing and toying with the whole of that sensitive area, until Judge grabbed her wrists.

"What are you trying to do," he asked in a voice heavy with passion, "force me to take you on the edge of the water, still full of soap?"

"No," she said cutely, and handed him the bar. "Stand still while I splash that soap off you."

And splash she did, as Judge returned in kind each wave of water sent his way.

"My turn. At last," he announced when the rain of water had ceased.

Judge worked the bar into a foaming lather of bubbles and began expert ministrations. He started with her hair, running the long strands between his fingers. He bent her over and rinsed the golden locks, feathering them into a floating halo. He righted her and moved to her ears, kissing and nibbling at each one in turn before applying the suds. He moved to the column of her neck, running his tongue the length of it before his fingers took over.

Over her shoulders, under her arms and to her breasts he moved, his mouth igniting each portion of her body prior to his sudsing her blazing flesh. She cried out her pleasure as he made soapy figure eights over her breasts and twirled her straining nipples between his slippery index finger and thumb.

"What are you doing?" she gasped as he nestled his face between her breasts and rubbed them against his cheeks.

He smiled up at her, a white foaming beard adorning his chin. "Can you think of a better way for me to wash my face?"

"Most definitely not," she mumbled, her throat choked with her growing appetite for the man. She closed her eyes and delighted in the sensations.

Judge returned to his duties, moving lower, careful not to send her into a spasm of laughter as he glided over her rib cage and down her sides to the flat of her stomach. Then he stopped, picked her up, and seated her on a rock at the edge of the pond.

Her eyes flew open as he pressed a kiss to her toes. "Haven't you forgotten an area?"

"Not I. Just saving the best part for last." He bent his head back to her feet. He kissed each toe and traced along the sole of each foot, before paying close attention to each again with his cleansing fingers. He then ran his teeth up and down her calf while he circled her ankles easily in his grasp.

Victoria was panting at the heights to which a simple task as was washing could lift her. She was sure she was going to scream out her need for him.

"I see you are all ready for me," he said in a husky voice.

"Oh, yes. Let's be done with bathing. You are about to drive me wild," she offered, in no more than a broken whisper.

"Only about to, huh?" He swooped her back into his

246

arms and set her down calf-deep in the water with orders to stand with her legs apart.

Victoria did as bade and, after he foamed her thighs and drew his fingers tenderly over the scar, quickly found herself moaning and dancing with the excruciating pleasure he was rendering her. His hands moved against her and into that most secret part of her, rubbing, twisting, and delving until she nearly lost her footing. He caught her just as she began to fall sideways into the pond.

Her body hot against his, she smiled into his azure depths. "I think you left out part of the treatment."

"The treatment?" He chuckled at her choice of words.

"Yes, *the treatment.*" Her expression cutely challenged him to come up with a more appropriate name.

"I think I'd be inclined to call it a prelude — to some serious lovemaking." He hugged her tighter, then held her from him. "Now what part of your luscious body could I have neglected?"

Victoria blushed hot pink from her head to the ends of her toes. "Ah . . . you did not . . . ah . . . do a thorough job with the last part."

"The last part?" A wolfish grin split his lips. "I thought I had covered it pretty thoroughly. But if you think not, I'll redo it. Satisfaction is always guaranteed, . . . I'll keep at it until you are completely satisfied." One hand released her and slid toward the mound glistening as the sun caught the tiny soap bubbles.

"No." She squirmed under his movements. "Not with your hand. Your lips."

Judge stopped and stared into her face. God, he loved her. "You like it when I use my lips?"

Victoria lowered her eyes. It was an admission she

247

could not bring herself to put to words. He might think her unredeemably brazen.

Judge would not let it rest. He wanted her to say it, to admit he did wonderful things to her body. He wanted her to feel totally and utterly free with him. For only then could they truly share themselves with each other. With the crook of his thumb, he raised her chin. "Don't be afraid to admit it, Victoria. Making love means you can let go of any inhibitions and fears you might have. It is a celebration to be partaken of fully, by both people."

She searched his eyes. He meant what he'd said. "I do not feel any inhibitions when I am with you. It is just that I do not want you to think I am . . . ah . . . too bold."

"Never would I think this woman too bold," he shouted to the sky. "Let's get you rinsed off, and then I am going to *finish the treatment* before we get down to making love."

He led her into deeper water, careful not to frighten her, and rinsed the soap from her body. Then he kissed her and picked her up against his chest.

Victoria could hear his heart pounding against her ear as he carried her to their bed, and set her down. He patted her dry, saw to himself, then lowered her against the blankets. There was no amusement in his face when he told her, "Spread your legs for me, Victoria," only burning desire.

He lay between her thighs until Victoria protested that she should be allowed to give pleasure to him while he was giving her so much delight.

"You are the most incredible woman I've ever met," he growled, moving so she could sample him at the same time.

Judge inhaled the sweetness of her arousal before he put his mouth to one swollen lip and sucked just outside her blazing core. She started to writhe, causing him to look up at her and place a stilling palm on her stomach. "We have a long way to go before you get excited."

"Too late. I am already excited," she moaned, returning to make him as ready for her as she was for him.

Judge had to hold himself on a tight leash, the way she applied her mouth and tongue to him, or he wouldn't be able to give her all the pleasure he wanted before being forced to seek his own release. Trying to ignore his own need, he left one hand to dip into her slippery wetness and moved to place his mouth to a waiting breast despite her objections.

She raked her fingers through his hair, tightening her grasp around the ebony strands as his delicious torture became more intense. Little pants coupled with moans and rose to muffled screams.

Playing and probing, suckling and licking, Judge applied himself to driving her beyond tremulous abandon, until she was kissing him wildly, writhing out of control, blind to everything except the sensations which engulfed her.

"I do believe you are ready for me," he growled low in his throat, close to urgency himself.

He poised over her and she guided him deep within her, circling him with her legs to take in all his length. She had never known anything so mind-shattering, so fulfilling in her life. She began to move with him, first long slow strokes, then shorter, harder, faster strokes. Grinding and pounding herself against him, desperately craving that ultimate sensation, she increased the savage friction until she was sure she would explode.

And then she did, straining and grasping him to her so tight that she screamed in unbridled ecstasy.

No longer able to stay himself, Judge unleashed his emotions. Wave after wave of bursting explosions rocked him violently, and he released all his passion into her.

No words could adequately describe what they had just experienced together. A glowing silence overtook them in the wake of their lovemaking, as their heartbeats gradually slowed to normal.

Judge lay the length of Victoria, gently nuzzling her hair, and relishing the aftermath of the most exquisite lovemaking he had ever experienced in his life. Suddenly, he clamped his teeth into his lower lip until he drew blood. The pain stopped him; he had almost slipped and whispered in her ear, *I love you*.

Chapter Twenty-seven

Bypassing Topeka, Judge and Victoria continued their journey westward. After making love to her the way he had, Judge vowed to keep her to himself until he could make a decision. With her confession about her father and financial position, Judge had been dealt another blow. Then there was Ozzie's part in this. A secret smile captured his lips. On the one hand, Judge would like nothing better than to cut the old timer's protruding Adam's apple out of his throat and feed it to the hogs. On the other hand, if Ozzie hadn't neglected to repay the loan, Judge never would have met Victoria. He ran his fingers through his hair. The conflict opposed his deep love for his land to his growing love for the Englishwoman. Their differences still seemed insuperable.

Victoria lifted her gaze toward the beating afternoon sun. Her eyes blinked against the glare as she gently rocked with the sure gait of the horse. She raised her hand to wipe the beads of perspiration from her forehead. Lassitude had long before invaded her to the bones. They had shared a horse since dawn at her request, and Victoria marveled at how easy it had been to persuade Jesse. Nestled against the strength of his chest, contentment, elusive since childhood, melted the last of her trepidation at being out in the middle of nowhere with a man she had met only a short time ago. The strength of his arms, surely earned from years of hard work on the ranch, held her with the ease of a caress.

"We'll camp here tonight," Judge announced, kissing the back of her ear.

He dismounted and helped her down. Victoria looked around her. The scene was the same she had seen for two weeks: a thick belt of trees near refreshing water. Her lips dropped. Although she'd never known such heaven, she could not neglect her responsibility forever.

"Jesse?"

"Ummm?"

"How much longer will it be before we reach Cheyenne?"

Judge could not put a name to the implications of what she was asking. "You growing tired of my company?"

"Never." Her gaze darted away to gather her thoughts. She fidgeted with the frayed fabric of her collar. "I could use some clean clothing." She paused. Truth and honesty were the foundations of love. "That is not entirely true."

He cocked a brow. "Oh?"

She followed the line of his tightening lips, her heart beginning to pound as she forced herself to continue. "Lani and Gerald are no doubt worried about me. And I must conclude my business transaction with the judge before control of Torrington Limited is lost to the family."

Judge's heart scorched inside at the ease with which she said that pipsqueak's name. Judge had thought, the way she'd come to him so willingly, that she no longer considered the English dandy her fiancé. A part of him had desperately wanted her to come to him as a woman unencumbered by circumstances.

He had forgotten what schemers all women eventually showed themselves to be. Yet another part of him instructed him to give her the benefit of the doubt, to let time settle all the nagging questions for him. After gazing on that incredible face for a moment, he selected the latter course . . . with a few exceptions.

"We'll be in Cheyenne in a couple more days. I wouldn't want you to be away from your precious fiancé for too long." The words slipped out before he could stop himself.

Victoria was so excited about hearing they would soon reach their destination that she completely missed his reference to Gerald, and the dark menacing tone of his voice.

"Since you suddenly seem to be so worried about your appearance, I know a farmhouse not far outside Cheyenne where we can stop. You'll be able to get a change of clothes — won't be anything fancy, like you're used to, but Betsy Lake's a clean, good woman who'd give anyone in need the shirt off her back."

Victoria looked shocked, causing Judge to amend, "Don't look so horrified, I didn't mean it literally. Gather some brush so we can get supper over with. It's been a long day, and tomorrow will be even longer if we're going to reach the Lakes' place by dark."

He spun on his heel and left her standing, staring

after him, not understanding what had precipitated such a sudden change in his behavior toward her.

As she went about her chores, his coolness began to grate on her. They had shared an idyllic two weeks, each seeming to anticipate the other's wishes, they were so close. Now, as they neared civilization, she wondered if he had been using her all along. She had bared her soul to him. They had spent hours talking about their childhoods. She thought she'd come to know him. She had even sympathized with his goal to someday own the largest ranch in the territory of Wyoming. Then it dawned on her. Of course! How could she have been so blind? He had been solicitous so he could somehow gain control of her inheritance for himself.

Victoria started to stir the beans with a vengeance, then decisively threw the spoon into the middle of the bubbling concoction and whirled around to confront him. No one was going to make a fool out of her and get away with it. Three feet from his bent form, she stopped.

She was out in the middle of the plains, dependent on him. If he realized she was aware of what he was trying to do, she could leave herself open to all sorts of unspeakable harm. She had to be careful until she reached the safety of the city.

Judge sensed her presence and glanced over his shoulder.

"Something you need?" He kept his voice unassuming.

"No. I merely thought I might help you make the bed," she said, catching sight of the blankets being spread out by those big hands. The bed. Their bed. Naturally, he expected her to share it with him. Well, she was not about to be used again!

254

"I've got it almost ready. Why don't you go wash up? I'll join you shortly."

Her breath caught as her mind revisited one particular bath they had shared. Despite herself, she warmed thinking about how he had soaped and delved into every portion of her woman's body. His fingers had ignited her senses; his body had awakened desires in her that she had never believed could exist.

Victoria mumbled her acceptance and left him to his task. With renewed dedication to her cause, she raced down to the creek's edge. Stripping off her clothing, she performed a hasty toilette before that cowboy could catch her in such a vulnerable position.

"What's your hurry?" Judge rasped.

Just fastening the last button at her throat, Victoria spun around. He was casually leaning against a cottonwood, his arms crossed over his chest. "What makes you think I was in a hurry?"

He shrugged, his stance impersonal despite his feeling she was up to something. "You're dressed already. I'd planned to give you a little help," he threw out with a wolfish grin, watching for her reaction.

Victoria stared into that handsome face. "I—I was hungry."

"For me?" The lips spread further.

Careful Victoria. Do not let him know you are aware of what he is planning. "You know you are at the top of my list," she said cryptically, a bit too cheerily.

The inflection in her voice warned him that something had definitely changed. Her eyes were too bright. She was too animated, almost jittery, and she'd dropped her arms so straight at her sides that she looked like a well-formed plank.

"Life holds many lists, Victoria."

255

"Hasn't the last two weeks made it perfectly obvious which list I was talking about?" she answered evasively.

He stepped forward and hugged her to him. Lifting her chin, he kissed the end of her nose. "Then we're in agreement."

"Agreement?" Her eyes wide.

"You are at the top of my same list." He paused. "Now, why don't you go get yourself some of the beans to tide you over, while I hunt up some meat. We'll need the extra nourishment if we are going to make the Lakes' place tomorrow."

Suspicious of his intentions, Victoria offered to accompany him only to have him put his arm around her shoulders and escort her back to the fire.

"It won't take as long if I go alone. Here," he ladled some beans onto a tin plate and handed it to her, "sit back and relax until I get back. Oh, and keep this gun at your side." He laid the pistol on the ground near her.

Fear that he was not planning to come back overtook her. She knew nothing of survival out here in the wilderness, other than what she'd learned from Jesse. They had only one can of beans left — not enough to last until she could locate a town. Back home, if she was hungry, she either rang for the servants or ordered from a menu. No doubt, she was at a real disadvantage out here.

"Don't worry, highness, I'll be back. You'll be safe as long as you stay by the fire. Animals are afraid of it." He laughed as the sudden expression of concern crossed her face. "You and I have some unfinished business." He winked at her, mounted his horse, and disappeared from view.

For an instant, as she watched him put distance between them, she wished male human animals were afraid of fire too. To further unsettle her, the words *unfinished business* circled her like a stalking mountain lion. Just exactly what *unfinished business* had he been referring to? Before spooning those awful beans into her mouth, her gaze scanned the area. Then she picked up the gun and laid it in her lap. . . .

Once out of sight of their camp, Judge kicked his booted heel to the horse's flanks. They had made camp a little over two miles from the nearest town, as close as he could figure. His stomach's growling reminded him that a hearty steak in town before he returned would fill his gut quite nicely. He decided that after he took care of his business, he would stop by a butcher shop and pick up a chicken. Victoria was such a greenhorn that it'd be easy to convince her the dressed bird was wild prairie fowl.

Guilt assailed him as he drew nearer the town. He'd left her alone to eat that tin of beans while he was about to enjoy a mouth-watering steak. Well, he rationalized, chicken fried over an open fire would taste pretty good too.

Victoria had lost weight during the last two weeks. Although she had assured him losing a few pounds would be good for her, when he'd made love to her, her ribs had been much too prominent. He liked his women with a little more meat on their bones. Yet regardless how Miss Victoria Elizabeth Torrington, named after two queens, looked, he'd love her, he grudgingly acknowledged.

The rest of the way into Greeley, Judge argued with himself whether he should go ahead with his plan. He had set it into motion before he'd left the ranch for New York; everything should be in place. But now he had fallen in love with the exasperating woman.

It seemed so devious, he thought, as he slowed the lathered animal outside a false-fronted building proclaiming good home cooking. Perhaps the plan could serve two purposes, he reasoned, securing the horse to the hitching post.

He went inside the gingham-curtained restaurant and sat down. The more he considered it, the better he liked it. Once he'd devoured the two-inch piece of meat and sopped up the drippings with slabs of warm homemade bread, he'd made up his mind. He'd go ahead with it. The plan would clearly demonstrate whether she was only interested in the land or whether, underneath that rigid determination of hers, she unqualifiedly cared for him as a man.

Intruding into Judge's musings, the rotund waitress asked, "Will there be anything else, sir?"

Judge pulled out the roll of bills he'd taken from the gunslingers and threw two down on the table. "Only if you can direct me to the telegraph office, then to where I can get a plucked chicken."

The waitress pocketed the bills, pleased by the tip the handsome stranger had left. "Telegraph office's down the street to the corner. Turn right past the mercantile. You'll find it on the end." Her thick brow crinkled. "As for a plucked chicken, the best I can suggest is to stop by the Widow Kennedy's place. North on the main road, outside of town a mile. It won't be plucked, but for a little extra cash she'll wring its neck for you and even make it into the best chicken an' dumplings you ever tasted."

"Thank you."

Judge went directly to the telegraph office to send off two wires. One went to Ozzie, who was to be waiting in

Cheyenne with Victoria's sister and fiancé, instructing him to take the pair on to the ranch and keep a close eye on them so that no more slipups occurred. He wrote out specific instructions detailing his plan. While the man went to work and tapped out the first message, Judge composed the other wire, to be sent to the Lakes, forewarning them of his arrival with a guest and requesting their cooperation with his masquerade.

The message complete, Judge handed it to the clerk, then snatched it back. At the bottom of the Lakes' lengthy telegram he added: PLEASE PURCHASE — Stop — AT MY EXPENSE — Stop — ONE VERY PLAIN CALICO DRESS — Stop — BETSY'S SIZE.

The clerk shoved his visor from his eyes once he'd finished the task. With a bemused expression on his face, he looked up at Judge. "Mister, I sure wouldn't want to be in your boots when that gal these telegrams are about finds out what you are up to."

Chapter Twenty-eight

Lani's green eyes glittered like wet emeralds at the old timer, as they sat in the sitting room of the luxurious Dyers Hotel. Gerald remained mute, shifting in his chair, his gaze darting restlessly between his dear wife, dressed in green frills, and the leathered face of the imposter who had helped that cowboy lead them a merry chase.

"It has been over two weeks and still we have not heard from Victoria," Lani cried, waiting for Ozzie to provide some sort of explanation to reassure her.

"Maybe she's got other things on her mind," Ozzie meekly offered in face of the little miss's growing anxiety.

"Victoria has never had anything on her mind but business matters."

Gerald winced under the force of her response, causing Lani to pat his hand and amend, "Except for you, of course, Gerald."

Ozzie's brow flew up in doubt. " 'Course."

"Victoria is the most dependable, loyal, faithful, individual I know. She is—"

"Sounds like ya're referrin' t' her as man's best friend," interjected Ozzie, making a feeble attempt to disarm her with a bit of humor.

"I say, Victoria could never be considered canine," huffed Gerald. *No. She is more leonine.* "Now, my good man, if you are not prepared to send out a search party, Lani and I will simply be forced to seek out a bobby to handle this whole bloody affair."

"A what?" Ozzie sent the sugar-coated dude a bewildered look.

"Gerald, I fear the Americans have another name for constable," Lani declared.

"Constable?" Ozzie scratched his ear.

Gerald gnashed his teeth. Americans were such an uneducated lot; they could not even comprehend the Queen's English. "Naturally, since you are not who you presumed to be, you no doubt know little about the justice system or its retainers."

Annoyed now, Ozzie pulled out his gun and twirled the cylinder, a big grin on his lips. "This here's all the know-how I need."

Gerald swallowed the lump of fear which always overcame him at the sight of firearms by announcing, "Lani, dear heart, this man is obviously an illiterate boor. Why don't we seek out someone capable of understanding simple English."

Scandalized, Lani implored, "Gerald, do not be silly. Aloysius has been very kind to us." She nudged his leg under the table with her slippered foot. "Explain to him what you meant. Then he can put his weapon away."

"Oh, very well. My good man, a bobby is a person who enforces the law."

"Well, why didn't ya say so in the first place." Ozzie winked at Lani as he holstered his pistol. "Yer talkin'

261

'bout goin' t' the sheriff."

"Yes. We shall go to the sheriff." Lani brightened now that she and Gerald had escaped unscathed. The Wild West certainly was an exciting locale to visit. Her friends would be awed by the stories she had to tell when she got home.

Ozzie's face slid into hard, straight lines. "Now I wouldn't go 'n do nothin' hasty if I was ya, Miz Lani."

"I would hardly consider waiting two weeks in this city for Victoria to arrive being hasty," Gerald replied. "Shall we go, dear?" Gerald took Lani's elbow and the pair rose.

"Just wait up." Ozzie stopped their departure with an outspread arm. "Sit yourselves back down."

"Give us one good reason why we should," Gerald stated firmly, his pride in his own capabilities developing after being away from Victoria's overpowering personality.

" 'Cause I got a telegram from Judge this mornin'," Ozzie admitted as a last resort.

Lani's eyes rounded and she took her seat without waiting for Gerald's help, much to his dismay. "Tell me, is Victoria all right? He has not hurt her, has he? Where are they? When will they arrive? Has he—"

Ozzie raised his hand to still the barrage of questions. "Judge said they will be delayed—"

"Delayed? Why?" Lani put the back of her hand to her forehead, swaying in her chair.

"Give me a chance t' finish 'fore ya up and faint int' a heap."

"Yes. Yes. Of course, do go on," said Gerald, secretly hoping the rancher had managed to sweep Victoria off her feet, thus saving him from the unpleasant task of breaking their engagement. He placed a reassuring arm around his delicate little flower. Lani was what a real lady should be: soft, pliable, and dependent upon him.

"It seems some of Jessup's men tried t' kill them, so they been takin' a 'round 'bout way t' get here."

Lani's hand flew to her heart. "Oh, dear Lord!" she gasped, fanning herself with her gloved hand.

"Don't ya worry none now, Missy, they're right as rain," Ozzie soothed.

Gerald stiffened, suddenly dropping his arm from Lani. He clasped his hands before him on the table and leaned forward, his eyes widening noticeably. "Did you say Jessup?"

"Yup. Why?" asked Ozzie, alert to the man's strange demeanor.

Gerald took a deep breath and forced himself to relax. "No reason, really. At first I thought you said Jesse. It seemed rather despicable of the bloke."

"I said *Jessup,*" Ozzie repeated, wondering if the man would be able to hear a buffalo stampede coming if it were no more than ten feet away from him. "Might oughta get your hearin' looked at."

"I well believe I may."

"Oh, please, Aloysius, what was in the telegram?" pleaded Lani, still visibly shaken. "May I read it?"

"First off, the name's Ozzie if we're goin' t' work t'gether. Next off, I got a plan that might interest ya two, seein' how ya seem t' be sweet on each other."

Lani and Gerald's mouths dropped open.

Gerald sputtered, "Devil take you if—"

"No, Gerald," Lani interceded. "I think we could use an ally." At Ozzie's blank expression, Lani clarified, "A friend."

" 'Course, I knowed that."

She sent her brightest smile to the old timer. "What is your idea?"

"Gimme your word ya won't go 'n spill the beans 'fore Judge's idea has had a chance t' work, and I'll tell what I got in mind."

"I trust you realize we must hear what you have on your mind before agreeing to any devilry, sir," Gerald insisted.

Lani shot Gerald a daunting gaze. He sank two inches into his chair, realizing his sweet, innocent girl had some of the same traits as her overbearing sister.

"Do not concern yourself, Ozzie. Gerald and I both promise, don't we, Gerald?" At the fire in her eyes, Gerald nodded meekly.

Ozzie took a deep breath. He had to take a chance. He needed their cooperation. Without it, they might accidentally stumble into the middle of Judge's ruse and ruin everything.

"As long as we see eye t' eye, this is what I want ya t' do. . . ."

Helene stomped back and forth in the hotel suite, so fiercely she could feel the floor shake beneath her feet. Her face flushed a deep crimson to match the rubies she wore at her neck and the elegant, red gown draped revealingly along her luscious curves.

"You might as well settle down, my dear. We won't be leaving Saint Louis for home until tomorrow morning," Luther Jessup remarked. Lying across the bed, his belly extended over his belt by a good three inches. His elbow was bent, his head resting indifferently against a meaty hand. A cigar hung from his thick lips. He was a silver-haired man of fifty-three, raw-carved despite the vast wealth he'd been surrounded with all his life.

Luther's father had come from the old country dirt poor and unschooled, and had built an empire out of the untamed territory of Wyoming. His father had been a man of lusty appetites, and young Luther had followed in the elder Jessup's tracks, eagerly taking advantage of several household servants. Luther had been taught to win, whatever it took; he had lived by that code his entire life.

When he'd first seen the beautiful, dark Helene she was mesmerized with Judge Colston, whom he'd hated since the younger man's birth. Luther had wanted her, and he'd won her from his despised rival. Now, as Luther watched another one of her tantrums spiral, he wondered whether possessing a wife young enough to be his daughter was worth the expense and inconvenience it cost him. And then there was the matter of her continued obsession with Colston.

Her voice rising, Helene swung around and glared at the crude hog she was tied to. "What do you mean *settle down?* If I want to pace, I'll pace! If I want to smash something, I will," she screamed, yanking the pear-shaped rubies from her neck and grinding the fine stones under her heel.

Luther watched her actions without emotion. If she wanted to destroy her own jewels, it was her loss. This time he'd not replace the pieces.

"Since you seem to have so much excess energy," he patted the bed next to him, "why don't you strip off that dress and join me?"

She cast him one of her most killing looks. "Can't you see I have other things on my mind right now?"

His face darkened at her rejection of him. "What's the matter? Colston turn you down for that Englishwoman?" he sneered.

Helene's face drained of color, turning pasty white. She glared her hatred for a full minute, contemplating all the nasty things she'd like to say, prior to composing herself and answering, "I don't know what you mean."

"Sure you do, *wife*. You didn't really think I have been blind to you and Colston, did you?" His smile twisted. He'd waited for years, silently biding his time, until he could spring just the right trap.

He'd been using specially hired ranch hands to lay claim to more and more land, then taking title to it himself. His spies had informed him that Colston had been to Washingtonn, D.C. to talk to government officials about his activities. His fingers itched. He was finally going to get his revenge and ruin Colston once and for all.

Helene sucked in her cheeks. "You're only saying that because you're jealous of the empire he built despite your efforts to stop him," she spat.

"Jealous? Of Colston? Of you and Colston?" He broke out into a hearty laugh as he ground the end of his cigar in the tray near the bed.

"Yes!" she screamed, the veins standing out in her milky white neck. "You're jealous because he's more of a man than you'll ever be."

The inclination to slap the smirking smile off those luscious lips nearly overpowered him, but he held back. She was the mother of his son, a child he dearly loved despite his knowledge of his wife's unfaithfulness.

"And that Englishwoman Colston seems to have developed an interest in is more of a lady than you ever were or ever will be."

"Why, you bastard!" She flew at him, her nails like talons.

Luther let her struggle against him. He easily could have ended her attempts to scratch him, but he enjoyed the fight, found it arousing. The harder she fought, the more his desire for her grew, until he could feel his need ready. With little difficulty, he pinioned her hands over her head, pressing her into the mattress, his bulky body the length of her.

"Get off me, you pig!" she spat.

"You have always made our lovemaking exciting. Or should I say our rutting?" he panted, pressing hot, wet kisses to the top of her breasts. "Life with you has never been dull. Perhaps that's why I keep you around."

"You'll regret this, I swear," she groaned, throwing her head from side to side to avoid his lips on hers. "I should leave you for this."

With one hand he kept her wrists captured and with the other free one grabbed her chin between hurting fingers. His lips smashed against hers in a brutal, punishing kiss.

"You'll never leave me. You like my money and all it can buy you too much," he triumphantly announced upon leaving her lips.

Helene's body began to relax. She smiled up into his disgusting, jowled face. Yes. She'd stay with him — for now. But if everything went according to her design, she'd soon own his empire, and, finally, possess Judge Colston as well.

Her smile was sweet, her eyes ruthless. She circled her arms around his neck and planted hot kisses on his face, whispering, "You're right, Luther. I'll never leave you. I'll always honor the vow I took when I married you: 'til death do us part."

Chapter Twenty-nine

His belly full and his plan in place, Judge returned to Victoria, whistling as he rode into camp. A plump chicken dangled from the saddle, freshly plucked and ready for the pot. She sat huddled near the fire, a blanket around her shoulders, the gun in her hands. A look of relief spread over her face as he appeared in the fire light.

"Thank goodness, it is you," she said, dropping the gun. Her heart had begun to pound at the sound of approaching hooves. She had been afraid she would have to use the pistol to defend herself, since it seemed unlikely that friendly riders would be approaching out of the darkness.

"Don't tell me you were expecting someone else," Judge teased, sliding from the saddle.

"And if I were?"

"I might have to get jealous," Judge said in a light voice, but his eyes spoke the truth of his inner emotions.

Victoria stepped forward. "What took you so long?"

"I stopped to dress the bird before returning, so I wouldn't offend your sensibilities."

"How thoughtful of you," she snapped.

"I'm so happy you think so. In that case, here," he pushed the bird at her, "you can cook it so we'll have food on the trail tomorrow."

Holding the chicken gingerly between her fingers, Victoria turned up her nose. "But I cannot cook. . . ."

They saddled up and left at dawn, putting many hard miles on the animals before the blazing sun was directly overhead. Beneath a few sparse trees, they stopped to rest the horses and have something to eat.

Judge took a bit of the proffered chicken. "You weren't kidding were you?"

"I do not know what you mean," she returned indignantly.

"You really can't cook." He threw the shriveled, tasteless meat down and pulled his gun.

Victoria's eyes bulged as she stared at the pistol pointed at her. "Just because I cannot cook, you do not have to be so upset about it. I did manage to heat the beans while we were on the trail."

"Don't move!" he ordered, cocking the gun and pulling the trigger.

Victoria screamed and collapsed.

When she came to, she was nestled in Jesse's arms, near a cookfire. She stirred, and he tightened his arms around her.

"I thought you were going to kill me."

"If I had to eat your cooking all the time I might consider it. But no, highness," he chuckled, "I was taking care of our lunch."

"Our lunch?"

A big grin stretched his lips and he moved to the fire to turn the meat cooking over the flames. "Yes. Rattlesnake. You'll enjoy it." He removed it, cut off a hefty chunk, and offered it to her.

"Rattlesnake?" she asked, faintly ill. "Are you certain it is edible?"

"More so than that chicken you cooked."

Judge took a sizable bite and started to chew. "Umm, good. Dig in."

Victoria watched him devour his portion, then turned her attention to hers. Hesitantly, she picked a bit of meat and sampled the rich flesh. "Why, this is good."

Judge smiled as she seemed to forget her high class manners, attacking the food with gusto. When they'd finished, Judge took his handkerchief, leaned over, and wiped the corners of her mouth. He handed her a canteen and she drank greedily.

"Looks like you're learning there is more to life than fancy gowns, crystal stemware, china, and linen tablecloths." Again he visualized her in a white apron, meeting him after a hard day on the range.

Victoria sat up a little straighter. "Just because I am forced to resort to dining with my fingers does not mean I intend to make a habit out of it."

"No. I'm sure you don't." He cast her a knowing grin which left Victoria strangely unsettled.

By the time they rode through the gate of the Lakes' farm, the sun was setting in a magnificent red-gold haze. Off in the field, rows of corn stood like green sentries. The weather-worn barn, which appeared as if it had endured many hard years, looked welcoming, as did the rough-hewn, two-story house next to it.

"How very quaint," Victoria observed.

Judge snapped in response, "If you can't be pleasant to the Lakes, then don't say anything at all."

She lifted her chin. "I beg your pardon. I am well-versed in proper etiquette. You need not concern yourself that I shall embarrass you."

As they neared the house, Victoria silently berated herself. She had been trying to make conversation, not denigrate the Lakes' home. Why was it every time she attempted to have any discussion with Jesse it became an argument? Maybe it was because their two worlds were so different.

The Lakes were standing on the broken-down porch when they dismounted. If Victoria hadn't known better, she would have sworn they'd been waiting for their arrival.

"*Jesse,* how are you, son?" Betsy Lake rushed forward and threw her arms around Judge. "We got your telegram this morning," she whispered into his ear.

"Bert." Judge pumped the slender man's hand.

Victoria noticed how well the pair seemed to fit together. Betsy Lake was about Victoria's height. Her skin, tanned and weathered by years in the sun, made it difficult to surmise her true age, yet Victoria guessed her to be in her early thirties. Her figure was nicely curved and she wore a neat cotton dress, much-patched but clean. Bert Lake was a little taller than Jesse, a bit thinner. He was perhaps ten years Jesse's senior, with neatly trimmed sandy hair and a mustache. His face was prematurely lined and his eyes were deep-set above full, smiling lips.

"Bert, Betsy, I want you to meet my bride, Victoria," Judge announced. "We've been traveling together for better than two weeks, from Saint Louis. If you have a spare room, a bed would sure be welcome. You know how hard the ground can be on newlyweds." He smirked.

Victoria was stunned silent. How dare he do such an outrageous thing after warning her to watch her tongue!

"Jesse, I think you owe this nice couple an explanation," she said through tight lips, waiting for him to retrace such a falsehood. Behind her indignation, his brazen lie gave her pause for reflection.

"We'll tell them all about it at supper."

"But—"

"Its all right, Tori. If it's one thing these good folks understand, it's two people in love."

Victoria opened her mouth, but shut it as Jesse pulled her to him and pinched her side, issuing a daunting look.

Once introductions had been made, the Lakes announced that they were just sitting down to supper and insisted there was plenty for everyone. Having eaten nothing but beans, her pathetic attempt at chicken, and rattlesnake for two weeks, Victoria decided to forgo demanding a retraction from Jesse until she could question him alone.

Betsy elbowed Bert in the ribs and said, "While Bert and I get everything set out on the table, why don't you two wash up at the pump. It's 'round back. There's towels on the line."

Judge grabbed Victoria's arm and escorted her toward the pump before she could offer further protest. When they were clearly out of earshot, Victoria swung on him.

"I demand to know why you lied to them."

272

"I was thinking of you," he said easily, and began to wash his face and hands.

"Me?"

"Of course. Here," he handed her the soap, "get busy. I don't know about you, but I'm starved."

"We are not going anywhere until you explain yourself."

"Look lady, you want to continue to be considered a lady, don't you?"

"My reputation is hardly in question," Victoria shot back, scrubbing her hands with a vengeance.

"Oh, I see. You'd rather have the Lakes think you were traveling with me, unchaperoned, for the last two weeks, just you and me. They aren't ignorant. They know all about the birds and the bees, and . . . love."

Victoria washed her face, which had turned crimson. She glared at him. He knew she did not want these kind people to think poorly of her. She fought an internal battle over the propriety of it all, finally rationalizing that it would only be for one night. She would never see them again anyway.

"Give me that damned towel!"

He chuckled at her language. "Seems you're changing in spite of yourself."

The inside of the house was decorated with odds and ends, and furniture Bert had crafted himself. Betsy had braided a rag rug for the front room, and had tatted doilies and sewn pillow covers. Her embroidery and stitchery added a homey air, and Victoria found herself admiring an intricate wreath, which Betsy told her she had woven from her own hair during the long harsh winters.

Supper over, Victoria put her fork down and, for the first time in weeks, felt as if she needed to loosen the

273

band around her waist. "That was delicious, Mrs. Lake." Victoria stood, her plate in her hand.

"Betsy, please. Now you just sit back down and relax. Bert and me will take care of them dishes. I know you must be plumb wore out and are anxious to get to bed."

Victoria shot an uneasy glance at Jesse, who remained all too smug. "No. Really. I want to help, actually."

"Nonsense. Bert, you clear the table while I show these two newlyweds to their room. You two just follow me." Betsy grabbed a lantern and started up the stairs before Victoria could offer further protest.

"Come along, Tori. I know how anxious you must be to get to bed."

Victoria shot daggers at Jesse as they made their way to a tidy little room at the end of the hall, away from the other upstairs bedrooms.

"Bert and me sleep downstairs, so you two won't have to worry none about disturbing us." She fluffed the pillows and pulled an embroidered cotton nightgown from the chest at the foot of the single bed.

Victoria's gaze settled on the single bed. One single bed. "Ah, we cannot possibly sleep in here," she muttered.

"Why ever not?" asked Betsy, startled by the woman's response. She studied her. She would never have guessed Judge would pick an Englishwoman. She was a beauty and, from the look of her, would be a dandy match in temperament for a man most thought no one would ever tame.

Betsy toyed with her ear. There was something unusual about the way Judge was acting. And that strange telegram he'd sent called for an explanation. But she and Bert owed him for lending them the money to save their farm, back in '78. They still hadn't been able to repay him, so she'd sagely kept from pressing him.

"Yes, Tori darlin', why ever not?" echoed Judge.

Oh, how Victoria would have liked to strangle that strong, handsome neck of his. "Because the bed is so narrow," she blurted out, sounding terribly uncouth.

"Don't you worry about that none." Betsy waved off Victoria's concerns. "Bert and me slept in that bed for six months when we was first married, and it served us just fine."

Betsy flitted about the room, opening the window and turning the bed back, over Victoria's protests. She was out the door for no more than two minutes when she returned with a very plain, blue calico dress in her arms. She shot Judge a conspiratorial glance. "You look as if you might enjoy a change of clothes. Why don't you take this."

"Oh no, I could not think of taking your things," Victoria protested. Betsy's clothing looked so worn that Victoria was sure the simple dress must be her best.

"I have others. If you don't let me give you this as a wedding gift, I'll feel very bad. Now, I want you to have it. It's the least I can do."

"You have already done too much," Victoria said, looking at the bed. "I shall only take it if you allow Jesse to pay you for it. After all, you have offered us your hospitality."

Judge peeled out several bills and ended the debate. "Thank you, Betsy. You have no idea how much the missus and I appreciate this."

Confused, Betsy said, "No, I don't suppose I do. Good night."

Victoria waited until she heard the woman's footfalls fade down the hall, then turned on Jesse. "All right,

Jesse, exactly what are you up to?"

"What do you mean?" He walked over and sat on the bed.

"This farm. Our 'marriage.' This room. This dress. *That* is what I mean. It is all much too convenient. You are up to something, and I demand to know what it is."

She was guessing. Judge decided to call her bluff. "Just be thankful you have a bed to sleep in tonight" He began to strip off his clothes.

"What are you doing?"

"Getting ready for bed. And I suggest you do the same."

"You are not sleeping in here with me."

"Why not? We've slept together before."

Victoria blushed to her toes. "That was a mistake."

Judge's eyes darkened and his gaze raked her. "No. It was no mistake, Victoria," he murmured. "Now, take off your clothes."

She stared at him a moment before silently admitting defeat.

"At least turn your back." Her heart was thumping wildly despite her resolve not to repeat the glorious lovemaking that had happened between them in the past.

Clad in only his trousers, Judge moved to stand in front of Victoria. Instinctively, she raised her fingers to the wiry hairs on his naked chest. She could smell the musky odor that was Jesse, causing her senses to reel. Standing mesmerized by his nearness, she watched as he began to unfasten the buttons down the front of her blouse. Her flesh flamed at his touch. She nuzzled her cheek against the back of his hand as he slipped the shirt from her shoulders. She was lost, just as she had been every other time he had come near her, until a knock at the door brought her rudely back to her senses.

Victoria scrambled to cover herself as the door opened and Betsy Lake peeked in. "Sorry if I interrupted anything," she said awkwardly. "I forgot to fill the pitcher so you two would have water." She went about her task with efficiency, then quietly slipped from the room.

"Now let me see, where were we?" Judge bent his head to kiss Victoria, but she stepped back and quickly slipped the cotton gown over her head.

"No. Please." She waited for a response. When none came, she continued. "I shall not try to deny I want you, because I do. Despite everything, I cannot seem to help myself," she admitted with great difficulty. "But tonight, while we are here, please, will you just hold me?"

A ragged breath escaped Judge and he whisked her into bed, cuddling his large frame the length of hers. She had made a profound confession tonight, bringing him closer to the knowledge that, whatever the outcome of the land dispute, he was not going to be able to let her go—no matter what he told himself. Words of love formed in his throat, poised on his tongue ready to escape his lips, but Judge forced them back. He had to wait. He had to be cautious and patient, he reminded himself. The two virtues he did not possess.

Victoria lay in his arms, relishing the feel of his warmth. He could have insisted on bedding her and she would have relented, that was how much resistance she had when it came to Jesse. He had not; he had respected her wishes. How many men would have had the strength to deny themselves under similar circumstances? It said a great deal about the man, and further complicated the love she felt growing for the big cowboy.

Tomorrow afternoon they would be back in civilization. The thought both excited and frightened Victoria. The opinions and values she had held dear for so long seemed to be changing faster than she could assimilate, but tomorrow she would once again be Victoria Elizabeth Torrington, named after two queens, a woman with a mission, a woman with responsibilities and obligations, a woman engaged to be married to another man.

Chapter Thirty

Judge dressed, and left Victoria to bathe the best she could using the pitcher and basin. His arms still warm from holding Victoria's body next to his all night, Judge headed down to join Betsy and Bert in the kitchen. Bert was out already, slopping the hogs. Betsy was alone, frying a mountain of pancakes, when Judge came up behind her and gave her a hug, which she promptly threw off.

"Now that we're alone, I think you might try telling me what's going on." She stood waving the spatula in her hand. "And I don't want no double-talk neither. Sit down and have a cup of coffee while you talk."

Judge complied out of longtime friendship with the woman. He took a sip of the hot brew and said, "Well, since I couldn't have you, Betsy, Victoria was my next choice."

"Don't try to pull the wool over my eyes, *Jesse* Judge Colston. That telegram you sent said a lot more than it didn't say. For instance, I know the two of you aren't married," she said pointedly.

Knowing she wouldn't accept anything less than the

truth, Judge poured out the story, save whether he was or wasn't actually wed to the beautiful Englishwoman, and their intimate relationship—that was strictly between Victoria and him.

Betsy listened, her arms folded over her chest. Then she added her own words of wisdom. "It seems to me that you could spare yourself a lot of grief if you'd sit down and talk it over. I like that gal. She's not out to cheat you. Besides, it isn't going to make much difference in the end anyhow." She served him a stack of griddlecakes and insisted that he eat while they were hot.

Judge crinkled his brow. People were always so free with their advice. "What do you mean?"

"If you're married, it don't matter. If you're not, the way you two look at each other, you soon will be. Any fool can see you two are in love. You two just have to admit it to each other. You know, playing with fire usually gets a body burned. Why not save yourselves a lot of trouble and just get it out in the open now?"

"Get what out in the open?" Victoria questioned, coming into the kitchen.

Judge sat at the table, nonplussed. Behind his indifferent pose, though, his breath nearly caught at the sight of Victoria in the simple calico dress. She appeared so different, dressed as she was, so natural, so lovely. His vision of her waiting for him outside the ranch house intensified.

Betsy started, then managed to compose herself, shadowing her eyes. "Your marriage, of course. Jesse told me it was a secret. That's why you were so bashful last night. But I always say that keeping secrets just ain't healthy for two folks so much in love as you and your man." She gave telling looks at Judge and Victoria. "Sit down and get some good food in you before you start out for town. *Jesse,* you can go visit with Bert before you leave."

A deep frown settled over Judge's face at being dismissed so readily. He sent Betsy a warning look, then grudgingly took his cup and left.

"He's quite a man, that one." Betsy piled pancakes on Victoria's plate.

"Yes, he is," Victoria said absently, and started dutifully pushing the food around her plate.

"Bert and me have known him a long time." Betsy took a cup off the shelf, poured herself some coffee, and settled across from Victoria. "He helped us save our farm after we'd given up. Been a lot of gals trying to get their hooks into him. Never seen him go to so much trouble for any of them like he's done for you, though." She closely watched Victoria's expression. " 'Course, he didn't bother to marry any of them."

Betsy was pleased with what she saw. The Englishwoman appeared quite unsettled; it was a good sign. "I'm going to give you the same advice I gave Jesse. When two people are as much in love as you and that man, it's important that you hang on to it. Don't let *things* get in the way of your love."

"I am afraid I do not understand what you mean," Victoria said, shaken at the woman's perception of her feelings for Jesse. She averted her face, replaying the intimacy which had spawned between them. Loving pictures of their time alone together developed before her, and she remembered her willing response.

Betsy scratched her head and sighed. She'd had her say. "Just mark my words. Oh dear," she suddenly jumped to her feet, "it is getting late. You two best be off if you're going to make it to Cheyenne this afternoon." Betsy fluttered about the kitchen and packed a basket of foodstuffs, before going outside where Judge was waiting with the horses.

Betsy hugged Judge and Victoria, then shaded her eyes against the glare of the sun as they mounted their animals. "Wait up just a minute, I'll get you a bonnet. You've already gotten more sun on that white complexion of yours than is good for you."

Betsy handed Victoria a blue pasteboard bonnet. Victoria tied it beneath her chin. She thanked the couple for their kindness and swung her mount around. Jesse was staring at her, a strange light in his eyes. The unspoken hunger in his face sent shivers down her back and she straightened in the saddle.

The bonnet added to Judge's vision of Victoria. He still worried that she was a schemer, but now a different feeling had emerged: an unwavering hope for their future together. He longed to prove that Victoria wasn't the kind of woman a part of him still feared she was.

As they rode into Cheyenne, Victoria was delightfully surprised. She had been led to believe that the city was quite uncivilized, but though there were few trees or shrubs, its wide streets were lined with a variety of good shops. Victoria's hand ran over the plain cotton dress she wore. It was so different from her usual attire. Yet it was so functional, even pretty in its own simple way. Although she had no intention of dressing merely to please a man, she had to smile at the effect the dress seemed to have had on Jesse.

They passed three hotels before Victoria spurred her horse alongside Jesse's. "Where do you suppose Gerald and Lani are staying?"

The question made Judge pause. "Anxious to see your fiancé?" he asked in a low voice.

"No. I . . . yes —"

His brows drew together darkly. "What is it, Tori?"

She sat straighter in the saddle under his close scrutiny. "If you are attempting to provoke me, it is not going to work. Of course, I look forward to seeing my family."

He spurred his horse ahead. She hadn't mentioned Gerald by name, and this gave Judge a small measure of satisfaction.

They rode through town until they reached a decorous street of sprawling mansions. Judge reined his horse through the heavy gates shielding a magnificent house which rivaled those of the East.

"Does this, per chance, belong to Judge Colston?" Victoria asked, astounded at the wealth displayed out on the wild frontier.

"The man is not as wealthy as you may hope."

"For your information, I do not care how much money Judge Colston has. I am only interested in disposing of the portion of his ranch which belongs to me. Rightfully, I might add."

Judge sighed at her dogged persistence with the topic. "I guess you'll soon see for yourself how much your portion of the ranch is worth."

Judge slid from the saddle and helped Victoria to her feet. His hands lingered around her waist, his eyes on her upturned face.

Awkwardly, her emotions in turmoil, Victoria broke the spell his touch threatened to weave about her. "Are Lani and Gerald staying here too?"

Skirting yet another question, Judge dropped his hands. "Before you see them I think we need to talk.

You have to admit that a lot happened to us while we were on the trail. A lot we need to discuss," he blurted out, wanting her to come to him now and bare her feelings for him.

"Jesse, please."

"Jesse, please, what?" he grumbled. "What are you trying to say? You had a nice little interlude and now you want to get back to your neat, smug, little life?" He grabbed her arms. "Is that what you are trying to say? Or could it be that a poor cowboy isn't good enough for you now that you are back in civilization?"

Tears formed behind her lids. She bit down on her bottom lip. Her emotions were too raw, too new to put them to words. "No. That is not true."

"Then what is true?" he demanded, pushing for some type of acknowledgment of what they'd shared.

She shook her head back and forth, taking in a ragged breath. She squared her shoulders and brushed off his grip. "Until I have met my obligations, I cannot think of myself and what I want or do not want."

They were met at the door by a servant informed of their arrival by the owner of the house, a friend of Judge's. Quite used to carved staircases and crystal chandeliers, Victoria did not sound forth the usual oohs and aahs. Her nonchalance caused the man to assess her more closely.

Higgins, as he had introduced himself, had been employed in Boston to come west with his employer. The butler still clung to the formal coat and starched shirt of his genteel past. Fielding the lady's questions, he explained that he had been instructed to receive them, conveying Mr. Hancock's apologies that he would not be in residence during their stay.

At Victoria's questioning gaze, Judge clarified, "The

judge often stays with friends when he is in town. I thought you might appreciate the change after staying in hotels since your arrival in this country."

"Yes. It was thoughtful of you. I would like the opportunity to freshen up a bit before we join the others."

"Very well, miss," Higgins responded, a confused expression on his face. There were no others, but his instructions had been quite succinct. He was not to offer explanations of any kind to the lady. In fact, he might have questioned the propriety of her station if not for her stately carriage. Higgins moved around them and had begun to ascend the stairs when the lady's resounding squeal halted his progress.

"My luggage! My luggage has finally arrived! I feared I would never see it, or the documents to the ranch, again." She rushed to her trunks and fingered the heavy cases almost reverently.

"You mean to tell me that all the while you ran around Washington, D.C. creating such a ruckus, you didn't have those blasted papers to substantiate your claim?"

"It did not matter. The papers do exist, and now as soon as we reach the ranch, Judge Colston will be forced to acknowledge our partnership. And I shan't have to worry about having that dreadful red suitcoat laundered, and I can return to some semblance of style," she announced.

Judge did not share Victoria's joy at the arrival of her bags. He liked seeing her in calico. It suited the woman he secretly hoped she was, underneath that iron exterior. If only she would continue to cast off the stiff airs of custom she had begun to shun while they were on the trail. With the return of her damned wardrobe and those documents, Judge feared the return of the hardened woman he had first met.

"Your luggage arrived but a short time ago, Miss, otherwise it would be awaiting you in your room. I shall see that it is taken up to you at once."

"Thank you."

They proceeded to follow the man to their guest rooms, and Judge found he would be forced to relinquish the closeness with Victoria he had come to relish. There would be no more nights under the star-studded prairie sky; they could no longer share the same blanket, a single bed, while wrapped in each other's arms. He watched the door shut him apart from her, and vowed they would not remain long in Cheyenne.

Instead of resting, as he had suggested Victoria do, Judge left the residence and went to the telegraph office to send off a couple more wires. It was now more important than ever that his instructions for preparation of the ranch he intended to show Victoria, be followed. Before returning to Hancock's place, Judge checked at Dyers Hotel to make certain Ozzie had left town, and then stopped by the marshal's office. There had been no trace of Clancy.

After Judge had bathed and changed into fresh attire, he joined Victoria in the library for tea. She was dressed in a tailored, navy blue, afternoon dress.

"I do hope you do not mind having tea in here. I asked if there was a book about Wyoming which I might borrow until Lani and Gerald return from their outing. Higgins was kind enough to allow me the freedom of Mr. Hancock's collection."

"Did you find what you were looking for?"

"He has many fascinating volumes, but nothing current on the area." She positioned two cups in front of

286

her on the tray. "Tea is such a refreshing drink. Since we seem to be alone at the moment, would you care to join me? I do detest taking tea alone."

Judge turned down her offer, poured himself a stiff three fingers of whiskey from a nearby tray, and swallowed the amber liquid. "Victoria, your sister and Pelthurst are not here."

"No. They must be out this afternoon, otherwise they surely would have met us at the door," she returned in misunderstanding, setting her teacup down."

"No, Victoria. They are not in Cheyenne."

Worry formed in the depth of her blue eyes. "But they were supposed to meet us here. The judge was supposed to see them to Cheyenne safely." Her color drained, leaving her deathly white. "They were not harmed by that wicked man you left by the river, were they?"

"No, Victoria," he said quietly. "No harm has come to them. While you were resting, I learned that they left with the judge for the ranch since they did not know when we would arrive."

"But Lani and surely Gerald could have waited here for me. I do not understand." She sunk heavily onto the leather sofa.

"Miss," interrupted Higgins, coming into the room, "I do believe that this may provide some sort of explanation. It was left for you yesterday." He offered her a note, added hot water to the teapot, and withdrew from the library.

Judge's first inclination was to grab the letter from her and read it. On the envelope, Victoria's name was written in the same swirling loops he had seen Lani make. It had indeed been penned by Victoria's scatterbrained sister. He could not be certain of the contents.

Judge shot a slitted glance at the scrap of paper held between those delicate fingers. All his carefully laid plans could come crashing down around him, if Lani had indeed managed to learn of his ruse.

"Why don't you fix yourself another cup of tea before the water gets cold," Judge suggested, as she set about tearing the missive from its encasement.

"Yes, I think I shall. But first, I want to learn why my sister did not wait in Cheyenne for me."

Chapter Thirty-one

Judge held his breath as Victoria's eyes scanned the note left her by her sister. What had started out as a simple trip to New York to thwart a spinster's attempt to steal part of his ranch, had turned into a terribly complicated mess. Another look at the incredible woman he had come to love halted his thoughts, and he waited for her to speak.

"This message confirms that they have gone on to the ranch to wait." A light of disappointment flickered over her face.

"Something wrong with that?"

"I suppose not. I just thought they might have wondered whether we had successfully eluded those men, and waited to find out, that is all."

She seemed so vulnerable at that moment. So alone without the support of family and friends, so unlike Victoria Torrington, that Judge moved to sit next to her on the sofa.

"Victoria, the judge knows I'd take good care of you.

No doubt Judge Colston figured it would be safer for them to wait at the ranch, in case there was some type of conspiracy."

"Oh, no." Her demeanor immediately changed to a protective hardness. "You do not think that dreadful man would try to harm my sister, since he missed his chance with me, do you?"

"If he had that idea in his mind, which I'm sure he didn't, the man wouldn't have a chance to carry his plan through once your sister is safely at the J Bar C."

"In that case, how soon can we be ready to leave for the ranch?"

Judge was amazed at the resilience Victoria possessed. At the same time, relief settled over him that he wouldn't have to come up with a ruse to keep her from exploring the city, where Judge was sure to run into acquaintances who might reveal his true identity.

"As soon as Higgins can pack up some food."

She swiveled to meet his gaze. "Would it be possible to travel in some other manner?"

Judge frowned. He took her to mean that she wished to separate herself from him. Perhaps she regretted their intimacy and wanted to make sure she wasn't placed in that position again. He'd find out. "Don't worry, there is no way two horses could pack all those trunks of yours."

Victoria let out a sigh of relief. "Thank goodness. While I enjoy riding, I cannot say it is my favorite form of long distance transportation in this warm weather."

Judge smiled at that, and rose to leave.

"Where are you going?"

"To hire a buckboard." Judge left to quietly outfit the buckboard he'd driven to Cheyenne when he and Ozzie had left for New York.

Much to Victoria's irritation, Jesse insisted they wait until morning to leave for the ranch. The sun had not yet risen when they bid Higgins farewell and pulled out of town. The buckboard was laden with her trunks, and Jesse had insisted that they tether their two saddle horses to the wagon. The shadows of night rapidly faded into the dazzling colors of day as the sun peeked into view and began its climb into a vast sky.

They stopped before noon so Victoria could rummage through her trunks. Judge took care of the call of nature in some nearby scrub, watered the animals, then waited patiently, sprawled out under a tree, until she rejoined him, a large shade umbrella in hand.

Judge pointed to the white umbrella. "That is what it took you so long to find?"

"Quite." Victoria dabbed at the perspiration beading her face. "I have already marred my complexion enough out here. And it appears it is going to be beastly hot today."

"Can't argue with you there." He rose and, to her surprise, began to unfasten the buttons at her neck. He had half expected her to step back out of reach and protest, but she stood before him, silent.

Her flesh was hot and moist beneath the fashionable jacket, sending searing messages through Judge's fingertips. Responding to her inaction, he drew the jacket off her shoulders and dropped it to the ground, along with the umbrella.

He opened the top of her blouse and massaged the column of her neck. Without conscious thought, he captured her lips and held them as he lay her down at the base of the tree. Joining her, he felt the swell of his need inspire his touch to grow bolder. When Victoria did not protest, his caresses moved to her breasts.

The thud of hooves in the distance caused Victoria to regain her head. She sat up and hurriedly straightened her attire, as three riders passed them on the road with grinning faces.

"We needed to rest the animals," Victoria lamely offered.

"Yes, ma'am." The eldest tipped his hat, not fooled for an instant. "We can see for ourselves the need you two had to take care of." They chuckled and rode off.

Victoria glared at Judge, her cheeks flaming at her uncontrollable passion for the American cowboy. "Why did you not say something in our defense?"

The moment had passed. Judge regained his feet and helped Victoria up. "I'm afraid you said more than enough for both of us."

For the remainder of the day, they continued in silence. Passing riders stared, curious at the sight of Victoria stiffly sitting next to Jesse, her large umbrella held over their heads. The countryside was flat, the roads poor, and the buckboard jolted continually. By the time they stopped at what Victoria described as a road ranch, she was road weary.

Disappointment echoed in the back of her mind when she learned that Jesse would sleep in a large public room with the other male travelers, while she was to be housed in a separate room. Supper was table d'hote, and proved to be wholesome fare.

That first night was sadly duplicated for the next three nights, until Victoria desperately longed to sleep outside under the stars, with Jesse beside her. Although he had not said more than casual words since those men had passed them on the trail the first day out, Victoria could feel his suppressed passion in the tenseness of his body next to hers.

"How much longer will we be traveling?" Victoria ventured to ask after they had left the last overnight stop.

"We should be at the ranch tomorrow. I'm afraid we'll be camping tonight. But you should find our spot interesting. We'll stay at the base of Independence Rock. It's a place where many of the emigrants who came across country in covered wagons stayed. Sort of a favorite place to rest before continuing along the Oregon Trail. Some call the landmark the Register of the Desert."

"Why is that?" she asked, her interest piqued.

"Because the huge boulder is covered with names of the people who passed that way. Many scratched their names and the dates right into the granite. Others painted their names with wagon grease. The Sweetwater flows close by its base. You'll be able to freshen up before we reach the cabin. By the way, there's not much in the way of facilities at the ranch. I'm afraid you might not wish to remain long."

"How far away are we once we leave Independence Rock?"

"From there we'll only be a half-day's journey from the ranch."

Victoria squared her shoulders. "Then if need be, we can always return to the river when I need to bathe."

Judge studied her. Nothing seemed to daunt the determined woman. Well, she was in for quite a surprise.

The weather was cooling fast as big, puffy, black clouds began rolling across the sky to the west. Off in the distance, lightning flashed, putting on an electrifying display as they stopped at the magnificent rock

293

formation.

Not waiting for Jesse, Victoria ran to the base of the rock, which covered several acres. Moss grew out of the many cracks in the granite mound's surface. Victoria climbed up its base and ran her hand along two of the names etched deep into the grain.

"Look there, carved near the top." She pointed in awe, despite the rudeness of the gesture. " 'Hunter Brody loves his Dancing Wind, Forever, 1847.' This is absolutely marvelous," she squealed, turning to come face to face with Jesse's strong features.

"I thought you might enjoy seeing it."

"I do. Would it be terribly presumptuous of me if I added my name, do you think?"

Her glee, almost childlike, unmasked another side of the complex woman, and at that moment Judge could not deny her anything. "I'll get a tool for you to work with."

While Judge set up camp under a sky darkening with the approaching storm, Victoria set to work. By the time supper was ready, she had added her name to the noble monument. She had selected an area near its base, away from the American pioneers' names, out of deference for their struggle to reach the western frontier. Before they ate, she proudly had Judge preview her work. When she again sought his counsel, he laughed at her determination that her marks be precisely placed.

Supper consisted of a tin of beans mixed with dried beef, and leftover bread, which Judge had secured from the last place they stayed. He handed her a cup. "Better get something hot in you. I'm afraid it's going to be a long, cold, wet night, the way those clouds are heading our way."

Victoria looked up at the sky, nearly an opaque black. "Thank you. It appears you are right. Perhaps we should travel on to the ranch house tonight."

"Not the wisest thing to do in a thunderstorm."

"Well, then, at least pull the wagon over by that stunted tree. It should offer some protection."

"You don't know the first thing about survival, do you?"

"I am not out in this godforsaken wilderness by choice."

Judge scratched his ear. "I guess I can't argue with that. But under a tree is the worst place to be in a thunderstorm; lightning strikes the highest point. We'll take cover under the wagon. It's not as high as that tree you suggested.

"But let's not sit here discussing the storm any longer. We need to get some rest before it hits. I made a bed up for us over there, under the wagon."

Without a word, Victoria positioned herself comfortably among the nest of blankets and held the corner up. "Are you not going to join me?" At his blank stare, she added, "We may need to share our body heat."

Judge laughed. "I guess you have learned something about survival out here after all."

They lay together watching the yellow bolts streak the sky until Judge could no longer stand the nearness of her without touching her. "Tori," he murmured, "let me make love to you tonight. This may be the last chance we have to be close to one another, and I need you."

Victoria remained silent, reeling from the simple confession which said so much. Strangely, she had been feeling the same way. They had bonded together while making the unscheduled trip from Saint Louis, and

Victoria knew that when they joined the others tomorrow, her life would once again fall into the path set for her.

Judge took her silence for consent, and began sweetly to torment her lips. The threatening storm raged above them, while Judge's gentle hands caused her to moan with ardor. Slowly, expertly, he applied subtle pressure to her breasts, causing them to stand erect in furrowed peaks.

Victoria's mind began sliding away amidst his ministration, and she moved in response to him without conscious knowledge. Her body came alive, rocking and swaying with his manipulations. First her breasts, then her woman's center, were set ablaze by the lightning in his touch.

Massaging, stroking, and dipping into her moist heat, Judge made her writhe, crying out with desire and begging that he join their bodies. Unable to delay his own supreme joy any longer, he clutched her to him and drove into her waiting core. She gasped at the power of his thrusts, then began to move in rhythm with him as he plunged farther into her welcoming tightness. Together they reached the heights of sublime ecstasy, shuddering at the overwhelming strength of their release just as thunder rolled overhead and lightning lit the black sky.

At the splattering of rain around them, Judge regretfully disengaged their bodies, using his to shield her from the cold. The storm built into a pouring rage, yet it could not compare with the tumultuous emotions raging within him. He finally fell into the quiet void of sleep.

Victoria awoke with a start from a dream in which she had been swimming — with good cause, she found.

She was lying in the midst of a puddle. "Jesse. Jesse!" She shook him until he opened his eyes. "We must get up. We are soaked!"

"So we are." He grinned, lifting the soggy blanket.

They crawled from underneath the wagon to be greeted by a brilliant sunny morning. Victoria's spirits sagged as she picked through her things. The storm had been so fierce that the rain had managed to seep into the trunks, leaving the contents nearly as wet as the dress she wore.

"Please. Forget about breakfast," she said, noticing Jesse's efforts to start a fire. "I would like to hurry along to the ranch so I can secure a fresh change of clothing." Sputtering over her appearance, she snapped, "I can hardly wait to return to civilization."

Judge's expression hardened. He threw out the water he had gotten for coffee and stomped out the smoldering fire. "Well, in that case, let's not spend any more time in this wasteland, your highness."

Judge quickly hitched the horses, and they spent several hours in silence, each fretting over the emotions which had entwined them.

It was two forty-five when Jesse reined in the horses outside one of the most dilapidated shacks Victoria had seen since her arrival in the West. The boards were precariously nailed to its haphazard exterior. Tattered, faded yellow curtains hung at the three very dirty windows. The entire structure leaned, causing Victoria to wonder whether a good puff of wind would blow the building over.

Victoria was hot and tired as she waited for Jesse to continue on their journey. Her dress was caked with dried mud stains, her arms and legs were streaked with smudges, and her shoes still sodden. "Why are we stopping at this disgusting shack?" she spat, when he made no effort to spur the team on.

Judge's lips split into a triumphant smile. "Because, your ladyship, you have arrived."

"Arrived? Arrived where?" she demanded, close to losing her temper.

"At the ranch, of course."

Chapter Thirty-two

Victoria stood in disbelief as she surveyed her surroundings with sinking hopes.

"What do you mean, I have arrived at the ranch?" she said angrily, voice raised. "I have arrived at *whose* 'ranch'? I use the term quite loosely."

"This is the J Bar C," Judge announced, expecting her to insist he head to the nearest town.

"But this is not a ranch. All that is here is a broken-down shack out in the middle of nothing but dried brush, and surrounded by a few scrawny cows and buildings in worse condition than this . . . this house." Shocked by the environs, Victoria swung her arm out to further indicate her point. "This cannot possibly be Judge Colston's ranch. There must be some dreadful mistake."

"There's no mistake, unless it is the one you made in thinking you were going to suck some wealthy rancher dry." The minute the words were out of his mouth, Judge regretted them, for Victoria's face faded from murderous red, to pink, to tinted white.

"I told you why I came to this country," she said

softly, walking over to the sagging front steps and sinking onto the splintered floorboards.

"Since you can see for yourself that you have nothing to gain by pressing your claim, perhaps you would be interested in returning to your precious civilization. Maybe Judge Colston will be able to scrape together a little something to help you out."

Victoria had felt a momentary defeat at the state of the house, but Jesse's suggestion of charity on the part of Judge Colston gave her renewed strength. Maybe the house itself was not worth much, but the land surrounding it had to have some value.

"Absolutely not. If necessary, I shall sell off my portion of the land," she announced, rising to stand her full height before the now glowering cowboy.

Incredulous, Judge choked. "You'll do what?"

"This land is as much mine as Judge Colston's. I shall simply sell my part," she repeated. "I am sure there must be someone at one of the neighboring ranches who might be interested in buying some of this land."

"Luther Jessup," Judge grumbled absently, before turning such an icy glare on her that Victoria could have sworn she saw pure hatred in his eyes.

"Who?"

"No one," he snapped and went to the horses to begin unhitching them. Why he thought he was in love with the schemer he could not fathom. He yanked her trunk from the buckboard, sending it to the ground with a loud thud.

"Just because you are upset with me, it does not mean you have to take it out on my luggage," Victoria snapped, rising to check the container for dents.

Judge grabbed her arm and pulled her up until she

was staring into his stormy face. "Of all the women I have ever known, you and you alone seem to have a special talent for making my blood boil."

"I could say the same thing of you." Never before had she met a man like Jesse; never before had she lost her heart. But she was not going to be driven from this land—not even by the man she loved.

She raised her chin higher. "Well, at least you are willing to concede I hold a special talent for something."

A bit of devilry turned his lips up at the corners. "Oh, your highness, I am willing to concede that you hold a very special talent for making my blood boil in more ways than one."

Victoria pinched her lips. She knew exactly to what he was referring. "You, sir, are without honor."

Judge glared down at her luscious mouth and snapping blue eyes. God, she was a beauty. She would never make anyone a compliant wife. And yet, despite the spats that continually erupted, he kept visualizing her as his woman. Perhaps it was because she reminded him of the land he loved so much. She was untamed, and could be hard and unyielding, though at other times, she offered more bounty than he had ever dreamed possible. In his arms, she was molten fire, eager to match his lovemaking, eager to give as much as she received. These thoughts cooled his temper.

He released his grasp. "Why don't I show you the barn while I tend the horses."

"I should like to wash first," she announced, keeping her ground.

"One thing you might as well learn right now, is that a man's horse is one of the most valuable possessions he has out here." The glimmer of an idea sprouted in his mind. "You can wait until *we* have seen to the animals' needs."

"We? I thought *you* were going to see to the horses."

"I've changed my mind. Since you insist you are part owner of this spread, you might as well start learning how to take care of it, Tori."

Judge handed Victoria the reins of the two saddle animals. They led the team toward the makeshift barn his men had tacked together, as his telegram had instructed. Ozzie had seen that the men followed through with his plan to have a line shack on the farthest, driest corner of the ranch readied for Miss Victoria Elizabeth Torrington.

"I intend to burn that damned red suit coat," she sputtered as they cooled down the horses. They watered them from four rain barrels, set just inside the barn door, and put them into ramshackle stalls with a supply of hay.

"I didn't know fancy Englishwomen were given to swearing," he smiled.

"You simply bring out my worst side," she defended, astounded at herself.

"And your best, I might add."

"You might not! Now that the chores are finished, I would like to bathe."

"I thought I told you there wasn't a stream near here."

"Surely there in running water in the house, is there not? This ranch of Judge Colston's cannot be entirely lacking amenities."

Judge grinned all the more. "See that little wooden building with the half moon on the door, about ten

302

feet from the back of the house?"

Victoria followed the line of his vision. "Yes. So?"

"So, that is as fancy as the amenities get out here."

Victoria narrowed her eyes at him and went to investigate the facilities. She opened the door, then immediately slammed it shut, stepping back and holding her nose. "Surely you must be jesting. I cannot possibly be expected to use something so, so . . . ," her voice trailed off as she searched for a word to adequately describe her horror.

"Something so beneath you, your highness?"

He was not going to make her lose her temper this time, she vowed silently. "Even in your country I thought more appropriate facilities would be available."

"Of course, if you prefer you can use the bushes."

She glared, but she was not going to give in to his attempts to make her leave the property. "I shall make do with what is available. Now, where is the water so I may bathe?"

Judge crossed his arms over his chest and leaned indifferently against the barn door. "You have already been making use of it for the animals."

Her brows flew up. "You mean we use the same water, from those barrels inside the barn?"

"You are quick this afternoon."

Victoria quietly counted to fifteen to calm her nerves before striding over to the barrels. She took a bowl hanging on a nail over the wooden cylinder and ladled two measures into the basin. She sunk the dipper into the cool water again and was about to add more when Jesse hollered at her.

"Just what do you think you're doing?"

"Just exactly what it looks like," she returned sarcastically.

"Well, you can pour that right back into the barrel."

"I will not."

Judge took hold of her wrist and dumped the ladle of water back into the keg. "Water is a precious commodity out here. If you haven't realized it by now, water is hauled in on the wagon. So starting immediately, you will be forced to ration it like the rest of us do."

Surely she wouldn't want to remain at the ranch under these conditions. Judge waited for her to request a ride to the nearest water. Her face had become suffused with a flaming red, and he had no doubt she would like nothing better than the comfort she was used to.

"The rest of you? Do you mean to tell me that there are others who live inside that . . . that house?"

"Not all the time. Most of the year it's just Judge Colston and me. But during roundup time the boss hires on three extra hands to help out."

Victoria let out a sigh. Sleeping arrangements were going to be unspeakably tight until her claim was settled. Attempting to ignore him, Victoria washed her face and arms the best she could. About to throw out the water, she halted when his voice assailed her once again.

"What do you think you're doing?"

"If you will excuse me, I was going to toss out the dirty water."

"I won't excuse you. You will save that water to use later if you think you are going to scrub up again today."

Victoria shot daggers at him, slamming the bowl

down, and headed for the house. Jesse's chuckle made her stop in her tracks, tempted to turn around and give him a piece of her mind. No. She would not give him the satisfaction. She continued toward the cabin. Upon stepping up on the stoop, she had to push her body against the door to force it open.

She put her palms to her cheeks. "Oh, dear Lord!"

Judge came up behind her. The men had done a better job than even he had expected. The one-room line shack was a disaster. A bed sat at an angle from the corner and was piled high with dirty clothes. The mattress appeared quite unutilizable, unless its stuffing could be gathered and slid back inside. A potbelly stove stood covered with opened tins and a pan full of food now fallen prey to a horde of ants. A handmade table and two chairs were littered with paper, dirty plates, and sundry items. An old sofa big enough for two people adorned the last available corner; it, too, had seen better days.

Judge hid a wicked grin. "What's the matter, Tori?"

She swung around to look at him. "You actually live this way?" She was horrified.

Judge felt a stab of guilt before remembering why he had brought her here. "I suppose it lacks a woman's touch. And it might stand a little cleaning."

"It might be better to burn it to the ground and start over," she said, surveying the shack's cluttered contents.

"Should I hitch up the team? No doubt you would be more comfortable if I took you back to New York, where you can take advantage of all American civilization has to offer. Then you can take the first ship back to England and your preferred way of life."

Even as Judge spoke, he knew he was being insincere. In reality, he did not want her to leave him—just to forgo her claim to his land. As he waited for her response, he wanted her to come to him, only to him. He wanted to hear that it didn't matter how they lived, or where, as long as she were with him. He had to beat down the desire to take her in his arms.

Victoria ignored Jesse's last stinging remark and watched her step, careful not to trip over the mess scattered about the floor. She picked up the articles of clothing, pushed back the rags which hung at windows too dirty to see out of, and walked over to the shelf, staffed with a full supply of foodstuffs. Once she had made a complete survey, she tossed a dirty shirt at him.

A puff of exasperation escaped her lips. "There is no doubt in my mind I would be more comfortable in a New York hotel," she began. "But you are going to find I do not give in so readily. After we get the table area cleared, I would like something to eat."

"If you don't like the accommodations, it'll be your responsibility to straighten them up," Judge announced, leaving her glaring after him.

A can crashed against the door as he shut it behind him, but Judge was smiling at her spunk despite himself. He waited for her to come out after him, as more banging and clattering issued from the shack.

He went to the buckboard and began unloading the rest of her luggage. Out of the corner of his eye, he noticed Victoria come out and lower herself on the top step. Another wave of guilt washed over him. He had been rather hard on her. God, how he wanted to whisk her away.

As Victoria sat with her head resting in her palms, watching that irritating cowboy she loved so bloody much batter her luggage, a fancy carriage drew up in front of her.

"Victoria!" squealed Lani. She alighted in pale green frills and joined her sister on the stairs, throwing her arms around Victoria. "I was so worried about you. Oh, sister dear, what have you done to yourself?" Lani chided, startled at Victoria's bedraggled appearance. "You have always taken such pains with your appearance."

Victoria bristled, but quickly smoothed at her lifeless blonde hair. "It is good to see *you* again, Alayne," she returned, suddenly realizing that she had been too distraught to notice the absence of Lani or Gerald and the judge.

"I am sorry. I did not mean anything by it. It is simply that you look so different," Lani amended.

"Considering the conditions under which we have been traveling, I would say my appearance is not out of the ordinary."

"Of course." Lani sneaked a peek at Judge. His face was shuttered, although his hands were rolled into tight fists. "Haven't you missed us, though?"

To Judge's chagrin, Gerald and Ozzie stepped out of the carriage at that moment. "Victoria, I say, you gave us quite a start running off with that," Gerald shot Judge a look of disapproval, "person."

Gerald shrank at the disapproving looks shot his way by the others. Judge then cast his dark look toward Ozzie, who shrugged.

"Oh, Lani, I have missed you terribly. I was worried, leaving you the way I did. Thank heaven Judge Colston brought you to the ranch." A question suddenly occurring to her, Victoria asked, "By the way, how long have you been here?"

Chapter Thirty-three

Lani's gaze shifted uncomfortably at Victoria's question. She bit down on her quivering lip before she managed to take a deep breath.

"Well, to tell you the truth, Victoria, Gerald and I are not staying here at the ranch, and neither is the judge," she blurted out, unable to think of an elaborate explanation.

Victoria shot a questioning glance at the judge, then back at Lani. "If you have not been residing here at the ranch, where have you three been stationed?"

Judge's murderous gaze settled on Ozzie. The old timer cleared his throat and attempted to satisfy Victoria before everything got out of hand. "They're stayin' at a neighborin' spread. There was just enough room for them. I met the owner in Cheyenne, and he suggested it'd be the best place for them since they was used to all the comforts an' all."

Lani quickly went on to explain that, unfortunately, all the guest rooms were now occupied. When Victoria suggested that they move to the J Bar C with her, Lani was quick to refuse, citing her weak and delicate constitution.

Although Victoria had never considered herself delicate or weak, she was not prepared to remain on a property so utterly run-down as this. "Well then, perhaps I shall return with you. This is a dreadful place."

Judge moved next to Victoria, casually leaned over and whispered, "What's the matter, Tori, can't you take it? You British too soft?"

Victoria straightened her posture. He had insinuated that the English were unable to cope, and in doing so had issued a direct challenge. "Lani, you and Gerald may return to the amenities you were enjoying, but I intend to remain right where I am. And you, Judge Colston? I hope you plan to return to your residence so we may conclude our business as soon as possible." She shot Jesse a heated look. "I have no doubt you are as anxious as I am to return to our normal lives."

Ozzie didn't hesitate this time. He knew what was expected of him, yet that little filly sure spoke the truth. No one wished more than he that this whole mess was settled so he could get back to worrying about no more than his horse and the grub Cookie served at the chuckwagon. "All in good time, little gal. All in good time."

Judge cast Victoria a wolfish grin. "I guess that leaves you and me, highness. Unless, of course, you are afraid to stay here alone with me."

"I say, this is highly irregular," Gerald protested. "You cannot allow this man to squire you about, unchaperoned, in this desolate wilderness."

"Jesse is not going to be squiring me about, Gerald. He will take up residence in the barn and continue his duties. This ranch obviously cannot afford any further neglect," she added for Jesse's benefit, forcing herself to accept yet another delay.

"But, Victoria—"

"No, Gerald. Until my claim can be settled, I have no intention of leaving this property." She linked her arms with Lani and Gerald's. "Do come inside and let me show you what I shall be left to contend with."

Once they had gone inside, Judge hissed, "What the devil are you up to, old man?"

Ozzie shrank at the vehemence of Judge's tone. "Nothin', boy."

"Nothing? Why didn't you tell me you were the one responsible for this mess? I know you got that money you loaned me to start my spread from Victoria's father, years ago. And, obviously, you forgot to pay the man back. Am I correct?"

Ozzie hung his head. "Sorry, Judge. I just up an' forgot."

"Why didn't you tell me the truth in the beginning?"

"Ah geez, I knowed I shoulda come clean. But I . . . I guess I—"

Judge sighed. "Forget it. It isn't going to do any good now. Just keep that scatterbrained sister and fiancé out of my hair."

"Judge," Ozzie's Adam's apple worked up and down at a furious pace.

Judge did not like the old man's nervousness. "Now what?"

"Lani and Gerald know who you are," Ozzie said rapid-fire, before he up and lost his guts.

"What?"

"I told 'em. But don't worry none. They won't spill the beans."

"Chrissake!" Judge exploded. "Get in there and get

them the hell out of here and back to the house before they ruin everything." Ozzie swung around to do Judge's bidding. He cringed as Judge snarled after him, "And *keep* them the hell away from here!"

Judge fumed while Ozzie made a hasty departure with his two charges. He watched the carriage disappear, then swung around to Victoria, only to have the door slammed in his face. As he raised his fist to pound against the portal, it opened and a shower of dirty clothes flew out at him.

"What the hell?" he snapped, gathering up the clothing.

Victoria stood framed in the doorway with her hands on her hips. "Since it appears I will be remaining here for a while longer, I intend to make this hovel livable."

"Then where do you want your trunks, ma'am?" He reverted to his most grating drawl. "I'm sure you'll want to change into one of your fresh dresses so you will feel more at home, Miz Tori."

"My luggage and your sarcasm will have to wait. Go fetch a bucket of that precious water of yours. If it's necessary, you'll bring another barrel full. I simply shall not begin rationing water until the filth that is this *house* has been scrubbed from every board."

"I didn't think one reared as you, highness, would know how to clean up after someone else—let alone yourself."

Victoria scowled. "There is a lot about me that you, apparently, do not know."

Judge shook his head, gracefully admitting defeat in this round of the battle. "Maybe not, but I have the distinct feeling I am going to find out."

Judge smiled to himself when she took up a broom and began furiously sweeping, surrounded by a cloud

311

of dust. He was heartened by her refusal to return to the many creature comforts the actual J Bar C provided. His hands in his pockets, Judge whistled as he strolled to the rain barrels. Victoria Elizabeth Torrington, named after two queens, defied every effort he made to classify her. She had more courage than many men he knew, more spunk, more grit, and, he rolled his eyes, just enough sheer cussedness to succeed — if she weren't up against someone just as damned determined.

Clancy gripped his gun so hard his knuckles whitened. He narrowed his eyes, slinking back behind the rock so he wouldn't be discovered among the boulders not more than a hundred yards from the line shack. It was a mystery to him why the boss wouldn't let him pick off such an easy target.

His lips tightened as he rubbed his pained knee. He'd get Colston. The bastard had crippled him with that shovel.

The son of a bitch Colston had left him in sheer agony, tied to a tree along the riverbank. Then he had had to endure the humiliation of that riverboat captain's snicker as his rescuer cut his bonds. Unconsciously, he fingered his knife at his side. He had taken good care of that captain. After the crew had set him ashore, he'd snuck back aboard and slit the captain's throat. The whore's son would never laugh at him, or anyone else, again.

Movement outside the shack brought Clancy back from his musings. He stayed hidden in his vantage spot for another hour, until he was sure he had seen enough to report back. Quietly, he mounted his horse and headed for Jessup's ranch.

Bent on the successful completion of his covert mission, he stopped at Colston's place to pay a call on one of the hands in an effort to learn what he could. He'd followed that fancy carriage with those two Brits and Osborne out to that broken-down shack, expecting them to return with the blonde. It made no sense to him that Colston and the woman would remain behind. But at least he knew where they were hiding.

By the time Clancy reached the J Circle L he was thoroughly confused. He hadn't learned anything the boss hadn't already told him. And although everyone knew where Colston was, the hands were to treat him like just another one of the boys. He realized that all the suspicions the boss'd had were correct. Colston was trying to put one over on that highfalutin' lady he'd been keeping company with.

He left his lathered horse at the stables and headed toward the main house. Standing in front of the stately two-storied mansion were Jessup and his wife, engaged in a heated argument. Never one to let an opportunity for useful information slip by him, Clancy slithered to the side of the house and listened.

"Why didn't you tell me what you were up to?" spat Helene.

"You're lucky you're still useful to me as Jeremiah's mother, or I just might consider sending you packing to a bordello, where you belong." Luther puffed on his cigar, his face white with rage. "Next time I catch you tying to sneak through my books, I'll rip that pretty little yellow frock right off that luscious body of yours and let the hands enjoy you, before I kick you out the way you came—with nothing!"

Helene's pretty face twisted. "I wouldn't even attempt to threaten me if I were you, Luther." She quickly readjusted her stance and slid her arms around the old fool. Sweetly, she cooed, "I know too much about your business dealings, darling. Besides, I know how much *you* enjoy this luscious body of mine." She rubbed against him, ignoring the heated stares she was receiving from the hands.

Luther pushed her back and slapped her, leaving the red imprint of his hand across her face. "You're a good piece of ass, I'll grant you that. But if you ever breathe a word about my business affairs, I promise you, it will be your last breath."

Holding her stinging cheek, Helene said, "What about Jeremiah? I'm his mother."

"Yes. He's the only decent thing you've done in your whole life. You're lucky I love the boy, or I might cast you both out."

"Luther, he's your son."

He chewed on his cigar, disgusted at the whore he'd married. She was a spitfire, dishonest, scheming, manipulative, and as close to evil as the worst. Perhaps that's why he kept her around. The plotting, no-good bitch reminded him of himself. "And as for Colston and that Torrington woman . . ."

Still arguing, the pair moved out of earshot. Clancy could only hear swatches of the conversation, but he dare not sneak closer. There was too much activity outside and he could not chance discovery. He cursed his luck. He'd hoped to listen to the entire argument. People often let slip things they wouldn't normally say when they were angry, and Clancy wanted to be in a position to take full advantage of any interesting scrap of information he could pick up.

Clancy rubbed his painful knee. There was more going on than what he'd been told by the boss. Colston's name was coupled with that English broad's in reference to some papers Jessup had in that office of his. Damn! He'd sure like to have about fifteen minutes alone with Jessup's personal accounts. Then he might be able to cash in by selling what he knew.

He didn't give a hoot who had hired him. There was no such thing as loyalty as far as Clancy was concerned. The only thing that mattered was that he wrung out as much hard cash as he could from whoever was paying. If it meant he sold out the one who had originally paid him, what the hell, he figured. His motto had always been: if you're going to get yourself mixed up in games, then you'd better be prepared to best the other players and come out on top — no matter what you had to do.

As he crouched back into the shrubbery to wait for the most opportune time to speak to the boss, twenty dollar gold pieces flashed before Clancy's eyes. Pressing his fingers together, he could feel the unparalleled splendor that cold, hard lucre could buy. Damn! He loved them cartwheels.

With a flashing hatred, Helene's eyes followed the overstuffed hog she'd married. Luther labored down the front steps, wheezing, and waddled toward the corral at the left of the house. He tossed the disgusting cigar he constantly chewed aside and took out a fresh one.

The bitter smell of his nasty habit was always about him, and Helene could still taste it from the last time he'd forced a wet sloppy kiss on her with those thick lips. His belly preceded the rest of him by a good three inches, causing her to recall the last time he'd taken her. She'd felt as if she were being ground into the mattress by his bulky form, while he'd grunted and snorted his satisfaction. She'd acted the fully sated lover, all the

315

while wanting to vomit as his meaty hands had groped her crawling flesh.

"Well, Luther Jessup," she sneered in his direction. "You may think you have the upper hand. But you don't, you old fool. You'll pay for the way you've treated me. And soon, oh yes, so soon, I'll have all your wealth and Judge Colston, too."

Chapter Thirty-four

For two weeks Judge watched Victoria ply her hand to the shack, scrubbing floors, washing windows, and fighting the dust which continually blew in between the cracks in the walls. The windows were adorned with the new curtains she had hand sewn from the skirt of one of her lovely blue dresses. She had rolled up her sleeves, tied back her hair, and gone to work.

Hands which once had been soft and well-manicured were now rough and red, the nails split. Dirt streaked her face by the end of each day. But she washed using no more than one ladle full of water, carefully reserving what was left for the few flowers she'd had him transplant from a blooming expanse near the stream where they'd gone to refill the barrels.

He had to give her credit. She had even taken over the cooking chores, making do with the old potbelly stove and few utensils. He had to smile at the meals she turned out: black, crusty beans, cremated bacon, bread which could have been used to border the flower bed outside the shack. Yet she hadn't given up and demanded he take over the food preparation, so he'd eaten her efforts without comment.

The sleeping arrangement was another matter. He'd bunked with the horses for about as long as he intended, he thought, stabbing at the hay and thrusting it into the stall. His temper at her insistence that he keep his distance at night was close to getting the better of him. He vowed that this enforced self-denial was about to come to an end. With a swipe across the beads of sweat dotting his forehead, Judge dropped the pitchfork and went to the rain barrel. Today would be a nice change from the back-breaking work Victoria had had him doing.

The cool water he splashed on his face was soothing on such a hot day. After washing his face and arms, and pulling a comb through his wavy black hair, Judge donned his chaps and tied a bandanna around his neck. Ready to fetch Victoria, he strode toward the house, only to be met on the steps by a vision in white.

One glance at Jesse and Victoria's vibrant smile faded. "Why are you not dressed?" she asked, appalled that they would no doubt be late.

Since Jesse had announced he was going to take her to an opera, Victoria had been looking forward to this day. She had taken special pains with one of her favorite gowns, a lace and satin off-shoulder creation by Worth. The flowing skirts were sprinkled with pink silk flowers. She had made every effort to cleanse her white umbrella to provide shade during their trip into town

Judge raised his brows. "I am dressed."

"What I meant was, shouldn't you be attired a little more formally to attend an opera?" she ventured. Jesse had been the perfect gentleman the last couple of weeks, gallantly working beside her to cleanse the ranch house from top to bottom, so she could not very well chide his efforts. That red kerchief he wore might

318

be the best clothing he had, she told herself. She had not noticed anything nicer and she knew the bag he'd had with him on the train had not yet been delivered.

"I think I'm dressed just fine to attend the opera we're going to. Though you might want to change your clothes. I don't think you are—"

"You do not have to think. I know perfectly well what attire is appropriate for an opera. I have undoubtedly been to many more than you have," she stated flatly, jutting out her chin.

Judge brought his palms up. "Have it your way. If you want to dress like that, who am I to try to tell a lady such as yourself what to wear?"

"Precisely."

As they headed for the opera, he thought she was the most obstinate woman he had ever known. He had been about to tell her what she was in for, but she, as usual, put up such a fuss he had decided to let her find out for herself. They'd make quite an entrance arriving as they were, the fine lady and the cowhand.

Sitting proudly erect with her umbrella in hand, her gown swept about her, Victoria would long be remembered as the best-dressed woman ever to attend the event. As they neared their destination, Judge wondered whether he should have suggested such an outing, and hoped that Ozzie, for once, had taken care of the details so that no one would slip up and call him by name.

"Why are we stopping here?" Victoria asked, annoyed at the side trip on such a warm day. She was already covered with a thin coat of dust and certainly did not need to stop at some dusty corral out in the middle of nowhere. "Shouldn't we hurry along before we are late?"

"We're not late. It hasn't started yet."

To Victoria's horror, Jesse jumped down from the buckboard and went to talk to a group of men sitting on a fence. She tapped her fingers, impatiently waiting for him to conclude his business so they could be off. Growing more vexed, she watched him head for a smaller corral where about twenty horses were housed, survey the animals, then head back toward her.

"Please, we must be going. I hope to get seats near the stage; I do enjoy opera so. By the way, Jesse, you neglected to tell me which one we shall be seeing." She took out a lace handkerchief and dabbed at her neck. How good it would feel to sit in a cool theatre and lose herself in the music.

"Don't worry, highness, I've reserved front-row seats." Judge reached up to help her down.

Victoria swatted at his hands. "What are you doing? Should we not be going now?"

"I told you we were going to the opera. Now what's the matter, have you changed your mind?"

"Of course not!"

"Then let me help you down before it begins."

Victoria's expression underwent a metamorphosis. "I have the distinct feeling I should have asked to which kind of *opera* you were referring."

For the first time since he'd met her, she was behaving reasonably in the face of her frustration. He should have explained what an opera was out West before he had brought her.

"Victoria, we're at the opera," he said sheepishly.

She slowly looked about her. She should have known! Jesse was not the type of man to enjoy a cultivated theatrical presentation. Patches of red worked their way up her cheeks. She was sorely tempted to give him a good tongue lashing. But working side by side with the big cowboy had given her an understanding of what this wild country meant to the man. She had slowly come to realize that there was more to life than being ensconced behind a mahogany desk in a spacious office, single-handedly building a shipping empire. She and Jesse were also building something back at the ranch. She could not quite put a name to how it made her feel, but warmth flowed through her veins just thinking about it.

Her smile was tight when she asked, "Exactly what is an *opera* out here?"

"Horse-breaking watched by people who sit on a fence surrounding it." He waited for her to start berating him, then added, "Bronco busting."

Victoria looked down at her gown. "I am not exactly dressed for *bronco busting*." She took a deep breath. "But if you will help me down," she swallowed, "I . . . I . . . oh, what does it matter, I shall take my place at that front-row seat you reserved."

A delighted smile that she was gracefully accepting the day's activities nearly set his heart on fire, and a glowing warmth radiated from his lips.

As Judge helped the spirited young woman onto the fence next to several of the outriders from his ranch, his dream of her standing on the porch of his house materialized stronger than ever. He was sorely tempted to throw off his masquerade as Jesse. No. He'd wait until tonight. As soon as Ozzie arrived, he'd order the old man to send Chang over to the shack with a special supper. He'd tell her then, and they'd settle the issue of the ranch so he could begin courting the lady properly.

Judge introduced her to the cowboys, then turned to leave as two fine buggies drew up a short distance away.

Lani and Gerald alighted from the first carriage. Judge's face hardened as Luther Jessup helped Helene and Jeremiah from the second. Before he left Victoria's side, Judge promised to direct her sister to her, and then left her with his men.

"Oh, Ju— I mean Jesse," squealed Lani, dressed in plain cotton and sporting a western hat. "This is ever so exciting! We have never seen anyone tame a horse before, have we Gerald?" She linked arms with the dandy.

Judge turned cold eyes on the English pipsqueak wearing denims and a plaid shirt. "I see you two have made yourselves right at home."

"Yes. We are having such fun at the ranch," Lani said, waving to Victoria. "Hello, Victoria. Oh, Jesse, we really must join my sister." She giggled as they left him and went to the fence by Victoria.

Judge pushed his hat back on his head and scowled as Ozzie approached. "How did the Jessups learn we'd be here today?"

Ozzie shrugged. "Don't rightly know, 'cept some of the men are chummy with Jessup's hands."

"Well, see that you keep them away from Victoria while I'm busy with the horses."

"Sure 'nuff."

Ozzie had already turned to head off the Jessups when Judge stopped him. "Ozzie, send one of the boys back to the ranch with orders to have Chang make a special supper and send it over to the shack tonight."

Ozzie's crooked grin lit up his face. "Ya two gettin' on a mite better, I see. Glad t' hear it. It's 'bout time." He chuckled, ignoring Judge's dark frown, and hurried off to carry out the brusque rancher's instructions.

After fielding questions about her inappropriate attire and how she had been getting on at the ranch with

Jesse, Victoria made room for Lani and Gerald beside her on the fence. They were so engaged in chatter that Victoria let the other people who had arrived in the fancy carriage slip from her mind, until the couple and their child climbed onto the fence a short distance from them and nodded a cordial greeting.

"We must introduce ourselves after the opera is over," Victoria announced. She stared at the boy, under five years old from the look of him. There was something about the boy's features which were reminiscent of what Jesse might have looked like as a child. But then she glanced at the child's father. The boy was a miniature of the big man, except for his blue eyes.

"Opera?" Gerald queried.

"Of course. This horse-breaking display we are about to witness is called an opera out here."

Lani giggled. "Do not tell me you are growing fond of living out here in America's Wild West. You have become so knowledgeable."

"Nonsense," Victoria insisted. But silently she admitted that her behavior had been undergoing a distinct transformation during the last month. "Now, hush up and watch the show."

All eyes turned to the first cowboy to come out the gate. A choking dust flew up around the wild animal as it bucked furiously, its hooves flying in the air as it tried to dislodge the rider seated atop its back. Hoots and hollers went up each time the horse left solid ground, sending the cowboy out of the saddle, his outstretched hand waving in the air, until the man was unseated and sent crashing to the dirt.

Victoria soon found herself enjoying the show and enthusiastically cheering each rider on, causing Lani and Gerald to gape at the change in the usually staid,

323

sober young woman. Rider after rider tried to best one another by remaining seated longer, only to meet a similar fate upon the ground.

When the men stopped for a noon break, Judge rejoined them, with a basket Chang had packed slung over his arm. "I've set up a picnic under that tree over there." He motioned to a lone pine away from the rest in attendance. Judge wanted Victoria as far away from the Jessups as possible, but as luck would have it, they stopped the small party near the end of the corral.

"Hello, *Jesse*," purred Helene, giving Judge a wink. She bent down and gave Jeremiah a gentle shove. "Run along and look at all those big horsies, honey. Maybe one of the men will let you ride one." She watched the boy scamper off, then her eyes settled on Victoria, whose arm was tucked into the crook of Judge's elbow.

If that pig Luther hadn't warned her not to ruin Judge's disguise, she would have taken pleasure in setting the English bitch straight about a thing or two. "And you must be Miss Victoria Torrington," she said cattily. "Luther and I heard you are staying out on the Colston ranch with Jesse."

Judge stepped forward. "Luther, why don't you and Helene come back to the corral with me? I have some interesting horseflesh I want to show you."

Luther took the cigar from his mouth; an evil smile twisted his lips. "Not now, *Jesse*." His gaze shifted to the woman. "Pleased to meet you, Miss Torrington." He offered his hand, ignoring Colston and enjoying his obvious discomfort.

The thought of finally having something with which to blackmail Colston appealed to Luther. At last, Colston was at his mercy. Suppressing the sudden urge to unmask the bastard now, Luther held himself back.

He'd play along with Colston's game until he was ready to make his move. Luther relished the idea of watching Colston squirm. The Torrington woman would never forgive Colston's deception, and the land would be his with little effort.

"I am Luther Jessup, and this is my wife Helene. I own the L Circle J, which borders Colston's spread."

Victoria crinkled her brow. "I do believe I have heard Jesse speak your name before, Mr. Jessup."

So she had been paying attention when he'd mentioned Jessup as one of the parties who would be interested in buying her portion of the ranch. Troubled, Judge listened while the rest of the introductions were made and Victoria invited the Jessups to lunch with them. Jessup was up to something, and Judge wondered what. Bothering him more, though, was that somehow the pair had found out about his ruse.

Gerald offered his hand. "Mr. Jessup, Gerald Pelthurst's the name. Could we have met somewhere before, sir?"

"The wife and I were recently in Saint Louis. I believe we stayed at the same hotel in that city. Perhaps it was there," returned Luther casually.

"Yes, of course." Gerald rubbed his temples and finished the introductions.

Chafing to rid himself of the Jessups, Judge was forced to sit through lunch expecting to be unmasked and wondering if Pelthurst was planning to go to Jessup as a buyer for his ranch. To his surprise, the conversation remained amiable. As they were preparing to return to the afternoon horse-breaking activities, Helene grabbed his arm in front of Jessup.

"Luther, why don't you assist Miss Torrington and see to Jeremiah, while I help Jesse by carrying the blanket back to the buggy."

Luther glared at Helene, then, a calculating grin on his lips, offered Victoria his arm. As they left Judge and Helene standing alone, Victoria looked back over her shoulder, staring at Judge, until her attention was drawn back to Jessup.

"All right, Helene, what are you and Luther up to?" Judge demanded. "And how did you know Victoria calls me Jesse?"

"Oh, Judge honey, a little old bird told us," she offered cutely.

He dug his fingers into her arm as he dragged her back toward the buggy. "If you don't want me to wring that beautiful neck of yours, you better talk."

"People are starting to stare." He squeezed harder. "All right," she hissed, grabbing her arm back. "One of our ranch hands overheard your men talking, if you must know."

"I don't care how you do it, but take Luther and your son and go home."

"Why? So you can have that Torrington woman all to yourself? What about me, Judge? What about us?" she cried.

He ignored her fit of jealousy. "What about you, Helene? Have you forgotten you're a married woman with a husband and young son?"

"Judge, that's what I've wanted to talk to you about. It's Jeremiah."

"Come on, boy, you're up next," hollered Ozzie, coming to get Judge. "Miz Jessup, I think your husband's lookin' for ya t' join him."

"You always pick the most inopportune times to show that ugly face of yours, you old coot," Helene sneered. "Judge, please don't forget, I must speak with you. It's vitally important." She gave Ozzie a curt nod meant to show her hatred, and stomped back to join her husband.

"She's up t' no good, I can feel it," Ozzie said, walking toward the horses with Judge.

"Quit worrying, she only wants to talk about Jeremiah. You know how much I like the boy."

"He's Jessup's kid. Don't go forgettin' that."

As they reached the corral, one of the hands was trying his best to hold a fierce black stallion which fought every effort to subdue it.

The whites of Ozzie's eyes doubled. "Ya ain't plannin' t' try and break that one, are ya? Ya know no one has been able t' soften that beast t' the saddle yet. And a lot has tried."

"You worry too much, old timer." Judge left Ozzie, swung up onto the top rail, and lowered himself onto the back of the mighty stallion.

Victoria screamed as the gate swung open and the horse charged forward with Jesse atop it. Bucking, wildly kicking, and turning around to bite its burden the black beast careened around the corral, putting up a vicious fight.

"Don't be so concerned, Miss Torrington," Helene cooed, noting the way the Englishwoman watched Judge with that special sparkle in her eyes. "*Jesse* is one of the best."

Helene had barely finished her sentence when, horrified, Victoria slapped a hand over her mouth to stifle another scream as the stallion gave a snorting kick. The beast sent Jesse flying over its backside to the ground, only to turn on the downed man and begin stomping him with its powerful hooves.

Chapter Thirty-five

"Oh, my Lord, no!" Victoria screamed. All morning she had attempted to keep her gown as clean as possible, but when she saw Jesse fall and that demon horse begin to slam its hooves down on his unconscious body, she forgot about the white gown and ran to him.

By the time she reached him, the cowhands had corralled the crazed stallion and led it away. Victoria dropped to her knees. Crying, she loosened his shirt and placed her palm on his heart. He was alive.

"He's alive. Hurry, bring a wagon. We must get him back to the ranch." Not waiting while the men ran to bring the buckboard around, she ripped strips from her gown and bound the gaping wound in his side.

Victoria was cradling his head, wiping the bloody streaks from his face, when Helene reached them. Luther, right behind his wife, held her back.

"He can't be dead. Tell me he isn't dead!" wailed Helene, causing Victoria to realize the dark-haired woman carried deep feelings for Jesse.

"He's still breathing," Victoria answered, sending a confused look at Helene.

"Come on, *wife,* it's time to go home," Luther snapped between his teeth, and dragged a trembling Helene away. As he helped his distraught wife and son into their buggy, Luther shot Gerald a narrowed stare. He ground his cigar around in his mouth, his expression cold and hard, before casting the butt into the dirt and joining Helene and Jeremiah.

"You three, lift him careful like. That's right. Watch his head. Ease him in the back there," Ozzie directed, once the buckboard had been brought around. Victoria sat in the back of the buckboard and bundled Judge as Ozzie slapped the reins over the horses' rumps.

It took close to three hours to transfer Judge from the corral and get him settled in Victoria's bed. Silently, Ozzie questioned leaving Judge at the shack, but Victoria dismissed him and sent him on his way.

"I'll get the doc and bring him out," offered Ozzie as he reluctantly left.

"Yes, Judge Colston, please do that. And do hurry."

When Victoria tried to remove Jesse's blood-soaked clothing she found the task impossible. Taking a deep breath, she went to the table, got a butcher knife, and cut his shirt and trousers off him. Without help, she had to tug to remove his boots. She stared down at him. Despite the bruises discoloring his muscled torso and the menacing wound in his side, Jesse was the perfect male specimen. With loving hands she bathed him.

Finishing up his bath, Victoria noticed that the nasty gash left by that monster horse had begun bleeding again. Unsuccessful in her search for any kind of bandage, Victoria rummaged through her trunk, then ripped one of her fine petticoats into strips. She worked with diligence to wrap him, often having to use her legs and body as well as her arms to get the lengths secured

329

around him.

A sheen of sweat glistened across his deathly pale face. She laid the back of her hand across his forehead. The heat of his skin blazed against her. She had to get that fever down. Remembering the baking soda on the shelf, she quickly ran to the rain barrel and returned with a bowl of cool water. She poured the white powder into the container and mixed it well, before dipping a cloth into the liquid and swabbing his fiery hot forehead. Then she fashioned a compress and laid it on his brow.

As she unfolded a sheet to cover him, she noticed that the wound still bled. She applied pressure, but the blood continued to seep between her fingers. Then she recalled that when she was a child, one of the servants had mounded flour on her finger after a playmate had accidentally snipped a hole in the fleshy part of her thumb while cutting dolls' clothes. She rubbed her finger over the grainy scar. Flour! It had to work.

She turned and ran for the sack in the corner, returning with a tin full of the white substance. Carefully, she eased the bandage from him and sprinkled the flour onto the gash. Over and over she repeated the process, until the blood began to coagulate, forming a semi-solid mass. Then she refastened a bunch of clean strips of material. To her relief, it worked. She raised the sheet to his gently rising and lowering chest.

Exhausted, Victoria pulled a chair over to his bedside and sat down to await the doctor's arrival, only leaving his side long enough to accept a basket of food kindly sent by a Chinese cook from a neighboring ranch. Periodically, she changed the compress. She worried whether he would live through the night.

And she prayed.

By the time the doctor arrived with Ozzie the next morning, Victoria sat slumped over in the chair, her head resting near Judge's shoulder.

"See? What'd I tell ya, doc. Them two's goin' t' be a pair, all right. That is if ya can save him for her."

"You know, Ozzie, I'll do all I can," Doc Lambert said. "Best get the little lady out of my way, first," the spindly man nearing sixty directed.

"Don't ya worry, I'll take care of Miz Victoria. But don't go forgettin' t' call Judge Jesse now, ya hear?"

The doctor frowned down his nose through his spectacles, but nodded his agreement before going to work. His stomach rumbled, reminding him how he had been comfortably seated at the dinner table in Casper when Ozzie, from the J Bar C, had barged into his home and hauled him away. Not that he minded. As a young doctor, he'd help deliver Colston, and he had always had a special place in his heart for the lad.

"What?" Victoria started as she was being lowered to the worn couch. Her eyes whipped opened to stare into the leathered, whiskered face of the judge. "Jesse. Is he—"

"It's okay, Miz Victoria, the doc's with him."

"But I must go to him."

"Ya lay back and rest. Ya ain't goin' t' be much good t' him if ya don't take care of yourself."

Despite the urge to ignore the old man's advice, Victoria forced herself to settle back against the pillows. He was correct, she did need her rest. She closed her eyes. Everything had seemed to happen so fast. One moment she had been enjoying the horse-breaking, then the next her world had suddenly shattered before her eyes, as that monster horse attempted to kill the man she loved.

"Well, will you look at that." Doc Lambert shook his head.

Victoria leaped from the couch, and she and the judge rushed to Jesse's side.

"What, doc?"

"Seems like there isn't much I can do."

"No!" Victoria cried.

"Don't worry, Miss—"

"Torrington. Victoria Torrington."

"Doc Lambert. Don't go getting yourself all riled up, young lady. I'd say you probably saved his life with that flour you used on him."

"Flour?" Ozzie scratched his head.

"Yes, this young woman packed that wound with the stuff and no doubt stopped Jesse from bleeding to death. Other than cleaning up the wound and giving him some medicine to keep him quiet and stave off infection, there's not much for me to do."

Victoria remained at Jesse's side while the doctor ministered to him. Once he slept peacefully, she made coffee, and the men enjoyed several cups before departing to return to town.

Victoria was bone-weary. But before she thought of herself, she had to change his compresses and attend his needs.

She lit the lamps and gathered her supplies. The warm light lent a heartening glow to his face, pale and shadowed with a heavy growth of stubble. As she bathed him, she found herself contrasting Jesse to Gerald. Jesse had such strength, an overpowering presence about him compared to Gerald, who had always leaned on *her* strength. The last month with Jesse had demonstrated the differences between the two men, and Victoria wondered how she ever could have thought Gerald the perfect match for her.

She lifted Jesse's wrist and began to scrub, remembering the gentle touch of his hands, his intimate, delving fingers. She bent over and slid the rag over his chest. His warm, moist breath whispered across the side of her cheek, sending rippling waves down her spine. With trembling hands, she finished her job, combing his hair, then lathering the shaving brush and applying a coat of the soapy foam over his growing beard. Tenderly, she scraped his dark visage clean and smooth.

Late into the night she hovered over him, until she thought she would drop. Easing back down into the chair, her head lolled to the side and she fell asleep.

For three days she repeated the process, unwilling to allow the judge, the concerned ranch hands, or her sister to help other than to bring in supplies, refill the water barrels, and take care of the animals.

On the fourth morning, as she moved about the shack with efficiency, Judge stirred and let out a pain-filled groan. He opened his eyes to see a vision standing over him, hands on hips.

"Oh, no, do not try to get up," she rasped, pushing him back down.

A sharp pain ripped through his side and Judge grunted. "What have you done to me, woman?"

"It is not what I have done, but what I am going to do if you do not stay put." At his look of confusion, she elaborated. "You went two rounds with a horse and lost."

"Did I put up a good fight?"

She let out a hearty laugh, tears threatening to spill from her eyes. His health was sure to return with his humor. "The best. You beat the day's record for staying in the saddle before that beast unseated you, then proceeded to trample you. The doctor from Casper patched you up, and the judge, and Lani and Gerald have helped out around here while you, sir, lounged in bed."

The door swung open and Ozzie stepped up. "I was listenin' just outside, and don't ya believe what she said for a minute. Miz Victoria is the one what saved that ornery hide of yours. She wouldn't let none of us near ya. Looked after ya all by herself, she did."

Judge's hand snaked down his side and returned with fingers lightly dusted with flour. "It looks like she used me for a bread board."

"A bloody loaf ya was too, boy. She stopped the bleeding with that there flour. Even Doc Lambert agreed that ya probably wouldn't be laying in that bed today if she hadn't see t' it that ya was well-cared for."

Judge wolfishly slanted Victoria a grin. "I guess there is more than one way to get into a lady's bed."

Victoria's color heightened and she slapped her hand to her chest. "Jesse. Please!"

Ozzie swivelled to look at Victoria. "Ya mind if I speak t' my foreman alone for a few minutes?"

"No . . . ah . . . no, of course not." She backed away from her patient, happy to escape from her moment of embarrassment, picked up a soft towel, and headed for the barn to see to her own needs.

Ozzie waited until he was sure she was a safe distance away, then said, "Judge, I don't want t' pry, but—"

"Then don't, old man."

Ozzie's Adam's apple bobbed. "Look, boy, I been doin' some nosin' 'round, and Helene is chompin' at the bit t' see ya. Jessup's got t' have somethin' up his sleeve too, not lettin' on he knowed who ya was the other day. But I'll be danged if I can find out what it is. If ya don't take care of business with Miz Victoria and soon, mark my words, somethin' awful's gonna happen. I can feel it in my gut. . . ."

"Oh, Gerald, Ozzie has gone over to see if he can help Victoria," announced Lani, sneaking into Gerald's room. She crossed over a fine native American rug, pushed back the heavy cotton draperies, and tiptoed over to perch upon the heavy four-poster bed in which Gerald lounged, propped against a mountain of pillows. "Do you realize that except for the Chinese cook, Chang, we are all alone in the house? Do you know what that means?"

Gerald pulled her to him, ignoring her squeals to be mindful lest he wrinkle the lacy creation she wore. "Yes, I know what that means, wife. It means I shall be able to remove your gown without worry." He grinned as his fingers made short work of the buttons lining the bodice.

Tumbling about the big bed, arms and legs entangled, they laughed together, exploring each other without hesitance.

"Wrap your arms around me, Lani," instructed Gerald.

Lani's green eyes deepened with color and she wound her milky arms about him, pulling his slender body to her. In turn, Gerald gathered her further into his embrace, murmuring in her ear, soft words meant to end their games so the final stage of lovemaking could begin.

Gerald's movements were awkward and broken, not imbued with the smooth sureness of one of vast experience. But to Lani, his fingers were fire, branding her

335

body as only Gerald could, until he sunk his staff deep into her and they moved with time's oldest rhythm.

Afterwards, lying next to his precious wife, Gerald teased at a loose curl. "Was it as good for you as it was for me?"

"Oh, yes, Gerald! And it will be even better when we no longer have to sneak about." She smiled into his eyes. "I shall be ever so happy when we have our own home, and Victoria understands and accepts that we are husband and wife."

"My Lani, I am ever so happy you came into my life." A burst of strength grasping him, Gerald added, "I think the time has come to tell Victoria she has lost me. Tomorrow we shall take the carriage over to where she is staying with that man, and have it out."

The smile slipped from Lani's face. She had waited to hear Gerald speak those glorious words, but tomorrow Ozzie had offered to drive her into Casper so she might shop at Judge Colston's expense. She so missed all the shopping sprees she had enjoyed back home in England, before her father's death, and this was her first chance to indulge herself since arriving in this country.

The western town certainly wasn't New York City or Saint Louis, so the trip shouldn't take more than a week by the time she visited the modistes and had had three or four gowns sewn. What was one more week? Hadn't she and Gerald waited this long? No, she decided, one more week could do no harm. Victoria would have to wait. This was an opportunity she just could not pass up.

"Gerald, sweetheart, would you mind terribly if we put off telling Victoria for one more week? Ozzie has invited me to go into Casper with him, and I do so want to take advantage of his hospitality and see as much of the West as I can while I am here," she said, carefully leaving out the details of the expense-paid shopping trip.

Gerald breathed a sigh of relief. His courage had already fled, and he dreaded facing the formidable Miss Victoria Elizabeth Torrington. And he had another matter to look into first; a matter which had troubled him since he'd first heard that bloke Jessup's name. "No. It is quite all right, love. In fact, I shall pack a bag and come with you."

"No! No, you must stay here," she gasped, not wanting him to learn beforehand of Judge Colston's generosity. Gerald's pride would be stung that he could not afford to buy her all the pretty things she enjoyed. "It would not present a proper appearance if you accompanied me — not until we inform Victoria, at least." She kissed him. "Besides, Gerald, I shall only be gone a week or two. What could possibly happen in that length of time?"

Chapter Thirty-six

"I am not staying in bed any longer!" argued Judge. "I feel fine."

"You may feel fine, but your body is not in any shape to undergo activity," Victoria insisted, standing over her patient with her hands securely settled on her hips.

"Oh, I don't know." Judge threw off the blanket, exposing his incredible male form. "I think I'm in pretty good shape."

Victoria gaped. There was no doubt he was a well-built male—exceedingly well-built! She averted her eyes.

"Jesse, please. I did not mean that you are not well turned. And please, cover yourself. You would not want to catch cold."

"Look at me, Victoria. You have seen me before," Judge rasped, snapping the sheet back over himself. "I said look at me!"

"Very well." She glared into those sparking blue eyes. "You may attempt to embarrass me all you care to, but you are not to leave that bed until you are completely healed."

He lay back, smirking. "When we first got here, you kicked me out of the house. Now you won't let me out of your bed. Hell, a man couldn't ask for anything better." He paused for effect. "Unless, of course, you would agree to join me."

"I will not!" She swung around and picked up his medicine and a spoon. "Open up."

Grinning, Judge allowed her to administer the medication. He puckered up his face. "What was that for?"

It was her turn to grin triumphantly. "It was a sleeping draught. That should keep you out of trouble for hours."

"Maybe so, but you are going to have to face up to the fact that, sooner or later, we are going to be together again, Victoria."

She had no answer to his statement. Instead she sat down on the chair and picked up a book, lingering by his bedside until he drifted off into a heavy sleep.

Once he was snoring softly, she busied herself around the shack. She hummed a gay tune as she clattered about the kitchen area, preparing the chicken the Chinese cook from the neighboring ranch had kindly been supplying.

The poultry simmering in a pot, she rinsed out a few of her unmentionables and hung them on a line Jesse had strung for her. Her indoor tasks finished, she checked on Jesse, then donned a pair of gloves and floppy hat she had earlier given up to gardening.

Puttering about the flower bed, she dislodged the few weeds determined enough to grow out on the Wyoming prairie. She raked up a well of dirt around each red Indian Paintbrush plant. Then she sprinkled each flower with the leftover water.

At the clop of hooves, she looked up, shading her

eyes against the glare of the sun. A fine carriage she recognized from the horse-breaking approached. Oh dear, her appearance was not fit for receiving visitors! She whipped off the flour sack she wore as an apron, and discarded her dirt-encrusted gloves and hat. She was still trying to repin some flyaway strands of blonde hair when the vehicle came to a halt in front of her. Victoria dropped her hands and stiffened her posture.

"Mr. Jessup, to what do we owe the pleasure of your visit?"

A cigar hanging from his lips, Luther lumbered from the carriage and removed a basket laden with vegetables. "Miss Torrington, I am sorry I hadn't the opportunity to come sooner after Jesse's tragic accident. But I'm sure you must be aware of the pressing obligations owning a ranch involves. My wife regrets that she was unable to come. She sent along a little something from the ranch." He set the container down as they continued to engage in small talk, watching her response.

Jessup'd had a man watching the line shack since Colston had been hurt. He'd been waiting for a more opportune time to approach the Englishwoman; he wanted her at her most vulnerable. But his impatience had driven him to take a chance this morning. Inwardly, he laughed. That black stallion had taken care of the accident he'd planned for Colston. Now all he had to do was get her signature on the documents authorizing the sale of her portion of Colston's ranch. He had to work fast, before the bastard regained his strength and ruined everything he had worked so hard for these last ten years.

Luther puffed on the cigar, causing Victoria to cough as the pungent smoke assailed her. "Mr. Jessup," she waved at the white rings drifting around her, "while I am certain we all have our vices, yours leaves me rather breathless, sir."

The bitch was implying he had a disgusting habit. His fists clenched at his sides. But he smiled, dropped the offending cylinder to the dirt, and ground it under his heel.

"I hope you will forgive me. I would have put it out sooner had I realized it was bothering you."

"Thank you, Mr. Jessup," she said coolly. "I have rarely been subjected to that base habit. You understand, gentlemen in my country generally do not indulge in the presence of ladies without first seeking permission."

"And how is Jesse? Is he up and about yet?" asked Luther, beating down the urge to remove another cigar from his pocket, light it, and blow smoke in her smug face. Over her shoulder, he glanced through the window, hoping to catch a glimpse of Colston.

Luther Jessup made Victoria feel uncomfortable. There was something quite ungenuine about him. "Jesse is feeling much better. I suspect he will be back to his duties in a day or two. At present he is resting. But if you would like to speak with him, I shall be most happy to —"

He put up a hand. "No, no, don't disturb him. Not unlike most men, I much prefer talking with a beautiful woman."

"Mr. Jessup, is there some specific purpose, other than to inquire after Jesse's health, of course, which brought you to the ranch this morning?" she probed, suspicious of his motives. "If not, sir," she picked up a bucket near the door, "I do have chores which I must attend."

Luther took the pail from her hand and started walk-

341

ing with her toward the barn. The building looked as if it had been thrown together, for ordinarily line shacks didn't have the luxury of such a shelter for the cowboys' horses. He had to give Colston credit. Whatever he was up to with the Englishwoman, he had planned well.

"Miss Torrington, I hope you do not doubt my reasons for this trip. My wife and I have known Judge Colston since he started his spread and have always been interested in his welfare."

They walked further, until Victoria took the bucket from the man. "I do thank you for coming by and bringing the fresh vegetables, but I really must get back to work now."

Luther was not going to be dismissed by a mere woman. "Let me help you, Miss Torrington. I'm sure a fine lady such as yourself is used to the finer things in life."

She disregarded his offer and began pitching hay. The bitch was ignoring him! Attempting to keep the hardening lines on his face impassive, he took the big fork from her and began feeding the animals.

"This is no kind of work for a lady."

As Victoria stood watching the man she guessed to be a little over fifty from his appearance, she had the strangest feeling. Although she did not like the man — his personality lacked warmth, and there was a cold, calculating quality about him which disturbed her — there was something about him which reminded her of Jesse. She studied him further. Yes, Jesse bore a slight physical resemblance to what Luther Jessup may have looked like as a young man, before his body had grown so out of proportion and his dark hair had silvered.

She picked up the bucket and began to fill it with water. "Mr. Jessup—"

"Luther, please, Victoria, if I may call you that."

"Mr. Jessup, we barely know one another. I think it proper that I continue to refer to you as Mr. Jessup, and must insist that you call me Miss Torrington for the time being," she returned. She had no intention of getting to know the man any better.

"Miss Torrington, in that case, perhaps you will accept my offer of hospitality. Come and stay at my home. I'll send several of my cowhands over to take care of your duties." He held up a hand. "No. No. Now, before you turn down my offer, think how much more comfortable you will be. I shall even provide you with your own personal servant during your stay."

"Mr. Jessup, while I appreciate your generous offer, I must decline. I am quite at ease here, and find the services of a personal maid unnecessary. I feel very much at home here, sir."

"Of course you do, my dear." The bitch! She was not cooperating at all.

"Mr. Jessup, if you have a point to make, I wish you would proceed. I must get back to my patient."

"I hesitate to mention it, but I hope you are aware that people have been talking about you staying alone here with Jesse. Mrs. Jessup and I only wish to . . . ah . . . shall we say, save your reputation from those wagging tongues who would mistake your well-meaning intentions."

The pompous pig! "I happen to be part owner of this property, and regardless of what anyone has to say, I intend to remain here."

At last, she had broached the subject he had come to discuss. He could see she was annoyed, but he knew her background. She was a shrewd businesswoman and had come to Wyoming to sell her part of the ranch and use the money to rebuild Torrington Limited. She would know a good deal when it was offered her.

Over her objections, he again claimed the bucket and took her arm with his free hand as they headed back to the house. "I didn't come here to discuss business, but rumor has it, Miss Torrington, that you are here in Wyoming Territory to sell your portion of Judge Colston's property. I might just be able to assist you."

"I cannot invite you in, Mr. Jessup. But if you will wait while I check on Jesse, I think I should like to hear what you have to say."

A conniving grin appeared on his face when she took the water and went inside. He was so close to success. He could taste it. He'd wrench the part of Colston's ranch containing the water rights away from that bastard before he knew what had hit him. Then he'd sit back and watch Colston fail; there would be nothing he could do about it. As a final blow, he'd tell the English-woman who Colston was, forever ruining Colston's chances with the woman.

A myriad of emotions circled Victoria as she took a handful of tea from the tin and poured it in the pot. She had come to this country to sell the land and save the family's business with the proceeds. Now that the opportunity presented itself in the form of Luther Jessup, she found it was not quite as simple as she'd thought. There were other considerations involved now. Her vision trailed over to her number one concern: Jesse. Luckily, he continued to slumber. She'd listen to Mr. Jessup; she owed that much to Lani and Gerald.

She set up a tray with the pot, cups and saucers, sugar, and napkins. She took the refreshments out to the steps and carefully shut the door behind her, so as not to disturb Jesse's rest.

"I am sorry, Mr. Jessup, I cannot invite you inside since Jesse is still resting. But if you would care to join me," she motioned to the tray and settled herself on the steps, "I would like to hear what you have in mind."

Luther's bones cracked as he lowered his heavy frame to take a seat next to the Torrington woman on the steps.

She poured the tea and offered him a cup. "Sugar, Mr. Jessup? I fear there is no cream."

"No, thank you. I like my tea strong and straight, with backbone." He sent her a knowing grin. "Just like I like my business associates." He took a sip. God, she made awful tea! He almost gagged it was so bad. Colston must have a stronger gut than he'd thought, for no doubt her cooking was no better.

"Shall we get down to business, Mr. Jessup?"

Judge awoke in a sweat and kicked off the extra blanket he found he had been covered with. Victoria. The woman was relentless. She'd either kill him or cure him with her efforts. The fragrant smell of chicken permeated the shack. She was cooking again. If he didn't get some good, edible food inside him and soon, he was sure he was going to waste away. She tried so hard, though. The sweet fragrance of tea filled his nostrils. His mouth felt like baked leather. Anything wet had to quench his thirst.

Disregarding Victoria's specific order to remain in bed, Judge rose. He located his trousers and slid into them, leaving them unbuttoned and loose around the tender wound, and headed toward the potbelly stove. As he passed the window, his attention caught at the sight of two heads, one blonde—Victoria—the other silver, and wavy like his own.

A scowl took hold of his features and he moved to stare out. Victoria sat next to Luther Jessup, a cup in her hand, intently listening to whatever Jessup was saying. His curiosity pricked, Judge unlatched the window and cracked it open. To his utter horror and disbelief, Victoria was discussing the sale of his property to Luther Jessup!

Judge's thoughts turned murderous as he heard the details of Jessup's proposal. The man must have learned about his efforts to prevent him from fraudulently laying claim to more land. Jessup was desperate to ruin him by getting a stranglehold on the water rights to the Colston ranch. Somehow, after the time Judge had spent with Victoria, he hated to believe she was about to sell him out. But there was no denying what he had heard. Well, he'd just see about that!

With practiced nonchalance, Judge opened the door and stepped out. "Hello, Jessup. What are you doing here?"

Jessup jumped and Victoria was startled, nearly dropping her cup in an effort to gain her feet. "Jesse, you are awake. I am so glad," she said, relieved that she no longer had to deal with the likes of Jessup alone. She went to him, but he pushed her away.

"I just bet you are," he scoffed.

Jessup noticed a chasm in their relationship. He hadn't gotten anywhere with the woman so far, but this could be a break for him. He rubbed his chin. He'd try to prey upon Colston's obvious annoyance at finding the Torrington woman speaking with him.

"I see you are up and about, *Jesse*. We were just talking about you." Luther's silent black stare issued a challenge.

"Jesse, please, you must not exert yourself," she urged. We were not talking about you." She swung on Luther. "Mr. Jessup, who was just about to depart, was merely attempting to be kind by offering to purchase my partnership in the ranch, that is all."

Luther stood up and nodded to Victoria. "Miss Torrington, please do give serious consideration to what we discussed." He gave Judge a curt nod and left.

Waiting until Jessup was well away from the ranch, Judge grabbed her arm. "All right, Miss Torrington, exactly what were you hoping to gain by giving me those knockout drops and then meeting Jessup under my nose?"

Chapter Thirty-seven

Despite the catch of her breath at the sight of Jesse's bare bronzed chest, Victoria seethed at the callous disregard for her that Jesse was demonstrating with his absurd accusations.

"What do you mean I was meeting Luther Jessup under your nose after giving you knockout drops?"

Every muscle in his body tensed, and though it took him most of his strength to remain standing, he was not about to let her stand over him at the moment. With his height, he hoped to intimidate her into telling him the truth.

"You, lady, insisted I take that foul-tasting liquid, then sat by the side of my bed until you were sure I was safely out of the way. Then what did you do, signal Jessup that the coast was clear?"

"Jesse," she said with a venomous snarl, her own temper rising, "for your information we are nowhere near a coast."

"Don't try to get cute with me. I want some answers.

And I want them now!" A sharp pain shot through his side and he had to ease himself back onto the bed. So much for that mode of intimidation.

"Are you all right?" She took a step forward, but his black scowl stayed her.

"Don't bother trying to change the subject." He grimaced at the pain, determined to ignore it and get some answers.

She threw him a disparaging look. "I am not trying to change the subject, as you so eloquently put it. And until you are able to act with civility, do not expect me to respond."

She whirled around and headed toward the door.

"No. Wait!" Judge grated.

"Wait? For what? To be yelled at and accused of feeding you knockout drops? Is that what I am to wait for?"

"No. Don't go," he said, softening.

"Then am I to assume you regret the disgraceful manner in which **you** addressed me a few moments ago?"

Judge had to swallow his words to keep from jumping up, pinning her down, and squeezing the truth out of her, she had so angered him. He'd never before laid a hand on a woman in anger, but no one before had made him want to, either. Slowly, he counted to twenty to temper his agitation.

He cocked a disbelieving brow. "No doubt you only had the best of intentions when you gave me the medicine."

"As a matter of fact, I had." She leveled him a cool stare. "Very well, now that we understand each other once again, I shall finish preparing your meal."

"What about Luther Jessup?" he asked, in a cautious voice meant to further disarm her.

She pinched her lips and stepped outside the door to retrieve the basket full of vegetables. "Mr. Jessup stopped to inquire after your health, and was kind enough to bring these fresh vegetables from his wife's garden."

Judge threw back his head and laughed. "Ha! Helene Jessup has never tended a garden in her entire life. As for Luther Jessup, he doesn't do anything unless he gets something out of it." A serious expression on his face now, he asked, "What did he want, Tori?"

"Since you obviously want something out of me as well, why not refer to me by my name?"

"Why can't you admit you rather like the nickname, Tori?"

Despite herself, her rigid stance relaxed and a smile tugged at the corners of her lips. "I have to say that you are the first person to ever coin such a name."

"And you like it," he probed.

Sincerity shone in his eyes. She sighed and bit her lip before answering, "Yes."

A concession. She had made a concession without argument. It was a step in the right direction.

"Tell me what Jessup wanted, Tori. It's important. The man has been trying for years to get his hands on Judge Colston's ranch."

There was honesty in his face. "The man offered to purchase my portion of the ranch. He showed me a map of the ranch, and the land he proposed appeared to be a far corner which borders his property on the northwest, I believe."

"What else was on the map?"

350

"I only was given a glimpse. He had it out for only a brief moment before returning it to his vest pocket."

Judge frowned, deep lines etched across his forehead.

"And are you thinking about selling out to Jessup? Because if you are—"

"Legally, a portion of the ranch is mine to do with as I please." She cut him off, wanting him to know that what she did with her inheritance was going to be her decision alone. "But, quite frankly, Jesse, I do not care for the man and have no intention of selling anything to Mr. Luther Jessup—unless I have no other options. There is something about Mr. Jessup which bothers me."

He'd see to it she had *other options!* "Many of the small ranchers around here share your opinion of the man."

"I have answered your questions truthfully. I think it is about time you answered mine," she said. "What is going on between Mr. Jessup and Judge Colston?"

Before his accident, Judge had been planning to tell Victoria who he was. He had been about to admit his ruse and tell her he had fallen in love with her. He had been going to bare his soul in the hope that she felt the same toward him. But long years filled with distrust were hard to break. And when he'd seen her speaking with his enemy, and so amicably, distrust had once again presented itself. He had to be mindful of what he told her until he could make arrangements for Ozzie to pay the damned money for the land. He now realized he should have done this in the first place; he could have saved himself the trouble he was now in. Of course, once the ranch issue was settled . . .

"Jesse?"

The dulcet tones of her soft voice snapped him back from his musings.

"Tori, Luther Jessup has been using his ranch hands to fraudulently increase the size of his ranch for years. As well as running the small ranchers off their land, I might add. Judge Colston is the only rancher in these parts determined enough to stop him."

Victoria watched him closely as he spoke. While she had no doubt he was sincere, his tale did not seem complete. "Is that the whole story?"

"No." He sighed. "Pull up a chair and I'll tell you." Once she was seated, he proceeded. "Colston got his start by rounding up mavericks. Jessup controlled the banks. That's where your father comes in. No bank would loan Colston money to start his ranch, so he got it from your father. Despite Jessup's efforts all these years, Colston's survived," he said, careful to leave out how well he had done.

Victoria listened as Jesse told her all about the ranch up to the time he and the judge had met her in New York. She found her sympathies with Judge Colston and the small ranchers increasing with each syllable. She then told him of losing her mother, taking over operation of the family business, her father's insolvency and death. She included Weatherby Hampton's visit, and how the men who had supported her father before his unfortunate investment were now set on wresting the business from her control unless she married her fiancé to put a male at the helm of Torrington Limited. She finally explained that the money from the sale of what was left of her inheritance was all she had to save the company and family from ruin.

It was out into the open. The story which had brought them together, placed on opposite sides, was now spread before them. The stone wall that had kept them apart had been dismantled with their cleansing declarations. If only it were the entire tale, thought Judge.

With halting movements, Victoria slipped her hand over his. Her touch sent the heat of a wildfire raging through him. The urge to rip her clothes off and lay her on her back raced through his mind, but he held himself back. No. He wanted her to come to him, to give herself willingly, freely.

For lengthy moments they remained, unmoving, gazing into each other's blue depths until Victoria said softly, "I do not know what to do."

The simple statement knotted Judge's stomach. "What do you want to do, Tori?"

Her lips trembled and she pressed three fingers to them to stop the quivering.

"No. Don't try to hide your feelings." He lifted her fingers from her mouth to his and kissed them.

Shattering emotions assailed her. All the reasons for fighting the feelings which welled inside her faded from her mind.

"What is it you want, Tori?" he asked again.

Her gaze broke from his, and she studied the ceiling until overcome by her own desires.

"You, Jesse. I want you to make love to me."

Once the words were out, he heeded no further restraint. His mouth lay siege to hers, her lips parting under the sweet, hungry assault.

Breaking their kiss, Judge rasped, "You know, for many years I believed all women were alike. But you are

353

different."

Again he joined their lips, his tongue dancing with hers until he left her lips and trailed a line of fire along her neck. His hands worked deftly to free her from the blouse which shielded her breasts from his touch. Then his mouth fastened upon the peaked buds.

Victoria needed no further prompting. She unfastened the remainder of her clothing and began to release Jesse from his. A grunt of pain stopped her.

"Your wound. I do not want to hurt you."

"Hang my wound." He pulled her back to him. "It's fine."

The wound stayed Judge's burgeoning passion from erupting into an immediate frenzy. The slow, stroking caresses of their explorations served to further heighten the tension. Their naked bodies became instruments of loving torture. Sensual fingers played across bare flaming flesh and dipped into crevices heated with molten moisture ready to be filled.

Unable to wait any longer, Judge knelt between her thighs and lowered himself into her. Her response was a murmur of love, spurring him to increase their pace while he sipped from the nectar of her mouth. Ecstasy consuming them, the rhythm of their movements grew until each was gasping in fulfillment.

Afterwards, they had fallen into an exhausted sleep. Upon awakening, Judge found his stomach echoed the hollow rumblings of a different kind of hunger.

"You are ready for lunch?" Victoria smiled, running her hand lightly over his chest.

Judge toyed with the golden strands of her hair. "We could try living on love alone for a while."

The implications of what he had just said made her

sit up. She had silently held those feelings deep inside her for some time. To hear them now, even spoken in a general manner, left her feeling almost giddy yet strangely unsettled.

"What did you say?"

He pulled her to him and kissed her properly. "I said we could try living on love alone."

"We could, but we might starve in the process." She broke free and dressed.

Judge propped himself up on an elbow to watch her graceful movements. "Oh, I don't know. You have a sumptuous body. I think I could feast on it for years and never get enough."

Victoria swallowed hard. She wanted to ask him directly if her interpretation was correct, but fear that she was mistaken held her back. Instead, she tossed him his denims and went to the stove. "Get dressed. It will only take me a minute to dish up lunch."

Feeling more content than he had since childhood, Judge followed her instructions. Still bare-chested and bare-footed, he took a seat at the table. Victoria filled two plates, set them down, and took a seat across from him.

Judge took one look at the food and smiled weakly. "I must say this looks . . . very . . . appetizing." He lifted his fork and studied the white mushy substance. If she weren't eating the same slop, he would have sworn she was trying to starve him. What she did to food was incomprehensible. He decided that next time he went for water, he'd ride over to the ranch and beg a care package from Chang. "What is it?"

Luther was steaming as he returned to his ranch after his unsuccessful try at obtaining Colston's land. He practically ran over three ranch hands while drawing the buggy to a halt in front of his house. He was so angry that he jumped down, red faced, and stormed into his office. No one, dammit, turned down Luther Jessup and continued to get away with it.

He slammed through the door and locked it behind him. He needed privacy to plot out his next move. He plunked down onto his leather chair before the huge carved desk. The bright sun streaming in through the large window behind him provided enough light to forgo the lamps situated at each corner of the desk. He had to have that land! He pounded his fist against the smooth surface. More than the land, he had to ruin Colston and force him to leave before the bastard's presence drove him crazy.

In a frenzy to rid himself of all Colston represented, Jessup took a key from his pocket and unlocked the drawer to his left. From it he took a big metal box, the contents of which he removed.

He shuffled through the wealth of papers and then began reading old records he had kept of his efforts. Somewhere in the letters was the answer to his present dilemma. He was so absorbed in the quest to ruin Judge Colston that he failed to notice the shadow that fell across his desk.

Outside the window behind him, Helene stood on a crate, straining to see what Luther was up to. He had returned to the ranch in such a state that he'd pushed passed her as if unaware that she was speaking to him. She knew he'd gone to see that Torrington woman, and when he'd looked right through her as she asked about

Judge's health, she'd been sure something was going on.

She had not yet had an opportunity to search his private office, he kept it locked up so tight. Given to rash behavior, when she'd seen him go inside and slam the door, she'd decided to try and discover the secret he kept hidden in the room.

Although she could not read any of the words on the papers he was studying, Helene now knew where he kept the key which would unlock the information she sought. She knew exactly where to look. All she needed was the opportunity.

Chapter Thirty-eight

Clancy rode from the Jessup spread burning mad. His last meeting with the boss had infuriated him. All he'd done was report that Colston hadn't returned to sleep in the barn once he was well enough and that the pair seemed to be getting mighty cozy. The boss had flown into a rage. But how could he keep them at each other's throats when he wasn't supposed to do more than hide out behind that damned rock and track their actions?

Wait, he told himself. Be patient a little while longer. But hell, he was sick and tired of being patient. He had a score to settle with that bastard Colston for crippling him, and nobody was going to tell Clancy what he could or could not do!

He stabbed his spurs into his animal's sides and headed back to where Colston and that Englishwoman were. There was no way in hell that he intended to wait any longer.

It was late afternoon when he reached the line shack

and surveyed the area. As far as he could tell, they were alone. His calculating smile glinted evil. He only had to worry about taking care of two people, although he wouldn't have minded plugging that old geezer who worked for Colston.

The Englishwoman was bent over tending those scrawny weeds out in front of the shack. She had her hair tucked up beneath the ugliest hat he had ever seen. Her baggy getup didn't do much for her shape neither. 'Course, in town, there were plenty of downright pretty ladies to satisfy his baser needs.

While he waited to find out where Colston was, Clancy checked his guns. Pity he didn't have a rifle with him; then he would've been able to make short work of them without ever leaving his hiding place. Colston was smart, and Clancy was going to make sure he was well prepared this time. There would be no more slipups.

At last! Colston. He looked to be pretty well recovered. The man walked from the barn into the fading sunlight. What all those women saw in him, Clancy could not imagine. Hell, he wasn't more than three inches taller, though his chest might be a little broader, his waist a mite slimmer. Clancy rubbed his stubbled jaw. Hell, Colston wasn't any better looking, at least Clancy didn't think so.

Completely unaware anyone was watching him, Colston toted a bucket to where the broad was working, and watered the weeds for her. Well, if that didn't beat all! Clancy was so mesmerized by the touching domestic scene that he nearly forgot what he'd come for. As he crouched, his throbbing knee and aching back reminded him.

He pulled his pistol from its holster, took careful

aim, cocking the hammer and easing the trigger back until the gun resounded loudly in his hand.

"My Lord!" Victoria screamed, slapping her hands over her head as a bullet knocked the gardening implement out of her hand.

Judge, who had been standing next to her, threw himself on top of her as three more rounds narrowly missed their mark. "Quick. Get inside!" he hollered, yanking her up after him.

Victoria stood still, planted to the ground, until a bullet sent dust splattering at her feet. She swung open the door and leaped inside, expecting Jesse to be behind her. More bullets ricocheted off the steps and the outside walls. When she discovered he wasn't in the house with her, she opened the door and called for him.

"Chrissake, what are you trying to do, get us both killed?" Judge shoved her back inside, joined her, and slammed the door behind him as another round of gunfire erupted.

"I was worried about you."

"Now's not the time. Get my guns off the rack," he ordered, panting.

Victoria straightened up and started for the gunbelts.

"Keep your head down!" he roared.

"Here are your guns," she spat, returning to hand them to him.

"Look, I just don't want you to take a bullet meant for me. If you stand in front of those windows you might as will pin a bullseye on yourself." He checked one of the guns and offered it to her. "I want you to hang onto this, just in case."

"Just in case what?" Her eyes were big and round and

frightened.

"Just in case that son of a bitch kills me and then comes after you. You do remember how to point it and pull the trigger, don't you?"

"Yes, but—"

"No buts," he said. After dropping a chaste kiss on her temple, he climbed out a back window.

A deathly quiet fell over the tiny house, and Victoria could hear her heart thudding. *Just in case that son of a bitch kills me and then comes after you.* The words hung like coffins over her head. Before she could dwell on all the ramifications, another round blasted against the house and tore in through the windows, shattering the dishes. Victoria flattened herself against the floor, wishing she had never heard of the Wild West.

Again a deathly silence fell upon the stifling room. This time Victoria had time to think about Jesse and the wonders of finding love out in this untamed country. She retracted her previous wish that she had never come to the United States, although she would never adjust to anything like this as part of life!

More bullets flew, but this time they seemed to fall short of the house. She ventured to peer out just as the flowers she had so lovingly planted were blown into a thousand shreds. Why, how dare they destroy all her work!

Angry now, she pointed the gun out the window and returned fire. She hadn't the foggiest idea where the gun was aimed, but it gave her a measure of satisfaction to let whomever was out there know she was not going to take what had been done to her garden lying down!

As Judge crept toward the grouping of rocks from which the bullets were coming, he realized, to his chagrin, he was having to dodge a wave of lead from an unexpected source: the shack. Dammit! Why couldn't she follow orders for once? If he didn't know better, he'd think she was trying to kill him.

Crawling on his belly, Judge inched his way to the rocks. No one was there. He surveyed the scene. There was a single pile of empty cartridges which told him only one man stocked them. It was then he realized he'd left Victoria alone. The man could very well indeed have left his perch for the shack. He looked up to see a wiry form inches from the front door, a hand reaching for the knob.

With a war cry piercing the air, Judge leaped from his spot and, ignoring the soreness in his side, sprinted toward the shack, guns blazing.

Clancy spun around just in time to face Colston, a snarl of hatred twisting his lips.

"You!" Judge said, a deathly rage shining in the cold depths of his blue eyes. "I should have known. Your boss pay you to come and finish the job?"

"What's it to you?" Clancy sneered.

"Nothing at all, since you'll never live to collect unless you tell me who hired you. Now throw down your guns before I plug you where you stand."

Sweat poured from the cowardly Clancy. He was a back-shooter. Facing a man fair and square wasn't his style, and he'd never regretted it. Slowly, he let the guns slip from his fingers.

"Now put your hands behind your head and kneel down," Judge ordered.

"You won't get anything out of me, Colston," Clancy sneered, groaning at the pain in his knee as he lowered himself.

At that moment, the crack of another bullet whistled through the air and struck Clancy through the neck. Blood spurted from a hole the size of a dollar, and Clancy grabbed the mortal wound, a horrified look on his face, as he fell into the dirt.

Judge dropped to Clancy's side as a cloud of dust from a big white horse's hooves obscured the unknown killer. Judge checked the wound. There was nothing that could be done for the dying man. "Clancy, can you hear me?" Judge urged.

Clancy opened pain-filled eyes and blinked. "I-I told you my-my life wouldn't be-be worth a . . ." After a desperate effort to speak, his voice failed him.

"You've got to try to tell me who shot you. You don't want to let that boss of yours murder you and get away with it, do you?"

Clancy tried to speak again, but words would not come, and blood gurgled red from the gaping hole.

Victoria stepped from the house, and Judge ordered her back inside with such authority that she immediately complied. He then turned his attention back to Clancy. "It was Jessup who shot you, wasn't it? Wasn't it?"

Recognition sparked into eyes already glazing over. Clancy tried to nod but his strength had ebbed. As his life's blood oozed onto the warm brown earth, Clancy lost his last battle.

"I knew it!" Judge snarled, wiping a hand across his mouth. A gun still dangling from his fingers, he climbed to his feet and walked toward the barn.

Victoria had been watching the gruesome scene from the window, and now stepped outside. "Jesse, you're not just going to leave this man here. Where are you

363

going?" she called out louder, when he failed to respond.

"To get my horse."

"Whatever for?" She ran after him, still in shock. "Shouldn't we get that man to a doctor?"

"The only thing he needs where he's going is a pitchfork," Judge drawled.

She caught up with him but had to practically run to keep up with his long, pounding strides.

"That's a horrible thing to say."

Judge's expression was black and hard as stone. "I should have killed him back at the river outside Saint Louis, and saved us all this trouble."

"You mean he was the same man?" she said in amazement, unable to identify the bloody body.

"The very same. Only this time Jessup did the killing before I could force the truth out of Clancy."

Judge reached the barn and saddled a horse, bridling another for the body.

"How do you know it was Mr. Jessup who did this?"

Judge was in no mood for questions and snapped, "I just do, that's all."

"How?" she demanded.

"I recognized his horse."

He led the animals back to the house and loaded Clancy's body before Victoria realized there was no horse readied for her.

"Where are you going?"

"To Jessup's to deliver what belongs to him."

His voice was filled with such venom that it frightened her almost as much as the shooting had.

"You are not going to ride over to his ranch and leave me here, are you?" she asked, fearing the answer.

Judge mounted and grasped the pack animal's reins in one hand. "You'll be safe here now. Jessup rode off right after he shot old Clancy. Don't worry, though, I won't be gone long."

"You won't do anything rash, will you?" Her voice cracked with dread. He stared at her for a moment with such cold hatred in his blue eyes that Victoria shrank back.

He softened at her utter look of dismay. "Don't worry, Tori."

Without another word he spurred the animals toward the L Circle J.

Anger and hatred boiled inside Judge all the way to Jessup's. He swiped a hand at the sweat on his forehead. Victoria could have been killed all because of the man's incredible greed and driving hatred. Had Jessup been in Judge's sights at that moment, he would have enjoyed killing the low-down bastard. By the time he reached Jessup's ranch, his temper had cooled little.

He rode his horse up the front steps to the door, past astonished cowhands gaping in disbelief. Ignoring the crowd which formed, Judge bellowed, "Jessup! Get out here! Now!" When no one came to the door, he shouted louder, "If you don't show your cowardly face, I'll smash your goddamned door down!"

The door slowly edged open and Helene stepped out. Surprise registered on her unusually white face. "Judge. I see you have recovered from your accident. To what do I owe the pleasure of your visit?"

"Where's that bastard of a husband of yours?" he pressed.

"He's not here. He left early this morning for the range, or so he said," she smoothly answered, without taking her eyes from the man she loved. "Why don't you leave *that*," her vision left him while she indifferently pointed to the body slung over the horse behind Judge, "with one of the hands and come inside . . . ah . . . without your mount, of course."

Judge was troubled at the ease with which she avoided asking what he was doing with a body strapped to his horse. "Another time, Helene."

She stepped forward and her hand went up toward him. "Please. Don't leave yet. You haven't seen Jeremiah. You know how the boy loves you." As a final inducement, she added, "He has missed you terribly."

There was still some humanity to Helene. Her face softened when she spoke of her son. It gave Judge pause to wonder what other feelings must lurk, untapped, inside her. He knew Jessup had never appreciated what he'd had in her. But she'd made the choice years ago, and had sold her soul for those silks on her back.

For the first time since she'd left him to marry Jessup, Judge discovered the animosity he'd held toward all women had vanished. A smile formed on his lips. Tori. Victoria. Victoria Elizabeth Torrington, named after two queens, was the cause. That marvelous, obstinate, irritating, determined Englishwoman had not only won his heart without even trying, but had healed it in the process.

Helene returned his smile, thinking it was for her. Hope. There was still hope he'd be hers, and it gave her strength.

"What are you smiling for, Judge?"

"I was just thinking about a woman, that's all," he answered dryly, his smile fading with the reality of

366

where he was.

"I don't need to ask who, do I?" She smiled widely now, assured of her position.

"No. You don't."

"You will stay for a while, won't you? I need to talk to you about Jeremiah, remember?"

"Can't. Just see that Jessup gets this. I believe it belongs to him." He dumped the body off his horse at her feet and wheeled his mount back in the direction of home and Victoria — without a single backward glance.

He was headed home. Home. To Victoria. His expression slid into a grim line. He still had to tell Victoria who he was and face the consequences of that razor-sharp temper of hers.

Chapter Thirty-nine

Helene squinted after Judge, watching him ride from the ranch. He had all but said the words that she'd longed to hear. He hadn't said her name when he'd mentioned he was thinking about a lady. But Helene knew she had been on his mind; he simply had to be cautious since she was still married to Luther. She hugged herself. Judge Colston would be hers, she knew it. All she had to do was to get rid of Miss Victoria Torrington and take care of Luther. Then they'd finally be free to be together. They'd have all the riches they'd ever need; they'd combine the two ranches into one vast empire; and they'd raise Jeremiah together.

Heartened by the new developments she had so besottedly imagined, Helene called over one of the hands.

"Have this . . . ," she looked down her nose at Clancy's remains, ". . . this carcass removed. It's littering my porch."

Helene watched with cold indifference as three men hauled the dead man off toward the bunkhouse. After

368

they rounded the corner she swung around and strolled into the house. Inside she clasped her hands to her heart. Judge. Judge had come to see her, she thought, dismissing the fact that he'd ridden his horse onto the front porch outraged, demanding to see Luther. No. The first opportunity he'd had to get away from the ranch after the accident, he had come to still her fears over the Englishwoman.

She passed Luther's office and unconsciously her hand went to her skirt pocket, fingering the cold sliver of metal there. When Luther had left early that morning he'd refused to answer her questions, telling her not to look for him until long after midnight.

She'd dutifully escorted him to his horse, expecting at least half a dozen riders to be waiting for him. But to her surprise, a single yawning cowpoke stood holding the reins to one of Luther's swiftest bay stallions, an unruly animal he seldom rode.

"You aren't taking the men with you this morning?" she asked, astounded.

"No, woman," he grated.

"Should I order several men from their beds and have them join you?"

"Not this time."

"But why? You rarely leave the house without a whole regiment of men with you."

There was not a hint of warmth to his voice when he answered her. "It's none of your concern." He reached out and pinched her cheek hurtfully. "If you know what's good for you, you'll get back inside and see to Jeremiah. You've been neglecting the boy lately, and I won't stand for it much longer."

He'd left then without so much as a good-bye. At

first she had considered asking the ranch hand if he knew where Luther was headed, but he seemed as bewildered as she. Instead, she'd gone back inside, thankful that for one day she would not be bothered by his incessant panting after her skirts.

Dressing in a fine cherry silk in the bath area between their two rooms, she'd found a key beneath the rumpled robe he'd left in a heap on the floor. It was the same key she'd seen him use to open the box he kept in his office. The key must have fallen from his pocket while he dressed, and the old fool had been in such a hurry he hadn't missed it.

Her thoughts returning to the present, Helene smiled, all warm and tingling inside. Life was about to be good to her again. For years she'd waited for the chance to rifle through his private papers. She removed the key she'd carried with her all day, drew it to her lips, and kissed it.

Without further hesitation, she slipped into the forbidden room. It was decorated with dark, heavily carved furnishings, plush sofas, and a massive desk. The time she'd spent outside Luther's window spying on him had been well invested. She did not have to waste time searching.

There was no rush. Luther wouldn't be home for hours, so she poured herself a glass of his finest brandy and stretched out on the sofa to enjoy it. After she'd emptied the glass, she went to the desk and seated herself in his ample chair, bouncing up and down.

"Soon this will be my chair and my desk," she said to herself, delighting in the smooth, hard surface against her fingers as she ran them along the edge of the exquisite piece of furniture.

370

No longer waiting, she took out Luther's precious locked box and set it on the desk. She worked the key in the lock, threw up the lid, and began to peruse its contents.

For an hour she avidly read his accounts, jotting down detailed notes on all his illegal activities. She had read through all his papers except the bundle of tied letters at the bottom of the box when the room dimmed with the coming darkness.

She could care less about his pitiful personal life and began laying the accounts back in the box. But something stopped her from leaving. It never hurt to know all there was to know about one's enemy. She lit the lamp on the desk and settled back to examine the missives that had been sent more than thirty-five years ago.

Her eyes saucered and her breath caught, threatening to strangle her, as she scanned the yellow pages filled with a woman's slanted scribbling.

"Oh, my goodness!" she mumbled, grabbing her throat. "I can't believe it!" As she read further, her mind spun with the thoughts of how she was going to use the incredible information to her best advantage . . .

Whistling to himself, Judge's thoughts were filled with Victoria as he headed to the shack. Earlier in the day when they'd made love, she had finally come to him as a woman unqualifiedly in love with a man. It hadn't mattered to her that she thought him a cowboy without worldly possessions. She had wanted him as a man, just as he'd dreamed so often lately.

The sun was sinking behind the hills when Judge noticed the lone shadow of a figure atop a horse, galloping toward him. Judge dismounted and drew his gun. With the sun at the rider's back, he could not make out who it was, only that the rider was not a horseman. He found a shielded spot behind a nearby tree and waited.

As the figure drew closer, a long pigtail wildly flopping in the wind from behind a funny cap became discernible.

"Chang!" Judge hollered to the little man, moving back to the road.

"Boss man. Boss man," panted Chang, falling from his precarious position atop the horse into a heap in the dust. He picked himself up and brushed off the loose black clothes he wore. "You got plobrems. Mighty big plobrems."

"Just calm down a minute," Judge advised, unable to understand the man, he was rambling so excitedly rapid in his thick accent. Chang's black eyes looked like onyx cubes as his heaving chest finally slowed. "All right, spit it out. What's going on that Ozzie couldn't handle this time?"

"Him gone to town with Engrish missy. Men, they come. Stear rots a cows."

"What?"

"Bad men, they stear rots a cows."

It took Judge a minute to interpret what the little man had said. Despite the years Chang had lived at the ranch he continued to have difficulty with the English pronunciation.

"Oh. They steal lots of cows."

"That what I say. They stear rots of cows. You come. Cowboys wait back at lanch. Come. You come now."

Judge shot a longing look in the direction of the

hack. He wanted to go to Victoria, but knew there was
o one to handle riding after the rustlers. He'd have to
ead up the men assembled and waiting for him.

"Listen to me, Chang. At the north line shack there is
pretty English lady waiting for me. The one I had
Ozzie tell all the men about?"

"Yes. Yes. I know. I send food, lemembel?"

"Yes, I remember. Good. I want you to go there and
make sure she is all right. Stay with her tonight, and tell
her I'll be back as soon as I can. Oh, and do not forget,
o Victoria, I am known as Jesse, Judge Colston's foreman. Any questions about that? I don't want any
lipups."

Chang grinned widely. Boss trust him to take care of
ine lady. Boss take him in almost eight years ago after
e brought to Rock Springs as strikebreaker in coal
mines, then fired two weeks later. Whites did not give
his people a chance, paying them little and treating
hem less than human. But not boss. Judge Colston
ave Chang after mob broke into his house and murdered his family. Chang heartbroken and inconsolable,
out boss take him back to ranch and treat him good.

"Top boss man rike missy? Yes?"

Judge had to laugh. "Yes, Chang, I like missy very
much."

"Then why you no terr hel the tluth?"

The one thing Judge had always liked about Chang
was his honesty. At that moment, Judge wondered
ndeed why he hadn't been straightforward with her.

"I made a mistake not telling her the truth," Judge
admitted, knowing what he said would go no further
han Chang's ears. "And I intend to remedy that real
oon. But it is important that she hear the truth from

373

me, so just be sure to watch your tongue."

Chang bobbed his head enthusiastically. "Boss ma lest assuled. I take good cale of missy."

Judge helped Chang back up on his mount and watched him canter off toward the line shack, bounc ing out of the saddle with each step the horse took Judge then turned his own animal toward home Home. The sound of it hit him as he rode. Home wa where Victoria was, and as soon as he'd handled thi latest problem with the rustlers, he was gong to settle things with Victoria as well. Judge sighed and looked back over his shoulder to catch one last fleeting glance at the wiry Chinaman heading in the direction Judge wished to be.

Chang grunted with relief when he spied the broken down shack in which fine lady stayed. He dismounted glad to set his feet on solid earth again, and led the horse down the last hill. He was not more than fifty feet from the house when he stopped cold, a shiver running through his entire body.

Pointed directly at his heart was the biggest six shooter he had ever seen.

"Do not come any closer," Victoria warned, the gun shaking in her trembling fingers.

Chang put his hands up in front of him. "It okay Missy. Ju . . . ah . . . Jesse, he send Chang."

She lowered the gun, her face filled with a wave of concern.

"Jesse? Where is he? He did not do something rash did he? Oh, dear, I knew it. I knew he was going to get into trouble when he left here with that body."

"Body?" he croaked. "Top boss man got body?"

She furrowed her brows. "Top boss man?"

Guilt and shame colored his face that he had nearly t the man who had become his family down.

"No, no, Missy. Chang mean Jesse. Jesse, he okay."

It was strange to hear Jesse, the judge's ranch hand, ferred to as the top boss man. She decided the little an must be mistaken, but there was something about sse's manner which caused Victoria to have a hard me dismissing it from her mind.

"You are Chang?" she asked, relaxing her stance nce she knew Jesse was all right.

"Yes, Missy. Chang."

She brightened. "Oh, yes. Lani has spoken of you. ou work at the neighboring ranch where she and erald are staying. Lani and Gerald have spoken very ghly of your culinary talents. I want to thank you for nding us those fine baskets of food."

"Yes. Yes." He bobbed his head. "Chang come flom eighboling lanch. I cook."

Victoria held back a smile with her palm, realizing s difficulty with the language. "Please, won't you me inside? I shall make us some tea and then you can ll me where Jesse is."

Chang followed the lady inside. But as he watched r start to prepare the tea he had sent over, he jumped his feet and insisted on doing the honors. She was out to make it so strong it could be baked into for- ne cookies.

Chang moved about the tiny room with practiced ficiency. In no time at all, he set a tray with the viting, fragrant tea upon it in front of Victoria.

Victoria lifted the cup and sipped the steaming liq-

uid. She had almost forgotten what it was like to b
waited upon. Strangely enough, it had not bothered h
taking care of someone else's needs — particularly sin
that someone else was Jesse, she thought sheepishly

"That is without a doubt the most refreshing cup
tea I have had since leaving England."

"Thank you, Missy."

At his questioning gaze, Victoria asked, "Is som
thing troubling you?"

In his broken dialect Chang inquired about the bod
and Victoria poured out the sordid tale of their tr
from Saint Louis. When she expressed her concern f
the big man, Chang told her about the rustlers, an
how the neighboring rancher had needed Jesse's hel
Chang had been sent to keep her company this evenin
he explained, since Jesse did not want her to stay alon
That Jesse was being so considerate made Victoria glo
inside.

Happy for the company after the events of the mor
ing, Victoria asked Chang about himself and how b
had come to Wyoming. Chang happily spent an ho
telling her how Jesse had rescued him, leaving Victori
to wonder about the man she knew only as Jesse. N
one seemed able to supply his surname.

"I cook you mear. We eat, yes?"

The prospects of eating something edible for
change further served to delight Victoria. Not about t
give the little man a chance to change his mind, Victor
handed him the basket of fresh vegetables which M
Jessup had been so kind to deliver before he had prove
so despicable.

"I am afraid we do not have any meat," she answered
misunderstanding his offer to cook the "mear."

"No meat okay." He smiled broadly, a gentle, tolerant man. "I cook." He held up a handful of vegetables.

In less than a half hour, Victoria and Chang sat down to a sumptuous feast of stir fried vegetables delicately spiced with sprigs of sage Chang had picked from the hillside.

Chang cleaned up the dishes, and they settled down to talk far into the night. The more Victoria questioned the wiry man about Jesse, the more evasive Chang became. Her head was filled with further troubled questions about the incomparable Jesse.

Chapter Forty

When Victoria woke, the room was filled with the inviting fragrance of fresh-baked biscuits and tea. She blinked her eyes open and looked around. Chang was not in the house. She shook her head. Although she had offered him the sofa, he had insisted on sleeping in the barn. Yet now the table was set, complete with fresh flowers. The room had been tidied, and through the window she could see the wash, gently blowing in the breeze, on the line Jesse had strung from the house to a nearby tree. The only evidence of the shooting that remained was the lack of glass in the windows. And in a neat stack beneath each window lay a pile of boards cut to fit the openings.

She stretched and climbed out of bed. Padding to the window, she peered out to see Chang busy hanging the last of the laundry. Once again the day promised to be hot.

Deciding to abandon propriety for comfort, Victoria rummaged through her trunk for clothing more suited to the climate. The coolest item in her wardrobe was the calico dress Betsy Lake had given her. She held the

imple garment up in front of her, a smile radiating
around her lips. Jesse liked her dressed in it. She slipped
t on, finding that the thought of pleasing him agreed
with her. Victoria finished her ablutions and went out
nto the sun.

"Chang, good morning. Won't you join me for that
wonderful breakfast you prepared?"

Chang nodded, and they had a delightful meal. Vic-
oria hid her disappointment that he would not shed
additional light on Jesse, no matter how much she
probed.

Shading her eyes, Victoria walked with Chang out to
nis horse. "Thank you so very much for all you have
done, Chang. And please thank your employer for
allowing you to keep me company."

Chang's grin widened at the thought of thanking his
employer. "Yes, Missy. Top boss man happy that I
come to keep you company."

There it was again, the title *top boss man*. Victoria
lid not attempt to further question him, although a
small voice within her told her something was amiss.

"I do hope Jesse and I shall have the pleasure of
eeing you again," she said, as he scrambled onto the
big horse.

A queer little smile across his face, Chang said, "Yes,
Missy. I rook folwald to see you again soon at boss
man's lanch. Then I cook good mear speciar fol you."

"I shall look forward to eating that special meal,
oo," she returned, and bid him good-bye.

She watched until the wiry Chinaman rode out of
ight, then turned to her ruined flower bed. She had
worked so diligently to create the small plot of beauty
next to the house, only to see it destroyed by that gun-

379

man. Well, she would just have to get started renovating. She donned her apron and her floppy hat, and pulled on her once magnificent theatre gloves, now stained from digging in the dirt.

Victoria had just knelt down to begin pulling the unsalvageable plants when the distant clopping of horses' hooves, mingled with the whirring grind of wheels against the ground, snapped her attention from her gardening. She wiped the sweat streaking her face and got to her feet. A plant in one hand, trowel in the other, she looked a sight as yet another visitor approached the secluded house.

"Good morning, Miss Torrington," Helene said sweetly, pulling the buggy to a halt in front of the Englishwoman. "My, my, I hope I haven't come at a bad time. You don't look as if you are prepared to receive callers," Helene added maliciously.

Victoria's mouth tightened. She knew she must look dreadfully disheveled and dirty, but this woman was not going to make her feel like a fishwife.

"Not at all, Mrs. Jessup. I have found that out here in the wilds, one must be willing to expect all sorts of callers, since there seems to be little tradition here of presenting one's calling card and waiting to be received."

Helene's amiable expression turned sour. "No doubt a soft, city woman such as yourself has been forced to make many concessions," she returned with a bitter tongue, alighting from the coach.

"Not as many as I had expected—especially with a foreman of Jesse's caliber around."

"I'm sure you find his work more than adequate."

"Why, yes. He does strive to please."

380

Helene's teeth clenched at the insinuation.

"Did I neglect to invite you in?" Victoria asked innontly, after Helene had taken it upon herself to move ward the door of the house. "How terribly inconsidate of me. Such a breach of proper etiquette." You obably have no conception of what proper etiquette anyway, Victoria thought behind her cool facade. Do come in, won't you? I must thank you for sending er those delicious vegetables. It was most thoughtful ' you."

Although Helene had not sent them, she smiled eetly. "Yes. I was worried *Jessie* wasn't being fed operly."

"You needn't have concerned yourself. I can assure u his needs have been well taken care of."

Victoria entered the house and seated herself on the orn sofa. She motioned for Helene to sit across from r on one of the hard chairs, so the woman would not inclined to remain long.

"Tea, Mrs. Jessup?"

"No. I didn't come here for tea, Miss Torrington."

"If this is not a social visit, then what did you come re for, Mrs. Jessup?"

Helene was irked. She had been itching for a fight all e way over here, despite having chided herself that e should subtly let drop her information and then ay the innocent when the fireworks started. Helene ted the cool manner in which the English bitch conued to conduct herself; it made her spoil for a battle l the more. Judge might be perturbed, but Helene ver doubted she could pacify him the way she always d.

"I came because I was curious, that's all." Helene

wanted to see the bitch work for what she was here [to] say.

Victoria was aware that the Jessup woman was pla[y]ing some type of game, and she found it tiresome. "[Is] this where I am supposed to ask why you're curiou[s] Mrs. Jessup?"

Helene glared and a huff of exasperation escaped h[er] lips. "I beg your pardon?"

"I would have thought you understood quite we[ll] Mrs. Jessup."

Helene's fingers itched to pull those blonde roo[ts] out. No. She must remain calm until she was ready f[or] their little game to end.

They eyed each other menacingly.

"Miss Torrington, I have merely been trying to [be] neighborly, since you don't seem to have made a[ny] friends and are all alone out here."

"If that is the case, thank you for your visit." Victor[ia] stood and moved to hold the door open for the woma[n.] "If you have nothing else to say, I must be returning [to] the repair of my flower beds."

Helene's color heightened to match the crimson [of] her fine morning dress. She was being dismissed. As [if] she were a servant, the Torrington woman was dismiss[s]ing her, Helene Jessup. No one treated her that way a[nd] got away with it. No one!

In a voice low and foreboding, Helene directe[d,] "Come back and sit down, Miss Torrington. There [is] still quite a bit I have to say."

Victoria stared at the glowering woman for a m[o]ment before returning to sit, straight-backed, on t[he] sofa. She prepared for what she was certain would be [a] most unpleasant interview.

382

"I think we can dispense with any further prelimiaries, Mrs. Jessup."

A gloating smirk transformed Helene's attractive aatures into a cruel, jeering mask.

"Since you leave me no means to put this delicately, I ppose you are going to force—"

"Force what, Mrs. Jessup? As I just said, if you have me here to tell me something, be out with it or leave. I o not have any more time to waste."

"Although I have to admit I can understand the ght attraction *Judge* appears to have for you, I simy can't imagine how you've managed to hold his intert this long. Unless of course, it is because you are ying to cheat him out of part of his land, and are still olding those legal papers he has spoken of."

"I am afraid, Mrs Jessup, I have not the foggiest idea hat you are rambling on about. I have not seen the dge for a number of days, and if he has demonstrated y interest at all in me, I can only assure those," ictoria looked pointedly at Helene, "who might find upsetting that I have no designs on the man."

"Oh, don't be so naive, Miss Torrington." Helene rew back her head and laughed.

Miffed confusion appeared in Victoria's eyes. "I supse it is time for me to beg your pardon."

Helene's vicious laughter grew louder. "You fool, I ave been talking about Judge Colston . . . better own to you as *Jesse*."

Victoria's body jerked at the news and she had to ruggle for control. "Mrs. Jessup, I do not know what nd of joke this is supposed to be, but I think it is time u leave."

"Not until I make sure you know how it is between

Judge and myself, Miss Torrington. You see, Judge ha
just been playing a game with you since he met you i
New York. He told me all about the English spinst
who was after part of his ranch.

"As a matter of fact, we've had many good laugh
over you, Miss Torrington. Judge and his foremar
Ozzie . . . oh . . . Judge Colston to you, switche
places. As far as Judge being a magistrate, the close
he has ever gotten to the bench was when he defende
one of the town whores a few years ago."

Helene got up and strolled about the little roon
"And as far as *this* being the ranch, you really have bee
a fool. This place is no more than a pathetic line shac
where the cowboys stay when they are checking on th
herds. Judge lives quite well. As a matter of fact, yo
silly sister and fiancé are staying in Judge's home rigl
now. . . ."

Somehow Victoria managed to sit through the rest
Helene Jessup's tirade without displaying the extensiv
hurt she felt. She had wondered why Chang had r
ferred to Jesse — no, Judge — as the top boss man. No
she knew.

During the trip, little things had bothered her abor
the man who professed to be a ranch hand. All along,
had seemed he'd had some power over the judge — th.
is, Ozzie. Now she understood why the man pretendir
to be Judge Colston had put her off when she ha
attempted to show him the legal documents proving h
claim. And then there had been those little commen
made by Bridgewater, Betsy Lake, the gunslinger, an
even the President of the United States.

My God, was she the only one who had not know
the truth about the man? She should have been mo

ognizant of his take-charge manner—of course, a anch hand would not behave as did Judge Colston, the wealthy rancher determined not to let some English pinster cheat him out of his property.

"What's the matter, Miss Torrington? Your face eems to be turning red," sneered Helene, returning to er chair. "Could it be that you are jealous that Judge oves me and always has?"

"I find that difficult to believe, Mrs. Jessup," Victoria said in a feeble whisper.

"Because I'm married to Luther? You really are naïve. Judge and I have been lovers for years. Luther has been just a pawn for Judge and I. We'll get his ranch and then combine our holdings into the greatest cattle empire in Wyoming. Why, Judge came to see me to discuss it just last night."

Victoria's chin began to quiver as she recalled how he had been adamant about not letting her accompany him yesterday, when he had supposedly been returning that gunslinger's body. God, he *had* gone to see that woman. Could Judge be everything Helene had said he was? Victoria chirped, "But you and Mr. Jessup have a son."

"Jeremiah?" Helene's lips drew up in brutal triumph. "Haven't you noticed the similarity between the boy and Judge, Miss Torrington?"

"Yes. But—"

"Then you've seen for yourself that he is the very picture of his father."

"I would assume he would be. But I fail to see—"

"He looks just like his father as a matter of fact," Helene said, without a hint of emotion.

"Yes, but—"

"His father is Judge Colston."

The full weight of the nightmare surrounding he threatened to squeeze Victoria's breath from her. At the horse-breaking, Victoria *had* thought the boy bore an uncanny resemblance to Jess . . . Judge, she admitted defeated.

With haunted eyes, Victoria said, "What kind of a man would let another man claim his own son?"

"I guess the kind of man Judge Colston is," Helene answered with a sarcastic sneer, shrugging her shoulders. Of course, she had left out one little detail: Judge did not know he was Jeremiah's father, and would not until the time was right.

Helene rose, satisfied that she had accomplished exactly what she had set out to. Victoria Torrington would be out of Judge's life, permanently.

On wobbly legs, Victoria rose and went to the door. She felt as if she were going to retch, and she could not let that despicable woman see how upset she was. Dignity was a matter of honor, and she would retain hers regardless of the inner turmoil which roiled in her stomach and had ripped her heart out.

"Since you seem to be through with what you have come here for, I suggest you do not delay your departure, Mrs. Jessup."

"Yes. Of course. It it time I should be getting back to my husband and son. I wouldn't want them to feel neglected." Helene sent Victoria an evil smile and swished through the door. Then she turned back and added, "I hope you found our little talk informative, just filled with neighborly tidbits you will find useful, Miss Torrington. Good day."

Once that horrible person had left, Victoria rushed

the bowl on the table and lost her breakfast. Then he sank onto the bed and stared blankly at the door, refusing to give way to tears. Tears were not productive. And henceforth, she was not going to let anything deter her from accomplishing what had brought her to this country in the first place.

She had been right all along to think one should never marry for love. What a fool she had been. What a silly, stupid goose. Well, no more. Her first course of action would be to marry Gerald and put a male at the helm of Torrington Limited in order to satisfy her creditors. She could then begin putting her life back in order.

Chapter Forty-one

Her mind churned with pictures of Judge Colston and Helene Jessup laughing at her, as he did the same intimate things to Helene's body as he had done to hers. Victoria's color heightened as she rushed to gather her things before that dishonest lout returned. All the while she tossed clothing into her trunk and somehow managed to get it into the carriage she had hitched up herself, she visualized how the pair must have laughed at her, and how they would enjoy their victory after she had gone.

"You are not going to get away with it, Judge Colston," she sniffed. Hot, salty tears rolled down her cheeks despite her resolve and she wiped them with the back of her hand, not bothering with the customary hankie. She bustled out of the house, leaving the door wide open in her haste.

Despite her immeasurable hurt, she feared she could not trust herself. She could not take the chance. She would not face Judge Colston until she was safely wed to Gerald. And she needed Lani around her right now. Remembering Lani's sketchy directions to the ranch — Judge Colston's — at which they were guests, Victoria

aid the whip to the horses' rumps. They kicked up a
dust cloud as she took flight from the shack the lout
had his men fix up just to cheat her out of her
inheritance.

How could she have been so gullible? Never, never
again would she fall prey to one such as Judge Colston,
first-class rake!

Judge was beat. He had been out all night, and there
hadn't been a trace of a rustler anywhere. They'd
scoured the countryside, followed the multitude of
tracks — but nothing. Not bothering to stop at his ranch
before returning to Victoria, Judge made only one brief
stop to bathe in a creek so he wouldn't smell like a
horse.

While he was stripped naked in a quiet spot just off
the road, the sounds of a buggy in a frantic hurry
assailed his ears. Normally he might have jumped into
his trousers and investigated, but not this morning. He
had important business to take care of. He was going to
tell Victoria the truth and resolve their conflicts. He
finished washing, picked the few red flowers growing
near the banks of the creek for Victoria, and rode to the
shack.

"What the hell?"

Judge leaped from his horse, dropping the flowers in
the dirt, and made a frantic dash inside the shack,
fearing that Jessup might have returned and harmed
Victoria. She was not there. He ran to the barn. No
Tori. He was about to gather the men and lead a search
party when he noticed the horses and the buggy gone.
Strange.

He went back inside the shack. There, he discovered

her clothes and trunks were gone as well. He wondered whether Chang had had anything to do with her sudden departure. Then the buggy he'd heard while bathing worked its way to the forefront of his mind. It had been headed in the direction of his own spread—at break neck speed.

Cussing his luck, Judge leaped on his horse and spurred it towards home.

Victoria gasped at the enormous size of the J Bar C ranch house. It was a sprawling affair, quite grand, surrounded by stables, a bunkhouse, a smokehouse and an ice house, and other assorted buildings. As she neared the main residence, Victoria noticed Gerald heading toward an awaiting carriage.

"Gerald! Gerald!" she hailed him, stopping the wagon and hurrying into his arms. "I have missed you terribly."

"Y-you have?" he startled.

"Oh, yes. And Lani, too. But no more. I have come to be here with you. And as soon as arrangements can be made, we shall be married."

"M-married? That is not possible now. I don't think that—"

"Nonsense, we shall be wed as soon as it can be arranged," she said, in the take-charge manner of the Victoria Gerald had known back in England.

"My, my, old girl, you haven't taken leave of your senses, have you?"

"I think I have only just got them back. Where is Lani?" Victoria asked, dismissing Gerald's feeble protests.

"Lani? She has gone to Casper with the judge for a

eek."

"I am afraid the judge is actually a man named Ozzie nd Jesse . . . ," her eyes snapped fire, "is none other han Judge Colston, the rotter."

"You don't say," stammered Gerald. "Are you cerain?"

Victoria took a calming breath and poured out the ntire story about Helene Jessup's visit, careful to leave ut that she had thought herself in love with that awful udge Colston. She concluded with her intention to narry Gerald—missing the look of horror on his ace—as soon as possible, and file suit in the territorial ourts.

"Victoria, I have an errand to run. Let me see you ettled and we'll discuss our nuptials when I return, vhat?"

"Of course. But there is really nothing to discuss. My nind is made up."

Befuddled and not a little upset over Victoria's sudlen appearance and plan to be married, Gerald esorted Victoria to Lani's room.

He left her there, excusing himself to resume his nission to confront Luther Jessup. Even if he hadn't letermined to go to Jessup's ranch that afternoon, Gerald had no intention of waiting for Judge Colston o discover what had happened and come after Victoia. Those two were sure to send sparks flying!

Sparks flew from beneath Judge's heels as he tomped into the house, shouting. Chang ran to the ource of the commotion, but was ordered back to the :itchen. Judge had seen the wagon out front as he eared the yard, leaving no doubt in his mind where

391

Victoria was.

"Victoria!" he hollered, searching through the hous and slamming doors like a devil twister.

Victoria had been trying to rest, but the instant tha familiar harsh voice assailed her ears, she stiffened Well, she would not keep Judge Colston waiting, th way he was bellowing like a wounded boar! She had a few choice things that she wanted to say to the man Walking erect, Victoria left the room, very much th Victorian lady, and came face to face with the glower ing rancher.

Judge's expression softened and a lump clogged hi throat when he caught sight of her wearing the calic dress he'd had Betsy Lake buy for her. "Victoria, w must talk."

"Talk? Talk!" she exploded, forgetting her intentio to remain chilly decorous. "Well, *Mr. Judge Colston,* have already listened to all you have to say. Now that know the truth about you, you will not have anothe opportunity to use and abuse my person further. You . . . you are the most disgusting excuse for a humar being I have ever had the misfortune to meet. And now if you will just leave this house, I — "

"Leave this house?" Judge's temper rose despite the knowledge she must be angry and hurt over his mas querade. "I am not going anywhere until you hear me out. Besides, this is my house."

"Oh, really? Why, I thought you resided at that hum ble little *shack, Jesse.*"

Judge grabbed her arm and, ignoring her protests dragged her into his study and slammed the door. He turned just in time to see her poised at the other end of the room, a vase in her hand. In defense, Judge put his hands up. "Now, Victoria, before you go and do some-ing rash—"

He ducked.

C-r-a-s-h!

The vase smashed against the wall right behind his ear.

"Listen to me—" Another object flew his way, and another.

Fighting off her attack, Judge managed to pull her to him. "Victoria," he gritted. "You've got to listen to me."

"No!" she screamed and struggled free. Hatred, hurt and humiliation glinting in her cold, blue eyes, she straightened her attire, then said with deliberate precision, "Your lady friend, Helene Jessup, paid me a call earlier today and we had quite an enlightening discussion, *Mr. Colston.*"

Judge tentatively reached out a hand, his own anger sapped by the weight of what he'd done. "Victoria—"

"No! I shan't listen to any more of your lies. I know all about you and what you are planning. All I want is what is rightfully mine. And if you try to deny my claim, I shall go to Mr. Jessup and tell him what you and your . . . your doxy are up to, before I file suit in the territorial courts and expose you and the family you are not man enough to claim. Now, I suggest you return to your line shack and remain there until my family and I have departed, which will be as soon as possible."

Before he could question her as to what she meant by referring to Helene, his family, and some plan, she stuck her nose in the air and marched off. Filled with the self-disgust at his own dishonesty, he let her go. She had just suffered a terrible shock. She would need time to cool off and collect herself before he could broach the painful subject of his deception again.

"Goddammit!" He pounded his fist against a tabl
before stomping out of the house. "I'm going to wring
Helene's rotten neck."

Judge mounted his horse and galloped toward Jes
sup's spread until he realized he would need time to
think before confronting Helene. He wheeled the ani
mal around and headed back to the shack to ponde
how he was going to convince Victoria to listen to him
He had lied to her about so many things. Loving he
was not one of them, and he vowed he would not let he
leave his house or his life.

Back at the shack, full of self-loathing for his deceit
Judge sat down with a jug kept there by the men. H
upended it again and again, ignoring the way he fel
about the evils of liquor, until darkness closed over hi
mind, obliterating the mess he'd made of things.

Gerald swallowed his apprehension and steered th
horses over in front of the magnificent Jessup man
sion. He had been bothered by nightmares since he'
first glimpsed the man. He had to get to the bottom o
his troubled thoughts.

No one seemed to be about when Gerald alighte
from the carriage and approached the door. Perhaps h
had been too hasty coming over here, he thought. Hi
nerve deserting him, he turned to leave.

"Mr. Pelthurst," a deep booming voice said from
behind Gerald. "I assume you're here to see me."

Legs trembling, Gerald pivoted and came face to fac
with the rotund, dark personage of Luther Jessup
Gerald's lips shook so, he could not speak.

"Won't you come in? I'm sure you haven't come al
this way just to leave again." Jessup's smile was evil a

e held open the door, and Gerald walked through as meekly as a lamb to slaughter. "We can speak in my private office."

Gerald pulled at his collar as he took a seat on the edge of the couch facing Jessup, who settled behind a mammoth desk.

"I say, since you appear to be devilishly busy, perhaps should return another time, actually," Gerald said hoarsely, rising to make his escape before it was too late.

"Don't be a fool, man," Jessup stayed him. He fixed two drinks, then returned to his seat. "To successful business deals." Jessup raised his glass, slugged the fiery liquid down, and sat staring at Gerald.

Gerald nervously imitated Jessup, but coughed as the burning sensation rode down his throat. "Mr. Jessup," Gerald began in a halting speech. "I do believe you may know why I am here in this official capacity."

"Official capacity?" Luther roared. "Pelthurst, you amuse me."

"Sir, I do not believe Miss Torrington will find it amusing to learn that you headed the delegation of investors responsible for her father's bad investments," Gerald said in a rush of words, before his courage totally failed him.

Luther listened patiently while Gerald explained that he'd first seen Luther while working as a clerk in Torrington's offices, five years ago. Gerald grew bolder, demanding to know if there was any connection between the failure of their business venture and Victoria's inheritance. Gerald had been listening to the J Bar C's foreman discuss the difficulties between the two ranchers when he had remembered Luther's name from Mr. Torrington's old records and correspondence.

As Gerald poured out the memories their meeting at the horse-breaking had evoked, it all seemed almost too fantastic. But it became more plausible that Jessup had intentionally ruined Torrington Limited when one knew that Mr. Torrington had refused to sell his holdings in Colston's ranch.

Luther laughed and agreed, to Gerald's complete shock. Luther continued to laugh as he told of trying for years to get a hold of Colston's ranch, and the lengths he'd gone to do it. "I tried to convince Torrington to sell his investment in Colston's ranch, but the old fool wouldn't agree. Then I discovered the man's one weakness . . . ." An evil smile twisted his lips as he said, "His wife."

"Mary Torrington? But she died in a tragic accident years ago," mumbled Gerald, finding their discussion all too incredible.

"Yes. I hear her coach was run off the road."

"How did you know that?" Gerald troubled.

"Because I was in the other coach," Luther said glibly. He went on to explain his part in it.

Gerald was mortified to hear that Victoria's mother had died, not of a simple mishap, but as the result of a carefully planned accident. Luther chuckled that it had taken some years, but he had finally managed to ruin Torrington. Then his face grew serious. He explained that he had not counted on the daughter's interference.

"You mean to tell me, sir, that you killed Torrington's wife, and ruined Torrington's business, merely because Mr. Torrington wouldn't sell you the papers he held on Judge Colston's ranch?"

"Let's see, how would you Brits say it? Oh, yes. Quite so, old man."

"My dear fellow, it all sounds rather mad."

396

"Not if you understand why I have to have Colston's ranch. But that is none of your concern, Pelthurst."

"You know I shall go directly to the constable." Gerald rose, frightened by the import of the information.

"Go anywhere you damn well please. There is nothing you can prove," Luther shrugged, "other than that I've tried to expand my holdings, as would any businessman." Then his face grew black with warning. "But if you are thinking about telling your story to anyone outside this room, I'd think again if you value the safety of that little filly you are so fond of."

"Victoria?" Gerald whispered, his hand at his throat.

"I ain't blind, man. Anyone with eyeballs can see you are sweet on that one you call Lani. Pretty little thing too," Luther added, with a leering grin.

Terror shook Gerald's heart, and he had to sit back down to compose himself.

"That's better. Now, let's come to an agreement that'll be acceptable to the both of us."

"You know I have no control over Victoria's inheritance," Gerald offered feebly.

"No. But you're her fiancé. Hampton suggested you two marry, which, incidentally, would put you in a position to help convince her to sell me the land. Correct?"

"How did you know about Hampton?"

"He represents my interests now."

"My word!" Gerald sighed. It was all beyond his comprehension. The one thing he knew for sure was that he had to protect his precious wife at any cost.

Chapter Forty-two

Gerald returned to the ranch with a pounding headache, uncertain what to do about what he'd learned. It had all seemed so simple when he'd first gone over to Jessup's to confront the man. If his suspicions were correct, Gerald had hoped to convince Luther Jessup to make restitution for what he'd done to Torrington Limited. Then Victoria could have returned to England and her precious company, and Gerald could have his own Lani openly. Never had he imagined Jessup's involvement had been so far-reaching, had included murder.

"I say, what do we do now?" he muttered, loosening his tie as he sank onto the sofa in the parlor to think.

"We get married," Victoria answered in response, coming into the room. "I have been waiting for you to return so we can begin making the arrangements."

"Married?" he repeated stupidly.

"Yes. Mr. Hampton said it would stall my father's creditors' demands if we married, so that is what we shall do."

"Yes, good, faithful, old Mr. Hampton. A paragon of virtue, what?"

Victoria ignored Gerald's ramblings about the English barrister and went on to half-heartedly explain about her plans to hold the wedding as soon as arrangements could be made. In her misery Victoria did not notice that Gerald, too, was wrapped up in troubled thoughts.

After Judge had left, Victoria had gulped for air. Within her, she had held on to a small measure of hope that he'd offer some reasonable explanation. She had expected him to deny all the things that horrible Jessup woman said. He had not. He had let her go.

Well, she was not going to drown in self-pity. She would marry Gerald and show Judge Colston that he had not meant any more to her than she had to him! Judge Colston had crushed her pride, and no man would ever do that again!

Gerald cleared his throat, snapping Victoria out of her reverie.

"Then it is agreed?" Victoria said absently.

"Agreed?"

"Yes, agreed that we shall marry."

"Marry? Oh . . . ah . . . ah . . . yes, yes, of course," Gerald stammered, unable to divulge to her that he was already married, and afraid Luther Jessup would harm Lani.

"Good. I shall send one of the hands into town with a message to the nearest minister."

Despite Chang's objections and hesitance, Victoria went ahead with the preparations. The messenger returned, after an overnight stay in town, with Reverend Blonsen's note, replying he would be happy to perform the ceremony day after tomorrow.

During the interim, Victoria drove herself relentlessly so she would not have time to think about her decision. At night, she fell into bed so exhausted that sleep welcomed her almost immediately. She sent a note to Lani, but determined not to wait if her sister did not return before the minister arrived.

"That is right, Chang. The wedding is to be this afternoon."

"But Missy, you wait fol top boss man. You no do this," Chang insisted.

"Chang, while I shall not forget all your kindness to me, I also cannot help but remember that you, too, were part of the deception Judge Colston engaged in. And while I would want you to be a guest at my wedding, if you continue to insist I cancel it, I shall simply be forced to ask you to leave until after the ceremony."

Chang's black eyes rounded. "Yes, Missy." He bobbed twice, then scurried for the stables.

Victoria heaved a sigh, sighting him as he rushed across the yard, Ozzie's goose hot on his heels. If she were not so wrung out over the situation she might have laughed, the way the wiry Chinaman and that goose seemed to have it in for each other. She should have known he would remain loyal to that rancher. At least, before he had run off, she'd had the little man bake a cake and decorate a table in the corner of the parlor. The couch had been shifted to make an aisle. Although Victoria did not expect any guests in attendance, other than a few ranch hands to witness the affair, she would have some semblance of a traditional ceremony.

This was her wedding day, yet she felt as if she were about to attend an inquest. She dressed in a solemn, dove gray, tailored suit which matched her bleak mood. Her hair she combed back into a severe style, so unlike

ne freely flowing curls she had become accustomed to
hile living at the shack with . . . No! She refused to
llow herself to think about the time she had spent
here. A loud rap at the front door ended her prepara-
ions, and she went to answer it.

"Miss Torrington?"

"Yes?"

"I'm Reverend Blonsen." The withered man of about
ixty-five introduced himself and followed Victoria
nto the parlor.

"Do you wish some refreshment before we com-
nence?"

The preacher patted his breast pocket. "Thank you,
ut I carry my own. For medicinal purposes only, of
ourse."

Victoria smiled weakly at the colorful man who was
bout to tie her to Gerald Pelthurst. "Of course."

Gerald joined them and stood fidgeting as half a
ozen cowpokes filed into the spacious house, hats in
ands, and plunked down on the seating provided.

"This it?" the reverend asked.

"Were you anticipating a crowd?" Victoria returned,
nnoyed at the amusement in the man's voice.

"This is Judge Colston's place. There's usually a
ouse full when he entertains. I expected him to be
ere."

"Well, he is not!" Victoria snapped. All eyes immedi-
tely fell on her. "Shall we get on with it? I should like to
et this over with as quickly as possible."

"Well, I'll be salt-petered," snickered the reverend
ood-naturedly. "And you, Mr. Pelthurst? Are you as
nxious as your bride to get the deed done?"

"I—"

"Yes. He is," Victoria answered when Gerald faltered.

Reverend Blonsen scratched his stubbled jaw. "I ca[n] see who plans to wear the guns in your family."

Victoria huffed with indignation. "I think we ca[n] dispense with further comments about our future mari[-]tal arrangements." She threaded her arm throug[h] Gerald's. "Are you ready, Gerald?"

Gerald had begun to perspire. He took out his line[n] handkerchief and wiped his brow. Everyone was starin[g] at him. What was he supposed to do? He was alread[y] married to Victoria's sister. How ever could he te[ll] Victoria to stop the wedding now? Good God, he swa[l]lowed, for the first time in her life, Victoria was count[-]ing on him.

"Gerald? I asked if you are ready," Victoria prodded[.]

Gerald looked over at the guests, who appeared a[l]most as ill at ease as he. He couldn't tell Victoria t[o] stuff it all now, could he?

"Gerald?"

His attention snapped back. "Yes. Yes," he uttered[,] as if in a trance.

Victoria's chin rose with stubborn pride. "Then w[e] shall proceed."

The reverend squinted watery eyes. "You two sure[,] now?"

"Quite."

As if she were standing apart from her body, Victori[a] watched as they all took their places. The reveren[d] moved in front of the fireplace. She and Gerald shifte[d] to stand before him. The man took out a well-wor[n] Bible, set wire-rimmed spectacles on his nose, and be[-]gan to read.

A thud at the entrance to the parlor brought Victo[-]ria's attention away from the minister. Unshaven, hi[s]

lack hair tousled, his cambray shirt unbuttoned halfway down his chest, Judge Colston leaned against the
oor frame, chewing on a length of straw. Behind
udge, Chang cast Victoria a guilty half smile and
linked into a back corner. Victoria stiffened and
urned back to the proceedings, her heart threatening
o stop.

The sound of a dish shattering interrupted the ceremony once again.

Gerald craned his neck. Lani stood framed by the
doorway, mortified, broken china peeking out of the
gift wrap at her feet. Her eyes had doubled in size in her
pale face and her lips were covered with shaking fingers. Her hand dropped and her mouth opened as
Judge's fingers closed around her arm. He pulled her
next to him, shushing her with his index finger. She
started to protest but Judge shook his head. Instead,
she bit at her fingernails.

The preacher raised his brows and looked amusedly
down his nose at the pair in front of him. "If we've had
enough interruptions, I'd like to get on with it. My
tongue's getting a bit dry, having to start and stop as
we've been doing." He settled pointed looks on Judge
and Lani. "You two back there going to sit down or
stand there gawking?"

Gerald sent Lani a silent plea as she and Judge
squeezed onto the couch with two of the ranch hands.
Gerald opened his mouth, but nothing came out. He
shook his head in defeated confusion and dropped his
eyes, numbed into inaction.

Victoria was too lost in the emotional turmoil
Judge's appearance had created to notice the disbelief
in her sister's eyes, or the fire in Judge's. Victoria kept
reminding herself that Gerald was what she had always

wanted in a man: someone who would not interfer
with the safe little life she had designed for hersel
Judge would never be a passive partner. He was contro)
ling and ruthless; he took what he wanted. He was not .
man to be led by the traditions which had ordered he
life.

It took every measure of restraint Judge possessec
not to throw Victoria Elizabeth Torrington over hi
shoulder and carry her off. He'd walked in to find he
standing before the preacher marrying that poor excus
for a man, Pelthurst, after Chang had found him at th
shack and spewed out the fantastic story, insisting h
rush home. Pelthurst. Judge itched to take tha
pipsqueak apart and show Victoria that Pelthurst
wasn't man enough for her.

Lani's expression was frozen. But Gerald was her
strength; he must have a prime reason for what she was
witnessing. Perhaps it had been orchestrated for Judge
Colston's benefit. He couldn't possibly be marrying
Victoria, could he?

"Judge, I saw your horse out—" Ozzie broke off,
stricken dumb by the scene. "Clifford?"

"Sit down, Aloysius! You're interrupting a man trying to do his duty by these two."

Thoroughly daunted by the old preacher he had
played cards with Saturday nights for over twenty
years, Ozzie's Adam's apple bobbed, and he sunk onto
a chair in the back of the room.

Once the snickers had died down again, Victoria
tried to focus as the minister droned on.

". . . If anyone can show just cause why these two
here should not be joined in legal matrimony, let him
speak now—"

In unison, four voices rang out. "I do."

Reverend Blonsen's eyes did a double take. His brows ose and his fingers plucked at the skin hanging loose round his chin.

"I see. There seems to be quite a show of force here ver one little wedding. Why I ever thought this would e a simple ceremony, I'll never know. For all this troule, the wedding is going to cost you double Mr. Pelhurst." He sighed, his eyes rolling over the four people ow standing before him. "If I didn't know better, I night think I had sipped a little too much sherry; I eem to be seeing double," he said to the two couples.

The reverend's eyes scanned the four people. The ride exuded nervous anger, the groom looked dumbounded, the other female anxiously fidgeted with her ingers, and Judge Colston had murder in his blue eyes.

"Let me see," Reverend Blonsen studied them a minute longer. "Since you," his gaze settled on Victoria, 'are the one most directly involved, we'll hear from you first, young woman."

All eyes bored into Victoria. She shot Judge a glance, then said. "Sir, I am afraid I cannot marry this man."

"So you said. Why not?"

"Because I do not love him."

"Then why'd you bring everybody out here today?" Reverend Blonsen countered, becoming perturbed.

"So you're finally going to admit it, huh?" Judge interjected through clenched teeth.

"You'll get your turn, Judge," the reverend said and turned to Lani. "All right, let's hear from you next, young lady."

"Haven't we heard enough?" Judge piped up again, noticing the crimson patches on Victoria's cheeks.

"I'll say when we have heard enough here," snapped the reverend, ready to lose patience. "Our Constitution states that everybody's got a right to say his piece. Besides, this is just starting to get interesting." H turned again to Lani. "Okay, miss."

Lani took Gerald's arm for support, then cried out "It is not miss, it is Missus . . . Mrs. Gerald Pelthurst.

"What?" Victoria gasped.

"Gerald and I were secretly married while we were in Washington, D.C. Victoria, I am ever so sorry, but we love each other. We were afraid to tell you because we did not want to hurt your feelings. But I belong to Gerald now. Tell them, Gerald," Lani chirped, her gaze of adoration glowing in her green eyes.

Gerald's mouth was clamped shut in shame. He had been about to forsake the vows he'd taken with the woman he loved. He hung his head, unable to offer further explanation.

The preacher scratched his jaw. "Mr. Pelthurst, if this is true, and you already have one wife, then what in tarnation do you want with a second one?"

The room exploded with laughter as Gerald stood shamefaced. "I say, this was a devil of an idea, I fear," he mumbled.

The reverend frowned. There was a great need for redemption here. He tented his fingers. "All right, Judge, it's your turn. Why are you objecting?"

Judge pushed Pelthurst aside to stand next to Victoria. Her face was flaming red. He wasn't sure whether he wanted to take Pelthurst's place as groom, or take her over his knee for this dumb stunt. But as he looked into her eyes, he knew that he loved the exasperating Englishwoman and always would. "Because I love her."

"Well, I'll be. Judge Colston in love," exclaimed the reverend, who had known Judge since childhood. While he had never approved of Colston's amorous dventures, Reverend Blonsen understood what drove he man.

The room rang with the roar of unrestrained laughter ow.

Victoria's head swiveled from side to side. Her sense f humiliation was nearly overpowering. She could ardly believe this was happening to her.

Judge's deep scowl silenced the men.

"Now that I've heard from all involved here, this is he way I interpret things," the reverend said importantly. "Taking into consideration that no one here wants you two to be married, and since I'm obviously not going to allow you to commit bigamy, even if you had a mind to; and since you two," he stared at Judge and Victoria, "seem to be in love, why waste all the food, flowers, and my time? I can marry you two and save myself another trip out here later."

"What do you say, Tori?" Judge uttered rashly.

Tension squeezed the muscles in Victoria's neck, sending a blinding pain up the back of her head. Judge Colston had deceived her. He loved Helene Jessup. He had a child by the woman, and they were scheming to get Jessup's ranch. Did Judge think that the only way to stop her from selling her portion of his ranch was to marry her?

"I think one attempt at a wedding is all I care to endure today, thank you," Victoria answered shortly. She marched from the room, unwilling to fall victim yet another time.

Chapter Forty-three

Noting Judge's barely restrained temper, the ranch hands wasted little time in skittering from the parlor and heading for the far reaches of the range.

Ozzie sagely escorted the preacher from the house before he could suggest any soul-saving measures, and offered to drive the man back to town. The crusty old cowboy was nobody's fool; he had no intention of being anywhere near the ranch when Judge Colston's tenuous composure turned to rage.

"Well?" Judge roared. "Isn't this your cue to disappear with your bride, Pelthurst?" Judge stomped over to the decorated counter, and grabbed up a bottle of whiskey. He then upset the table in his anger before swinging on the couple, a black glower punctuating his features.

"What are you waiting for?"

"Gerald?" Lani, gulped her fright and pushed at Gerald's sleeve, urging him forward.

"Colston, old man, I daresay, we hope you do not intend to give up on the old girl."

Judge slitted his eyes at the English dandy. Although he'd like nothing better than to squeeze Victoria's lovely white throat at that moment, Judge wasn't about

408

o hear anyone defame her.

"Pelthurst," Judge began much too calmly, warning the couple to be wary. "Before I lose my temper completely and do something I'm sure I'll never regret, I suggest you get the hell out of my sight."

Gerald took a step backward.

Menace in his arctic blue eyes, Judge snarled, "And I'd better never catch you referring to Victoria as the old girl again. Do you catch my drift, old man?"

"Q-quite so."

Judge splayed his fingers through his hair and waited to be left alone. The moment stretched and the pair stood rooted to the floor. Since Victoria's harebrained sister and that pipsqueak of a husband of hers didn't seem to have any intention of getting out of his sight, Judge discerned he'd have to be the one to leave. He had unfinished business to settle with Helene anyway. He set the bottle back down. Liquor was the last thing he needed now. Problems weren't solved with alcohol; they were only compounded.

Gerald looked longingly at the door, then into Lani's imploring eyes. He had already let her down once today; he would not do it again, regardless of the price to his person.

"C-Colston. Wait. P-please," Gerald said in a choked voice.

Judge pivoted, his lips drawn into a thin line.

"Please. This is important," Gerald pleaded.

"What would you have to say that could possibly be of any interest to me?" Judge shook his head and turned back toward the door.

"It has to do with Luther Jessup." The words rushed from Gerald's mouth.

"Why, I just spent time with him while I was in

Casper," Lani added, surprised that Gerald had mentioned the man.

Judge's interest was pricked. He pulled the double doors together, completely unaware that Victoria had returned to the entrance of the parlor unobserved, and had been quietly listening to the conversation. Judge motioned for the couple to sit on the couch. Folding his big frame down onto the arm at the far end of the sofa, Judge leaned toward the huddled pair, missing the creak of the doors as they opened an inch.

"All right," Judge said darkly. "What is it you have to tell me about Luther Jessup? And Lani, when did you see Jessup in Casper?" Judge added, a flicker of suspicion entering his mind.

Gerald squeezed Lani's trembling hand and patted it with his other one. This was his chance to redeem himself in her eyes, although he knew his information would devastate his darling wife.

"A day, or maybe two, after Ozzie and I arrived. Or was it three?" Lani shrugged. "I saw Mr. Jessup ride into town and stop at the land office. He was most gracious. He invited me to join him for dinner at the hotel." Lani went on to explain how he had introduced her to the best dressmakers and had kindly offered to escort her about.

"What time did Jessup leave you?"

"Let me see." Lani pressed an index finger to her lips in thought. "We had dinner about two o'clock. I remember because we had just left the most pleasant modiste. . . ."

As Judge listened, pieces of the puzzle of Clancy's killing no longer seemed to fit together with pat precision. Although the young woman expressed confusion over the time period, Jessup's presence in Casper would seem to rule him out as the murder suspect.

Judge thought back to that day. He had been certain Clancy was silenced by Jessup before he could talk. He recalled how Clancy had said his life wouldn't be worth a scrap from a female's love letter if he talked. The killer had been waiting, watching for some reason, and had ridden Jessup's horse. But was it Jessup? The English pipsqueak's grating voice broke Judge out of his reflections.

"I say, this is a bit much."

"The horse that Jessup rode into Casper—do you remember what it looked like?" Judge questioned Lani, ignoring Pelthurst.

"I really am not sure. It could have been brown or—"

Judge moved to the very edge of his seat. "What about white? Could it have been white?"

"Gray perhaps. I do not remember, actually," Lani started to get flustered. "I am sorry."

"Steady on, girl." Gerald patted Lani's shaking hand. Then his expression grew fearful. "You must stay away from Luther Jessup, Lani. He is a dangerous man," Gerald advised. That the blackguard had been acquainted with Lani made his threat all the more vivid to Gerald.

Judge's brows drew low over blue slits. "How do you know Jessup's dangerous, Pelthurst?"

Gerald fingered his collar. "Back in Saint Louis, I thought I recognized the man's name when Aloysius mentioned it. He was one of the men your father and I made that disastrous investment with, Lani."

If their conversation hadn't been so serious, Judge would have had to smile at Pelthurst's referring to Ozzie as Aloysius. The old timer detested the name.

"You mean he was one of the men involved with

bankrupting Torrington Limited?" Lani shrieked, grabbing her throat.

"Worse." Gerald went on to describe how Jessup had ruined the company when Torrington had refused to sell his interest in Judge's ranch. He told of Mr. Hampton's visit, which had precipitated their trip to America, and the barrister's part in the dreadful muddle, including the reasons for Victoria's insistence that she and Gerald wed. Of course, Gerald did not mention his suspicions that the wedding had as much to do with what Victoria had learned about Judge Colston as with her desire to save Torrington Limited.

Gerald then detailed his visit to Jessup's ranch. Before telling the worst of it, he encircled Lani in the crook of his arm. Then he forced himself to relate the horror of Mary Torrington's death, and Jessup's demands and threats against Lani.

"No!" Lani wailed, burying her face against Gerald's chest. Sobs wracked her body so loudly that the occupants of the room did not hear the gasp from the other side of the door.

As Gerald unfolded his tale, Judge recalled that Jessup had been in England on business at that time. "You mean to tell me that Jessup killed Victoria's mother and ruined Torrington Limited, all because Torrington wouldn't sell his holdings in my ranch? And then he instructed you to get Victoria to sell her holdings or he'd hurt Lani?"

"Yes." Gerald stroked Lani's beige curls while she continued to sob.

"Dammit!" Judge jumped to his feet and paced back and forth about the room. His head spun with the extent of Luther Jessup's depravity. But something else bothered him as well. Had Jessup been in Casper the

412

lay Clancy was killed? If he was, could he have ridden to the line shack in time to murder Clancy? Judge's mind whirled until he reached a decision.

Judge swung toward the doors.

"Where are you off to?" Gerald asked.

"I'm going to pay a visit to the one person who can clarify Jessup's activities, as well as explain what had Victoria so upset by her visit."

"Who are you going to have a go at?"

"Helene Jessup."

"But what about Victoria?" Lani ventured.

"I love her," he said without reservation. "I intend to marry the exasperating woman despite her objections."

The thud of booted heels stomping toward the door caused Victoria to dash into the kitchen. Panting and holding her midriff, Victoria stumbled to a chair and crumbled onto it. Her head in her hands, she fought to keep down the bile churning in her stomach.

"You okay, Missy?" Chang asked, startled by the sudden appearance of the pale young woman. "I get top boss man."

Victoria's head snapped up. "No!" At Chang's look of consternation, she added, "Besides, Mr. Colston has left the ranch and won't be back for some time. Please. If you could get me a spot of tea, I shall be quite all right in a few moments."

Chang hesitantly nodded. As he passed the window on his way to the stove, he caught sight of Judge Colston atop his finest palomino, streaking from the ranch in a thick haze of dust.

A mixture of emotions barraging him, Judge spurred the great palomino toward the L Circle J, prepared to have it out with the Jessups. The grueling afternoon sun beat down on Judge, and sweat poured down his face.

Judge had always known that Jessup seemed obsessed with destroying him, but that he would murder an innocent woman just to gain control of his land was nearly beyond belief. Judge drove the animal onward.

Warming yellow light glowed from the Jessup mansion as Judge neared the ranch, just after sunset. Purple shadows stretched from the outbuildings and the boisterous voices of the hands rang out from the bunkhouse. Jessup's hired guns were preoccupied and shouldn't cause interference.

To be certain he would not be interrupted when he confronted Helene, Judge dismounted a safe distance from the buildings and hid his horse. Without so much as snapping a twig beneath his heels, Judge advanced toward the house. Furtively, he peered into a window. Helene sat alone at the head of the immense dining table, regally attired in fine aqua silk, sipping from a crystal goblet. Judge crept the rest of the way around the house. Jessup was nowhere in sight. Although Judge itched to get his hands around Jessup's neck, he had to talk to Helene first.

Judge bounded up the front steps, taking them two at a time, and tried the carved door. It was unlocked. He slipped inside, and with a casual air, sauntered into the dining room.

"Good evening, Helene."

She started, then, eyes devouring Judge, ran her tongue over her lips. "Sit down, love."

"I'll stand."

She lifted her glass. "Wine?"

"No."

"In that case, to what do I owe the pleasure of this rather unorthodox visit?" she crooned, unaffected.

414

"I want to talk to you. Now."

Helene dismissed the servants. She had always been careful with her clandestine dealings. Her plans required that she keep her intrigues secret.

"All right, lover." She expelled a bored sigh. "Whose hide are you out for this evening?" At Judge's scowl, she added, "I do hope it's not mine."

His scowl deepening, Judge spat, "First, we'll start with you telling me what you said to Victoria that made her so upset."

Helene swallowed back a sudden lump of fear. "And second?"

"Second, we'll talk about Luther."

Her lips curved into a petulant pout. "Why don't we talk about us?"

"I've told you, Helene, there is no 'us.' " He glared at her, then realization hit him. "Is that what you told Victoria? Something about us?"

Helene's chest heaved. At least that Torrington bitch was out of the way now; she wed someone else earlier today. "What does it matter what that woman thinks now that she's married to that Englishman?"

"Victoria didn't marry the fool. If you know what's good for you, Helene, you'll tell me what you said to her."

Helene's face flamed as he grabbed her shoulders, drawing her to her feet. It didn't matter that he was furious with her, she loved his touch. She rubbed her cheek against the back of his hand. "I told her the truth," she scoffed, throwing back her head.

His fingers bit into her. "What truth?"

Helene straightened, reeling from the vehemence in his voice and the violence in his touch. Her stance became rigid. This wasn't the ambience she had hoped for, but now she would have to tell Judge about Jeremiah. She could put it off no longer.

"I told Victoria that you have other commitments," she said craftily, slanting him a sly glance.

"Helene—"

She stepped back out of his reach. "All right," she spat. "I told her that Jeremiah is your son."

Shock, fury, then disbelief, shadowed Judge's face. Obviously, he was not convinced. His fists flexed. "I ought to wring your neck, Helene." In an instant, he had swooped down on her and was dragging her toward the door.

"What do you think you're doing?"

"I'm taking you back to the ranch so you can tell Victoria the real truth!"

Helene flung her arm out of his grasp. "I told her the real truth! You are Jeremiah's father. Think about it. Doesn't the boy look like you? Why, even those silly ranchers' wives commented about the resemblance at the last fair we attended, remember?"

"He resembles Luther," Judge insisted.

Now was the time to ruin Luther once and for all. Now was the moment to drop the explosive bit of information she had learned from his letters. "Of course he does. Luther is his grandfather."

"What the hell are you up to?" Judge roared.

"It's time you know the truth."

Judge pushed her into the library and slammed the door. None too gently, he shoved her down on the sofa, looming threateningly over her. "If you are lying, I warn you, you'll regret it."

"I'm not lying." Triumph glittered in her eyes. "Think back five years and how we spent those four months together while Luther was in England doing business.

416

Jeremiah was born full term, seven months after Luther returned, making it impossible for him to have fathered the boy."

Not waiting for his reaction, she charged ahead with her tale about discovering Luther's missives. "I wasn't going to read them because they were so old. But since I had the time before he returned from Casper — that day you left Clancy's body on my doorstep, remember?

"Well, anyway, Luther had written to some friend all about how he had forced your mother, a lowly servant in his parents' house, to have sex with him. It detailed how he was forced to pay the Colstons to send you away. There was even a letter from your mother pleading with Luther not to tell your father. Let me see." She paused to let the effect sink in.

"Another letter described how much Luther had hated having a bastard son under his nose all these years since you returned, which I guess explains his obsession with trying to ruin you. Oh yes, it explained his cattle rustling operation too. Even those illegal land claims had been obtained so he could squeeze you out. I never realized how paranoid Luther was until I read his correspondence. The fool made copies of every letter he ever sent."

"How do I know you're not making all this up?"

"I knew you'd need proof, darling." She walked over to the book shelf and removed the letters she had hidden there. Handing them to Judge she said, "Here, read them for yourself."

Judge rubbed his temples after studying the letters. Folks' comments about Jeremiah. The date of the boy's birth. Jessup's blinding hatred. His mother's protectiveness of him. His "father's" drinking. Being sent away to school out East. It all made perfect, terrible sense now.

The horror wrinkling Judge's forehead caused Helene to smugly proceed. "Why do you think Luther wanted me?" she added, hoping her remark would have the desired result. "So he could hurt you."

Judge sat down heavily next to Helene, trying to absorb everything. He had come here to clarify what had transpired between Victoria and Helene, and to find out about Luther's whereabouts when Clancy was killed. Helene had instead blown the foundations of his life apart.

"I can see that you finally believe me, darling."

Considering everything Helene had told him, his eyes hardened to blue ice. In a dangerously low voice, he said, "Why didn't you tell me this before?"

"I wanted to. Honest I did."

Helene's feigned tears flowed freely as she watched for Judge's reaction. "I started to tell you a number of times over the years. But last month I finally realized I had to get Jeremiah away from Luther before he harms the boy. Luther is crazy!" she cried.

With deadly calm, Judge asked, "Where is Jessup?"

"You know he never confides in me."

Judge jumped to his feet, cast her a look of total disgust, and swung on his heel.

"Where are you going? Aren't you going to stay and talk about Jeremiah?"

"Not now." Without so much as a backward glance, Judge left Helene staring after him.

Chapter Forty-four

Judge's troubled thoughts raced faster than Firebrand as he rode back to his ranch, determined to clear his head before talking to Victoria. Jeremiah, his son. Jessup, a murderer, defiler of his mother, his real father. The cool night air brushed his face and, moonlight illuminated his path as he attempted to assimilate what Helene had told him into a course of action.

Judge rode directly to the barn, coming upon Ozzie snoring loudly against his saddle, one arm flung over that blasted goose, which eyed Judge like a watchdog. Dismounting, Judge lit a lantern and nudged the old man with his boot, causing the bird to hiss.

"Wake up! I think it's about time you told me the truth," Judge snapped sharply. "And hang on to that goose before I beat Chang to it and cook that ornery creature myself."

Ozzie stirred and protectively wrapped his arms around his pet as Judge crouched back on his haunches. "I knowed I shoulda told ya 'bout Miz Victoria, an' all, from the first. Gosh, Judge, I swear, I didn't have no idea she was goin' t' try t' marry that Pelthurst fella."

"I don't want to talk about Victoria. I want you to tell me about my mother and *father.*"

Ozzie snapped wide awake, his Adam's apple ticking like the second hand on a fine timepiece. He had known that letter from England might just stir up everything about Judge's past. "What do ya mean?"

"I think you know exactly what I mean. You knew my parents a long time ago; before I was born, you three were close."

"Yeah. But I don't rightly know what you're gettin' at."

"Don't play games with me. Helene dropped quite a stick of dynamite on me earlier tonight. I know Luther Jessup is my real father. That's the reason he has tried to destroy the ranch all these years — because he hated having to look at a bastard son. I know that's why my "father" drank himself to death, and it's why my mother was allowed to remain on a corner of Jessup's spread until she died. And I finally understand how those two poor people, who never had more than a dollar to their names, managed to scrape enough money together to send me back East to school. I was supposed to remain in the East, wasn't I?" Judge demanded. "But what I don't understand is the part you've played in all this."

Ozzie hung his head, nuzzling the goose much as a child clings to a security blanket. There would be no escaping Judge this time. "Boy, you wasn't supposed t' ever find out."

"Why? Why, old man?"

"I promised it t' your ma. She loved ya. Wanted the best for ya. Even your pa, although he weren't your real pa, he loved ya; it just sort of ate him up. That's why he took t' the bottle. Jessup paid them hush money t' send ya away 'cause as ya got older ya started t' take after

420

Jessup, with that dark hair of yours. Folks was beginnin' to ask a heap a questions, what with your yella-haired ma and redheaded pa. They was both my friends, so I promised your ma t' look after ya should ya ever come back. But I've loved ya like ya was my own, boy."

"Didn't you think I had a right to know who my real father was?"

"Why ya askin' all that now? Ya cain't change nothin'."

Judge expelled a weary sigh. "No. I can't change anything with Luther Jessup, but I can with Jeremiah."

Ozzie furrowed his brow. "Jeremiah? What does Luther's boy got t' do with ya bein' Jessup's son? 'Cept course that makes ya two half kin."

A harsh laugh fell from Judge's lips. "Jeremiah's my son. And a boy should know who his father is," Judge said, realizing that his remark applied to both father and son.

Ozzie's chin sagged. "Ya mean that—"

"Yeah. I'm his father and Helene is his mother."

"Geez, if that don't make a hen lay eggs. How'd ya find that out?"

Judge settled back, obviously relieved to be able to discuss the news with the old timer, and spilled the entire sordid tale of his trip to the Jessup spread earlier.

"What ya goin' t' do?" Ozzie asked when Judge had finished filling him in. "And speakin' 'bout what your goin' t' do, what 'bout that she-devil Helene? You're not goin' t' do nothin' rash, are ya?"

Judge regained his feet. He stood ramrod straight; his posture unbending. "Tomorrow I'm going to pay a visit to Jessup and claim my son. And you can quit worrying about Helene. She's not for me. I'll help her out financially if she wants to get away from Jessup.

421

Nothing more."

"Gosh! They'll never let ya have the boy," Ozzie troubled.

"I'll fight for the boy if I have to. I won't have the child learn of his true father the way I did," Judge said between gritted teeth.

Ozzie mulled over their conversation. It was good to have it out in the open while the boy was a young 'un. And it seemed to have done the hard rancher good somehow. Added more direction to his life. As long as there was the chance that there could be a child running about the ranch, Judge ought to have himself a right good woman to keep him in line, figured Ozzie. "What 'bout Miz Victoria? What ya goin' t' do 'bout her?"

The old fire returning to Judge's eyes, he scoffed, "Once I take care of Firebrand, I intend to see to the matter of Miss Victoria Elizabeth Torrington, once and for all!"

"Shouldn't ya ought t' wait til she gets up? Ya know how them wild fillies can be when roused."

"Don't worry, I'll treat her just like a wild bronc."

"Aim t' do a bit a tamin', huh?"

Judge laughed. "One can never tell with Victoria."

"Remember, sometimes a gentle hand can keep ya from gettin' throwed."

"I'll keep it in mind."

"Oh, say Judge, I brought a couple of telegrams from town for the two of ya." Ozzie scrambled to pull the forgotten papers from his pocket.

Judge waved him off. "Not now. I don't need any more distractions right now, and neither does Victoria."

It was nearing dawn by the time Judge stabled the horse and left Ozzie to head for the house. On the porch to the left, Gerald and Lani rocked in each other's arms on the wooden-slatted swing, enjoying a peaceful interlude out in the cool night air, after making love for hours. Gerald's head bobbed up in surprise at the sound of footfalls approaching the house at this hour.

"Colston, Lani and I want to thank you."

Judge moved closer to the cuddling couple, surprised that they weren't in bed, which is where he'd have Victoria if she were married to him. "What for?"

"For helping us to become so splendidly happy. If it hadn't been for you and coming to America we probably never would have married," Lani cooed, stroking her hand along Gerald's smooth cheek. "Very likely Gerald would have been married to Victoria by now."

Concern thinned Judge's lips. "How is Victoria?"

"Dash it all." Gerald sighed. "We have not had the opportunity to speak with her. After you left, she locked herself in her room, refusing to come out or talk to us."

"Well, she's going to talk to me."

Gerald watched Judge disappear inside the house. Gerald dropped a kiss on his wife's lips. "Doubtless you know they are about to have a rather indelicate conversation. It would seem sensible if we returned to our room."

"Yes, I am afraid there is about to be a devil of a fuss."

He gave her breast a light squeeze. "And do you realize, old girl, this is the first night I have been allowed to spend the entire night with my wife without sneaking about?"

Lani giggled. "Oh, Gerald. You are so wonderful. Do let's hurry along so we have time to do it again before the sun comes up."

"Right you are."

Gerald whisked Lani up into his arms and hurried down the hall to their room, past Judge, who was pounding on Victoria's door with one hand, a large silver platter in the other.

"Victoria! Open the damned door before I break it down. You are going to talk to me whether you want to or not!"

Victoria turned the latch and seated herself on a tufted velvet chair. Judge burst into the room and stood staring at her, the sterling platter held before him to ward off any projectiles which she might decide to hurl his way. Soft lamplight flickered over her features. She had curled her legs beneath her cloud-blue wrapper, which she held tightly closed at her throat. Her face was puffy and red from crying, although she seemed to be rigidly composed now.

"Victoria, I don't want another argument," he began trying to remember what Ozzie had advised about a gentle hand.

"Then why did you attempt to break into my room?" she snapped.

Judge rolled his eyes. "Christ! Here we go again. I did not attempt to break into your room!" he roared.

"No? What would you call battering against my door at this hour? Then entering with a . . . a shield of sorts. Come prepared, did you?"

"It was the only gentlemanly thing to do, considering the accuracy of your aim."

Victoria sucked in a breath. "No self-respecting gentleman would think of visiting a lady until she was prepared to receive him, much less forcing his way into her boudoir at this hour."

"And no self-respecting lady would lead a gentleman to think she cared for him and then up and jilt him at the altar!"

Lights went on throughout the house as the combatant voices sliced into every room. Chang made a pot of coffee and sat down at the kitchen table with Ozzie and the other hands, calmly taking bets as to who would have the last word.

Gerald and Lani drew the covers over themselves. They were too busy, lost in their own lovemaking, to be concerned with Victoria and Judge.

Victoria squared off against the rancher. It was easier to hide behind her anger than to dwell on how very much she had been hurt by his deception. The accusations and indictments flew back and forth until both became winded and red in the face. Neither one had scored a clear-cut victory when Victoria snipped, "And what of your family? Did you intend to keep that from me, too?"

Judge sat down on the bed as if he had been punched in the gut. "God, Victoria," he said in a whisper, halting further comment from her momentarily. "Why are we arguing again? I didn't come here to discuss my family, as you put it, but since you are going to become my wife, you have a right to know."

Her fists balled at his supposition that she would simply accept him, but she held her tongue.

"Contrary to what Helene may have told you, I just learned Jeremiah is my son tonight. And now that I know, I'll never hide his true identity from anyone. Tomorrow I plan to talk to the Jessups about custody. A child has a right to know who his real parents are. . . ."

Stunned by the sincerity and conviction in his voice, Victoria moved to sit on the edge of the bed. She listened as he told her about his long relationship with Helene. There was an unspoken pain, something he was holding back, and it surrounded each word with a

425

hurt that went even deeper than his discovery of his son.

She waited until he had finished, then probed, "I believe you have told me the truth. But is it the truth in its entirety?"

Judge stared into her face. Before him sat the woman he wanted to spend the rest of his life with; she deserved to know he was the son of the man who killed her mother and caused her father's death.

"No, Victoria. There is more. Tonight I also learned I am Luther Jessup's son."

Victoria's hand flew to her mouth at the mention of Luther Jessup. "The man responsible for my parents' deaths?" she mumbled without conscious thought.

Instinctively Judge reached for her and pulled her trembling body into his embrace. "Oh God, Victoria, you knew?"

"I overheard you talking to Gerald and Lani after the wedding was called off."

"I am so sorry about your family."

"Thank you." She sniffed, but held back the sobs threatening to overtake her. She swallowed and, before she could reconsider, said, "I also overheard what you said about how you felt for me. Did you mean it?"

"Mean what?"

"When you said that . . . that you love me."

He squeezed her hand, then pressed a tender kiss to the inside of her palm. "Heaven help us, yes I do."

"I love you too," came her simple declaration, void of all pretense.

The overpowering emotion elicited from their revelations brought them together in a searing kiss, leaving them breathless as they dragged their lips from each other.

"Oh, Judge, we have so much to talk about."

He sat back from her in order to keep temptation at

bay. "Then let's get everything out into the open, once and for all."

For over an hour they discussed the Jessups and her parents; she showed him the documents and he admitted they were valid, explaining Ozzie's role in it. Their intimate conversation was cleansing, laying clean the wounds which had brought them together.

They relived their journey, encapsulating all their escapades: the encounter with Clarissa in New York; the reporter; President Arthur, and Chief Justice Waite; Bridgewater and Buck in Saint Louis at the firehouse; Betsy Lake, Judge's visions of Victoria in calico waiting for him on the porch; Clancy; and the time they'd spent at the line shack together. The stories, told from each other's perspective, gave them a better understanding of what drove each of them. And suddenly, no topic was taboo.

"Victoria, about Gerald and the wedding—"

"The wedding was a mistake, as would have been marriage to Gerald. Even if he had not been already married to my sister," she added. "I was hurt and wanted to salvage my pride. I watched Lani and Gerald from my window earlier. They belong together."

"He never was man enough for you," Judge stated flatly. He still thought Pelthurst little more than a puny pipsqueak, but was willing to give the man the benefit of the doubt now that the Englishman was married to Victoria's sister.

A weak smile toyed with the corners of her mouth. "You mean man enough for *Miss Chastity Iron Drawers?*"

He hugged her to him, unable to stop himself. "Those men were fools."

"Yes. Well, now I shall be able to return to England and prove them all wrong when I rebuild Torrington

Limited, correct?"

"No. Give Pelthurst a chance to prove he's a man. Let him take over operation of your father's business, because you're not going back to England. I've already told you that you are going to marry me, which means you'll be staying here on the ranch."

Victoria pulled away from his arms. It was much too difficult to think clearly when he held her. "I never agreed to marry you, sir. And even if I did, we could never live anywhere but in England; it is my home."

"Sir? Sir! I'd say we are way beyond that by now!"

"Don't you take that tone with me, you . . . you cowboy . . . !"

Ozzie had just collected the bets he'd won and was counting his money when, again, raised voices boomed into the kitchen. Chang snatched the cash back. "Not so fast. They not done yet!"

"Ya want t' take odds on how long it'll be 'fore them two's hitched?"

Chuckling good-naturedly, houseboy and foreman settled back to enjoy the escalating beef between the two bosses, certain the rousing arguments were going to become a common occurrence within the household.

"You don't have enough money to go back to England without getting your portion of my ranch. So it looks like you are going to be here for a very long time to come." Judge folded his arms over his chest. He had to admit he delighted in matching wills with someone so equally suited. This time he could not afford to lose. What's more, he did not intend to!

"Oh, I do not think so," she returned, with too much confidence to suit Judge.

Judge cocked a brow. Now, what the hell did she have up one of those satin sleeves of hers this time? "Don't

428

count on it, Tori," he warned.

"But I am. I have a lady's prerogative on my side."

Judge narrowed his eyes. "Meaning?"

"Meaning that I plan to return to England quite shortly, as a matter of fact. You see, I have business matters to settle there, and an American husband to introduce to my brother Edward. Then I shall return to Wyoming, to make sure my husband handles my inheritance wisely," she said with a straight face.

"Oh, you shall, shall you?" He grabbed her to him without ceremony and thoroughly kissed her. Breathless, he said, "I take it you have finally accepted my proposal."

"Proposal?" she squeaked, incredulous. "You call your commands a proposal?"

"And that acceptance of yours. What would you call that?"

"I'd call it what you deserve."

"God, I love fighting with you." He laughed. "But this is one time I think I have something much better in mind."

Judge pulled her down across the bed and as he rained kisses upon her face, his fingers adeptly peeled away her nightclothes.

Never one to prove a passive participant, Victoria divested Judge of his clothing. Her hands roved about the thick nest of hair covering his chest. "I have never ceased to wonder at your beauty," she rasped, her passion rising.

"That's supposed to be a gentleman's line." He drew her back down, fastening his hungry mouth on the crest of her nipple.

"I am not so sure I want a gentleman in bed," she moaned at his tender advances. His heated touch enraptured her and she thrust her hips against the hardness of his arousal.

"That's good," he groaned, "because I plan on teaching you things a gentleman would never dream of." His explorations grew more impatient as he slid his fingers down her belly and dipped into ready flesh.

She began to squirm against his palm. "Does that include riding and roping?"

Judge raised himself between her welcoming, open thighs and smiled down into her searching face. "I don't know about roping. But we'll begin with your first lesson on riding broncs right now." He clasped her to him and rolled beneath her, lowering her down onto him.

In the next instant all playfulness left them and their bodies took complete control of their minds, banishing the lighthearted side of their lovemaking. Intensity built with the impaling thrusts, which spiraled them until ecstasy wrought its careening release.

Coming back to earth, Victoria nuzzled his neck and whispered garbled love words. As dawn broke in through the windows, just before she fell into a contented slumber, she murmured, "I intend to go with you to the Jessups."

"Yes, my precious Tori, I knew you would," he crooned. He waited for her breathing to become measured before he rose and silently dressed.

Chapter Forty-five

A grim line to his features, Judge reined the golden palomino back the way he had come but a few short hours before, passing one of Jessup's riders with no more than a cool nod. Judge was too absorbed in his own plans to stop and pass the time, as often was the custom despite the hostility between the neighboring spreads.

Judge had been in such a rush to be away from the ranch before Victoria awoke that he had again brushed off Ozzie's efforts to thrust the crinkled telegram into his hand. Whatever it was, it could wait.

He'd left instructions to keep Victoria at the house, if possible. Victoria. His fantastic, marvelous, incredible woman. He spurred his animal into a gallop. The sooner he got this business over with Jessup, the sooner he could make Victoria his wife. Judge laughed to himself. His lawyer had been right when he'd instructed Judge to marry the lady. Of course, there'd be hell to pay when she discovered he'd left without her this morning.

"Good morning, Chang." Victoria stretched, entering the kitchen and taking a place at the table. "Has Judge had breakfast yet?"

Chang shifted uneasily from foot to foot. "He gone, Missy."

"He left without me?" she sprang to her feet. "How dare he! Chang, have a horse saddled for me while I change," she ordered, flouncing past Lani and Gerald.

"Victoria, please talk to me," Lani pleaded.

"Later, love." Victoria hesitated at her door. "Lani, do not worry. I am happy for you and Gerald. But I am in a dreadful hurry at the moment."

"I say, where is she off to in such a dither?" Gerald asked, watching Victoria disappear into her room.

Lani shrugged. "You never can tell with Victoria."

Victoria threw on her smartest navy riding habit.

She ignored Ozzie's pleas and his efforts to thrust a telegram into her hands, insisting, "I do not have time now." He helplessly watched her leave the house and mount her horse.

She was going to catch up with Judge. She would not be denied the right to face her parents' murderer.

Victoria urged the horse along the road Ozzie had said would take her to the L Circle J. A rider neared her as she rode. The hulking man drew up to Victoria and tipped his hat.

"Ma'am."

"Good day to you, sir."

"You the English lady stayin' at Colston's place?"

"Yes."

432

"Here." He thrust a slip of paper toward her. "Miz Jessup sent this here little billet-doux for you." Without waiting, the man rode off.

Victoria opened the sheet and scanned the page. It requested that she meet Helene at a spot near the SweetWater River to discuss Judge's son. It threatened that if she did not come alone, Helene would take the boy away and Judge would never see him again. At the bottom of the note, Helene had traced a map of the location where Victoria was to go.

Victoria furrowed her brows. She could give the missive to Judge and let him deal with Helene, but Victoria knew how he would feel about her threats. Although she did not like the Jessup woman, Victoria owed it to Judge to at least hear the woman out. She would try to thwart any plans Helene might have to take the boy away. Her mind made up, Victoria studied the map, then turned her horse toward the Sweetwater.

Seated at his desk, rummaging through his personal papers, Luther's head snapped up at the sound of shattering glass. "What the hell do you think you're doing?" he sneered.

Helene shrugged. "I've always hated that vase. It was one of your favorites, wasn't it?"

Fire spewed from Luther's eyes as he rose. "Why you bitch. I'll teach you to. . . ."

Helene raised the gun she'd hidden in the folds of her skirts and pointed it at the bastard. She did not notice the paper which fell out of her pocket. "You'll never ever threaten me again, Luther." Her eyes traveled to the contents of the box fanned about the desktop. "Going over your private papers? They're not so private

433

anymore. I read them, including all those letters of yours. Tsk, tsk, tsk. You really shouldn't have kept such incriminating documents . . . oh, and I told your bastard son all about them, too."

"And what about your bastard son?" he bellowed. "You knew?"

"Of course I knew, you stupid bitch! I've known all along. I used you to keep Colston's son away from him. And now, after all these years, when Colston finds out, he'll hate you for it."

"Judge knows." She waved the gun at him. "You're finished, Luther. Judge and I can finally become a family and rule over an empire."

Luther threw back his head and laughed. "I have to give you credit. You've got more guts than I thought. But you'll never have Colston," he sneered. "Unless I miss my guess, he prefers the Englishwoman. Now put that gun down so we can settle this," he snarled and started for her, confident in his position.

Helene pulled the trigger, blasting her hated husband in the chest. She moved to stand over the fallen man, and when he reached a bloody hand out to her, gasping for help, she shot him again and again, until the pistol was empty. Casually she picked a Derringer off his desk and was about to pump that into him too, when pounding footsteps stopped her.

Helene swung around, hiding the handgun in her skirts. The household staff stood staring at her. "He was going to kill me," she cried, rushing past them. She ran up the stairs and bundled Jeremiah into her arms. Frantic to be away, she hurried to the buggy she had ordered earlier, and drove the horses from the ranch in a cloud of dust.

Judge noticed a buggy racing toward the Sweetwater

off in the distance, as he closed the gap between the two ranches. Someone was in an awfully big rush, but Judge had no time to allow his attention to be diverted. While he rode, he'd had time to put all the pieces together, and he didn't like what he'd come up with. If his suspicions were correct, Victoria could be in a great deal of danger.

Cowboys and household staff milled around the grounds by Jessup's house, as Judge approached the front door casually, so as not to arouse suspicions. Strange. Jessup was not known for allowing his hands to dawdle.

"Where you think you're going?" A gruff voice behind Judge called out.

"To talk to the Jessups, if it's any business of yours."

"Ain't no use going inside then."

"Oh?"

"Neither's there."

"Where are they?" Judge demanded, moving closer to the hostile knot of men.

"I'd say, Jessup's probably in hell by now. And his wife hauled her son out of here like her tail was burning."

"What are you talking about?"

The cowpoke shrugged. "Jessup's dead. His wife killed him, then ran off. Simple as that."

Judge's heart thudded against his rib cage as he bounded up the steps to see for himself. Inside Luther's private office, Judge found the big man's body in a puddle of blood, six holes blown clean through his chest. He knelt down and checked for a pulse; there was none.

"You'll never hurt anyone else again, Jessup," Judge said without remorse.

As he turned to leave, his eyes caught sight of a folded slip of paper near the body. For a reason unknown to him, Judge bent down and picked it up. Scrawled over the page in flowery handwriting was a note addressed to him from Helene, imploring him to meet her at their secret spot next to the Sweetwater River. She had gone on to state that it was vastly important for their future.

"Jesus," he gasped. Judge dropped the thin sheet of stationery to the floor and ran for his horse. Helene was desperate, and there was no telling what she would do next. In her state of hysteria, Helene might even harm the boy. He jumped onto Firebrand's back, shouted for one of the men to ride for the sheriff, and rode hell-bent toward the Sweetwater. Thank God, Victoria was safe back at the ranch.

Victoria dismounted a safe distance from the river, where the water ran deep and swift. The bank was dotted with scrub cottonwoods and hefty boulders. Anxiously she waited, careful not to venture too close to the edge of the fleet-flowing Sweetwater, named for a bag of sugar dumped from a donkey's back into its waters. Since her mother had drowned, there was nothing sweet about rivers, as far as Victoria was concerned.

She had stood at the appointed spot only a matter of minutes when Helene arrived. Leaving Jeremiah in the buggy, Helene joined Victoria. Eyes thick with hatred assessed the Englishwoman who would dare try to steal her man.

"I'm glad you came so promptly. And you did come alone, as I directed, didn't you?" Helene looked about hem to make sure her instructions had been followed.

Victoria stiffened her back and raised her chin. "I did not come here to pay a social call. Do get on with it. Did Jeremiah accompany you?" Victoria asked, catching sight of the boy, now playing in the sand with a tin cup, a short way away.

"You're a real uppity one, aren't you?" Helene hissed, ignoring the bitch's inquiry about her son.

Victoria stared the woman down. "I beg your pardon."

"You thought you could get your claws into Judge Colston, didn't you? Well, you're not going to."

"If that is all you brought me out here to say, then I can assume this interview is over. I have important business with your husband, Mrs. Jessup."

Not about to let the woman walk away from her, Helene grabbed Victoria's arm and swung her around. "You have business with *me*, Miss Torrington," Helene sneered. "Besides, I'm afraid you'd find my husband rather . . . shall we say . . . unresponsive."

"You are becoming quite tiresome, so kindly state your business and let go of my arm."

Helene looked at the river and back again at Victoria. Madness overtook her features, lending her face an evil cast. "Clancy told me you have a fear of water, Miss Torrington."

Fear began to course through Victoria's veins. Something was very much amiss in Helene Jessup's demeanor. "Clancy?"

"Why, yes. The gunslinger I hired to kill you."

Victoria's gloved hand flew to her lips. "My lord, you were the one who hired that dreadful man? We thought your husband was responsible."

"That's the beauty of it. Everyone thought it was

Luther. And they always will. I took pains to make sure Luther takes all the blame. You understand, a dead man can't talk. And after I kill you, Judge and I can finally be together with the empire I've always dreamed of—and our son, of course."

"You *killed* your husband?"

"I see by your face that you must already know about Luther being Judge's father. Don't let it upset you. After all, Luther did murder your mother and destroy your father. I'd say I did society a big favor. We might look upon it as justice, don't you think?"

"I think you are quite deranged!"

Seething, Helene pulled the Derringer on Victoria. "We've spent enough time talking. Now get into the river. I want your death to look like an accident."

"No!" Victoria screamed, but she was forced to back slowly toward the water as Helene advanced on her.

"Further. Or I swear I'll pull the trigger. I've killed before, and believe me, I'd enjoy killing you."

Victoria was encompassed in a snare of terror. She cast the river another glance. She could charge Helene. But there was no doubt in Victoria's mind that Helene would shoot her. She'd have to brave the river and hope Helene's attention could be distracted long enough to allow Victoria to wrest the gun from her. Her legs barely supporting her weight, Victoria stumbled down the bank and knee-deep into the water.

The swift current immediately swept Victoria off her feet. She screamed and clawed at the bank as she was drawn into deeper water. Her skirt was wrapped around her struggling legs, sinking her beneath the rough surface. Clawing upward, Victoria broke above the water to hear Helene's shrill, vicious laugh. Dragged downriver, Victoria caught hold of a heavy root sticking out into the water. Her hands closed around it as the choking liquid rushed past her at chin height.

The beat of hooves forced Helene's attention from the drowning Englishwoman. She hid the gun in her skirt and rushed toward the buggy as Judge slid from his horse.

"Judge, you are too early," she cried, praying the bitch would disappear before he discovered what she was about. "You were not supposed to be here this soon."

"Help! Help me!" Victoria shrieked.

Helene grabbed his arm to stay his efforts to save the Englishwoman, but Judge threw Helene off and dove into the chilling water. His heart leaped as panic for Victoria's safety drove him to her side. With superhuman effort, he pried her fingers from the root and fought to pull her to safety.

"Stop! You can't save her. She has to die so we can be together. No!" Helene screamed from shore.

Panting, Judge dragged Victoria and himself to land. His breath ragged, Judge raised himself up on his elbows and glared into the face of the stranger Helene had become.

"She tried to kill me," Victoria gasped in between choking, coughing breaths.

"She's lying, Judge! I swear."

"Christ, Helene," Judge shook his head, "I wish she were."

Sobbing, Victoria jumped into the verbal melee. "She's the one who hired Clancy. All that time he was sent to kill me. And she murdered Luther Jessup."

"I'm afraid she also killed Clancy. Isn't that right, Helene?"

"How could you know that?" Helene blundered, before she realized what she was saying.

"Clancy hinted it was you when he said his life wouldn't be worth a female's love letter. But it didn't mean anything until after I talked to you. You mentioned Clancy and let slip that you knew Luther was in Casper at the time Clancy was killed. After I started thinking about it, I realized you knew too much about Clancy, and had lied to me about knowing Luther's whereabouts that afternoon.

"When I saw that note you must have dropped near Luther's body, asking me to meet you, there was no longer any doubt about my suspicions. Luckily, I arrived in time to stop you from harming Victoria."

Unconsciously, Helene's hand snaked down to her empty pocket. The note. She had forgotten to send it, and yet her own handwritten words had destroyed her chance to be with the man she loved.

"They deserved to die and so does she," Helene burst out. "Clancy failed to kill that English bitch, and Luther would have taken our son. Don't you see," she began to plead. "I've solved all your problems. Me! I helped you! I took care of the man who has been rustling your cattle and making those fraudulent land claims in order to ruin you. Luther was a common murderer, can't you understand?"

"So are you, I'm afraid."

"Noooo!" Helene's piercing screech rent the air as it ripped from her lips.

Her eyes wild, Helene barreled toward them, giving Judge hardly enough time to yank Victoria out of the madwoman's path. But to his amazement, Helene rushed past them and flew into the water, where Jeremiah had just tumbled in, the tin cup in his hands.

The river wasted no effort in its attempts to lay claim

to a victim this day, even if its offering was just a small, guiltless child. The boy flailed his chubby little arms, helpless to fight against the mighty churning foe.

Judge raced into the river after Helene, and the current carried the three of them off. It all happened so fast. Helene reached Jeremiah and, with all her might, shoved him toward Judge. Her momentum pushed her under the surface. Judge managed to get the boy to shore, then plunged back into the river after Helene. Time and again he dived, searching for her.

She was gone. The Sweetwater had claimed Helene's life in lieu of her son.

Gasping for air, Judge returned to shore. The boy was quietly sucking his thumb in Victoria's arms. He hugged them both. "Come on, let's get Jeremiah back home."

"Judge, the river's bad," the boy whimpered, raising his arms. Judge took the boy to his hip, and together, he and Victoria walked to the buggy. "Where's Mommy?"

"Your mommy had to go on a trip, son. But don't worry. This nice lady and I are going to take good care of you," Judge crooned, settling the boy in the back seat of the carriage.

Judge helped Victoria aboard, tied their horses behind the coach, then climbed up beside her. He shot one last glance at the spot which would no longer provide the peace it had since he was a child. Now, Victoria would become his refuge. They traveled in silent meditation until the boy fell into an exhausted sleep.

Victoria covered Judge's hand with hers. "She did love her son."

Judge sighed. "Yes. Helene finally thought of someone other than herself. It was the one time in her life she did something without first considering what she could get out of it," he reflected.

The rest of the way back to the ranch, they discussed the events which had drawn them into tragedy, laying to rest their remaining questions and residual feelings.

Waving the two forgotten telegrams in his gnarled hand, Ozzie rushed to meet them. "You two got t' take these. I got one for both a ya." He passed them out, then spied Jeremiah. "Where ya two been? And what ya doin' with the boy?"

"Let's get him to my room. Then we'll tell you everything, old timer."

Seated in the parlor for three hours with Ozzie, Lani, and Gerald, Judge and Victoria answered questions about the incredible events which had transpired over the last few months, and related their plans to be married immediately. Judge allayed Lani and Gerald's fears about their future with the news that he would provide financial assistance to help them get started rebuilding Torrington Limited. Concluding the grueling interrogation to everyone's contentment, Judge explained his plans for Jeremiah: Jessup's land would be held in trust for the boy, who would never be sent away to school.

"Did ya two open those danged pieces of paper I been totin' 'round yet?"

"Oh? No." Victoria tore into hers. Excited, she clasped her hands. "It's from Edward. He's coming over! Judging from the date of this cable, he should be here any day." She turned to her affianced and squealed. "Would you mind terribly if we wait to be married until my brother arrives?"

Judge had read his telegram and answered, "Looks like we're going to have two important visitors for the wedding. President Arthur should be arriving about the same time."

442

"Plesident Althul?" Chang croaked as he came into he room with refreshments. "I cook mighty fine food. I make his favolite. Flied lice—"

"Flied lice?" Gerald squeaked, visions of such a dish squirming before his eyes.

"Don't you like flied lice, old man?" Judge poked fun at Gerald's gullibility.

"Fried rice, Gerald," Victoria informed him softly. "Fried rice."

"Yes. Yes. Flied lice and goose."

"But there is only one goose within fifty miles of here," Victoria announced.

All eyes shot to Ozzie.

Horrified, Ozzie's Adam's apple bobbed and he jumped to his feet, his face carmine. "Oh, no, you don't! You're not goin' t' touch a feather on my goose's tail."

"Sit down, ord man," Chang said in his thick accent. "I cook you goose anothel day," he trumpeted to resounding laughter.

Noisy confusion erupted about the room. Everyone seemed to be talking and giggling and arguing and planning all at once. Excited disagreements arose over the accommodations for the president, guests to be invited, food to be prepared, and a whole assortment of related topics. Ozzie and Chang bickered. Lani flitted about. Gerald spouted ideas for the business. Voices rose and bounced off the walls until Judge clamped his hands over his ears and rolled his eyes, swearing fifty people must be crammed into the parlor.

He'd had enough! He grabbed Victoria's arm in midsentence and dragged her to a spare room, despite the babbling entourage which trailed after them. Without reservation, Judge slammed the door in Gerald's startled face.

"At last." Judge turned the lock and swung around to face Victoria. "I have you alone."

A conspiratorial grin crossing her lips, Victoria said, "That was not very polite, the way you shut them out."

"It wasn't meant to be polite, my dear. It was meant to get the point across."

"And that is?"

He pulled her against the length of his hard body. "That I have urgent needs which won't wait until the wedding. So what do you think of that?"

She closed her arms around his neck. "I think that we should not waste any more time talking," she murmured against his lips.

Just before the delicious sensations of Judge's lovemaking overtook her, Victoria's last rational thought was that tomorrow she would slip into the blue calico dress and stand on the porch, waiting for him to return from the range. Or, better yet, she would ride out to meet him.

HISTORICAL ROMANCES BY VICTORIA THOMPSON

GOTHICS A LA MOOR—FROM ZEBRA

ISLAND OF LOST RUBIES
by Patricia Werner   (2603, $3.9)

Heartbroken by her father's death and the loss of her great love, Eilee
returns to her island home to claim her inheritance. But eerie things beg
happening the minute she steps off the boat, and it isn't long befor
Eileen realizes that there's no escape from *THE ISLAND OF LOST RU
BIES*.

DARK CRIES OF GRAY OAKS
by Lee Karr   (2736, $3.95)

When orphaned Brianna Anderson was offered a job as companion to th
mentally ill seventeen-year-old girl, Cassie, she was grateful for the non
troublesome employment. Soon she began to wonder why the girl's family
insisted that Cassie be given hydro-electrical therapy and increased doses
of laudanum. What was the shocking secret that Cassie held in her dark
tormented mind? And was she herself in danger?

CRYSTAL SHADOWS
by Michele Y. Thomas   (2819, $3.95)

When Teresa Hawthorne accepted a post as tutor to the wealthy Curtis
family, she didn't believe the scandal surrounding them would be any concern of hers. However, it soon began to seem as if someone was trying to
ruin the Curtises and Theresa was becoming the unwitting target of a
deadly conspiracy . . .

CASTLE OF CRUSHED SHAMROCKS
by Lee Carr   (2843, $3.95)

Penniless and alone, eighteen-year-old Aileen O'Conner traveled to the
coast of Ireland to be recognized as daughter and heir to Lord Edwin
Lynhurst. Upon her arrival, she was horrified to find her long lost father
had been murdered. And slowly, the extent of the danger dawned upon
her: her father's killer was still at large. And her name was next on the
list.

BRIDE OF HATFIELD CASTLE
by Beverly G. Warren   (2517, $3.95)

Left a widow on her wedding night and the sole inheritor of Hatfield's
fortune, Eden Lane was convinced that someone wanted her out of the
castle, preferably dead. Her failing health, the whispering voices of death,
and the phantoms who roamed the keep were driving her mad. And although she came to the castle as a bride, she needed to discover who was
trying to kill her, or leave as a corpse!

*Available wherever paperbacks are sold, or order direct from the
Publisher. Send cover price plus 50¢ per copy for mailing and
handling to Zebra Books, Dept. 2906, 475 Park Avenue South,
New York, N.Y. 10016. Residents of New York, New Jersey and
Pennsylvania must include sales tax. DO NOT SEND CASH.*

HISTORICAL ROMANCES BY EMMA MERRITT

RESTLESS FLAMES   **(2203, $3.95)**

Having lost her husband six months before, determined Brenna Allen couldn't afford to lose her freight company, too. Outfitted as wagon captain with revolver, knife and whip, the single-minded beauty relentlessly drove her caravan, desperate to reach Santa Fe. Then she crossed paths with insolent Logan Mac-Dougald. The taciturn Texas Ranger was as primitive as the surrounding Comanche Territory, and he didn't hesitate to let the tantalizing trail boss know what he wanted from her. Yet despite her outrage with his brazen ways, jet-haired Brenna couldn't suppress the scorching passions surging through her . . . and suddenly she never wanted this trip to end!

COMANCHE BRIDE   **(2549, $3.95)**

When stunning Dr. Zoe Randolph headed to Mexico to halt a cholera epidemic, she didn't think twice about traversing Comanche territory . . . until a band of bloodthirsty savages attacked her caravan. The gorgeous physician was furious that her mission had been interrupted, but nothing compared to the rage she felt on meeting the barbaric warrior who made her his slave. Determined to return to civilization, the ivory-skinned blonde decided to make a woman's ultimate sacrifice to gain her freedom — and never admit that deep down inside she burned to be loved by the handsome brute!

SWEET, WILD LOVE   **(2834, $4.50)**

It was hard enough for Eleanor Hunt to get men to take her seriously in sophisticated Chicago — it was going to be impossible in Blissful, Kansas! These cowboys couldn't believe she was a real attorney, here to try a cattle rustling case. They just looked her up and down and grinned. Especially that Bradley Smith. The man worked for her father and he still had the audacity to stare at her with those lust-filled green eyes. Every time she turned around, he was trying to trap her in his strong embrace.

Available wherever paperbacks are sold, or order direct from the Publisher. Send cover price plus 50¢ per copy for mailing and handling to Zebra Books, Dept. 2906, 475 Park Avenue South, New York, N.Y. 10016. Residents of New York, New Jersey and Pennsylvania must include sales tax. DO NOT SEND CASH.